A Touch of Spring Fever

Howard Bushart

Acknowledgements:
My gratitude to all the Gypsy Rhythm Writers wherever they are;
Author's Ink group; Barbara Reaves Koloski and Anne-Marie
Novark; Kay Daly; Kathy, Janis, and everyone who's supported
and encouraged me over the years.

Cover art by Kara Griffen.

Truitt's song is a variation of "Our Goodman" an Irish tune of the
mid-1700s.
Tildy's song is a variation of "Siúl a Ghrá" another Irish song of
the mid-1700s that has many incarnations.

Brother Maynard Publishing

ISBN: 0990522709
ISBN-13: 978-0090522706

Dedication:

For the family—living, dead, and yet to come.

CHAPTER ONE

It was warm where he sat in the half darkness of the barn and that was by design. Truitt McBride had situated the work bench out of the weather, almost dead-center of the structure and ringed by piles of loose hay, a wall where the harnesses and other livery items hung and a crib that went from floor to loft. Though he could hear the wind outside, had felt it earlier, he didn't need to feel it to know that it was sharp, stinging. It didn't take much of the "sight" to know that. This time of year and this time of morning it couldn't be anything else. But that really didn't matter. He sat at his workbench, in the bright glow of yellow light from a coal-oil lantern hanging from a rafter peg. The workspace was snug all year round. The lantern light was more than enough to work by and he didn't need illumination for anything else. He spent part of every day of his life moving about the barn and the shadows held no secrets for him.

Freshly-oiled leather harnesses glistened on his workbench as Truitt ran a rasp over the precisely-honed edge of the turning share of his plow. The gleaming steel had no more need of sharpening than his harnesses had of oiling but that wasn't the point. Every spring since he was strong enough to hold a turning share in a furrow, he hitched a pair of mules to this ancient plow. Every spring since he was strong enough to keep the blade in the soil, he broke ground on the small farm nestled in the valley between Devil's Saw Ridge and Hog Heaven Hill. Both the plow and the land had belonged to Truitt's father, and to his father before him. Now they belonged to Truitt and in the natural order of things would one day belong to his sons Walter and Amos. He hoped so anyway. Walter and Amos; his sons come hell or high water. Now there was a real chore if he needed one. If only he could get them ready to go as easily as he did the tools or the mules.

Like his father and grandfather, and all the McBrides for as far back as Truitt knew, Walter was tall, dark, thin, and with good enough looks to catch the eyes of the ladies. Amos, on the other hand, was more like his mother's people, tall and thin enough to be McBride stock but with the same thick red hair and splash of punctuating freckles that jumped up from time to time in his maternal lineage.

Everyone in the valley waited for Truitt to begin plowing and he knew that. It did not feel like a responsibility or a burden. Not really. He had a knack, which he could in no way explain, for knowing exactly when to start. It was a feeling more than anything else, this sense of timing that had proven pin-point accurate over the years. He knew, knew with every bit of himself, the very moment when soil, weather, water, and God All Mighty came together in the great rebirth. He was as heavy with the knowing as the crops in harvest time and it felt to him that he was a part of a collective gravidity that overwhelmed him no matter how often he experienced it. When Truitt broke ground the frosts were over. There would be no late freezes to turn the soil to stone, to murder fragile, young plants in their earthen cradles. As inexplicably as ever, Truitt knew today was the day. And that knowing was as reliable as the seasons themselves. It was the "sight" and he was not the only man on the mountain to possess it or, perhaps, to be possessed by it.

Truitt stepped outside as he finished his coffee. The mountains towered darkly on the gray pre-dawn horizon and his breath clouded in the morning air. He shivered slightly and walked back inside for his jacket. The mules snorted and stamped inside their stalls, every bit as impatient as he was for sunrise. In less than an hour, the sun would climb into the sky, beginning the morning-long process of burning

6

the mist from the fields. By mid-morning it would fill the valley with pleasant warmth but, for now, the chill overwhelmed the gray world outside. Truitt sat his coffee mug on the workbench and shrugged into his coat. Before leaving the barn, he took a short nip from the bottle he kept upon the shelf next to the workbench, just a precautionary nip against the spring chill.

The whiskey burned pleasantly inside him as he walked toward the pig pens. There was some corn left in the pigs' crib and the porkers would appreciate a few ears. Truitt's pigs were every bit as bad as the most shrewish nag. He had to feed them first thing in the morning or else be ready to put up with their squealing complaints for the rest of the day. Of course, they squealed every time they saw him anyway, taking him for a soft touch no doubt, or soft in the head but the squealing never bothered him much if he'd fed them. In fact, it usually didn't bother him at all. Like his Aunt Tildy always said, "you can't heap guilt on an innocent soul".

Though no one could rightly accuse Truitt of having an innocent soul, they couldn't accuse him of ignoring his livestock either. And all the dishonest livestock in the world—lined up upon whatever side of their enclosure Truitt was on at the time and thrusting their perpetually moist and dirty snouts between the rails to tell every passerby their shamefully fabricated lies of deprivation—just couldn't make the accusations stick. Pigs, as far as Truitt was concerned, didn't have an honest bone in them and were worse than housecats when it came to their disregard for the truth.

Truitt sang softly in his off-key voice as he walked across the dew-wet grass that soaked his overalls from mid-shin down.

"Well I come home a Monday night, drunk as I could be,
I spied a horse out by the barn where my horse oughta be,
I called out to my little wife, "Explain this thing to me,
Why's that nag out by the barn where my nag oughta be?"

"Ye're naught but a shameless drunk and ye can't even see,

Tis no more than a milk cow, yer granny sent t'me."
I've traveled this wide world over, a hundred miles and more,
but a saddle on a milk cow's back I've never seen before.

Truitt stopped singing abruptly. "Amos, that you boy? I'm having to line you up with a fence post to see if you're moving."

Truitt grinned wider, expecting a smart reply from his younger son but he got no reply at all. This irritated him.

"I suppose I should be grateful you got your lazy ass up at all."

There was again no response. Truitt felt suddenly apprehensive. Whoever it was standing by the pig pen, it was neither of his sons.

At first, he thought he might be mistaken, that it was simply a trick of the early light but as he moved closer, he saw a small man, much smaller than either Walter or Amos. The man said nothing and didn't move a muscle but Truitt could feel the stranger's eyes on him.

Truitt stopped. Inside the pen, he could see the carcass of a pig lying in the mud and his anxiety was replaced by anger. If Truitt hated anything on God's earth, it was a thief. Lordy, he wished he'd brought his gun. He was unarmed and more the pity. If he'd brought his Long Tom he could have peppered the little man's backside with some birdshot. It wouldn't damage the fellow as much as give him something to think about for a few days.

On the other hand, a good, old-fashioned and sincere ass-kicking would likely be just as effective.

Truitt picked up a length of fence-rail from a pile on the ground and swung it a couple of times like a ballplayer stepping up to the plate. He liked the feel of it. The length of rail should do the trick and get the man's attention right enough. Though he could not see well enough to tell, he could still feel the little man's gaze. He felt it the way a jaybird might feel the gaze of a tomcat and he didn't like it one bit. Damned if he was going to break weak on his own land because some sneak-thief half-pint was staring at him. He gripped the fence rail tightly in his right hand and took a resolved step toward the pen.

8

"Looks like you done come to the wrong place lookin'
for free bacon, shorty. You'd do well to get the hell away
from my pigs if you know what's good for you."

The little man stepped forward to meet him, totally
ignoring the club in the irate farmer's hands.

"I ain't playing," Truitt said. "I'll tear your ass up like a
new ground."

Truitt brandished the rail like a war club.

"I mean it, Junebug. You'd best be clearing out if you
know what's good for you?"

The little man didn't give much credence to Truitt's
threats. He strolled a bit closer to the fence. This bothered
Truitt. It bothered him a lot. The man was not intimidated
at all by either Truitt or his threats. He fixed Truitt with a
gaze that stopped him in his tracks.

The stranger was not a man at all, but a youngster,
twelve, no more than thirteen-years-old. Fresh blood
dripped from the boy's chin and there was a tacky stain on
the front of his filthy shirt. Truitt's legs almost buckled.
The kid's eyes were harder than any eyes he had ever seen.
No wonder he had felt them so. And they spoke to him,
promising him more than he ever wanted to imagine.

The kid pulled his lips back over a pair of canine teeth
that would have looked right at home in a mountain wolf. A
low snarl rumbled up from the boy's chest and squeezed
through the glittering ivory of his mouth as he took another
step forward.

"Oh?" the youngster said his voice as sharp and
dangerous as the Reaper's scythe. "And do you know what's
good for you, old man?"

Truitt stepped back and dropped the fence rail.

The boy's snarl intensified until it became a howl as he
rushed forward to vault the rail fence. Truitt never saw him
leap the fence. In fact, he never saw him rush forward. As
soon as the boy took a second step, Truitt spun and headed
for the safety of the house. Though he had at least forty
years on the kid, Truitt ran like a young buck. The boy
could not close the distance, then Truitt hit his stride and the
race was on.

* * *

"What in the hell is that?" Amos McBride said as he rolled from his bed. Reeling sleepily, he didn't take time to dress or put on his boots as he stumbled to the door. His mother, her two sisters, his grandmother and his older brother were also hurrying toward the front door. They could hear the screams, hair-raising and terrified out in the yard.

"Oh, Lordy, that's Truitt," Ellie McBride said to Amos as she hurried out the door. Amos and Walter followed. Walter, anyway, had the good sense to grab a weapon, his double-barreled Long Tom twelve gauge. But he was much too astonished to use it.

While still a hundred feet from the farmhouse, Truitt screamed frantically for help. With his eyes focused on the front door and the sound of the wind and his own voice in his ears, he moved like no one in the family had ever seen him move before. Sleepy-eyed and confused, they milled on the porch and barely got out of his way as he vaulted the steps and hurried past them.

Walter finally shook off the fog of sleep long enough to kneel at the edge of the porch and rest the Long Tom on a railing as he aimed the weapon into the darkness. Walter thumbed back the rabbit-ear hammers and placed his fingers on the twin triggers as Amos, too, moved quickly across the porch and crouched behind the railing as if it might afford protection.

Amos was unarmed and the hair on his neck and arms tingled and rose but he could see nothing. He waited for the boom of Walter's shotgun. It never came. Seems there was nothing to shoot at.

"Who the hell's out there?" Walter demanded. "You'd best sing out and let me know. Else, by God, you're singing in a heavenly choir by breakfast." But there was nothing, not a heavenly choir, not a chirping bird. The morning was as still and quiet as any other morning. Except for the noise his mother was making.

"Now if that don't beat all. Truitt? Truitt, what in the world's wrong with you," Ellie shouted as she entered the house. She would have slammed the door behind her, but Amos caught it and started to follow her inside.

Ellie had barely cleared the door when Truitt suddenly rushed out again, colliding with Amos and nearly knocking him down. He ripped the door from Amos' hand and pushed it open as wide as possible.

"Hurry, hurry, get on in here!"

Wilda and Margie, came inside followed by their mother, Mabeline. Mabeline Williams, stopped just outside the doorway to spit a stream of snuff over the porch rail before crossing the threshold.

"Now what's got into him?" Margie asked, of no one in particular.

"Corn," Mabeline said with disgust, spitting another stream of snuff. "I always told Ellie he was low-down and now the good-for-nothing's got the rum-fits."

Truitt grabbed Amos and shoved him forward through the door, then followed him.

"Is he gone?" Truitt asked as he bolted the door.

"Is who gone, you damn fool?" Mabeline answered, over Ellie's shoulder. "There ain't nobody out here but us."

Truitt didn't answer. He was obviously rattled.

"Who in the world did you see?" Ellie asked, pressing for an explanation. She was usually tactful in dealing with her family, a careful and diplomatic mediator most of the time and skilled in drawing what she needed from the more-often-than-not stubbornly hard-headed members of her clan. But this wasn't a usual circumstance. Truitt ignored her as he headed straight for the bottle on the pantry shelf. His hands shook as he uncorked it.

"Whatever could have scared you so?" Ellie asked again, taking the direct approach as she pulled up a kitchen chair for him.

But he did not sit down. He paced instead. Truitt took a long drink of whiskey and wiped his mouth with his sleeve. "I don't rightly know," he said. "But you all seen it, didn't you? That thing out there in the pig-pen?"

"I didn't see a thing, Papa," Walter said, looking to his brother Amos for support. Amos merely shrugged, spreading his hands and shaking his head.

Truitt paced up and down, clearly rattled, as he recounted the experience, pausing from time to time for another shot from the bottle. He looked into Ellie's eyes and saw the confusion as well as the skepticism there.

"But we didn't see anything," she said. "The only thing I saw was you running and carrying on like nobody's business."

"It was out there, Ellie, I swear to God it was. Didn't you even hear it? Howling like—like some kind of banshee or something. Jesus. I'll bet that's what it was. I thought that was just an old story. But Lordy, Ellie, I just saw one. That's no good. The only time a banshee comes around is when somebody's fixin' to die."

"Well, *he* wasn't no banshee," Ellie said. "Banshees are women."

"Sure enough," Wilda said.

"And if you catch *her*," Margie added, "*she* has to tell you who it is that's gonna die."

"Oh, bullshit," Mabeline said testily. Mabeline stomped across the rough wooden floor and squared herself around to face her son-in-law. She stood nose to nose with him, her face just inches from his and jutted her jaw forward, challenging him.

At just a hair over six feet tall, Mabeline Williams could stand eye to eye with almost any man in the valley. She was a big women but she moved even bigger. Her heavy, lurching gait was distinctive, intimidating and misleading. She could not have weighed more than two hundred fifty pounds or so but she moved like she weighed half a ton most of the time. When she didn't, look out.

"Well this one wasn't about to catch no Banshee. That's if there was one and there ain't. You got no sense at all, Truitt McBride, and never had any. I always said that. Ain't I always said that, Ellie?"

She did not wait for her daughter to reply.

"This fool ain't seen nothin' that didn't come from the bottom of that bottle of his. Remember how his uncle Flannery used to carry on about bugs and boogers and what not when he had the rum-fits? Well, it must run in the family because this one's no different. I always told you,

12

Ellie, I always told you. I always said this is a sorry excuse for a man."

"You hush, woman," Truitt said, angrily. "I don't have to take a thing from you while I'm under my own roof. I got half a mind to put you out there with that thing."

Mabeline totally ignored the threat as she settled herself down in the chair Truitt had passed on. She was not about to let things lie. It was not in her nature. Mabeline Williams, as far as Truitt was concerned, would argue with a stump—and cuss one, too.

"Anybody who ever said you got half a mind was talking out of pure Christian charity," she said.

She sat directly across from Truitt and glared at him. And Truitt glared back. There had never been any love lost between Truitt and Mabeline Williams. Things had certainly not improved between them in the three years she and her two daughters had been living with him. Truitt always figured that Mabeline had badgered her husband to the point that there was nothing for poor old man Williams to do but die in self-defense. Pretty much everyone in the valley could agree that Mabeline, whatever else she might be, was a bit of a ring-tailed bitch. The soil had not settled on Sean William's grave before his son, Freeman, had turned his mother and sisters out of the home—at his wife's generally strident request.

Truitt, weak and foolish as he was sometimes, allowed Ellie to convince him to take her family in. Truth was—at the time anyway—Truitt hadn't taken a lot of convincing. He honestly did feel sorry for the women. Besides, he figured that if he held out the olive branch, so to speak, then Mabeline would likely take it, at least under her current circumstances, without ripping the arm that held it from its socket.

Too bad he didn't know as much about women, particularly this one, as he did about crops. It wasn't long before he began to feel a deep resentment toward Freeman for starting the chain of events which led to Truitt sharing the same roof with Mabeline. But, at the same time, he also held a grudging admiration for the man. Freeman displayed remarkably good sense.

Mabeline looked steadily at Truitt with her surly expression. Then something happened behind her eyes and she sat bolt-upright. Truitt noted the change in her expression as a shocked look appeared on her face and hardened into anger. She leapt to her feet, sending the straight-back chair clattering across the floor behind her.

Although a stout woman, she was toughened by years of hard work and her ponderous way of moving about belied an innate quickness and agility when she was so motivated. She crossed the floor in a flash and swung at Truitt's head with a roundhouse right that just barely clipped him as he ducked out of the way. Still his momentum caused him to stumble and he sprawled on the floor.

"Here, that's enough of that," Ellie said, moving quickly to intervene.

"You no-good, son-of-a-bitch," Mabeline said, looking down at her son-in-law as Amos and Walter immediately moved to either side of Mabeline, prepared to restrain her if the situation escalated. But Mabeline seemed content to drop the assault, content at least to drop the physical assault.

Truitt made no attempt to rise though he did sit up.

"You see," Mabeline said, standing over Truitt and pointing her finger at him imperiously. "You see what you've gone and married, Ellie? There's nothing out there that's not supposed to be there. There's nothing out there that hasn't always been there and anybody with a lick of sense knows that. But if there was a . . . a banshee or a . . . a crazy boy or whatnot, then this spineless coward would have shut us all out there with it just to save his own worthless hide."

Truitt's face grew red.

"It, uh, it wasn't exactly like that. I was tryin' to get my gun. Nobody brought a gun outside did they?"

"I had my gun," Walter said.

"Well I didn't see it anyway, even if you did."

"You can surely go to hell for lyin' same as for anything else," Ellie said.

Truitt was about to continue pleading his case when he was interrupted by the sound of heavy footsteps on the porch. Heads turned toward the doorway even before the sound of the loud knocking.

"Don't open the door," Truitt said, rising to his feet as Mabeline walked over to answer it. "Damn it, Mabeline, don't you open that door.

Mabeline looked over her shoulder and raked her once again terrified son-in-law with a look of contempt.

"Who is it?" She called out.

"Mrs. Williams? This is Percy Way. Can I come in?"

"Come on in and make yourself at home," she said, as she threw the bolt. She turned and swaggered past Truitt making sure he felt her disdain as Percy entered the room.

Percy was accompanied by his brother Bill and their cousin, Ernie Weems. All three were armed.

"I hope we ain't come at a bad time," Ernie said. "Seems some strange doings around last night."

"Y'all noticed anything peculiar?" Percy asked.

"The only thing peculiar round here is this fool," Mabeline said, nodding toward Truitt. "Claims he seen some kind of ghost, or goblin, or crazy boy or something."

"And, I did, too. He had long teeth, like some kind of animal, growled like an animal, too. Killed one of my pigs then come after me. I think he would've killed me, too, if I hadn't outrun him. I can't get none of these hard-heads to believe me."

"I'd believe him," Bill said. "That pig of yours is deader'n hell all right. We seen it when we come in. And Ernie and me run three fellas off one of my cows this morning. If we hadn't shot at them, they'd probably got after us, too."

"It made me sick," Ernie said, placing his hand on his stomach and grimacing, "what they was doin' to that cow and all."

"Percy? Are you all right?" Ellie asked.

Percy did not look all right. Truitt thought his strained expression was a mite more than a body would expect for somebody who'd only lost a cow.

"I don't think so, Ellie. We're looking for my daughter, Chloe. She didn't come home last night."

CHAPTER TWO

Although it was just past ten o'clock, the morning had already been a long one, perhaps the longest of Amos McBride's nineteen years. He sat atop the railing of the fence, his shotgun resting across his nervously bouncing knees as he looked down at the carcass of his father's sow. This was no butcher job like he had ever seen before and he had seen plenty. His older brother Walter paced slowly around the fence line, examining the ground.

"What do you think, Walter? A cougar? Maybe a bear?"

"It's a man, I reckon." Walter answered as he squatted down to examine the ground around the dead sow. "If it was a bear or a cougar, it sure covered its tracks."

Footprints covered the muddy ground like red ants on a picnic biscuit. Walter made a production of his tracking efforts, however, squatting back on his heels and peering at the prints as if they were hieroglyphs that spoke only to him. The truth, of course, as Amos knew well enough, was that even at the age of twenty-five, Walter still liked to play at wild Indian. He stood slowly, still staring at the ground.

"You and me seen about all there is to see around here as far as animals are concerned, I reckon. And I expect that there's nothing at all in these parts able to kill a three-hundred pound hog—nothing but a human being. Besides, you just can't argue with the fact that whatever killed that there pig was wearing boots."

"You know, Walter, I can see that from clean over here."

"Well, then, there you have it. All we have to do is find him."

"Not a thing to it," Amos replied. "All you gotta do is follow those tracks away from here and up those rocky-ass slopes yonder. Course, the tracks won't stand out there as good as they do in the soft mud and pig shit, but I got faith in you."

"And I got faith that you never let not knowing what you're talking about get in the way of your talking about it."

Walter turned and walked away leaving Amos to his own pursuits. Of course, they would track the boy down. The kid sure had some answering to do. But there were other more pressing concerns for Amos right now, more important questions. For instance, there was the whole thing about the strangers with the teeth.

At first Amos thought his father was pulling his leg but as far as he could tell there was no joke, no funny twist to the story. He did not care much for the idea that his father had gone crazy but that was the most likely explanation. All except for the part that there, lying at his feet, was a huge pig, dead as any bacon he had ever seen, with dozens of small boot prints in the mud around it.

Amos really did not know what to think. But the very last thing he wanted to consider was that something might have happened to Chloe Way. And he did not want to consider this because he could not remember a time when he had not been in love with her.

Chloe was the baby, the youngest of Percy and Agnes Way's seven daughters and two years younger than Amos. The Way girls were something. Kinder members of the community described them as "wild". Other, more judgmental, individuals favored harsher terms. And, of the whole beautiful bunch, it was Chloe who, as her mother put it, was the pick of the litter.

Amos didn't consider himself worldly by any account and he reckoned anyone who did was stretching the description to a snapping point. But he wasn't at all surprised that Chloe's beauty gave her a certain power over men. It certainly gave her power over him. But he was even less surprised that the relentlessly independent young woman had no qualms about using that power anytime it was to her advantage and he couldn't help but admire that.

In any case, by the ripe old age of seventeen, Chloe Way already had years of experience as a scandalous woman. At least she had the experience of dealing with a scandalous reputation.

Amos had heard many rumors about her but as far as he was concerned rumors were all they were. A running joke in the valley named Percy's shotgun as best man at the five older girls' weddings. And his own grandmother, Mabeline Williams, had tagged Chloe with the less-than-flattering nickname of "Family" Way, claiming it was only going to be a matter of time until Chloe got herself into that kind of trouble. But Amos did not hold with Mabeline's theory and, even if he did, it would not matter. All Chloe had to do was smile at him and he would forgive her anything. Amos always hoped, if Chloe were indeed to find herself in "that" kind of trouble, that he would be the one responsible, or at least the one blamed.

But Chloe was different from other girls he had known, no doubt about it. She had the independent streak about her that set her apart and perhaps was the catalyst that caused the more active tongues to wag. Chloe had a mind of her own and she was as hard-headed and bold as any man Amos had ever met and almost on a par with her sister Sara.

As it happened every time Amos thought of her, he remembered the incident two years past when he and Walter happened upon Chloe and some of her sisters swimming in the lazy flow of Seven-Mile Creek. From his hiding spot in the thick foliage, Amos watched the girls swim and splash about. The white flash of skin, bright and brilliant among the shadows of trees over water, made him dizzy with feelings he had never known and couldn't explain.

The girls lolled in the shallow water where a patch of sunlight found its way through the gnarled branches of the tall oaks. They lay on their backs with their legs spread slightly and at each little movement one of them made, the motion of the water caused their breasts to move as if

18

independent of the rest of their bodies.

Amos paid careful attention to every single detail of the scene and even more attention to the construction of the memory but mostly he paid attention to Chloe. Her long, wet, almost but not quite auburn hair hung straight down to dangle into the creek when she tilted her head and the same movement caused her white breasts to thrust forward, rising from the water. Her green eyes were concealed by a lazy droop of eyelids made heavy by the warm summer sun. Grains of sand dotted her cheek and droplets clung to the fine, microscopic down of her glistening skin. Scissoring her long legs slowly back and forth in the shallow water, she exposed the dark triangular patch at the juncture of her thighs.

Amos was buffeted by emotion, steam-rolling over him, pulling him in every direction. Not the least of these emotions was a bone-deep sense of loneliness which took him completely by surprise and filled him with the strangest ache he could ever have imagined. He wondered if what people called love was just a faith that there was a "someone" out there and that the "someone" would keep them from that loneliness, a killing sense of isolation and disconnection.

If Chloe could do that for Amos, if she would do that for Amos, then how could he not love her? That didn't seem quite right to him but that was as far as he had come with it. And, if this was love, it sure made the crotch of his pants tight. Amos was given to ponder that, too, but about that time Walter decided to have some fun and stepped out into the open in plain view of the girls.

"Morning, ladies," he greeted them loudly.

The girls' reaction had been instantaneous as they squealed and splashed out into deeper water, sinking up to their chins for concealment and crossing their arms tightly over their breasts; all of them but Chloe. She stood in the knee-deep water, looking calmly at Walter, her steady gaze causing him to blush and drop his eyes. Then she turned to Amos, who still knelt in the underbrush.

"Good morning, gentlemen," she replied softly, perhaps even cordially, as if they had met one another on the way to a church social.

But there was more than that. Even as she stood in the shallow water, as naked as the adoration on Amos's face, she was in charge and she knew it. She lowered her head for a moment and Amos didn't know what to expect. Typical of Chloe, she did the unexpected. Chloe turned her brilliant green eyes on him and smiled. He could have died on the spot.

Amos couldn't take his eyes off her as she waded calmly out onto the opposite bank and strolled over to a pile of clothing, as casually unconcerned as if she had been alone in her own room. She faced him as she stretched her arms above her head and slid into her light cotton dress. The fabric clung to her wet skin and once again Amos became aware of the lump in his throat.

Chloe cocked her head to one side and smiled brightly.

"Bye, Amos," she said. "I hope this gives you gentlemen something to think about from time to time."

And then she was gone.

Boy, had it ever given him something to think about.

Even now, sitting on the railing and looking at the dead sow, the thoughts of that afternoon elicited a hot rush of blood in his veins. God, he hoped nothing had happened to Chloe.

The men crossing the yard caught Amos' attention. Percy and Bill approached the hog pen each wearing a similar grim expression. Truitt stood on the porch, shotgun slung over his shoulder while he stuck the second of two revolvers in his belt before hurrying down the steps to catch up with the others. Finally Walter and Ernie followed, chatting and joking as they approached.

"Old Truitt was moving was he?" Ernie asked, grinning broadly.

"Moving?" Walter said. "Friend, you don't know nothing. There ain't a thing in God's mountains that could've caught up with that man. You'd need a racehorse to talk to him, much less catch him."

The two laughed together but Amos failed to see the humor. Truitt obviously did not either. A stern look from his father silenced Walter and Ernie followed suit. Neither spoke again as they joined the rest of the group at the pig sty. Truitt leaned against a fence post, looking silently into the pen. He stepped back and kicked the bottom rail, shaking the whole enclosure and almost spilling Amos into the rancid muck.

"Dang," Truitt said, angrily. "That was my best sow."

Without another word, he turned and walked away, marching in the direction of Hog Heaven Hill. Amos, along with the others, followed without further discussion. Hog Heaven Hill, the tallest of the mountains ringing the valley, was still dwarfed by the looming giants of the range stretching westward in the distance. Steep and heavily wooded, it was a rough climb. Amos did not ask where they were going. Though no one had told him, he already knew. They were in for a long walk and an equally long climb up the forested slope to the small clearing where Aunt Tildy Garrett's cabin stood.

There may have been a river or two in the country that was older than Matilda Garrett, but Amos didn't know the names of them. He also knew of no one as old as his father's great aunt. For that matter, he knew of no one who actually knew Tildy's age. If he had to bet, he would wager she was a hundred if she was a day. She was not sure herself to hear her tell it. But she had been in her fifties when the sound of Union cannons drifted up from the lowlands and the valleys and meadows had been strewn with the dead.

Amos remembered his grandfather saying what a fine figure of a woman Tildy had been in her prime and how he had once been caught spying on her while she bathed. Grandpa McBride cackled over the beating he had received for his effort and maintained it had well been worth it. Amos shuddered. It would take a hell of a beating to force him to watch the old girl bathe.

Tildy was rumored to be "strange." And he had heard people say this, though never to her face, ever since he could remember. Amos had been nine years old when Walter explained to him what people meant by "strange".

"You know," Walter said. "Just strange. She ain't got no use for men. Never has."

"So what's strange about that? I ain't got no use for

21

women. Does that make me strange?"

Walter laughed.

"Naw, that just makes you a kid--a ignorant one at that. But Aunt Tildy's got a yen for women. She treats them like a man would treat them. Understand?"

Amos shook his head.

"Damn, Amos. You can be dumber than a whole sack full of rocks sometimes. Aunt Tildy's queer, boy. She likes to take other women to bed."

That news shocked young Amos to his shoes. Living on a farm, he had a more than passing acquaintance with the mechanics of sex as it was practiced by barnyard animals. So, with a child's logic, he moved to the next frightening assumption. *Aunt Tildy had a penis.* For a while, he avoided the old lady with the same self-conscious horror with which he avoided a dose of Castor Oil. Of course, he now understood.

At least he understood what "strange" meant even while he doubted he would ever understand what "strange" was like. But he knew what it meant when people thought you were different. It meant talk behind your back, bad names and bad stories told to everyone but you. It meant bearing a cross that was not of your own making. And Aunt Tildy bore it well, without complaint, without explanation, without apology and without shame.

Amos walked quietly with his shotgun over his shoulder as they entered the woods to climb the slope of Hog Heaven Hill. The terrain was steep, an exhausting trace under the best of conditions, even more tiring with the sun almost directly overhead. The path twisted past swaths of loose rock, around sharp bluffs and impenetrable tangles of undergrowth that had to simply be gone around.

But Amos paid no mind to the terrain, as trackless as he had told Walter it would be, or to his own weariness. His mind was still on Chloe and he hoped Aunt Tildy would be able to help. Strange or not, Aunt Tildy knew more about all sorts of things than anyone else in the county. Many believed she had the "sight" and that was true enough he guessed.

That wasn't entirely true either. He damned well knew

she had it. If anyone could explain these recent odd occurrences, it would be her. Amos never had to struggle to frame a question or make a point with Tildy as he often had to do with other members of his family. Aunt Tildy knew what he was thinking most of the time—at least when he was around her.   And while he was never actually comfortable with that reality, he had to accept it because that was the way it was and what else can a man do with a natural fact?

He had no doubt she simply knew other things as well. Amos comforted himself with the thought that she would likely know exactly what had happened to Chloe and, even more importantly, where to find her. He would not consider any possibility beyond her safe return to her father. That was the first thing, the important thing. Make sure Chloe was all right and get her home. After that, he had a bone to pick with his friend Burl Tanner.

CHAPTER THREE

Tildy Garrett sat on the porch, rocking slowly in her chair. Tall and gaunt with iron-gray hair that matched her gray eyes, she was not a particularly impressive woman at first glance. But Amos had more than first-glance knowledge of her and she was, in his estimation, a most remarkable woman. A plain dress of light blue cotton hung on her slim form where her breasts had withered away to nothing. Her chest as far as Amos could tell was as flat as his own and, Granddad's stories notwithstanding, he could not imagine Aunt Tildy ever having a womanly figure.

Sun-darkened, rough and deeply-creased, her skin resembled rain-soaked leather. And today Amos was uneasy at the sight of her. It wasn't her shape or the texture of her skin that bothered him. It had more to do with her bearing and her eyes. Tildy's eyes were deep, gray, and timeless. They lacked the rheumy emptiness he found reflected in so many other ancient eyes. There was life and plenty of it stuffed into the leather sack that was Tildy Garrett. And it shone in her eyes, eyes that would be at home in a face as young as his own—a face as young as Chloe's. They were the old woman's most distinguishing feature. That and the fact she still had all her teeth.

Tildy raised her hand to shield her eyes and the men crossed her small yard to where she sat on the porch. Amos followed along behind them.

"Come on up and sit a mite," she said, in a voice tremulous with age. "I've been expecting you."

Truitt led the way, climbing the short stoop and bending to give Tildy a peck on the cheek before pulling up a chair.

"You're just as pretty as ever," he said.

Tildy smiled, waving a hand to dismiss the compliment. "Yep. And you're just as full of flattery as a flatland peddler—bullshit, too."

Truitt didn't deny it and Tildy cleared her throat. "You men got the look of them with something on their minds."

Amos hung back, but he wasn't hiding from her. It wasn't possible for him to hide from her. He could feel her awareness swimming around the edges of his own and knew that all of the talking coming his way was just something for the others. Tildy already knew what he knew and a damned sight more. That was the way it worked between them he guessed. He looked up at her and she smiled at him.

"Hidey. Amos," she said.

"Hidey, Aunt Tildy."

Percy laid his shotgun on the rough plank floor of the porch and squatted next to it leaning against the railing.

"There's been some awful strange doings down in the valley last night," he said, taking tobacco and rolling papers from the pocket of his coat. He continued to talk as he rolled a cigarette. "My baby daughter's missing. She went out walking with Duncan Tanner's boy, Burl, last night. She ain't come home yet. I reckon I'm looking for her."

"That ain't all," Ernie said. "Livestock's been killed by some kind of—some kind of—" he paused, searching for a word that he simply could not find. "Hell, some kind of something or other. They look like men but they sure don't act like no men I've ever seen."

"We thought you might be able to help us out," Percy said, lighting his smoke and passing the works to Ernie. "The only thing we know about any of this is we don't know a damn thing. Even less about where to start doing something about it. Folks say you got the sight and I reckon I believe them. After all, you did know we was coming and all."

"The only sight it took for that is right here," she said, pointing to her eyes. "I may be old but I'm not blind. I can see the whole valley from here and I've been looking in on you boys all morning and watching you climb through that stretch of trees for the last hour or so. But maybe if you can tell me a little more about what's going on, we can figure it out."

Amos thought the men must have felt a little foolish, at least it seemed that way to him. Here they were, out in the bright daylight in front of God and everybody, talking about things which had sounded real enough in gray twilight but as false and unbelievable as anything dreamed up by frightened children here in the old lady's front yard. Tildy listened politely and impassively through most of the telling, occasionally nodding or clucking sympathetically.

But she was particularly attentive when Percy discussed Chloe's failure to return from her walk with Burl. Amos again felt an unwelcome twinge of jealousy at the mention of Burl's name. Burl knew how Amos felt about Chloe and he went to call on her anyway. Amos burned with anger every time he thought about it.

Of course it was true that he had never actually told Burl how he felt about Chloe—in fact, Amos had never told anyone—but it somehow made sense to him that Burl would simply know about his feelings and respect them. Surely he could tell. And whether or not Burl knew or what he knew or when he knew it was all beside the point. There was going to be a reckoning.

The men finished speaking and Tildy drew a plug of sweet-twist tobacco from her apron pocket and bit off a chew.

"I figured it might be something like that," Tildy said, rocking back in her chair and chewing thoughtfully. "Them things were vampires."

"They were what?" Truitt asked.

"Vampires."

"What in the world is that?" Ernie asked. "Sounds like some kind of foreigner or something."

"At one time they probably were. But we're all

26

foreigners sometimes or at least somewhere," Tildy said. "Vampires are a bit different."

"I'd say they're a damned site different," Truitt said, turning to Amos.
"Vampires are those old blood-sucking boogers your grandad used to scare you with in them stories he told— before I had to make the old man stop. I didn't think you was ever gonna get a full night's sleep again."

He did not have to explain to Amos, nor remind him. Amos remembered well enough his grandfather's stories. So well, in fact, that he was still grateful that he shared a room with his older brother.

Truitt turned back to Tildy and shook his head. "Tildy, there ain't no such things; that's all made up to scare young uns'."

"Well, those stories sure enough scared me when I was young," she said. "But my own grandaddy swore they weren't made-up. He said that vampires were thick as flies at a church social back in the old country and that there used to be a lot of them around here, too, before they all got killed or run off."

She leaned forward and turned to Amos, looking intently into his eyes.
"That was a long time ago, before my time, when things got so bad that folks started hunting them down. Those that weren't killed run off, scattering way back in the mountains. I hear tell some come back from time to time, though I can't rightly say I ever seen one myself. Anyway, it's a long story."

Amos was standing even before Tildy was finished speaking. Tildy smiled. Filled with the same anxieties and concerns he shared with the others, the fact that he knew beforehand what she was going to ask of him and was already prepared to carry out her request was not really in his consciousness.

"Amos, why don't you run fetch some cider before we get too far into it?"

"Yes, ma'am," Amos said.

But Amos did not hurry to carry out the task. In fact, he dragged his feet. Amos dreaded the chore he had been assigned. The well-house was dark, cool and—for the first time—ominous as he nervously stepped inside to retrieve the jug of hard cider. It was not Amos's first trip into the structure. The first time, his mother had been standing just outside the door where he could speak to her. Since then he had needed no companion to complete the trip.

Until today.

Now the darkness closed around him and the skin on the back of his neck tingled as he moved quickly through the shadows. He almost dropped the cider jug in his haste but he could not move half as quickly as he desired. All he wanted in the world was to be back in the sunlight.

He felt Tildy's presence, her thoughts moving about on the perimeter of his own. Almost as if letting him know that everything was fine, that Tildy trumped the possibility of vampires. Tildy's mental voice was a comfort even if he was the only one who could hear it.

The word "vampire" buzzed in his mind like a blue-bottle fly. He tried to attach it to images. Though he pictured many horrors, the one that stuck in his mind was the imagined reality of the tow-headed boy his father had described. A boy with tusks like the ivory of a walrus Amos had once seen in a book. Amos tightened his jaw as he banished the ridiculous picture from his thoughts. He would not let such silliness deter him from his errand. Tildy brought glasses out onto the porch and soon everyone sat with a glass of cider waiting for her to elaborate.

"A vampire's an awful strange creature. A corpse come to life that can only stay alive by drinking the blood of the living. I figure they're a lot like a mad dog. If one gets hold of a man and drinks his blood, well, of course, the man dies. But he don't really die exactly. He'll turn into one of them. They're crazy as mad dogs, too. They'll take anything that bleeds—man, woman, child—don't make a bit of difference. They say any one of them is strong as ten men and you just about have to kill them every way there is to die before the damn things stay down.

"Grandaddy said, when they drove them out the first time, they had to hunt them down in daylight and drive stakes through their hearts. He wasn't lying about that. I seen his face. It was no lie. He said some were people he'd grown up with, people he cared about, and he hinted that during that time some innocent folks got staked along with the guilty. There was a week or two of slaughter and they were gone. Old folks said they run off to the high mountains yonder. Like I said, I hear they come back from time to time."

"Aunt Tildy, if they're so hard to kill and all, how come that young one didn't just follow me into the house and kill the whole family?" Truitt asked.

"Yeah," Bill said, patting the butt of his shotgun for emphasis. "And them me and Ernie run across this morning flat hauled ass when we cut down on them."

"Hard to say," she said, thoughtfully. "Maybe it was too close to daylight–they have to hide in the daylight or the sun burns them up–or maybe it was something else. It seems I recall a vampire can't just up and come into your house. It has to be invited. Maybe that one this morning figured you wouldn't be inviting him in."

"At least they got some manners," Truitt muttered.

"Anyhow, if you want to do them in, then you got to find where they hide in the daytime and drive a stake through their hearts. A stake'll do her, or sunlight. Some claim crosses and garlic will do the trick. Grandaddy swore by Holy Water."

"What in Hell's Holy Water?" Bill asked.

"Near as I can figure, it's something you got to get from a priest. He has to pray over it or something. But if you don't go that route, they won't stay dead. Just putting a bullet in them won't do the trick."

"And just where in the world are we gonna find a priest?" Truitt asked. "We'd likely have to go all the way back to Ireland. There ain't been a Catholic of any kind in these parts since your granddaddy's time."

"That's God's own truth," Ernie said.

Truitt shook his head and pursed his lips for a moment, not looking at Tildy. "I don't believe I've ever heard so many outlandish stories at one sitting in my life," he said.

Aunt Tildy sat up rigidly and gave Truitt a dirty look. Before she could speak, Percy tossed his two cents in.

"No disrespect intended, Tildy, but I don't know if I

believe any of this either."

Tildy looked steadily at Truitt, who looked away. Then she turned to Percy.

"Do you men believe your own eyes? Did some little fella kill Truitt's sow last night? With his teeth? Did Bill and Ernie run a couple more off a cow this morning, doing the same thing?"

No one answered. Tildy's face softened as she spoke to Percy.

"Are Burl and Chloe missing? You men come all this way to ask me what I know and I told you all I can remember. They're only things that were told to me. It might all be true or it might be the deepest bullshit you ever stepped into. How about you all explain to me what in blazes is going on and I'll see if I believe you."

Percy looked down at his boots and said nothing. Everyone fell silent for a while, as if digesting the information.

"I don't know what to believe either, boys," Ernie said. "The only thing I know for sure is that I want to get home before dark and we got a bit of woods to cover if we're going to find Chloe before then."

"You ain't never lied," Bill agreed.

"You all should've got an earlier start then," Tildy said, squinting at the sun riding lower on the horizon. "The best thing would be to stay here and start out early in the morning."

Percy, too, gazed at the sun.

"We appreciate it, Tildy," he said, turning back to her. "But I can't stay here not knowing what's happened to Chloe. Besides, we all got families, all except Ernie, and they're alone. We'd best be getting started back."

"Yep, I reckon you had at that. But not till you got something to eat. It won't take a few minutes. Amos, come on with me while I rustle something up."

Amos followed her around the house to the shallow root-cellar which had been laboriously hewn into the hard, stony ground. He did as she instructed, fetching the several articles she wanted and bringing them out. He was not as nervous about the dark as he was before. Tildy's presence was a calming one and Amos felt safe with her standing outside the cellar door. It did not make sense that he would feel safe. After all, a strong wind would no doubt blow Aunt Tildy away. But he felt safe anyway.

"They ain't stories," Amos said, standing just inside the cellar with his hands full.

"No, sir, they ain't. Just ain't no use arguing about it is there? They'll find out soon enough."

Perhaps Aunt Tildy's self-sufficiency put him at ease. He could not help but admire the way such an old woman, with no man around, could get by so well up here. He exited the cellar and carried the provisions into the kitchen where Tildy took ham and fresh eggs from the larder. Amos stayed with her to help prepare the meal.

He levered the pump handle up and down until a rust-red flow of water sputtered through the opening, built to a steady stream and cleared as the iron deposits became more diffuse. Tildy filled the coffee pot and placed it on the stove. She hummed to herself as she measured out the coffee. Amos knew the tune and hummed with her.

Tildy began to sing and Amos did as well. Together they moved back and forth between the English and the Gaelic, the old Irish ballad of a woman and her lost love. Amos was captivated by the sound of the old woman's voice which was high and clear and sounded nothing like an old woman's voice.

> *Shule,shule, shule agra*
> *Only death can cease my woe,*
> *Since the lad of my heart from me did go*
> *Go thee thu Mavourneen slaun.*

> *I'll dye my petticoat, I'll dye it red,*
> *And round the world I'll beg my bread,*
> *Till I find my love alive or dead*
> *Go thee thu Mavourneen slaun.*

By the time, he finished setting the table, Amos had ceased singing altogether. Tildy didn't seem to notice. When she sang it was as if she became someone else, maybe something

31

else, something not fettered by such things as time and ill-health. Amos sat in a straight back chair and watched her. It occurred to him that she was beautiful and that he was just now learning how to see her. Tildy, inside herself and oblivious, paid him no mind all.

Come, come, come my love
Only death can cease my woe,
Since the lad of my heart from me did go
Fare thee well my dar—ling.

No more am I that blooming maid,
That used to roam the valley shade
My youth and bloom are all decayed
Fare thee well my dar—ling.

Amos turned away from Tildy as she finished the song and cleared his throat. It was a waste of time, of course, because Tildy knew exactly what he was feeling and thinking and it did him no good to try to hide anything from her. Still, he would make a go at it. Tildy passed behind him and paused only long enough to trail her hand over his head and down to and across his shoulder.

Go thee thu Mavourneen slaun.

He swallowed the lump in his throat and concentrated on the table cloth.

He held a suspicion that the old oil cloth spread over the table had been there forever. At least he couldn't remember any other one. The cover was a floral pattern, tinged yellow with years and the smoke from the wood-burning stove. It was blue, like the summer sky, with green leaves and red and yellow blossoms scattered across it. Whoever designed it must have spent some time lying on the ground and looking up at the sky through a canopy of roses.

"So, you're in love with Chloe," Tildy said, placing another platter on the oil cloth.

Amos had turned his attention out the kitchen window. The panes of glass, like the table cover, were stained yellow with accumulated smoke.

"Huh?" He heard her well enough but was stalling for

time.

"So you're in love with Chloe."

"Well, I don't reckon . . . I mean, I never said nothing like that."

Tildy laughed.

"Oh, yes, you did. Your eyes done all the talking and it sure enough don't require the "sight" to see that clear enough. If vampires don't get hold of that Tanner boy, I reckon you'll do a right good enough job ripping his throat out with your own teeth."

Amos blushed and turned away. He wondered if his feelings had been that obvious to the men.

"There's nothing to be ashamed of. It's natural for a young man to feel the way you do and that Chloe Way is a looker."

Amos looked quickly up at her, again experiencing the hot flash of jealousy. The look was not lost on Tildy. She smiled as she read the thoughts racing across his mind and reflecting on his face.

"Nah, Amos," she said, placing an arm around his shoulder. "It's not like that at all, boy. I'm an old woman and my sporting days are done. Besides, I never bothered nobody that didn't feel the same way I did. Chloe's not that way."

"But Sara is?" Amos said, impulsively.

Sara was Chloe's sister and the next youngest of Percy Way's children. Like Tildy, Sara also never had much use for men and folks said that Sara, too, was "strange." But Amos was now embarrassed that he had even asked the question. In the first place, he knew well enough that Sara longed for women. In the second place, he knew well enough what Tildy was going to say before she said it. That was what had bothered him all these years. He knew Tildy's answer before she spoke just as she knew his. Talking was just a formality and a comfort.

"You know that good and well for yourself. But if you need somebody to say it then I reckon that's something you ought to ask her," Tildy said, out of politeness rather than necessity.

"You do have the sight."

"Yeah, that I do and so do you. For that matter, Truitt has a touch of it himself but he won't listen to it. Least not too much. Only when it comes to things like knowing when it's planting time. I reckon it runs in the family. He just gets a feeling. I get that, you get that. And you know it's not like folks think. I can't run around reading everybody's mind all the time and neither can you. The thing between you and me is a sometimes thing and it's special."

"I know," Amos said.

"I don't know where Chloe is but I know she's all right. So do you."

"I know that, too," Amos said. "Still I'm afraid for her."

"And it's natural that you are. But you're going to cross paths with her soon enough. And you and me both know things are going to get a damned sight worse before they get any better. There's a darkness coming down on us, Amos and it's like nothing we've ever seen before."

She didn't need to convince Amos. Maybe she was convincing herself.

"Your guess is as good as mine about how it's going to end, but we both know it's a ways from being over. Maybe you should be afraid for all of us."

Amos nodded his head and did not ask for explanation. He was afraid for everyone.

"What about you, Aunt Tildy? You're up here all alone. If those things come from the highlands yonder then they're sure going to pass through here both coming and going. Will you be all right?"

Tildy's hand moved involuntarily up to her throat and Amos detected a fleeting moment of fear in her expression.

"That's another one of those things I don't know."

"Come on back with us then. You'll feel a lot safer down in the valley with other folks."

The old woman laughed again and shook her head.

"My mind's still quick, boy, but these old legs are plumb used up. You're going to have a tough enough time getting home before dark without hauling me along. The best I could do for you would be to slow you down and guarantee the night would catch you. Besides, if there's any truth to what I've said, then I'll be safe enough here. If not, I might feel a little safer in the valley but I wouldn't be any safer than if I sat out on the porch and waited for them. If I'm wrong, nobody in the valley–or anywhere else for that matter–is going to be safe."

Amos nodded somberly. He was taking the situation more and more seriously by the moment. If Tildy was right, all hell might be breaking loose in the valley by nightfall. Although Amos was quite anxious to leave, he was still very much concerned for Tildy's welfare.

"I don't much like the idea of you staying up here by yourself. What are you going to do if some of them things show up?"

"Well, I won't be inviting nobody in that I know is dead and that's for sure. I'm going to put me a cross on the door and if anybody wants to come in, including you or anyone else who leaves here today, they're going to have to kiss that cross. I've got no need at all to go outside during the night."

"But what if you're wrong? What if none of that works?"

Tildy pulled at her chin for a moment while she pondered the question. Her eyes looked far beyond both Amos and the stark green mountains framed in the small window behind him.

"I've been alive a long time, boy. I don't rightly know how long, myself. But I plan on dying soon. When that happens I'm going on to my reward, whatever that may be, but if I got a say in it, I plan on staying as dead as I can as long as I can. The thought of getting up in a day or so and dragging this old carcass around looking for blood for an eternity or two don't much appeal to me. I'll wait for them to come and they will. When they do, I'll find out if what I heard is true I guess. But I'll guarantee you this: If I can't keep them out, the last thing I'm going to do is stick my brother's old Navy Colt to the side of my head and pull the trigger."

Amos looked at Tildy with shock written all over his face. Suicide simply was not done. It was the surest way of damning a soul to hell than almost any other sin imaginable. Suicide could not be justified under any circumstances. He opened his mouth to convince Tildy of this when she raised her hand and waved him off.

"I know what you're going to say. I've heard it all my life. Let me tell you this: If I die at the hands of a vampire, I'll live as a killer for God knows how long—maybe forever—and that's not right. It's not right and I'm not going to have it. God will understand. And if he don't, well, I guess I've done gone and wasted my whole life praying to some hard-ass with no sense at all."

With that remark, Tildy turned to finish setting the table. Seemingly without concern, she had just combined the unpardonable sin of suicide, or at least the threat of it, with the equally unpardonable sin of blasphemy; and all in almost the same breath. Amos did not know what to think but he held his peace.

Sitting at table with the others, Amos sensed their desire to be on their way. The meal was not a pleasant one, nor a sociable one. The anxiety around the table was as high as the afternoon sun. Everyone wolfed their food and Amos did the same. With the meal behind them, no more time was wasted. Each thanked Aunt Tildy, both for her hospitality and for the information. As they walked away towards the woods, he turned to wave goodbye.

Tildy stood on the porch, alongside a rough-hewn column post. She seemed very small, very fragile. Amos had a feeling he would not see her again. Not something he could explain, just a vague sense of knowing that was not at all clear, not at all comforting. The men walked quickly into the tree-line as the sun rode lower on the serrated mountain skyline, red light creeping up the eastern slope leaving darkness behind it. Halfway down the mountainside it was apparent to all of them they would never make it back by nightfall.

CHAPTER FOUR

In the cool shade of the trees, Amos walked as silently as his companions and just as deeply lost in his own thoughts, thoughts of the imagination-straining history of vampires as told by Aunt Tildy. Here, walking through the familiar surroundings of the tall oaks and conifers, it was tempting to think it all ridiculous, tempting but not useful. Even if he had never heard of any such things before today—at least this side of fairy tales.

In his limited educational experiences, he had heard of a people called "Masai" who lived across the ocean in the land of Africa. He had seen pictures of them; a lean, tall, black race who wore the skin of animals and brightly colored home-spun cloth. The book said they raised cattle and counted their wealth in cattle. He had been fascinated by the pictures, especially of the statuesque Masai women with their close-cropped hair and bare breasts.

Many nights, he had dreamed of Africa, of living like a Masai, of wearing skins and hunting lions with the wicked long-blade spear they called an assagai. He had been in the fourth grade when he tried to explain those dreams to his teacher. She had laughed.

"Well, Amos, I think there are parts of that life you'd like and maybe some other parts you wouldn't like so much."

"What wouldn't I like," he asked, finding it difficult to believe that there could be something to dislike in anything so obviously adventurous.

"Blood," she said, grinning at him ghoulishly.

"Blood?"

"It's a staple of the Masai diet. Cattle are much too valuable to be killed very often for food. The Masai make shallow cuts in the throats of the cattle every now and then, drain some of the blood and mix it with milk. The Masai drink blood, Amos."

The thought of drinking blood made his stomach lurch. He abandoned all hope of becoming the world's first, red-headed, Scot/Irish, Masai warrior. He had not thought about the dreams in years but now they all flooded back; vampires, Masai, blood. If the Masai were a race of vampires, one would never know it from the pictures and when a Masai died, he stayed dead. Amos almost hoped Tildy and the rest were crazy. It would be easier to deal with.

Somewhere within him he knew better and that was the thing he just couldn't get around. It didn't matter what made sense. It didn't matter what folks thought. It didn't matter anything really. What is simply is and that's about the end of it. He didn't like it any better than the next man, providing the next man didn't like it worth a damn either, but he did have to accept it. The truth was that vampires, or whatever anyone wanted to call them, turned out to be real.

That's truth for you—painful, uncomfortable and unavoidable. Like knowing the truth that everyone has to die or that a whole new kind of monster was down in the little valley between Devil's Saw Ridge and Hog Heaven Hill. The truth was, as Aunt Tildy pointed out, the situation was far from over. In fact, it had hardly begun.

The lengthening shadows in the woods didn't do much to quell Amos' nerves, or the nerves of any of the others for that matter. He did not know to what extent the others believed this vampire business, but the tension he felt in them was real enough. No one disclosed what they were thinking or feeling and no one had seen anything unusual so far. But everyone, including Amos, no longer carried their weapons in the casual, over-the-shoulder position, but held them at ready.

"Listen," Truitt said, holding up his hand to halt the men.

From deep in the woods came quick, sharp yelps like the barking of a small dog.

"Oh, shit," Ernie said, as he looked quickly about. "You boys hear that? A fox barking and it ain't even dark yet. Lordy, that's a bad sign."

The yips and yammers of the fox came faster for a few seconds then silence. The group moved on again, picking up the pace as they moved through the trees. They had gone no more than a hundred yards when the high-pitched shriek of a screech-owl split the air; another night sound, another omen.

Amos pressed his thumb against the hammers of the Long Tom as his fingers curled tightly around the stock and gripped the triggers. Other than the sounds of the fox and owl, everything in the forest seemed as usual. The squirrels played in the branches and cotton-tail rabbits, fragile nerves breaking at the very last moment, leapt from places of concealment to scamper several yards farther away to hide again. Night came on quickly as the group moved through the ever-deepening shadows, over the leaf-strewn ground and picked their way through the woods.

It was totally dark by the time they reached the edge of the meadow. Through a break in the trees, Amos saw the clearing where the fields met the forest. The dim light of the quarter-moon provided little illumination but anything was better than the choking darkness which enveloped him at present. Each second seemed an eternity. His fear intensified with every step and the closer he came to the edge of the woods, the more he felt he would never make it out. By the time he broke free, his heart pounded with the force of a trip-hammer.

Amos drew a deep breath as he moved out of the tree-line. He relaxed his grip on the Long Tom, feeling the tingling in his hands as surging blood began to circulate again. Right hand gripping the barrels, he swung the gun up to rest across his shoulder. The relief he felt was unbelievable. He felt as if a three-ton weight had been lifted from his shoulder. In an almost giddy elation, he started across the field. He had been expecting all hell to break loose since sundown.

And then it did.

Hell broke loose from the trees in the form of shadows,

39

bursting howling and raging from the cover of the forest to race across the meadow toward Amos and the others. Amos realized, to his horror that though the apparitions looked like men and ran like men, they snarled and growled like animals. They were not legends, gleaned from an old woman's fertile imagination; not characters cooked up to frighten gullible children; they were real. And they were killers. And they were here. He flipped the shotgun down to ready and fired both barrels.

The recoil staggered Amos back but he saw one of the ghostly forms take the load of buckshot. The shot stopped the creature suddenly; lifting it from its feet and slamming it to the ground like a vicious, charging dog stopped by its chain. It did not move. In an instant, Amos reloaded and fired once more. Another figure went down, leaped up again and retreated into the woods.

There was something familiar about the second creature. The way it looked; the way it moved. Burl Tanner? Could it have been Burl Tanner? That was not possible. Was it? Amos had no time to further consider the question.

In seconds, the air filled with the resonant boom of shotguns and the sharp smoke of gunpowder billowed around them stinging Amos' nose and eyes. As he reached into his hunting sack for more shells, Amos saw Ernie and Percy firing away to his right, in the opposite direction of the first assault. Amos realized, with horror, that there were even more of them. As he spun to face them, he was tackled from behind.

Amos rolled with his assailant across the long grass of the field and wriggled furiously to break the creature's grip. He leaped to his feet the moment he fought free. His shotgun lay ten feet away and he made a desperate dive for it. The vampire also found his feet and, as Amos leaped for the gun, the vampire made a swiping attempt to grab him. Amos felt the creature's nails rip across his back as it clutched the fabric of his shirt and tore it.

The shirt tore free and Amos landed hard. Though rattled, desperation again drove him immediately to his feet. Somehow he held his shotgun. As the vampire rushed him again, he brought the barrel crashing down on its head. The skull cracked. Amos heard it as the monster crumpled to the ground. Amos reached for the shells in his hunting sack only to discover the sack, too, had been lost in the struggle. He was now unarmed. Amos turned and ran for the trees.

* * *

Truitt didn't have time to see how the others were faring. He barely had time to wish he had brought his repeating rifle. He fired both barrels of his shotgun at the first onslaught, re-loaded once, and then the creatures were upon him. He fired the shotgun once more then drew the revolvers from his belt. A quick, as well as an accurate marksman, he drew blood every time he fired the pistols. Truitt blazed away as fast as he could thumb the hammers and find a target. By the time the cylinders were empty, the remaining vampires had fallen back. Now he stood in the field, trying to determine the fate of his companions.

Two figures approached through the lingering drifts of smoke. He drew a bead on them with the re-loaded Colts and cocked the hammers.

"That you, Truitt?"

It was Ernie. Following him was Walter. Truitt looked beyond them but saw no one.

"Where's your brother?" Truitt asked as Walter drew nearer.

"I don't know," Walter answered. "We can't find Percy either."

"But those damned things drug old Bill off in the trees yonder. I seen them do that," Ernie said.

Ernie and Walter trailed the frantic Truitt as he ran from body to body in the meadow and scanned the treeline every few seconds. Seven bodies lay in the field but their companions were not among the dead. The young boy Truitt had seen that morning was, however.

"Dang. This one's just a kid," Truitt said. "I ain't never killed a kid before."

"I ain't sure we killed none of them," Ernie said. "Aunt Tildy says they won't stay dead unless we put stakes through them and whatnot."

Walter stood alongside a body, first giving it a tentative kick, then rolling it over with the toe of his boot. He knelt beside the body and looked it over. "Ain't enough heart left in this one to stake with a matchstick. I hit the son-of-a-bitch smack in the middle of the chest from not ten feet away with a load of double-aught. He's got a hole in his chest a blind man could piss through."

"You're sure right about that," Ernie said, stepping over to take a look. "You won't find a solid piece of this old boy's heart big enough to stake with a matchstick."

Truitt barely glanced at the body as he stepped around it.

"Is it just me," Ernie asked, "or do all these bastards look for real dead to you all?"

"They do to me," Walter said. "What do you think, papa?"

"I think it's time we found your brother." Truitt checked the revolvers again. They were as ready as the last time he'd checked just a few seconds before.

Walter rose to his feet and looked at his father. "I don't think we ought to go anywhere right now but back to the house. I ain't so sure Aunt Tildy knows as much about these things as she lets on."

"Can't see that matters too much," Truitt said. "We got things to attend to."

"We should find out," Walter said. "I think we ought to take one back to the house and watch him to see what he does."

"Ain't you been listening to me?" Truitt asked, sticking his guns back in his belt. "Load up, Walter. We won't be going nowhere till we find Amos."

Walter and Ernie looked at one another. There was resolve in Truitt's voice and once he made a decision it was next to impossible to persuade him to reverse it.

Walter tried.

"Listen to me, Papa. I think as much of Amos as you do. He is my brother and all but we don't have much choice. The women are home alone. They need us."

Truitt considered it a moment. He had not thought about the women. Still, his primary concern was with Amos.

"Your brother needs us, too. I'm not just going to up

and leave him here."

"Truitt," Ernie said, "if those things drug him off like they done Bill, then maybe you won't like what you find. You heard what Tildy said about them that's killed by vampires."

"Yep. And I heard what Tildy said about bullets not killing them, too, and look at these."

Truitt swung his arm in a dramatic sweep indicating the bodies as he made his point.

"Just stop and think for a minute," Walter said, also gesturing to the fallen vampires. "I must have shot this many myself. They weren't trying to duck no bullets. How many did you shoot? Ernie? Amos? Percy? Bill? How come there's only seven here? Hell, there must've been two dozen to start with and I reckon we shot them all. How come there's only seven here?"

"I got no time for riddles or arithmetic lessons," Truitt said, angrily.

"Listen," Walter continued. "Listen to what I'm saying. We still don't know what we're dealing with. How come some are dead and some ain't? What if they don't stay dead? What if they get up while we're standing here? Papa, what if those others give up on us and go on down to the valley where pickings are easier?"

Truitt seemed unsure of himself at this point and Ernie joined in.

"Not ten minutes ago there was six of us. Now there's three. I'm damned near out of shells. There's no moon to speak of tonight and we got no light. There's no way we're gonna find nobody in those woods unless we step on them. Now, you tell me what in the hell good we're gonna do staying here and gambling these things don't come back?"

"He's right, Papa. We need to get on home."

Truitt jammed the other revolver into his belt and angrily picked up his shotgun. His eyes glinted with fury through the gray smear of powder-smoke covering his face.

"Get on home? Get on home? What kind of home am I supposed to get on to? You expect me to just walk in the door and tell Ellie to fix me some supper? No need to set a place for Amos, though, I got him killed tonight. Is that what you want me to do?"

"Papa I—."

"I ain't about to do that, Walter. You hear me? I ain't about to." Truitt turned away from them and wouldn't look at either one. "I'm going to find my boy, alive or dead I'm going to find him. Now, if you're coming load up and let's go. Otherwise, just leave me the hell alone."

Ernie and Walter hesitated, not really sure what to say or how to say it. Walter finally broke the silence.

"What if he ain't neither, Papa?"

"Huh?"

"What if he ain't neither. Neither dead or alive?"

"There's nothing we can do, Truitt," Ernie said. "Not tonight. We can come back and look tomorrow, with more shells and more men, and with the sun, but we ain't gonna find nothing but trouble tonight."

"Well then," Truitt said. "I guess I'll do it on my own."

"Papa, you need to listen to me," Walter said. "I love you and I love Amos. I'd go to hell with either one of you and I'd go to hell for either one of you but what will mama do if those things show up and we ain't there? Grandma won't stop them by herself."

"You know that's right, Truitt," Ernie said. "There ain't one thing we can do for him tonight but get ourselves killed."

Truitt seemed to sink back in on himself as he considered the situation. Finally he nodded. He turned and walked away, toward home.

"Come on, Ernie," Walter said. "Let's take this little one with us."

Truitt stopped, half-turned and called over his shoulder.

"Not the boy. Leave him lay. Take any of the others you want but leave the boy lay."

Truitt said no more as he again turned away from them. Walter and Ernie looked at one another and Ernie shrugged as he turned to another body. Walter held the shotguns as Ernie slung the corpse over his shoulder with a grunt.

"Dang. You sure got yourself a big one."

* * *

44

Amos ran blindly through the trees, unaware of the branches whipping harshly across his face, his body, gouging into his flesh and tearing his clothing. Numb to everything but fear, he crashed through the easily avoided underbrush, his breath coming in whistling gasps as he held his course in a panicked bee-line. At one time or another he had covered every inch of these woods and knew them as well as anyone could but, in his present state, he had lost all sense of direction. He made so much noise himself that there was no way to tell if he was being pursued. His terror promised him he was.

He clutched the empty shotgun, holding it close to his body as he dodged a tree which seemed to spring from the night to block his path. Any minute now, he expected a snarling shape to detach from the shadows. His legs pumped furiously as the ground fell away beneath his feet and he had no time to realize he had stampeded off a bluff before the ground found him again and slammed him into unconsciousness.

He was still unconscious, still lying at the foot of the bluff when a young woman came out of the trees to kneel beside him. After a bit of effort, she hoisted Amos onto her shoulder and bore him away into the darkness.

CHAPTER FIVE

Truitt looked over his shoulder every few minutes for the rest of the long walk home. He hoped that Amos, Bill, and Percy would catch up with them before they reached the house. Even though he agreed to abandon searching for them, he had not agreed to abandon hope. Each time some wild thing rattled a bush or a gust of wind shook the trees that hope would burn brighter. But with each step closer to his farm, he felt just that much more distant from his friends and from his youngest son. The world had changed today and would never be the same again. And he would have to adjust to living in this new world, this new reality and he had no idea how to do that.

The night sounds were mocking. Crickets, cicadas, and the occasional sound of whippoorwills, sounds he had always found pleasant, had taken on a spiteful tone. Truitt put one foot in front of the other mechanically as he trudged homeward, more from instinct than intent. The treacherous sun had long since stolen back the warmth of the day and carried it away behind the mountains. Late March wind, whistling down from the peaks had a sharp sting to it as it whipped across the forested slopes.

Walter and Ernie followed several yards behind Truitt, taking turns carrying the body of the fallen vampire. At last they saw the lights from the window of the McBride farm and a wisp of smoke rising from the stone chimney. The three paused for a moment. There was no exchange of words between them but each envisioned the difficult time they faced with the women. As they walked into the yard,

Walter paused, shrugging the body from his shoulder. It hit the ground with a meaty thump.

"This ought to do it," he said. "I'll hang a lantern on the porch and we'll be able to see from the front window. I don't want it too close to the house because it might upset the ladies. If this son of a bitch so much as twitches, we'll shoot it, stake it, burn it in the sun, cut it up and feed it to the hogs or whatever else we gotta do to make sure it stays dead."

Truitt nodded. As they neared the house, the door opened a crack and Ellie McBride peered out. She had been watching from the window.

"That you, Truitt?"

"Yep, it's us."

The door swung open and a rush of light from the coal oil lanterns flowed out and over the steps to bathe the hard-packed dirt and sparse grass in a golden glow that was almost tangible warmth. Almost. The trio walked inside and, seconds later, a muffled shriek escaped the house, riding the wind to the far reaches of the valley.

* * *

The morning sun spread its warm illumination across the floor and over the eyes of Walter McBride. He blinked slowly as he woke, squinting up at Ernie Weems. Ernie sat in a kitchen chair, pulled up by the window, looking out at the body lying in front of the house. "Anything happened yet?" Walter asked, stretching and sitting upright on his pallet of blankets spread across the floor.

"Nope. He's just as dead as he ever was. The sun's been up nigh onto an hour and he ain't so much as smoldered yet either, much less burned up."

Walter poured them both a cup of coffee from the pot sitting on the black iron stove. The coffee had been made the night before and was thick, black, strong. He crossed the room and sat the cup of the potent brew on the window sill in front of Ernie.

"There you go. If this shit don't kill you, you ain't gonna die."

Ernie raised the cup to his lips and took a small sip. Grimacing at the bitter taste, he turned his attention again out the window to the prone form in the yard.

"You reckon only the live ones burn up in the sun?"

"Maybe," Walter said, "But I got me a sneaky suspicion that it's more likely that none of them burn up in the sun."

In a short time, the family began to stir. Truitt and Ellie came downstairs, both having aged years overnight. Ellie's face was swollen and puffy, eyes red from crying. She seemed to walk about in a trance and Truitt appeared to have fared little better.

Walter did not think any of it had sunk in yet as far as he himself was concerned. Amos was gone but Walter felt nothing. Margie was the last to stir, entering the living area from the large room built onto the kitchen to accommodate her, her sister and her mother.

Margie was a quiet woman and her silence was unremarkable but her mother, Mabeline, was another matter. Mabeline always had an opinion, always had something to say; but not this morning. Not aloud anyway. She had not spoken two words to anyone since they had come home the night before. But every time one of them met her eyes, he became aware of the accusation there. Few words were exchanged by anyone as the women set about the task of preparing breakfast. Truitt poured a cup of coffee and joined Walter and Ernie at the window.

"Still dead is he?" Truitt asked.

Walter nodded.

"Well, then, I don't imagine that we need to worry about that one doing anything. I'll fetch in the lantern. Get some breakfast and we'll get started."

He did not wait for a reply as he padded across the floor and out the door in his bare feet. He stood on the porch dressed only in his pants as the air, still damp and crisp, raised goose bumps on his exposed flesh. Truitt took the lantern down from its peg and blew it out.

Very slowly, he scanned the entire area and detected nothing—no movement, no silhouettes on the horizon, nothing out of the ordinary; nothing other than a dead pig in the sty and an equally dead man, or something, in the yard.

Some folks might be tempted to find that odd under certain circumstances, he guessed. Truitt saw nothing else and turned to go back inside.

It never occurred to him to wonder if perhaps he was being watched.

* * *

Bill Way watched the house from the concealment of the deep shadows on the western side of the barn. He had been no more than a couple of hours behind them since he had awakened beneath the trees, awakened into the life. And, like Truitt, the world would never be the same for him again. But, unlike Truitt, there was no confusion in Bill's mind, no conflicts nagging him, demanding recognition, resolution—other than one. Overnight, his world had become much more primitive, simpler and decidedly much more savage.

Already the ties with his prior life were broken and, though the memories of that life still existed, they were not cluttered with superfluous sentiments or feelings of nostalgia. He had fought with all he had the night before but had been overpowered by sheer force of numbers. Bill had been dragged, kicking and screaming, from the meadow and into a new existence.

The last memory of the Bill that was, was the vision of a terrifying face looking down into his eyes; a face with fresh blood dripping from the chin. Bill knew it was his own blood dripping onto him from that face. He sank into darkness. All his fears, all his concerns, everything he shared with the others had been left in that darkness; everything but the anger. He had been abandoned, left to a fate he had no way of understanding. Bill did not begrudge anyone the change, but it was the principle of the thing. They should not have run out on him.

He had picked himself up from the ground and started for the McBride farm. He knew the men would go there and he had nothing left to fear from the beings the old crone called vampires. Several of the creatures, temporarily satiated, reclined in the shadows and watched dispassionately as he stood to leave. He understood them now—they understood each other.

Whatever he had become, it felt good. He was more aware of everything around him than he had ever been before in his life; more aware of his strength; more aware of his hunger. It was the new-found hunger as much as his sense of outrage that pulled him into the meadow, across the valley, and into the shadows of the barn where he now stood. It was a powerful thing, growing by the minute. He watched the house a few moments longer then started across the yard.

* * *

Truitt sat at the table while Mabeline and Ellie served breakfast. Everyone stared at their plates, enveloped in a deep, uncomfortable silence; the strained silence of death-watch.

All there was to say had been said the night before. Truitt had explained, in minute detail, the events of the day. The visit to Aunt Tildy, what she had told them, the ambush at the meadow; and the more painful account of the loss of half their group had been discussed from every angle. Then there had been the grief of Ellie and the anger of Mabeline to deal with. The men attempted to address that grief in the way of men, helpless before the pain of women, and offered optimistic lies for them to cling to, slim threads of fictional hope to ward off the pain.

Now there was nothing left to say.

They ate silently, eyes focused on their plates. Perhaps the world had narrowed. Perhaps all there was or would ever be again existed within the confines of the rough, pine-planked farmhouse.

There was a comfort of sorts in the meal. The food, prepared and served in the same routine, predictable manner repeated daily for years, now seemed to be of deep, almost ritual importance. The absolute familiarity of it became an anchor, a proof, if anything could be offered as a proof, of a reality which once existed. Mabeline brought the pot around with fresh coffee and, as she moved from place to place refilling each cup, her actions imparted sympathy, comfort and reassurance. The soft clinking rattle of the silverware and the pungent aromas permeating the house were reminders of life.

Truitt looked up at the sound of heavy steps on the porch. A quick glance at Walter and Ernie told him all he needed to know of their alarm. Truitt's first thought was of the body lying outside and his food turned bitter in his mouth. Mabeline took a step toward the door, coffee pot still held in her hands, as the knocking began. Truitt's mind screamed "no" but his lips had no time to form the words.

"C'mon in," Mabeline said loudly.

The door was ripped off its hinges as Bill Way stalked into the room. A tall man, well over six feet, Bill was thin as a rail, yet he tossed the heavy door to one side as if it were no more than a piece of kindling. He paused as he stepped inside, dried blood staining the front of his clothing and bits of leaves clinging in his hair. Pale blue eyes burned into Truitt as Bill raked the room with an intense gaze. His voice had lost all trace of the pleasant soft-spoken tone Truitt was accustomed to and sounded hard, savage.

"Looks like you boys lost me last night. Well, no need to fret none. I found my way back--just in time for breakfast."

Mabeline screamed, dropping the coffee pot as she retreated backwards covering her face with her hands. Bill made a guttural noise, almost a growl as he crossed the floor, advancing on her. He seized her roughly as Ernie flung himself across the room to intercede. Bill swung his arm almost casually, striking a vicious blow to Ernie's neck, catching him in mid-leap and smashing him to one side to crash on the floor. Ernie landed in a crumpled heap.

Bill pulled the squealing, squirming Mabeline toward him and bared the long fangs which had not been there the day before. As he brought his head forward to strike, Truitt snatched up the shotgun, leveled it and fired both barrels.

The concussion shook the room as Bill's head exploded in a cloud of red mist. His legs took several steps back, as if he had been shoved, before they buckled and his body toppled heavily to the floor. Mabeline, too, reeled backwards, spattered with gore, to tumble over Ernie's chair. She lay where she had fallen, hands clenched into fists and screaming incoherently at the top of her lungs.

"Shut her up," Truitt said angrily. "Shut that idiot up."

Wilda and Margie knelt by their terrified mother, attempting to calm her down. Mabeline would have none of it. She screamed until she was out of breath and sobbed when she tried to catch another. Her head had been within inches of Bill's when Truitt fired and bits of what once had been Bill Way clung to her hair, her face, her clothing.

Margie, busily wiping her mother's face with an apron, found a sliver of bone embedded in Mabeline's cheek and retched. Clamping a hand over her mouth, Margie rose quickly and ran from the room.

Truitt shook with a rage that quickly displaced his fear. He turned his glare from the hysterical Mabeline to the body of Bill. With a curse, he crossed the floor to the body.

"You no-good son of a bitch," he said, kicking Bill's corpse. "Have I ever treated you anyway but good? Have I, goddamnit? What'd you come here for? Didn't you have the whole Smokey Mountains behind you? Couldn't you have gone off there? Why in the hell did you come here? Why? Why?"

Truitt punctuated each question with a brutal kick to Bill's rib cage. With the force of each kick, blood leaking from the ruined head spurted intermittently like water from an air-locked pump.

" You . . . no . . . good . . . son . . . of . . . a . . . bitch."

Walter stepped forward and took his father's arm, tugging him gently but firmly away from Bill.

"That's enough, Papa. There's no call for that. The poor bastard can't hear you anyway."

Truitt looked at Walter and the others as if he were seeing them for the first time. He seemed to deflate.

"Truitt," Wilda said, kneeling beside Ernie's prone form. "Somebody better tend to Ernie. I think he's hurt bad. There's blood running out of his ears."

"He's hurt?" the recovering Mabeline bellowed. "He's hurt? What about me I'd like to know? That thing was all over me. Blowing his stinking breath in my face and trying to bite me while you all were squalling and carrying on and thinking about yourselves. I almost got my damned head blowed off."

Truitt felt murderous as he turned toward her.

"How'd he get in? Huh? How'd he get in the house in the first place? Didn't I tell you they can't come in unless they're invited? Didn't we stay up half the damned night telling you that? And what do you go and do? Why you just invite him right in. C'mon in, Bill. Glad to see you ain't dead anymore. Hungry? Well, you just make yourself at home and slaughter some of the family."

"Hey, I never said—" Mabeline began.

Truitt cut her off as he took a threatening step toward her. "You let him in. You let him in. I should've waited until he had his teeth in your neck and shot the both of you. And if you don't hush, I swear to God, I'll throw you out of this house if the devil and all of hell is out there. Do you hear me?"

Mabeline backed away from Truitt, the second time today that anyone in the room had ever seen her back away from anything or anyone.

"I didn't know. You ... you said they said they couldn't stand the sun and all. I didn't mean—."

Truitt would not hear it. All his fear and anger was directed at this one target and he would not let it go.

"You never mean a damned thing, woman. Now I said hush and, by God, I mean it."

"That's enough," Ellie said angrily. "I've heard enough. Don't we have enough to worry about without you two going on like that? Now, Ernie's hurt bad and I need some help."

Ernie lay on his right side, facing the wall. A trickle of blood ran from his left ear, down his face to puddle beneath his head. Truitt took Ernie's arm and pulled to roll him over. The torso twisted with a grinding of bone but Ernie's head did not move with it. All tone left Ernie's limbs with the barest of a tiny tremor and he lay limp and immobile.

"Oh no," Truitt whispered, releasing Ernie's lifeless arm.

"What is it? What's the matter?" Mabeline asked.

"His neck broke, Grandma," Walter replied. "Sweet Jesus, his neck broke."

The rest of the morning passed like a dream; at least for

Truitt who moved about woodenly with no real sense of purpose. The trauma had taken its toll on everyone.

"Why did he have to come here?" Truitt asked of no one in particular.

"I don't think he could help it, Truitt," Ellie said. "I just don't think he could." She sat down across from him, disbelieving eyes wide in her pale face. "Bill Way's always been a good man. It wasn't his fault those things done that to him. But I don't think he'd ever do anything to hurt anybody if he was in his right mind and the Good Lord knows he wasn't in his right mind. It could just as easy have been you or Ernie or Walter or—."

She didn't finish her thought. She didn't have to.

Ellie's face crumbled and she began to weep again. Truitt turned away from her. He couldn't think about it. There was no time for that. No time for grief. No time to be anything other than hard. He walked into Mabeline's room where Ernie was laid out on the bed. Walter sat beside the body staring at the still form and not quite believing that Ernie Weems was gone for good and all. Truitt put a hand on Walter's shoulder.

"C'mon, boy, we got work to do. Let's get Bill and Ernie out to the smoke-house. I don't know exactly how much we can count on what Tildy told us, but we won't be taking chances. We're going to build ourselves some crosses and circle the house with them. Nobody, and I mean nobody, else is coming in here."

They carried the bodies out, storing them in the fragrant space of the smoke-house and started for the tool-shed at the side of the barn. It was clear Walter was more than a little troubled.

"Papa, I don't think Tildy knows what she's talking about. I mean about staking these things and them burning up in the sun and all."

"Don't matter," Truitt said grimly. "We know the damned things die and, if they come around here, as long as we have ammunition we'll stack them up like cord wood."

54

CHAPTER SIX

The world staggered its clumsy and formless way through Amos's bleary eyes and into his unprepared brain like a drunk playing blind man's bluff. He thought he saw a woman. Or maybe it was women since he seemed to see several of them. Amos closed his eyes tightly. Everything hurt. Even his hair felt terrible. The darkness was no comfort at all and he opened his eyes again. Nope. Not women. Woman. Chloe to be exact.

Amos raised himself on one elbow and the movement sent a fresh explosion of pain galloping cruelly across the tender regions inside his cranium. He gagged, got dizzy, and quickly lay back down again. The vague figures moved against the dark blur of the forest and coalesced into Chloe again. Amos just lay for a moment, retreating to the edge of oblivion until the images of the attackers bursting from the tree line flooded back into his mind with crystal clarity.

Maybe he hadn't been rescued.

"No! No, get away from me," he shouted, struggling to rise. His legs gave way and he crumpled to the ground almost on top of his shotgun. He grabbed the weapon, planting the butt onto the ground and pulled himself up, hand over hand, to a standing position.

"Why, Amos McBride, what a mean thing to say."

Amos's mind cleared three big steps behind his vision as he focused on Chloe. He barely had time to feel the pleasant, odd emotion he guessed was love before his new-found terror reasserted itself. Swaying unsteadily, he held the shotgun by the barrel and swung it back like a club.

"If you try to bite me, Chloe, I swear to God, I'll knock your brains out."

Chloe laughed.

"Bite you? That hadn't occurred to me." She grinned at him. "Sounds interesting, though."

Amos squinted as he looked at her smile. They were the same even white teeth he was accustomed to seeing. He looked at her carefully but could detect nothing out of the ordinary. Still, he remained cautious.

"Well, you don't rightly look like one of them but Aunt Tildy says that if a vampire gets hold of you, then you turn into one, too."

"Vampire?" Chloe said, with a puzzled expression. "Are you talking about the men that got after me and Burl?"

"They're not men. At least they're not like the kind of men we're used to."

"That's crazy," she said. But she stopped and thought about it for a moment. "Crazy, but true. You know some things I don't?"

She stepped forward but Amos stepped back. Again he raised the shotgun like a club.

"Damn it, Amos what's wrong with you? That fall addle your brain?"

"I mean it, Chloe. I'll brain you. I don't rightly know for sure what's going on but I'm not taking chances. You've been out here the better parts of two nights."

"So?" Chloe said, placing her hands on her hips. "What're you getting at?"

Amos was a bit flustered. He was also dizzy. He lowered himself carefully to the ground. "Well, you've been out here the better part of two nights," he said again as if that made some point. "Two nights and all."

"So?" Chloe said again.

"Well, so you don't really expect me to believe that nothing happened do you?"

"I don't rightly give a damn what you believe," Chloe said, tossing her hair back with a shake of her head. "I don't care what you think, Amos McBride. You're an idiot. But if my Daddy ever hears of you talking to me this way then you'll wish one of them things had got hold of you."

"You're not a vampire?"

"I'm not a—what? What kinda craziness is this? Sweet Jesus, you look more like one of them—whatever they are—than I do. Look at yourself. You're a mess. And here I go risking my hide like some damn fool to drag you over here where it's safe. And look how I get treated."

Chloe's outrage teetered on the brink of sincere self-pity.

"Well?" She demanded.

Amos didn't answer. But he did take a look at himself. As well as he was able, anyway. And Chloe had simply stated the obvious. He was a mess. The front of his shirt, what was left of it, was tacky with blood and he put his hands to his face to feel the swollen puffiness of his split lips. He also discovered, to his dismay, he had lost at least one tooth and part of another.

"Dang."

"Oh, that's not all, dear heart. Your nose looks like it might be busted," she leaned down over him and made a show of inspecting his features. "Mmmmm-hmmmm. Eyes are black. A lump the size of a tomato on your head. About that color, too."

"All right, Chloe, I get it. Dang," Now the fright was past and Amos began to seriously take stock of his aches and pains. He was rich in inventory. He had difficulty breathing. A sharp pain stabbed through his left side as he drew a breath and he wondered if maybe he had broken some ribs as well. He, too, felt a little sorry for himself as he looked up at Chloe.

"I'm sorry," he said, with a helpless shrug he hoped was endearing. "I don't reckon that fall knocked much sense into to me at all. I was just scared. Nothing more than that."

"You think I'm not? You're right about one thing, though. They're not people. Not like any I've ever seen before. What did you call them?"

"Vampires. Aunt Tildy says it's like some kind of fever. Once you get it, you run around all crazy, drinking blood and doing all kinds of foolishness. You have a hard time dying after that, too."

Chloe rolled her eyes. "Well," she said, sitting down

beside him. "I've had all kinds of fevers, including a touch of spring fever now and then, but I've never had anything like that or even heard of it."

"Me neither."

Amos peered about into the darkness as he listened attentively to the sounds of the night. Maybe it was the fall, but he was still disoriented.

"Chloe, you said we're safe here. Where are we?"

Chloe looked worried and she scooted up against Amos and placed her palm on his forehead.

"You mean you don't know? We're at Baptizing Creek. You've been here hundreds of times."

Amos's confusion struck a sympathetic chord with Chloe and she brushed his red hair away from his face to peer at the prominent knot between his eyes. She nodded as if the cursory examination had actually told her something.

"You might want to stay up a while after taking a lick like that," she said.

But Amos was not paying attention. He looked around him trying to place his surroundings in context with the mental map he carried in his head. Baptizing Creek ran through a meadow almost at the foot of Hog Heaven Hill. In the summer, Baptist and Holiness preachers held revivals here and the word of God was bellowed throughout the valley, echoing deep into the mountains as the warm summer breeze took on the faint odor of fire and brimstone. People gathered in the clearing for sermons, hymns and–in the case of the Holiness flock–to pass from hand to hand the deadly Eastern Diamondbacks as a demonstration of their faith.

The creek itself flowed slowly, meandering down from the mountains, twisting like a snake's track through the tall grass of the meadow. Baptisms were conducted in the cold, clear, waist-deep water. In the center of the meadow, marking the sanctity of the clearing, a large oak cross rose twenty feet into the air. Twisting his body to look behind him, Amos could see the cross framed against the night sky twenty yards away.

"A couple of them chased me in here," Chloe explained. "I was out walking with Burl and they jumped us. Burl tried to fight them off but I ran. I'm scared they done something awful to Burl."

"Awful enough," Amos said. He could see the "what" in her eyes but she did not ask directly and he did not volunteer.

"I ran as hard as I could," she said. "I could hear them behind me and I knew I was about to die. I just don't have it in me to give up, I guess. I didn't slow down a minute when I hit the creek but just splashed right on across. They didn't follow. I heard them howling and carrying on behind me and I turned to look back. I don't reckon they can swim because they didn't cross." She paused a moment and wrinkled her forehead. "But that don't make sense," she continued. "They saw me cross. They knew the water wasn't much more than belly deep. It don't make sense that they were afraid does it? Still, they ran up and down along the bank but they didn't come after me. I expected them to go find some other way across but they never did. I don't know where they are now. Don't matter, I guess. They can't come across and I can't leave."

"Wait a minute," Amos said, suspicious again. "You had to cross the creek to get me."

The bluff he had fallen from was a good two hundred yards from the boundary of the creek. There had been no light to speak of and Chloe would have no way of knowing it had been him tumbling down through the brush. Chloe saw where his thoughts were taking him and headed them off.

"Yes. I had to cross the creek for you."

"Why? If you were as scared as you say you were? Why did you? There's no way you could know it was me. How'd you know I wasn't one of them?"

Chloe looked into his eyes a long moment before answering and Amos again felt the rising unease. It would really have been nice to have found Chloe under circumstances where she wasn't scaring the living hell out of him from time to time.

"I don't guess I could have known for certain. Just a feeling. See, I don't think they're afraid of anything—well nothing but the creek, I guess. They're not like you and me, not even when they are afraid, if they are afraid. I don't know. You screamed when you fell. You were screaming even before you fell. You were scared, Amos. As scared as anybody can be. The scream told me. It was human. Human like the people I've always known."

Amos's cheeks reddened. There was more than one way to get a girl's attention, he guessed. But there was no denying it; he had never been more terrified in his life. With no desire to pursue the subject, Amos turned to conjecture.

"Maybe they can't come in here because this place is like a church."

"What's that got to do with anything?" Chloe asked.

"Something Aunt Tildy said. Seems these, these, whatever they ares, can't stand anything religious. Crosses and holy water and whatnot will kill them."

"You don't say," Chloe said, sarcastically. "Then all we have to do is build a couple of crosses to carry with us and we can sashay on out of here and scare the dickens out of any booger-bear between here and the house. Now there's a plan."

Her sarcasm was lost on Amos who missed it entirely.

"I'm not in much shape to march anywhere right now," he said.

"Good God Almighty, Amos. That's about the silliest thing I've ever heard of. You walk over to the other side of the creek toting a cross for protection and those monsters will be on you like ducks on a June bug. I think——."

Amos raised his arm and waved her off. He was suddenly nauseous, light-headed. Chloe saw his distress and reached out to help him. He let her assist him as he stretched out in the cool grass. The stars in the dark sky swirled and flickered as the dizziness stole his reason.

"I gotta lay down," he said, already lying on his back. "I don't have the energy to argue with you tonight."

Nausea and vertigo struggled for the right to deal him the most misery. A pounding dark horse of a headache entered the fray. He rolled slowly over onto his stomach and heaved but there was nothing to disgorge. The light meal from earlier in the day was gone. His body shook as he retched again, again unproductively. Amos tried to concentrate, to locate some part of his body that did not ache. He was unsuccessful. He groaned.

"I know," Chloe said, as if speaking to a child. "I know. It'll be all right, now."

Amos rolled back onto his back again, gulping as deep a breath as his injured ribs would allow as he fought the queasiness. He closed his eyes and let his head loll back. It was going to be a long night.

"You don't have anything to eat do you Amos?" Chloe asked, touching him lightly on the arm. "I'm Godawfully hungry."

Amos's eyes popped open as he instinctively brought his hand up to cover his throat protectively. He looked suspiciously at Chloe for a moment then relaxed.

"Naw," he muttered. "Nothing that you haven't already had the chance to get I reckon."

Chloe gave him a puzzled look that he never saw as he drifted off to sleep.

* * *

When Amos opened his eyes, the sun was up and glaring. He would have liked to think that the warmth of that sun would relieve the pain and stiffness of his battered body. It didn't. Chloe had apparently been awake for some time. She sat by the creek next to a small pile of dark, empty fresh-water mussel shells. The pearly, blue-white interiors of the shells contrasted sharply with the dark exteriors and caught the sun, reflecting it in a bright glow as if they were incandescent. Chloe turned toward him as he stirred and popped one of the bi-valves into her mouth.

"Want one?" she asked, while opening another. "They don't taste like much but they're filling."

Amos shook his head.

"All I want to do is get back to the house. I think we'll be safe enough. Aunt Tildy says vampires can't come out in the daytime. The sun will burn them up."

Chloe, chewing a mussel, looked up angrily and started to speak. She coughed, choking on her breakfast and held up one finger, waggling it severely in Amos's direction as she swallowed.

"Now you listen to me, Amos McBride. Don't you start that nonsense with me this early in the morning." She got to her feet and kicked at her pile of mussel shells as she strode into him. "Now what kind of creature have you ever seen in your life that'll curl up and die just because a little sunshine lands on it, huh?"

Amos, taken aback by her anger, backed away from her.

"What in the world's wrong with you?" he asked, sincerely. "You sure are acting strange."

"Me? Me? I'm acting strange? I'm probably the only person in the whole valley this morning who ain't acting strange. I'm not the one running around here willing to risk my neck—and yours, too, by the way—on some silly old woman's fairy tales. Why don't you wear a chicken bone or a rabbit's foot around your neck, huh? Or maybe you can just cross your fingers and whistle. That's likely to work just about as well as a cross, which by the way, is probably not at all."

Amos grabbed her shoulders and pulled her toward him. She was on the verge of a full-blown rage. He tried to hug her but she pulled furiously away and turned her back on him. Amos let his arms fall to his side and he stood looking at her blankly as she pulled herself together. When she turned again, her face was pale, sorrowful, afraid.

"I'm not leaving here, Amos. Not now, not later. And I don't recommend that you do either. I don't know anything at all about the 'vampires' your Aunt Tildy told you about but them that got after Burl and me were out in daylight bold as brass."

"That can't be," Amos said, unwilling to let go of the comforting thought that there was safety to be found in the light of day.

"Well, I reckon it can be."

"You're sure about that are you?"

"Of course, I'm sure. I was there. Remember?"

The new information added an unwelcome wrinkle to the whole situation that Amos had not counted on. He considered the situation for a moment.

"Dang. Maybe Aunt Tildy was wrong about that."

"Maybe Aunt Tildy was wrong about everything."

"Well, what do you suggest?" Amos said, growing a little angry himself. "We sit here and eat those damned mussels for the rest of our natural lives? We've got to do something don't we?"

"I don't know, Amos. Surely someone will come along for us by and by. All I know is, I ain't crossing this creek."

Amos stalked several yards away and sat down with his back to her. He felt a growing sense of resentment for her, as if her disclosure of the daylight attack had somehow created the situation they found themselves in. Certainly, the disclosure had destroyed his most comforting level of security and he felt as if Chloe had indeed taken away his rabbit's foot. Well, he wanted it back. He wanted to lash out at her, to strike back at her as if she were the enemy. The enemy. What were they dealing with here? What could they do really? If the things—men, animals, whatever they were—could come out in the sun, then Aunt Tildy had been terribly wrong. And, if Tildy were wrong about such a vitally important detail, then how could he assume her to be right about anything?

What was valid? Maybe Tildy had been wrong about the idea that vampires needed an invitation to come in. If so, his premonition about not seeing her again could prove to be false as well. He did not welcome the thought of such a reunion. But what if you did not change? All of his experience, everything he had ever encountered in his life, every sense he had told him that if you were dead, you stayed dead. All the old religious stuff about resurrection and judgment aside, it just made no sense at all that you were not only reborn but transformed as well. Perhaps . . . no. Everything was conjecture. Maybe if a vampire killed you, you stayed dead. Maybe not. On one hand, this; on the other, that. Who knew? But there was one thing that was fact. He had seen them, fought with them. He had seen Burl Tanner and there was no way he could pretend that away.

He picked up a stone and tossed it casually into the air, catching it again as he squinted into the sun, across the creek, toward home. Nope, no way of knowing anything.

Maybe even this place would not be safe after all. Maybe some of the other vampires, some who were not as finicky about getting their feet wet, would come by. He looked up at Devil's Saw ridge. There was the rock; here was the hard place.

Chloe's shadow fell over him as she came up from behind. She waited for something, he did not know what. Maybe she wanted to hear a plan, a suggestion, maybe an apology. He had nothing to offer in any category. Maybe she wanted him to tell her it would be all right. He did not think he could do that. Confusion and frustration mounted in him and he refused to look at her. She just stood there. He whipped his arm forward, hurling the stone out into the creek.

"I don't know what to do either," he said.

He looked down at her shadow, the dark twin mirroring her every movement as she knelt beside him and reached out for him. Even in the light of day, he felt a thrill of apprehension course through him. Dear God, was it going to be this way for the rest of his life? Her hand on his shoulder was warm, a comforting weight that anchored him to the earth as she stretched out beside him.

She pressed against him, holding him tightly, as he held her. It would be hard to say who was comforting whom. And it didn't matter. Not really. All that mattered was need, one for the other. Chloe pulled back to raise herself onto an elbow and look down into his eyes.

"Well? Aren't you going to tell me that everything's going to be all right?"

"Sure. If you want me to."

"Of course, I want you to," Chloe said. "I don't know about you but I'm scared to death."

"Okay. We're going to be all right. Everything's going to be just fine."

"Men are such liars."

Amos grinned in spite of their predicament. It hurt.

* * *

Tildy stood on her front porch looking down the

64

mountainside toward the valley. Hanging from a nail driven into the door was the silver-plated crucifix her brother, Delwin, had brought home as a souvenir of the war with Mexico. She held his Navy Colt in her hand. The night would prove to be a long one. As the last of the sunlight fled the mountain passes, she knew darkness had overtaken the men before they made it out of the woods. Already the stars were appearing.

She stepped through the door. It would be a clear night, a chilly one as well. Tildy lit the kerosene lamp sitting on the table and placed the revolver alongside it. The light dancing on the slick surface of the oil-cloth caused the colors of the flowers to glow. Red roses became liquid puddles and Tildy thought of blood as she took the speckled enamel pot from the stove to pour a cup of coffee. How much of what she had told the men did she believe herself? Any of it? All of it? So much sounded like utter superstitious drivel–absolute nonsense.

It occurred to her, as she sipped her coffee, she had nothing else to go on. There were no other explanations. The flickering lamp cast shadows, moving, swaying across the room as if they were animate things. The small, blue flame had a hypnotic quality. Her jumbled thoughts slowed and became quiet as she stared into it. Eventually her eyes became heavy and she fell asleep.

The spring winds blew down from the highlands sweeping across Hog Heaven Hill and swirling into the valley below. They met the sounds of shouts and gunfire half-way up the slope and carried them away toward the valley, away from Tildy. She nodded forward in her chair. Early morning, before dawn, her body began to twitch. A light sheen of perspiration coated her face, beading on her upper lip, and she rolled her head from side to side. Percy Way was dead. Bill Way was dead. The scent of blood reeked to the heavens. Slowly and determinedly, she fought her way back to consciousness.

Tildy heard herself moan. She opened her eyes. Her coffee cup, still half-full of cold coffee, sat on the table and she had no idea how long she had been asleep. Getting up slowly, she refilled her cup. A slight twinge in her bladder reminded her that in another hour or so she would have to relieve it. The coffee would not help matters any. To hell with it. If worse came to worse she would dig out the chamber-pot or find something else to use as a slop-jar. She squinted at the face of the old grandfather's clock in the sitting room and smiled. She wondered if she would ever stop doing that. The damned thing had not worked in nearly twenty-seven years. She still nursed the coffee when the sun rose.

Tildy stood and arched her back, feeling, as well as hearing, the snapping and popping in her joints and vertebrae. Old or not, there were few things more pleasant than a good morning stretch. Blowing out the lamp, she left the Colt lying on the kitchen table and started for the door.

She stood on the step a moment sniffing the air. Just as sweet as ever. And the skies were just as clear, just as beautiful, as any she had ever seen. Smokey-white wisps of clouds drifted over the peaks, dissipating into thin, gauzy smears against the blue until eventually disappearing. Tildy stepped down into the dew-damp soil, walking slowly across the yard to the outhouse.

The dream occupied her mind. Things often came to her in dreams. Once there had been a time she had tried to ignore them, at least the unpleasant ones, tried to pretend they bore no weight. It had been a fruitless endeavor, however. No matter how she chose to react, the dreams, visions really, were always on target. Tildy was not always thankful for her gift, if indeed it was a gift. Sometimes it felt like a curse.

She entered the outhouse to relieve herself. The dream had been vivid. Tildy heard the screams as if she had been right there with Bill and Percy at the moment of death. Shadows slid through the darkness of the trees, taking on horrific shapes to fall upon the men and tap into the streams of life. The crimson flows, released, brought life to one, death to another.

No, it was not quite that simple, not quite that clear. Life to both perhaps—or maybe death—maybe something else entirely. Powder smoke, blood and fear mingled with the odors of the damp spring air and fertile earth creating an overwhelmingly powerful aroma of life and death, blended in such a way she could not tell where one ended and the other began. The images haunted her. Perhaps that was the true nature of things.

A long time ago, Tildy had been tempted to think growing old would entail some profound change apart from the physical. She would be wiser, feel wiser, know things due to experience and time. But that was a false belief, the unrealistic expectations of youth.

How could it be her body had come so far and yet her mind lagged equally far behind? How could it be she could feel so lost, so helpless, so confused, so young while still carrying her ancient baggage? Where was the magic threshold she was to cross? Why did she now think of her father, of comfort, of a far-away, long-lost self she could never go back to nor be free of? Of a lover, long since buried in the earth?

If she could not tell where things began and ended in this life, how could she puzzle out the image of life and death, tied as closely together as a team of mules and pulling in the same direction? Maybe there was more to it than a body's meant to know.

Tildy shuffled back across the yard and it came to her, streaking across her mind and exploding like a Fourth of July skyrocket. Her life was over. No matter what else happened, no matter what precautions she might take, no matter what final resolution might be achieved, no matter anything, she was not going to survive. The impact of her revelation stopped her in her tracks and took her breath away.

Of course. The thoughts of her father, her brother, her lovers, other times and other Tildy's, they were all there for her to look at, for her to say goodbye. Each step closer to the house was also a step closer to the magic threshold–the final knowing or the final nothingness. She spent the rest of the day with her thoughts and nightfall brought her peace. Of course, she would die. It was right. It was fair. She smiled as she lay down for the night.

Tildy was no longer afraid.

CHAPTER SEVEN

Percy Way was reborn on a bed of pine needles.

Beneath the trees, at the foot of Hog Heaven Hill, he opened his eyes, peering into the darkness, amazed to find he could see quite well though it was still dark. Dying hadn't really been so bad. Not nearly as miserable an experience as he'd always believed. In fact, at the time of his last breath, he had been aware of an erection. Nope, it wasn't bad at all–except for the fear.

His fear had caused him to abandon his brother, all his companions, and flee headlong into the forest. The fear caused him to scream shamelessly and plead for his life as he was dragged down from behind. The fear caused him to void his bladder as he recognized one of the faces descending on him as the face of Burl Tanner. Percy had screamed for Chloe to save him, assuming she was still with Burl. Burl laughed as he tore into Percy's throat and Percy's fear numbed him to any pain as he sank into oblivion.

He sat up to discover he was not alone. Burl sat among several men and two women seated a few yards away. Percy ran his fingers through his dark hair and brushed the pine straw from his shoulders. Was it his imagination? His thin hair was thick again, full in a way he hadn't known in more than twenty years. He felt a new energy, a sense of elation. Since childhood, Percy had always been "stout," overweight, short-winded, flabby. Now he felt strong as an ox. It was surprising, unexpected, and totally exhilarating.

"What happened?" He asked, looking over at Burl.

Percy was startled by the sound of his own voice as he rose to his feet.

Burl laughed.

"Well, you could say you've changed a mite over the last little bit, Percy."

Percy had known Burl Tanner since the boy had been born twenty-two years earlier. He looked the same as always. The lean face and clean features were those of the boy he had always known--until the muscles crawled under the skin and hardened into a frightening visage that was totally removed from anything Percy recognized as Burl Tanner; until a purple blush flushed over the skin like a dog-tick full of blood; until Burl's canine teeth descended, like a cat unsheathing its claws and indented the man's lower lip. Then Percy saw an entirely different entity than the Burl he had always known. Percy brought his hand up to his own mouth to discover he was similarly endowed.

"Don't reckon I need to worry about vampires no more do I?" He asked.

"Naw, Percy, I don't reckon you do."

* * *

Amos finally gave up on his attempts to persuade Chloe to come with him and she, in turn, abandoned her attempts to get him to stay. He waded the creek and headed for home while she sat on the bank eating mussels. She was afraid to go and afraid to stay. As Amos crossed the clearing and disappeared into the woods, Chloe wondered if she would ever return from her walk with Burl Tanner.

Burl was no different from any of her other suitors. He would play whatever game he had to play in order to get what he wanted. She understood that. She had always understood. So she was not particularly taken aback by Burl. He was a nice enough sort but nothing special. Besides, she held the same power over him she held over most men and she understood that power as well.

In the mountains, young women become old women in almost no time at all. Girls were expected to marry and

begin raising families almost as soon as childhood ended—
sometimes even before. A woman who reached the age of
twenty without having either a man or a child or two of her
own was generally viewed as flawed in some manner,
therefore undesirable, or, worse yet, "strange." She knew
she would have her power and be free to use it for only a
short time and she gloried in wielding it during her period of
grace.

Her relationships with men thus far had been merely
games, a type of combat really. She feinted and parried with
her weapons, her body, her eyes, her laugh, her voice, her
movements, as she circled to look for openings. The men
did the same, each exciting the other. In a way it was a
dance as well. Her walk with Burl had certainly been a
dance. They had moved over the road toward Baptizing
Creek, stepping across the wagon ruts, bodies moving in
sensuous, exaggerated grace, carefully casual contact of
hands, hips, legs, in a ritual old as the mountains looking
down on it. A game Chloe found exciting.

She knew what men desired of her, what they expected,
what they would do anything for. From her earliest
childhood she had been told by her mother, her sisters, or
any woman she had ever talked with for any length of time.
Chloe learned to be adept at reading the eyes of men; for it
was there she found the desire which empowered her. She
discovered it in the eyes of her father, as he looked at her
sisters, and finally as he looked at her. And she avoided him
as she attempted to avoid the awareness of his desire.

Burl, too, desired her. He was transparent as any
window. So did Amos McBride. But something was
different with Amos. He loved her and she knew it. He did
not love her body nor was he in love with the idea of being
in love—Chloe was familiar enough with both those
situations. No. Amos McBride loved her. He loved her in
spite of his family and hers, in spite of her reputation, and
this made him different from any other man she knew. She
loved him, too, at least as far as she understood love, and
that set him apart more than anything.

But Amos, for whatever reason, never made a move.
He did not come to call on her and, since she had been ten

years old, anytime he ever encountered her he blushed fiercely and could hardly speak. His shyness often seemed stupidity to her. She smiled and flirted and flirted and smiled—once even while naked. What other signal could she give him? Still Amos remained either totally blind or totally paralyzed. Either way the results were the same. So what was a girl to do?

Burl, though, was another matter. She kept him wavering back and forth between the belief that she would rebuke him and the belief that she would not. Chloe had not been sure herself. After all, she started her own fires and men were merely the kindling. But she never knew exactly when that might occur. With Burl she never had a chance to find out.

Two men suddenly appeared from the brush alongside the road and ran toward them. Burl placed himself between them and her. She had never heard of bandits or robbers in the valley before but maybe Burl figured that was what they were. Maybe he figured he had nothing for them to take whereas Chloe had. If that had been the case, he figured wrong.

So Chloe found refuge at Baptizing Creek. Why had Burl refused to run? Some silly man thing no doubt. She heard him scream. Maybe she would hear him scream forever just as she would always hear the snarls and threats of the killers. Why they could not cross the creek was beyond her. All that mattered really was that they could not.

She spent that night and all of the next day alone in the meadow. During the second night she heard screams again, and gunfire this time, a short, violent cacophony of sound.

She had just settled down to sleep when she heard the last scream, much closer than the other screams, and the crashing of the brush as Amos tumbled down.

Of course, she had not known it was Amos at the time. Someone had fallen and lay at the base of the ridge among the greasewood and small pine. If she crossed, she would do it blindly and if she guessed wrong it would cost her life. Thinking back, she wished she had been as sure of what she might find as she had led Amos to believe. Halfway across the stream, she picked up a large rock from the bottom and carried it with her. It had to be a human being, someone in danger, someone terrified. The cry had been one of stark terror.

Chloe reached Amos and leaned down to turn him over, still gripping the stone in her hand. She leaped backward as he groaned and a stream of blood ran from his mouth down both sides of his face. She raised the stone, prepared to strike, and slowly drew closer. The blood was his. Chloe would never tell him how close he had come to death at her hands that night.

She dropped the stone and raised him to a sitting position. Keeping one hand on his shoulder for balance, she moved around in front, squatted and pulled him over her shoulder. Chloe used the butt of the shotgun to lean on as she rose to her feet and balanced the unconscious young man. She shrugged her shoulders several times to adjust the weight.

Amos had a good thirty pounds on her, but she was accustomed to hard work and her fear added considerably to her strength. In fact, the fear made for light work as she covered the distance back to the creek almost as quickly as she had alone and unburdened.

The night closed in on her as she neared the creek. Snarls and crashing in the brush echoed in her ears and she felt heavy, rumbling footsteps shaking the ground as she ran. Chloe braced herself to be seized at any moment as she crossed the creek and dumped Amos unceremoniously to the ground. She turned to look behind her. Nothing. The only sounds were crickets, cicadas, the ragged chorus of peeper and rain frogs concealed in the darkness. Fear does funny things.

She took a handkerchief from Amos's pocket and wet it in the creek. Tears spilled and she resented them. She felt them a collective weakness. But, she was no longer alone and that was a good thing. God knows, anything beats being alone. She cleaned him up as well as she could.

Now she was alone again. The damned fool just had to go as if the world depended on it or something. There was nothing she could do to convince him to stay, including making love to him. But that wasn't an entirely wasted effort on her part for many reasons. Chloe smiled. She had a feeling he would return. What they shared, whatever it was, had changed them both.

Chloe sat a moment staring in the direction Amos had gone. Tossing the remaining mussels into the creek, she stretched out on the grass. There was nothing to do but sit and think, or try to sleep. She sought the oblivion of sleep.

* * *

From the mountainside above the ridge, Percy Way could see most of the valley and all of the little clearing at Baptizing Creek. He'd been sitting and watching for some time. He turned his head slowly, following Amos as the young man crossed the creek and walked into the trees. Amos carried his shotgun and by the time Percy made it down to the valley, his young companion of the night before would be out of the trees and into the meadow on the other side.

It was too risky to chance. After all, it would be dark again by and by. Chloe, on the other hand, was unarmed and Percy now wanted his daughter more than he ever had before.

He rose and started down the slope.

* * *

Chloe lay with her eyes closed for a long time before sleep came. She wondered about her father. Amos knew nothing of his companions' fates following the encounter with the vampires and his narration did little to set her mind at ease. Chloe had to cling to the belief that the men were armed, capable and adequately able to defend themselves. She had to believe they would be coming for her, perhaps searching for her at this very moment. Amos would probably run into them himself and bring them back to the meadow. Cloaked in the protection of their strength, she could leave here, return home. The nightmare would soon be over. The men would find a way to deal with it.

She slept, dreaming of home, running through her

father's fields with her sisters. The voice of her father carried on the breeze, rustling through the corn.

"Chloeee."

Her eyes flew open.

"Chloeee."

Chloe sat upright, gaping at the familiar figure nearing the creek with the sun at his back. She recognized him in an instant but there was something different about the way he carried himself. Inexplicably, she felt the hair rise on the back of her neck and she shivered.

"Daddy?"

"Where in the world have you been, girl? I been looking high and low for you. Come on now. It's time I was taking you home."

"Daddy?" she said again, not completely free of the bonds of sleep.

"What's wrong with you, Chloe? I said let's go. Your mama's worried to death."

There was something different about Percy's voice. She could not quite put her finger on it. Something. Something new but something missing as well. The feeling. His voice was smooth, hypnotic, and persuasive and the words were comforting but it was strangely dispassionate, cold. A dead voice.

Yet she was drawn to the voice anyway, drawn to her father. Her fear paralyzed her again as she started to rise and froze in a half-crouch. She squinted across the distance at his face but it was lost in the shadow of his hat brim, concealed in a harsh halo of afternoon sun.

"I can't. I don't think I can move. I'm too scared. You come to me"

Percy paused at the edge of the creek, standing in a wide stance with his hands on hips. Odd. Where was his gun? If it was as dangerous over there as she and Amos believed, it seemed her father was taking a terrible chance.

"Scared of what? I'm standing right here. Ain't nothing gonna bother you. C'mon, now. I didn't think I'd have to be bringing no sugar-tit to a grown girl."

Chloe rose to her feet and took a hesitant step in his direction. Even as she moved, she knew something was very, very wrong. He looked different. He sounded different. He was unarmed in an extremely dangerous situation. And, though she did not want to consider it, it seemed that Percy could not cross the creek.

"I'm coming," she said, moving to the edge of the stream. She pulled her dress up high over her slim legs as she waded out into the chilly water. She shivered but with much more than cold. "Don't hurt me," she said, the plea coming from a place inside her she did not understand, a place inside where honest awareness lived apart from wishful thinking. "Please don't hurt me, Daddy."

Percy laughed softly.

"I'm not gonna hurt you, baby. I'd never hurt you."

Her mind filled in the emotional void with feelings she wished to be there. This was her father. Of course, she was safe with him. The soothing voice filled her senses as she made her way across the creek. It filled the universe and there was no other sound in the world but that comforting, compelling voice. Percy moved closer to her as she neared the shore.

"C'mon, you're almost there. C'mon now just a mite further. Now give me your hand."

As she extended her hand, her left foot slipped forward over the slick stones, toes slamming hard into a large rock. Chloe stumbled backwards, dropping the raised fabric of her dress into the stream. Arms flailing like a windmill in a cyclone, she tried to regain her balance. Swaying unsteadily, she stopped, spreading her legs wide against the insistent tug of water. Percy leaned forward and Chloe shielded her eyes with her hand as she looked at him.

Now she saw his face.

Twisted and savage, eyes shining with a predatory fury she could never have imagined, Percy's visage loomed large filling her eyes, her soul. To her horror, his teeth descended and his red tongue snaked out between the fangs which filled his mouth. Oh, God, he was licking his lips.

"No, no, no, no, no!" she screamed, scrambling back for the safety of hallowed ground.

"Goddamn you, bitch, get over here!" Percy roared. "You can't stay there forever and if you don't get over here right now, I'm gonna make it harder on you than you can believe! You hear me, goddamnit?"

Chloe gasped for breath as she fell into a sitting position, her long legs splayed in front of her. With an angry shake of her head she threw her hair back over her shoulder.

"You go to hell, if you're not already there you bastard."

"You think you're safe there?" Percy asked, in a mocking tone. "You think that ground's holy? Well, it's not. Not no more it's not. You fixed that, whoring with that McBride boy."

Chloe's mouth dropped open in shocked surprise as Percy continued his verbal barrage.

"I saw you, you little slut. Laying out here in broad daylight screwing Amos right into the ground. Moaning and carrying on like your sisters. You're every bit the whore as any of them. Even your mama. Any place you set your feet is dirty."

As she rose to her feet, Chloe was unaware of how much she parroted Percy's mannerisms. Just as he did, she stood with her feet planted wide apart, hands on her hips and leaned forward when she shouted back at him.

"Then why don't you come get me then? If you can. Come on, get your feet wet."

Percy stalked up and down the bank but he made no move toward the water.

"Yeah, that's what I thought," Chloe said. "This ground's holy all right. Holy enough to keep the likes of you away."

Percy bellowed in rage and charged the creek. With a squeal, Chloe stumbled backwards, lost her footing and fell on her backside. He stopped at the edge of the stream and looked at her with an amused expression.

"No hurry," he said, after a moment. "I don't reckon you're going anywhere are you? Nope, I don't reckon you are."

Percy turned and pointed up at Hog Heaven Hill. "Burl Tanner's up yonder and he's waiting for you. Bill's up yonder and he's waiting, too. You can bet your sweet ass I'll be waiting. You're never gonna be able to leave this place. You know what I'm gonna do in the meantime?"

Chloe covered her face with her hands and did not reply.

"Look at me!"

Her head jerked up, eyes fixed on Percy.

"I'm gonna go up the mountain and visit that old queer woman who lives up there. I'm one man she'll pay attention to, by God. And I'll likely look up Amos and his folks, too. But you really won't ever know where I am will you?" He laughed and slapped his thigh. "Naw, you won't ever know. Hell, I might be miles away from here or just inside them trees. But, you know what, now that I think about it, I bet I'll always be with you. What do you think? Asleep or awake, I'll always be just over your shoulder."

"You won't get away with this. The other men will hunt you down. Amos is coming back for me. He'll find you." Her threats were empty, as empty as she felt. Percy noted the change and played to it.

"I don't reckon it matters much who finds who, girl. It's all gonna end up the same. You can save yourself a lot of grief by just wading on back over here. I won't hurt you, Chloe. No more than I have to. And it's not all that bad, really it's not."

Chloe felt her resolve weakening as she listened to him. This was a dangerous indulgence. His voice alone, without the persuasive words, was again hypnotic, soothing, fatal. She tore her eyes away from him and covered her ears as she shook her head violently. Turning her back to him completely, she shouted over her shoulder.

"You can wait till Hell freezes over. I'm never coming to you."

"Have it your way," Percy said, shrugging his shoulders. "I can be patient. Maybe you'd rather have Amos over here? I can arrange that. All I have to do is wait in the trees. He'll be along by and by I reckon. But I got plenty of time, an eternity, in fact. Right now, I guess I'll go see what your mama and sister are doing. You think they'll invite me in? I'm betting they will. Won't they be surprised to see me? Yeah, I'm betting they will be."

Turning to face him again, her alarm was written all over her face.

Percy smiled. Chloe had given him what he needed.

"You can't do that," she said. "You love her . . . you took vows."

"Only till death do us part, girl. Only till death do us part." He laughed again, a vicious sound. His face hardened into a savage mask, his voice dropping until it was little more than a guttural growl. "I kept up my end of the bargain—we've parted."

"I'll kill you. I swear to God, I will."

"Kill me?" he said, laughing again. "Why, I'm already dead, sugar. As dead as you're going to be, whether you stay here or not. As dead as them two sows back at the house are about to be. Gotta go, Chloe. I'm late for supper—real late."

Percy turned and walked away.

"No, damn you," Chloe shouted, leaping into the creek. "You leave them alone, you good for nothing bastard."

Her anger, as well as her fear for her mother, blinded her to her own danger as she splashed hastily toward the monstrosity that had recently been her father. Percy's eyes shone with anticipation as he hurried back to meet her on the bank.

When she saw him tower over her, hands raised into the air like talons, she knew she was lost. But then she had been lost since the first day this whole thing started. She tried to turn back and lost her footing. He caught her by the arm as she slipped and slid on the slick bottom.

"Suppertime, bitch," he said, snatching her from the water.

Chloe kicked her legs across the surface of the stream as he dragged her up on the bank. One kick sent a rooster-tail of water splashing over him. He screamed, abruptly releasing her as he stumbled backward, wiping at the water on his face. His waving arms knocked his hat from his head and a malodorous vapor rose from the skin that blistered and peeled before her eyes. He took a bandanna from his pocket, rubbing vigorously at any spot the water touched. Chloe crossed the stream and watched in disbelief from the safety of the meadow.

Percy bared his teeth in a snarl as he walked back to the edge of the creek and bent down to retrieve his hat. The left side of his face—from the scalp-line on down beneath his collar—was raw and red as if he had been scalded. He looked at her with utter hatred in his eyes.

"You're dead, Chloe. Deader than I am. This place is all you're ever gonna know from here on out. If you try to leave, I'm here to tell you, I'll be waiting. Reckon I'll be going now, I gotta see your mama."

He turned away, took a couple of steps, then turned back to her again with an afterthought.

"Know what?" he said. "I ain't even gonna use these." He raised his right hand to his mouth and thumped the end of a canine tooth. "I'm just gonna rip that bitch apart. Same for your queer sister. I'll give them your love."

He ambled unhurriedly away without another word. Chloe watched as he followed the direction Amos had taken earlier. Her legs trembled as she reeled away from the rippling boundary that now marked her world. Collapsing under the large wooden cross, Chloe gave way to tears.

She finally knew what it felt like to give up.

* * *

Agnes Way busied herself with the task of preparing the evening meal. She did not have to think about what she was doing; she functioned by rote, routine ingrained with years of practice. In fact, not thinking was the point.

Sara watched from her chair by the window. She knew her mother was comforting herself. Any time there was trouble—a death in the family, an argument with Percy, another one of her daughters married off—Agnes would turn to cooking and cleaning. Sara had developed the ability to measure the degree of her mother's anxiety by the time and effort she put into these tasks. She knew, by past observation, the anxiety was extreme.

Agnes set the table with enough food for an army, let it set twenty minutes or so, then began to pick it up again. She smiled over at Sara.

"I think I'll put all this back on the stove. I know Percy will be hungry as any wolf when he gets here and Lord knows Bill will eat anything that ain't nailed down."

"Here, let me help you," Sara said.

"No, baby, I'll do it. You go on up to bed and lie down. You look plumb tuckered out."

Sara doubted that she looked plumb tuckered out, but she did not argue. More than likely, her mother did not want to share the make-work tasks with her. As it was, Agnes was running out of things to do and having to repeat chores she had completed earlier. That suited Sara just fine. She never found a fraction of the comfort in routine her mother did.

Upstairs in her room, Sara lay back across her bed. It was true she was concerned for Chloe—that was real—but the only concern she had for Percy was for her mother's sake. As for her own feelings about him, she did not give a Tinker's damn if he ever came back. Everyone in the valley thought so much of him. They certainly did not know the Percy she knew.

He had made his first advance on her when she was only twelve. At first she enjoyed the extra attention he paid her but it was not long before things got ugly. Sara had never been able to figure out why he picked her if, indeed, she had been the only one. There was no way for her to know for sure unless she came right out and asked her sisters. She was too ashamed to do that.

Once, while he was making a fuss over her, she met Ima's eyes and thought she saw pity there. Ima turned quickly away and refused to look at her again. Sara never mentioned it to anyone and none of her sisters so much as hinted at any impropriety on their father's part. It had been more than four years since she had put an end to it but it seemed like last night.

She awakened in the middle of the night to find him beside the bed with his hands under the covers. His touch roused her, caressing her thighs and kneading her breasts. Rolling away, unable to hide the fury any longer, she sat bolt upright pulling the quilt tightly around her.

"You get the hell out of here," she said.

The words were out before she had time to think, almost of their own accord. Percy was drunk and he reeled slightly as he rose to his feet. A look of anger played across his face, replaced quickly with a crooked leer he obviously thought was a smile.

"Now, baby, don't be like that," he cajoled, leaning over the bed toward her and attempting to stroke her hair.

The smell of the whisky washed over her like a sour wind, fueling the rage inside her.

"I mean it," she said, placing her hands against his chest and pushing him back. Her voice was controlled but even and there was no mistaking the fury there. "Get out of my room and leave me alone."

"So you think you're grown enough to give me orders," he said, his own voice low, slurred yet very threatening.

"I'm grown enough to know what we've been doing's not right. I've known that for a long time and I'm not putting up with it no more. Now you get out of here or—."

"Or what?" he said, harshly. "What are you gonna do? Tell your mama? Do you think she'll believe you?"

"I don't know who'll believe me but I'll guarantee you this; I'll tell everybody in the valley who'll stand still long enough to listen. Even if they don't believe me, it'll make for some right dandy gossip anyhow."

Percy clenched his fist, bringing it so near her face that she could smell the odor of dirt, feed, and sour mash.

"One time, girl. You open your mouth one time and I'll kill you."

"Then you got it to do. I'm here to tell you, I'm not putting up with no more. If you want to kill me go right ahead--then try explaining that to folks while you're at it. But if you so much as lay one hand on me again without killing me, then there's going to be hell to pay."

Percy shook with anger as he stared down at her, arms hanging limp at his sides. She fought to keep from trembling. He looked for any opening, any trace of fear, any wavering on her part. If she provided the slightest opportunity, the slightest weakness or hesitation, then all would be lost. She looked into Percy's eyes and behind the anger she touched his fear of discovery. Sara pressed her advantage.

"I've seen the way you been looking at Chloe, too. You had best think twice, old man. The same goes for her. I'll bet with two of us talking we stand twice the chance of finding someone to listen."

She held her ground as Percy turned and stormed from the room. He never bothered her again but the mutual and intense dislike between them became a bit obvious for those who cared to note it. Agnes did not care to note it nor did Sara's sisters. Sara had made a half-hearted attempt to keep up appearances for a while but soon abandoned that as well. In any case, the word "daddy" always stuck in her throat from that point on. Percy had given her enough of men to last a lifetime.

The upper room had grown hot, stifling, over the course of the day and she got up to open her window. It was near sundown and Sara stood a long while looking through the glass without seeing anything. Why had he chosen her? What was wrong with her? What was it about her that would make him do such a thing? It was a question she had pondered since the age of twelve and would likely never be able to answer.

A rapping at the front door came stealing up the stairway followed by her mother's voice.

"Is that you, Percy?"

"Yep, it's me."

"Well, what are you doing knocking for goodness sakes? C'mon in the house."

CHAPTER EIGHT

Amos walked through the trees holding the empty shotgun as if it were loaded. His right hand curled around the butt, fingers gripping the triggers and thumb resting on the rabbit ear hammers. Should anyone, or anything, happen to observe him as he walked, he hoped to give the impression of being armed and ready. Held in his left hand, along with the barrel of the gun, was a cross, crudely made of small pine sticks tied together with a bit of flannel from the tail of his shirt. With a pine-twig cross and an empty shotgun, Amos wouldn't have given himself much of a chance in a confrontation with a pissed-off billy goat much less anything else. He just didn't feel good about the world or his place in it at the moment.

Contrasting light and shadow spread endlessly beneath the canopy of branches and Amos stayed in the sunlight as much as possible. Though he tried to be alert, his mind kept turning back to Chloe. She adamantly refused to set one foot beyond the boundary of the creek. Maybe it was for the best. Why expose her to any unnecessary danger if her sanctuary seemed safe enough for the moment? That is, of course, if there was any such thing as a safe place anymore. Only God knew or maybe even He did not. The best that Amos could hope for right now would be to make it home in one piece and bring back some reinforcements.

A small animal, rustling in the brush, quickly brought his attention back to matters at hand. If he did not keep on guard, he might not make it out of the woods. Constantly turning his head, he quickened his pace. He wished desperately to be back in the open and struggled with an almost overpowering impulse to run. He reminded himself of the night before and how the fear had almost gotten him killed.

He paused to look up at the clear, high, blue sky as he composed himself. It just wouldn't do to lose his head under the circumstances. He pulled his shirt tail up to examine his ribs. It no longer hurt to take a breath, at least not too much, and he did not think anything was broken. An ugly purple bruise did, however, cover the entire lower portion of his rib-cage. If nothing was broken it was a wonder. The swollen lips and gums continued to bleed sporadically but that had not seemed to bother Chloe.

Chloe again.

It was not as if she had never invaded his thoughts before but now it was a whole new push of fresh, vivid memory that drove every other thought—even thoughts of self-preservation—to the edges of his consciousness. What a strange way for a man to lose his virginity. In spite of present difficulties and immediate concerns, Amos felt a rush of elation.

He seemed to have left his body at the point of climax and he had never, never in his entire life experienced anything so absolutely intense. For a few seconds the whole world and everything in it had gone away and nothing remained but motion, breath, soft warmth and sensation. The second time took a little longer and the third time longer yet.

God, he loved that girl.

A shadow fell over him and Amos almost cried out as he whirled, swinging the unloaded shotgun in a wide arc. The force of his blow spun him around as the gun moved without resistance through empty space. Tangling his feet, Amos stumbled, falling heavily to the ground. The crow called loudly as it settled on a high branch to look down at him. Apparently the bird was unimpressed by the empty weapon. This bird came as close to sneering as any Amos had ever seen as Amos picked himself up and slapped the dust and pine-straw from his clothing.

"Dang," Amos said. He felt a bit embarrassed. He sighted down his finger at the crow and dropped his thumb like a hammer. "Boom," he said softly.

The crow got the message. It launched itself into the air, wheeling silently out of sight. If Amos hurried, he could be home and back before nightfall. He did not want to be caught in the woods again tonight. For that matter, he did not think he would ever want to be in the woods at night again.

In a short time, he stood at the edge of the large meadow where they had fought the vampires the night before. The spring breeze rippled the long grass, blowing his red hair back from his face. Still a bit sharp with the recent memory of winter, the breeze also brought the smell of the blood staining the front of his shirt and of the death still lying concealed in the grass to his attention. The afternoon sun warmed his back and shoulders as he started across the field but a cold shiver ran up his back in spite of the sun.

The bodies lay where they had fallen. Everything Tildy had said about vampires not staying dead rushed into his consciousness and spun there like a dime-store top. With his heart in his throat, he approached the questionably-slain with the shotgun drawn back like a club. Tildy was wrong. These bodies had been lying in the meadow with the sun beating down on them all morning and it had not fazed them a bit. Not a one of them smoldered or was even singed. Still he moved cautiously. Lying ten feet or so from the nearest body was the hunting sack he had lost the night before. The strap was broken.

Amos fished a couple of shells from the sack and, feeling a little more secure with a loaded weapon, repaired the sack by slitting it and tying the strap back securely through the slit with a double knot. Having the wherewithal to at least fight back lifted his spirits immensely.

He thumbed the hammers of the Long Tom as he drew close to a fallen vampire. It lay on its back, lips frozen in a snarl, dead eyes staring away into the nothingness of death.

He kicked it with the toe of his boot. Nothing. Pulling a strand of grass, heavy with seed, he knelt by the creature raking the grass across a dead eye. Again nothing.

He moved from body to body with the same results.

Amos examined the last one more closely. It had taken a round in the side of the head.

It was as dead as Granddaddy's pecker, as dead as anything Amos had ever seen. Tildy was wrong again. Bullets killed them and he took some comfort in that, but the sun did not bother them, which meant others might be watching him and licking their chops at this very minute. He did not like that idea at all. Amos looked at the crude talisman he had carried away from Baptizing Creek thinking of what Chloe had said.

"Now what kind of critter on God's green earth will burn up in the sun? Or curl up and die at the sight of a cross?"

Well, he had bet his life on it and he was wrong. And if he were to have met one of the monsters in the woods, he would have paid that debt. Tildy was only a crazy old woman after all. Maybe these things she called vampires were something else entirely. Maybe everything she had said was only bits and pieces of legends, fairy tales, stories she had heard and gotten confused in her mind. Bullets killed them. As long as he had shells he was all right. He tossed the pitiful talisman into the air and caught it again.

"I guess the Good Lord does take care of drunks and fools after all."

He let the cross drop onto the body of the fallen vampire.

A sizzling sound startled Amos and he watched in amazement as the cross burned into the chest of the vampire, sinking down into its body. He could not believe his eyes. The body began to decay and fall apart, the long period of decomposition accelerating into a matter of minutes. Flesh, organ, clothing, everything, falling apart, rotting into nothingness as Amos stood mesmerized four feet away. The bones even split, coming apart with loud pops.

Startled, Amos jumped backwards and his heels came down on a small log. The log rolled and Amos hit the ground unceremoniously while managing to smack himself between the eyes with the barrel of his shotgun on the way down.

"Shit," he said, raising himself to one elbow. Rubbing his forehead, he quickly glanced about in embarrassment. No audience—at least no audience that he could see.

Amos rose shakily to his feet to inspect the area where the body had lain. Cross and body were both gone. Completely gone. Nothing remained but a scattering of dust among the grass. That, too, began to disappear as the wind carried it away. Amos did not know what to think as he again started for home.

He found Percy's hunting sack lying a few yards away and slung it over his shoulder. The sack contained a full box of shells, as well as a number of loose ones, a tin of matches and an almost full pint of whiskey, all of which might come in handy.

As he walked on he came across another body, lying apart from the rest. He stood for a moment looking down at the dead face. Sharp teeth protruded from the blue lips beneath glazed eyes faded an even paler blue. If he were to guess, Amos would say the man was not much older than himself. He wore the tattered remnants of a Confederate uniform, even though the war had ended over forty years ago.

Amos wondered if the man had indeed been a soldier—maybe even a Tennessee boy? Did vampires really live forever? Who knew? Had the soldier been afraid? Thinking he might die on a battlefield somewhere? Maybe even one at home? God, could he ever have imagined the hand Fate was going to deal him? Did he know, or even care, who won?

His body was never found. Did anyone mourn for him? A wave of pity swept Amos away. He did not know if it was sadness for himself, for the soldier, or for all of mindless creation. He struggled with his tears as he rose and walked away. He wished he had the time and the tools to bury the soldier.

There was plenty of daylight left as Amos drew near the house, more than enough to see that something strange had been going on. Amos stood near the pig-sty, looking in at the dead sow.

She had been rolled over on her back and staked to the ground with a sharpened fence-rail. The body of a dead man lay some distance away toward the house. It, too, was staked. Amos felt a start of fear when he first saw the body, concerned for his father and brother, but, as he drew nearer, he realized it was the body of another vampire.

He turned his attention back to the house and noted the erratically spaced fence of hastily-hammered crosses surrounding it. Apparently Truitt had survived the nocturnal onslaught. Breathing a sigh of relief, Amos started across the yard to the house.

* * *

The morning had been busy. Truitt and Walter stored the bodies in the smoke-house and Truitt had staked them both, then the sow and the man outside, and erected the fence of crosses before coming back inside. They found Ellie with a bucket and scrub-brush fighting a losing battle with the blood-stained planks of the floor. Truitt took a bottle from the pantry and sat down at the table.

"Well, what now?" Ellie asked, abandoning her task and joining him.

"We sit, I reckon. We got plenty to eat. And enough shells if worse comes to worse. I think we'll be pretty safe here. We got those crosses up and all."

"If they do any good," Walter said. "You sure are putting a lot of stock in those things."

"They're not likely to hurt," Truitt said, though he doubted their effectiveness himself.

"Truitt, what in the world's happening here?" Ellie said. "We got dead people on our hands for Christ's sake."

"They're not exactly people, Ellie."

"So you tell me. Try explaining that to old Sheriff Murphy if he comes around, why don't you? Cause I'll flat out tell you that they look like dead men to me and I reckon they'd look like dead men to him, too. Close enough for a hanging anyway."

Ellie had a point.

"We'll cross that bridge when we come to it, if we ever do. We got problems enough as it is. I think it best we should just ride it out here for now."

"How long will that be, Papa?" Walter asked. "Is this going to blow over today? Tonight? Next Tuesday?"

"How the hell should I know? You know as much about this as I do."

"That's what I'm saying. We ain't the slightest notion on any of it."

Truitt slid the bottle across the table to Walter. "Listen, I know you're scared but Tildy said we'd be safe inside if we don't invite them in."

Walter took a swig from the bottle, set it back on the table and wiped his lips with the back of his hand. The raw liquor flushed his face.

"Yeah, I know. But maybe that only works if you got a front door, which we ain't. There's just too damned many maybes, Papa. If we had some idea of how long this was going to last, then staying here might be a good idea, but we don't have the foggiest notion. I think we ought to get on out now."

"Well, I don't know—."

"Looky here. It don't make no sense at all to wait till we're short on food or ammo or till we're ass-deep in vampires. I think we ought to get on out while we can—get on out while we still got our mules."

"I don't know, Walter, maybe we—."

"Damn," Walter said, leaping to his feet and startling his parents. "The mules. You don't think they got the mules do you?"

"Lordy, I hope not," Truitt said.

"I better check."

"You be careful, boy," Ellie said. "I don't want anything happening to you."

Walter crossed the room and picked up his shotgun, breaking it down to assure himself of the load. He clicked it closed again and rested it over his shoulder as he headed for the door, pausing for a moment to grab a handful of extras shells from the pantry. Truitt watched him go. He felt mentally paralyzed, incapable of any decisions. Walter's arguments made sense and the idea of staying terrified Truitt every bit as much as it did Walter. The difference was the idea of leaving terrified Truitt even more. Walter had been gone a full five minutes when Ellie turned her head to look out the window.

"Good God! It's Amos!" She said, on her feet and headed for the door almost before she got the words out.

Truitt intercepted her.

"Wait, wait. You stay in the house, Ellie. I'll go out to meet him."

He backed away. Slowly, hands held palms down in front of him as if prepared to tackle her. Ellie stood looking at him with a puzzled expression until he suddenly turned, grabbed his shotgun and darted out the door. Ellie bolted right behind him.

"Truitt!" she screamed, as her sisters blocked her way. "Don't you hurt him, damn you! Don't you hurt him!"

* * *

"That's far enough, Amos."

Walter stepped out in the open from the corner of the barn, shotgun leveled at his brother's chest. Amos noted the drawn back hammers and knew only an ounce or two of trigger pressure stood between him and doomsday.

"Hey, Walter, it's me," he said, managing a smile in spite of the situation.

"I know who you are. Didn't I just call you by name? And I said that's far enough, by God."

Amos froze. He hadn't expected anything like this. From the look in his brother's eyes, Amos knew Walter was not fooling around. Pleading his case was going to be a tricky proposition but Amos was prepared to try. He never had the chance as a commotion on the porch caught both his and Walter's attention.

Their father stood on the porch saying something to Wilda and Margie who were attempting to drag Ellie back in the house. Ellie had attained the space where the front door used to be and held on with both hands while she strained against her sisters' efforts. Truitt crossed the porch to stand looking out at the stand-off involving his sons.

"Papa, I'm home," Amos said in bewilderment.

"I can see you are," his father answered, gesturing toward the front of Amos' shirt with his hand. "And I can see what you been doing, too."

"Oh, naw. It's not like that at all. That's my blood. I got a little banged-up last night but I'm all right—just some bark knocked off. I got clean away and I found Chloe, too."

"More likely she found you. And when she found you, we lost you. I can see what you are now and you got no place here anymore."

"But Papa, ain't nothing wrong with me. I mean, I am a little busted-up, like I said but, hell, it's no worse than that. Come on, go with me. I'll take you to Chloe and she'll back me up."

Truitt shook his head, eyeing Amos coldly.

"Looky here," Amos insisted, "you're making a mistake. A bad mistake. Come on go with me."

"Why? So you can get me away from here where those things can get hold of me like they done Bill? Like they done you? You turn and get. I'll not be saying it more."

Amos was not quite ready to give in. But before he could continue his argument his grandmother stepped in, stomping across the porch to confront Truitt.

"Have you lost what little sense you had to begin with, man? You can't let that thing walk away. You saw what Bill was like didn't you?"

Truitt glared at her without saying a word.

"Grandma's right, Papa," Walter shouted. "We can't just let him walk away. He'll come back sooner or later, maybe with some others. We can't take that chance."

"You're talking about my son, Goddamn it!"

"For once in your life be a man, Truitt," Mabeline said.

Truitt ignored her. Amos saw his father wavering and knew the next few seconds could be his last. Mabeline, as usual, pushed Truitt a bit too far.

"Bust his ass!" she screamed. "Suck up what little balls you got and shoot him or else give me the gun."

Truitt whirled on his mother-in-law and shoved her,

perhaps harder than he had intended. She staggered against and over the porch railing to land in the yard amidst a cloud of dust. Walter froze in gape-jawed astonishment. None of them had ever seen Truitt raise his hand to anyone, much less a woman, not even under the direst of circumstances.

Amos, on the other hand, was looking for an opening and Truitt provided it.

As soon as Truitt moved, Amos did, too. He did not know how the debate would end but he felt it in his best interest to be elsewhere when the decision was made. The action on the porch distracted Walter for just that split second that Amos needed to get the edge.

The boom of Walter's shotgun split the air, reverberating through the valley. As Amos ducked around the corner of the smoke-house, the shot tore into the rough lumber, exploding the wood into splinters raining down in his hair. Keeping the smoke-house between himself and his family, Amos ran in the direction of Baptizing Creek until he was well out of shotgun range. Standing in the field, he caught his breath enough to shout back at the house.

"Screw you, Grandma!"

CHAPTER NINE

Amos sat in the meadow and uncorked the pint of whiskey. The sun sank behind the mountains and the darkness would soon be coming. What now? Was there anywhere left to go? If he had tried Percy's there was no way he could have made the creek by nightfall. Bill's place was further yet. Besides, maybe the Way brothers had been taken. If so, according to Tildy, they would become vampires themselves. Now there was a reunion to stumble into after dark.

Tildy never mentioned how long the transformation might take, if there was a transformation. She had been wrong about the sun, right about the crosses, wrong about the bullets. Jesus. Everything was doubtful.

He took a drink, swallowing quickly as the whiskey burned its way down, stinging the raw tissue of his lips and gums. Amos gagged and coughed.

"Dang," he said, catching his breath.

He corked the bottle and stood up, gathering his gear. First, get to Chloe. She needed him, or perhaps he needed her. Either way, together they might be able to make some sense of all this. More than anything else, he needed to be clear of the woods before full darkness. And, to that end, he needed to hurry. He headed for Baptizing Creek.

If he were lucky, he might meet reinforcements. If his luck was gone to Texas, well, no telling what he would meet. In any case, if he met anyone at all, he preferred that it be in what daylight was left to him. He made good time.

The reception at the farmhouse had not been what he expected. He could have imagined himself answering questions, explaining events, reassuring everyone perhaps and maybe even rallying the troops for a rescue party. Things had just not worked out that way. The last thing he ever expected was running for his life while his family argued over whether or not to kill him and who would do it.

He tried to justify their behavior to himself. They were afraid. No doubt of that. Something had happened at the farm and, after all, he did look a mess. He could not really blame them for their suspicions. After all, he had done pretty much the same thing with Chloe. But the fact remained that he did blame them. He was hurt and angry. They would not listen, would not give him the chance to explain. Walter had shot at him for Christ's sake, his own brother. And his grandmother had encouraged him. Amos felt terribly alone.

He entered the woods half-a-mile up from the spot where he had come into the meadow earlier that day, just in case someone might expect him to take the same route back. At least that was what he told himself and it was a good explanation. It just was not the truth. The truth was that he had absolutely no desire to pass by the bodies again. Several yards into the woods, he found Percy's canteen. A short distance further in, he found the man's Long Tom. Apparently Percy had abandoned them in his flight. The shotgun was still loaded. Amos carried it with him.

The taller trees swayed in the stiff breeze blowing down from the mountain. Like before, Amos sought the open spaces, avoiding the underbrush and thickets. Halfway through the woods, he startled a young cottontail, which startled him, in turn, by exploding from beneath a small patch of briars to scamper across the floor of the forest. Amos swung the shotgun to lead the rabbit and fired one barrel. The shot hit the rabbit in mid-leap, rippling the fur along the animal's body like a sudden gust of wind.

It did not flinch, twitch, or even blink, but it was dead as it hit the ground, coming down and somersaulting forward as if it had clumsily tripped on something. Amos half-expected it to get up and continue on its way. It did not. It lay where it had fallen, motionless, warm, limp. He picked it up and placed it in his sack.

And death is like that, he thought. Really like that. Going about your business one minute, tits up on the ground the next. Of course, he did not like to think about it but it really was that simple. The simplest thing in the world. A fragile heartbeat away. Frightening.

He felt no pity for the rabbit. It was food. That, too, was simple, the natural order of things. Besides, what kind of life is running and hiding and hiding and running? Maybe that was a question everyone in the valley would be asking before the week was out. Maybe people were food, too. Maybe people had just gotten stronger, better at protecting themselves, far removed from other creatures that preyed on them. Maybe people had simply forgotten that fact. Well, Amos had been reminded. A new hunter was in the woods and Amos was the rabbit. He was food.

* * *

If her parents were speaking, they were whispering and, if they were whispering, it was because Chloe had not come home. Either Percy had not found her or, if he had, something terrible had happened to her. Sara knew had Chloe returned intact, the big do downstairs would leave no doubt in anyone's mind of her homecoming.

Sara listened closely as she stood by her window. No sound. She turned to open a drawer of the oak chest next to her bed and removed a light cotton gown.

At one time loose and baggy, coming nearly down to her feet, the gown was now hardly past her knees and was more than a little threadbare from frequent washing. Sara pulled the gown over her head, dim moonlight passing through the fabric, outlining the curves of her body.

She heard the creaking of the stairs. Not wishing to give the impression of eavesdropping, nor anxious for any bad news, she quickly climbed into bed and pulled up the covers, feigning sleep. A shadow in the hall could be seen through the space at the bottom of the door as her mother stopped just outside.

Wait until tomorrow, Mama, Sara thought, closing her eyes tightly. *Wait until tomorrow to tell me Chloe's dead.* Sara heard the latch give way as the knob turned with a soft rattle of metal. Lying still, she waited for her mother to speak.

Percy stood silently in the doorway.

Her room was dark, bathed in shadow. Dim light from the lamp downstairs crept weakly into the corridor, flickering behind him. She lay on her side, eyes now open and facing away from the door. Not now, Mama. Not now. She tried to keep her breath, sleeper-even, sleeper-deep. She even feigned a soft snore. But she heard the faint whisper of bare feet on the floor, sensed the presence of another in the absence of that sound.

There just was no escape from bad tidings. She rolled onto her back.

She gasped when she saw Percy. He stood motionless, watching her with a quiet, intense patience. She sat straight up in bed, covering her breasts with her hands as if she were naked.

He was.

The son of a bitch was stark naked. It took a moment for this thought to gel in her mind. His erection swung pendulously from side to side as he moved to the side of the bed and stripped the covers away. Good God. Chloe missing and the low-life tries something like this.

"You," she said, angrily, as if it were an indictment.

"Yep, me."

"You get out of here or, I swear to God, I'll go right down and tell Mama."

He threw his head back and laughed.

"Call any dance you want to, baby girl. She's a laying down there on the floor by the front door. She was just tickled to death to see me. Flat tickled to death."

Percy usually came to her drunk. But he wasn't drunk tonight. Something about him was different though and the difference was ominous. His low, cold voice drew her attention to his face. She could see it clearly as he drew nearer.

"Oh, my God."

"Yep, you might say that," he said, laughing again.

"My God, what's wrong with you?"

"Can't you tell?" he said, bringing his hand down to grasp his penis.

She screamed as he fell on top of her.

"Some things just don't ever change, Baby Girl."

* * *

Something was wrong.

As Amos grew near the creek, Chloe stood on the opposite bank watching him nervously. She was in a state. He could tell by the tense posture, the fidgety motions of her hands, all the small cues that combined to create an almost visible aura of unease that hung about her.
The gunshot. Of course. She had heard him shoot the rabbit and now she was frightened.

"Hey, I'm all right," he said, forcing a smile as he drew the rabbit from his sack and held it in the air. "Just bringing in some dinner."

He stepped into the stream to wade across and Chloe fairly collapsed with relief. She could no longer hold back her tears and Amos hurried to comfort her. He did not ask what was wrong. It was not tact on his part but a bone-deep clumsiness in the presence of Chloe that was contaminated by a serious desire not to know what had happened in his absence. So he held her and let her cry until she ended the emotional outpouring with a tremulous sigh against his tear-sodden chest. She sniffed and pulled away from him.

"You didn't see my daddy out there anywhere did you?"

* * *

There was no time to waste. Sara slid into a pair of pants and tucked the tail of her flannel shirt into them before pulling on her boots. She slid out the window, turning to reach up and grasp the facing as she placed both feet on the bottom of the sill. Slowly, she released her grip, balancing precariously as she reached for the edge of the roof. Her fingers wiggled several inches short of the flashing. If she were unable to reach the roof, her only option would be to leap to the ground and hope that she did not break anything. Even if she were to make the jump safely, her chances for survival looked slim.

Crouching slightly on her perch, Sara eyed the flashing for a moment. There would be only one chance. She took a deep breath and jumped. Sara caught the gutter and felt the sharp edge of rusty tin as it sliced across the palm of her left hand. She did not cry out. Her feet crashed into the side of the house with such force that surely it rattled the windowpanes in every room of the structure. Sara held her breath. If Percy heard her, she was sure, it would all be over.

Without wasting a moment, she strained, pulling herself upward while pushing at the wall with her feet. Finally, she threw one leg over the edge of the roof and swung herself up. As she lay panting on the shingles, she peered over the gutter, half-expecting to see Percy stick his head out the window and look up at her.

God, let me be going crazy, she thought. *Please don't let any of this be real.*

She pulled the tail of her shirt out of her pants and pressed it tightly into the palm of her injured hand. That wound, however, was the least of her problems.

Percy had raped her, throwing himself upon her, pinning her to the bed in spite of her best efforts to resist. It was just another taking. And, God knows, he had taken everything from her he could; her innocence, her virginity, her childhood, her self-respect, and now her mother. Sara almost sobbed. There was nothing left but her life and her future. He couldn't take anything else and she wasn't sure she cared anymore.

Why did he seek her tears? Her suffering? Why now? Why then?

"Some things just don't ever change, Baby Girl."

No kidding? She could swear to that.

I would have loved you, you son-of-a-bitch. You rotten bastard. I wanted to love you. I tried to love you. Oh, God help me, I'm still trying.

Her struggles had always seemed to amuse him. He laughed as he spread her legs and entered her. Every other time he had ever come to her, he had been oh, so careful, restrained, mindful of every little noise the bed might make and even of his own breathing. This time there was no restraint, no attempt at any sort of self-control. No, this time he thrust himself into her in a measureless eternity of rasping breath and creaking springs. The sound filled her head. It filled the entire world.

She ceased struggling, allowing herself to become numb as he labored over her. The physical change in Percy—the teeth, the wound on his face—should have terrified her but she had distanced herself too far from the situation to react. A string of saliva ran down Percy's chin to drip on her forehead. Her mother's blood was smeared from his chest to her's. Percy groaned as he finished, rolling away from her.

"Damn," he said, looking at Sara and grinning. "I didn't really expect that. Didn't know I still had such foolishness in me. Or in you anyways." He laughed, amused by his own wit.

Sara did not move as he rose from the bed. Her eyes followed him, however, and he noted that. He shook his head as he stared down at her.

"You don't get it, do you? Of course you don't. How could you? Well, don't fret none, Baby Girl. Your Mama will be getting up in a while and coming to see you."

The mention of her mother brought Sara back. She sat up in bed and pulled the coverlet to her chest.

"What did you do to her?" she asked, her voice sounding strange and distant in her own ears.

"Brought her over with me. That's all. Ain't a wife supposed to be with her old man?"

He had gone crazy. There was no doubt about that.

"I'm going to kill you," she said evenly.

"Yeah, you and Chloe both. I'm gonna lose a lot of sleep over that. This time tomorrow, you'll be just like me and you won't see a thing wrong with any of this. We'll all be a family again soon enough and you'll understand. Right now, looks like something else has come up again."

He pushed her back on the creaking mattress.

Sara shook her head to clear it of the ugly scene as she

flattened herself on the roof. He said there were others, like himself, others who were waiting outside. She had seen nothing so far, no one, even though she had checked the window periodically since he left her room. Even if there were—and she did not know if she believed him since she had never given anything he said much credence—it was likely that if she stayed inside, she would certainly be raped again and probably killed as well.

The beast that had been her father was insane. He murdered her mother, drunk her blood to hear him tell it and Sara believed that all right. He had her blood on his chin, his chest, his fat belly, even his balls. Sara had no doubt her mother was dead. And, if that was not enough to convince her of his insanity, there was his insistence that Agnes would somehow come back to life.

But insanity did not explain the teeth, the strength. There was no way to explain any of that without accepting that Percy was no longer human. Sara crawled softly across the roof to settle into the shadows against the stone chimney.

"Son of a bitch!"

The angry shout startled Sara. She had lain pressed against the cool stones for quite some time and, though unable to sleep, she had been successful in losing herself in the soft silence of the night.

"You can run for now, damn you, but you're mine. You hear me, Baby Girl? You're mine," Percy shouted, his head hanging out the window.

The rage in his voice frightened her more than anything she had ever experienced. Whatever else he was, he was dangerous. She tried to become smaller, squeezing herself as well as she could into the shadow of the chimney. Seconds later, she heard the door bang against the side of the house. It sounded as if the door had been torn from its hinges. She crept forward to peer over the edge of the roof.

Percy had indeed kicked the door off its hinges. As she watched, he kicked it off the porch as well, sending it spinning across the yard. He followed the door as if it were a hated enemy and kicked it again, splintering the wood. Percy peered into the darkness in all directions and Sara held her breath with the knowledge that his night vision, too, was that of an animal.

But he did not look up. The raw wound on the side of his face was healing quickly even though the ashen face itself was more ghastly with the glistening fangs and the strange purple blush that spread across his face like a contagion. His long shadow spilled across the entire length of the yard and was joined by another long shadow. Agnes Way stepped into the light and together they headed for the barn.

Sara had to stifle an impulse to call out to her mother. Percy was dressed again and Agnes wore the same clothing she had been wearing earlier, only now stained with blood. She was so pale. Something inside Sara told her she could not believe her eyes. Her mother walked and no doubt talked but she was dead. Even as Sara witnessed her walking across the yard, Agnes was dead. Percy had been telling the truth for once in his miserable, vicious, and wasted life. Sara watched as her parents entered the barn.

Almost immediately, a panicked braying ensued. One mule came running through the open barn door, kicking out with its hind legs as it ran. It was followed by the second of the pair, trailing its companion with Percy hot on its heels. Sara's stomach lurched as the mule wheeled. Agnes clung to the animal's neck as her skirts popped and whipped around her in the night wind. Sara turned her head away as they pulled the mule to the ground.

CHAPTER TEN

Burl Tanner pulled up his overalls and fastened the bib. A pack of tobacco and rolling papers fell from the pocket. As he bent to pick them up, it occurred to him he had not had a cigarette in two days. In fact, he had completely forgotten he was a smoker. He brushed his sandy-brown hair back from his face and smiled to himself as he sat down on a rock. He rolled his smoke, fished a match from his overalls and raked the head across the rock he was sitting on. The match ignited in colors, spitting from a ragged, hissing flare into a steady flame, reflecting in the eyes of the woman on the ground. Burl drew a deep lung full of sharp smoke and blew it out. It was the best he had ever experienced. Today every experience was the best.

The woman lay on her back with her legs drawn up. Though naked, she made no attempt to cover herself as Burl looked down at her. Her name was Rachael. He had not known her name when he had first had sex with her. He did not know anything about her at all other than she was as he was and what that meant was a mystery to him. But he knew he wanted her. And she wanted him and that was enough. As for the rest, Burl was finding out more about who he was—what he was—with each passing moment. And, to his surprise, he liked it.

A moment of pain; a moment of utter terror; a moment of darkness, of nothingness, and then life—it all made about as much sense as the life he had left behind and that would have to be enough. He had died beside the road, Chloe's screams mixing with his own, echoing inside him, filling his mind. When he opened his eyes again, he was in the company of the two men who had "killed" him. They sat a few feet away, watching him patiently. Surprisingly, he felt no fear in their presence.

"It's about time," one of them said, rising to his feet. He was a tall man, rangy, with dark brown, almost black curly hair that fell over his shoulders. The stranger smiled at Burl's confusion. The second man, several inches shorter than the first and more solidly built, strode over to Burl and extended his hand. Burl allowed himself to be hauled to his feet. Without another word the two started for Hog Heaven Hill. Burl, just as silently, followed them.

No one explained anything to him until they joined with some others but he felt as if he were beginning to understand without explanation. There seemed to be a strange type of knowing between them, almost like reading one another's minds but not quite, yet still something more as well. He understood they had taken something from him but they had given him something in exchange. Something he had not sought but had accepted immediately. Unlike Bill and Percy, Burl had no unfinished business, no left-over agenda from the life that was. He left that life behind as casually and without regret as if he had discarded a worn-out shirt.

Born again. He had never felt better in his life.

He had been present, watching, sitting silently beneath the trees like the others when Bill awoke. He could see that Bill brought his anger with him. Though

103

the man had never said a word, Burl had known. It could not have been clearer if Bill had made a speech. Bill was going after those who had abandoned him, as if it made a difference now. His anger would kill him and Burl knew that as surely as he knew the sun set in the west.

As Bill walked toward the valley, Burl turned away, knowing Bill would die twice in the space of twelve hours. The strangers watched as well. Burl could sense, in this strange new way of knowing, that they, too, knew Bill was doomed. He had also been there with Percy. There was an almost parental impulse to be there, as if awaiting the birth of a child. In a very real sense, that was exactly what he was doing, waiting for a child. A child conceived in the process of feeding. His boy, Percy Way. Burl had brought him over himself and felt a bit of a vested interest in him.

If he thought of the awakenings in terms of birth, then both Bill and Percy were stillborn, dead from the moment they opened their eyes. Percy's lust tied him to the old life as surely as Bill's anger tied him. Everything Percy had tried to keep secret in his other life was now an open book. Percy apparently felt no anger, no sense of betrayal, nothing but the need to possess, nothing but raw desire. He, too, walked away alone. Burl, however, was content to stay.

In any number of ways, the new life felt no different than the old. Screwing and eating, eating and screwing. The impulse was disguised a little better in the world he had left behind but, still, it was the driving force of existence. He also found a bond of community, perhaps as strong, maybe stronger, among his new companions. To be present at the awakenings was to greet the newborns, to welcome them into that community; if they were suited to it. Unlike Percy and Bill, Burl was more than suited to it. He was born for it and knew it the moment he was born into it.

Burl followed the others and when the opportunity to feed presented itself, he did not hesitate but fell to the task as if he had been doing it all his life. He'd even been shot in the process, taking a round of buckshot in the shoulder from Amos McBride's shotgun. He knew how Amos felt about Chloe. Smiling at the thought, he wondered if Amos had recognized him through the haze of smoke, fear, and night. And, if he did, had he taken any satisfaction from it.

Then there was Percy Way.

Burl had no thoughts of converting Percy at the time. In fact, at that particular moment, Burl did not give a damn and whether Percy was reborn or dead forever was immaterial to him. He would not have thought twice about taking Percy's life under any circumstances. Nor was he moved by Percy's pleas. The man's panic only served to increase Burl's excitement. Here was power, raw, relentless, and intoxicating; he was unstoppable.

Tossing the cigarette aside, Burl sat down beside Rachael and smiled at her. She smiled back and it occurred to him that none of it mattered really. His shoulder wound healed in no time at all, as had the wounds of the others who had survived. If the heart was intact and the brain intact, there was no need to consider other damage.

And he had already died once.

How many other people have the opportunity to die twice? And, apparently, death was perfectly safe. In fact, it was euphoric. As his old life slipped away, Burl had been as giddy as a kid discovering corn-liquor for the first time. After that, anything else had to be gravy.

Rachael had approached him while he waited for Percy to come around. He watched her as she moved toward him, unbuttoning her blouse as she walked. Silently she knelt before him, her breasts bare, jiggling with her movements as she reached down to loosen the buttons at the crotch of his overalls. He felt himself grow hard in her hand.

Several amused spectators watched as she brought her mouth down on him, their faces reflecting an interest that sparked like embers behind their eyes. Burl, lost in physical sensation, became aware of every nerve in his body to an extent he had never before experienced, an extent he never could have imagined. As he slipped further and further into a world rapidly narrowing into feeling, he noticed others similarly engaged. Two men were with the remaining woman, other men with other men. The rules were different now. He accepted them without question.

Throwing his head back, the stars dancing across the dark sky flooded his eyes, swirling into a single, brilliant, point of light. The whole universe concentrated within him, pouring back out again as he thrashed and jerked in the bed of pine needles.

A short time later, Burl took a little more stock of his companions. The shorter man was Frank; the tall, lean one, Aaron. Burl and Rachael sat with them, eating the berries she had picked and some hard-tack from her provision bag. There was nothing to drink. The closest source of water was Baptizing Creek and Burl knew instinctively it was of no use to them. Burl, rolling a smoke, noticed Aaron watching him. As he reached into his pocket for a match, he offered the pouch to Aaron.

"Thankee," Aaron said, taking the pouch. "Won't grow worth a damn in the high country. Too rocky, I'm reckonin'. Damn me if I had any good smokin' tobaccy in years."

He busied himself with rolling one of his own. Burl found himself wondering, for the first time, just who in creation he had taken up with. They sure didn't sound like they were from around these parts—Aaron, particularly with his strange accent and odd manner of speaking. Aaron passed the pouch to Frank and held his hand out for a match, which Burl supplied. Aaron lit his smoke, fixing Burl with a steady gaze.

"Ye'd want t'know a thing or two would ye?" he asked.

Burl was taken aback initially but he quickly made the connection. If, after only two days, he was able to simply know things, then it only stood to reason the others would be more accomplished at it.

"Yer alive," Frank said. "You was dead and now you ain't. A mite puzzlin' ain't it?"

"Yep, now that you mention it, it is a mite."

Aaron leaned back, taking another drag of his cigarette and smiling at Burl.

"I'm reckonin' we all puzzled over how we came t'be and how in bloody hell it all happened. I know and ye can hold it t'yer heart. But there really ain't no explaining it. Weren't one of us comin' in different from ye', kickin', screamin', nastyin' our britches n' fightin' t'beat hell. How or why ain't in our ken."

"Kind of like getting struck by lightning is it?" Burl asked, grinding the remnant of his cigarette beneath his boot.

"Ye could say so. For them that's gettin' struck afresh anyway. Them that's been struck, well, now we tote the lightnin' and it comes with an accountin', rules to foller ye might say."

Burl threw back his head and laughed.

"Rules? They damned sure slipped right by me. I saw Frank and another fella doing things to each other I never would have imagined two days ago. For that matter, Rachel here was just doin' things to me I couldn't get done in a New Orleans whorehouse. I'm not one to bitch, mind you. I like this here life just fine so far but I can't say I've seen anything that would lead me to believe that there are rules. If I remember right, you and old Frank, without so much as a 'howdy-do' sort of had me for supper while I was out walking with my girl."

Frank chuckled and even Aaron's somber face split into a grin.

"Ye'll do, old hoss," Aaron said. "By God, ye'll do."

They talked for a while and Burl felt like a schoolboy. But there were too few answers to his many questions.

"As ye see," Frank said, "we don't know a hell of a lot more about this life than we did the other one. Come to think of it, neither one makes too damned much sense. I reckon a feller's got t'play the hand he's dealt."

Burl said nothing. He took his pouch from his pocket, rolling another smoke.

"How come we can't go in somebody's house without being invited?" Burl asked.

"I don't rightly know," Aaron said. "It's just one of them things."

"Well, what would happen if a body was to just go ahead and do it anyway?"

The other members of the group looked at one another with shocked expressions. It had never occurred to any of them to question this particular injunction.

"Well," Frank said hesitantly, "I don't think nobody knows that either. I'm betting it ain't good, though. None of us has ever done it."

"Besides," Aaron added, "it wouldn't be sportin' would it. Even as poor a creature as a bloody rabbit's got a hole t'go in ain't he? None of us would do such a thing even if it din't call the wrath of God down on us, which, ye'll understand, it will. It just ain't done."

Burl exhaled a cloud of smoke, leaning slowly toward Aaron with a grin on his face.

"And none of you ever bother children either. So how come we had the boy, the one that got killed down

108

in the valley the other night?"

Aaron brushed his hair back from his face, his expression somber.

"Well, I'll tell ye plain. I had a couple of young uns myself when I come into the life, over Chicamauga way, and I didn't much cotton to the idea of leaving 'em. Kinda like that Percy feller. But it ain't right to take the young uns and damn me if it's practical either."

Aaron looked away, obviously in the grips of some emotion.

"I missed my children a slew a years," he said, staring off into the distance. "Missed 'em so much I had t'go back. Even talked to my eldest boy. Here I was, lookin' t'be thirty years or so and spendin' the time of day with the old, old man I'd bounced on me knee and played peek-n-boo with. I started cryin' right in the middle of it. My child reckoned me crazy I'm thinkin'. Just sitting, passin' time about no particular and I bursted out a weepin'. It was too much. I come back three years later when they buried him, but I ain't been back since. Won't be either."

Seemingly embarrassed by his disclosure and the direction the conversation was going, Aaron cleared his throat and spat, then smiled at Burl before continuing.

"Ye know I wanted 'em with me but it just ain't right. A young un is a young un and a bloody pain in the arse from any which way y'see 'em. But they tend t'grow outta it. Poor old Dwayne, the boy got killed t'other night, never got the chance. Lad was only thirteen when he come over and after some seventy-odd years he never got more'n a couple years growth on his body. It's like that with us. I don't know why. If an old-timer comes over, the life makes 'im younger. I'm reckonin' I look younger now than I did when I first crossed that crik. But it takes the young uns forever t'grow up."

"But that's not what I'm asking," Burl said, getting

109

back to his original question. "How did he wind up coming over in the first place?"

"We got us a crazy preacher a few years before we got Dwayne," Frank said. "Lordy, did that man carry on. We brought him and Rachael over at the same time. Rachael here was a fallen angel," he nodded in her direction. "As you can see, she was a pretty little whore and was doing all right till she got religion. She fell in with this preacher man who worked real hard to save her soul, mainly so he could get to her ass. We run across 'em in a little clearing over near the Georgia line. They were naked as jay-birds and screwing till times ain't long. Whooooo, you never seen a man lose a hard-on so fast in your life.

"This here preacher, Truman by name, was already crazy as a Betsy-bug and that didn't have a thing t'do with us. He stayed with us for a good while but I never did think he was quite right. First damned thing he done was bring an old gal he'd run across over—which was okay with us, as far as that goes. But he also brought her son, Dwayne.

"Now, like Aaron was saying, a kid can be mean and nobody'll argue that, but when you stay a kid as long as Dwayne, well, mean ain't the word for it. He got older in his head but all he ever had was that little old kid's body. Yeah, he got mean, all right. But Dwayne was sad, too. Pretty lonesome most of the time. He knew he'd lost somethin' he couldn't ever get back. I think he might've even got himself killed on purpose. He was always taking risks.

"Anyhow, this preacher never did have any doubts about the life or who we were. In fact, he used to tell us all the time. Said we was the damned, cursed in the sight of God, abominations upon the earth, cut off from the light, bound for hell-fire and all kinds of nonsense.

"Well, we never paid him much mind but Dwayne's

mama bought all of it and asked for more. She was real concerned for her soul. Ended up following him all the way down the mountain to get baptized in that creek yonder. Well, the rest of us couldn't miss that show, so we followed 'em."

Burl looked up wide-eyed. The creek was poison for them, even he knew that. He had known it from the moment he opened his eyes to the life.

"You don't mean to tell me they walked out into that water?"

"That's exactly what I'm telling you."

"Jesus Christ, what happened?" Burl asked, incredulously.

"Well, it was a damned short show, I'm here to say," Aaron interjected. "The bloody fool waded out into the stream and the water boiled around him, steam rolling up and all. The woman got scared, tried to back off, but Truman wouldn't have it. He snatched her off the bank before she could spit. Dragged her out there with him. I'm reckonin' none of us ever seen anything like. I'm tellin' ye he caught her by the scruff a'the neck and shoved her under."

"All the while the meat was cookin' off his bones," Frank said. "And when he brought her up, it was just like he promised. By God, she was a changed woman."

"Damn," Burl said, with a low whistle. "What then?"

"The last we saw of 'em," Franks said, "his legs give out and he fell down into the creek still holdin' onto the woman. The son-of-a-bitch was hollerin' 'hallelujah' all the way down. The woman was a hollerin' too."

"Aye, but not hallelujah," Aaron added.

"Reckon he was right?" Burl asked as he stood.

"About what?" Aaron said.

"Are we the damned?"

CHAPTER ELEVEN

By the time Wilda and Margie had dragged her back inside the house, Ellie was furious. She fought them every step of the way, her struggles increasing two-fold when she heard the shot fired outside. She was on the attack when Truitt came through the door, and he immediately caught the brunt of her rage. He made no move to protect himself as she charged forward, slapped him across the face and drove him against the wall. Her blows cracked like pistol shots, four in quick succession, jerking his head, turning his cheeks bright red. By the time she was restrained by Walter and Margie, she had managed to split his lip and blood trickled down his chin.

Ellie spun on Walter, pushing him backwards with a surprisingly powerful blow. She caught him in the middle of the chest, knocking him to the floor.

"I guess you think you really done something don't you? You big, hard men. You really done something."

Mabeline, a bit worse for wear herself after tumbling from the porch, tried to calm her daughter down.

"Now, baby. Walter and Truitt was only doing what they had to do."

Ellie pulled away from her and started for the door.

"Why in the world I talked Truitt into letting you stay here, I'll never know. You've been a pain from day one. You and these two fat, useless sisters of mine."

No one moved to stop her as she started out on the porch. Ellie stopped and turned back to face them.

"Was that some egg-sucking dog out there a minute ago or was that my son?"

No one answered.

"I hope you're all real proud of yourselves, real proud. Now, where is he? I'm going to go tend to him."

"He ain't out there, Mama. I didn't shoot him. I couldn't."

"What do you mean?"

"I mean I didn't hit him. I just shot over him, to run him off. He went across the fields yonder." Walter pointed out toward the western mountains.

"Well, thank God for that. If any of you ever hurt my baby, I won't be responsible for what I do to you."

* * *

Sara woke with the sun in her eyes. She sat back against the stone chimney for a moment, then stood and scanned the entire perimeter of the countryside surrounding the farmhouse. She detected nothing but, still, it took a while to work up the courage to move. Every time she tried, she thought of Percy, striding around the corner of the house, insane grin on his face, to welcome her back into the family. She pulled her boots off and dropped them to the ground before taking a final look around. Nothing at all stirred, not even a bird. Clutching the mortared stone of the chimney, she swung herself around, bare toes gripping the uneven surface as she climbed to the ground. She still moved cautiously, though quickly.

The carcass of the mule, abuzz with blowflies, lay twenty yards away. Sara averted her eyes as she entered the house. Dark smears of blood stained patches on the rough floor and the drone of an errant blue-bottle

113

fly filled her ears. Without any hesitation, she hurried up the stairs to her parents' room to rifle through their cedar chest. It only took a moment to find what she sought.

The forty-four caliber Colt revolver, well-oiled and glistening in the light, felt heavy in her hand. She sighted down the blue steel barrel as she held the bulky weapon at arm's length and swung it. A portrait of Percy and Agnes hung on the wall and Sara brought the weapon to bear on Percy's chest.

"This time I got something for you, Daddy."

She stuck the Colt in her waistband, collected all the cartridges she could find and headed downstairs. In ten minutes the farm was behind her as she started down the road with a few light supplies stuffed in a beat-up fabric satchel. She turned to look back. Home. All she had ever known. She felt a slight twinge of nostalgia but the feeling was fleeting, quickly replaced by a surging sense of freedom. Leaving was a final thing. She would never be back. She kept her eyes focused in front of her as she walked down the road.

Not once did she look back again.

* * *

Sunrise found little change at the McBride farm. Mabeline, Wilda and Margie stayed in their room. Ellie remained in hers. Truitt, banished from his own bed, had slept in shifts with Walter, taking turns watching. He watched Walter sleep, lying on the pallet, next to the stove. Sipping at his coffee, Truitt thought of Ellie's parting remark and it still stung. She had made it plain she was glad Amos had escaped. He was, too. There was no way he could have pulled the trigger on Amos. Not if the fate of the entire world depended on it. Obviously Walter could not do it either. He was not the best shot in the world, but blind-drunk and

114

shooting left-handed, Walter could not have missed at that range. Wherever Amos was, whatever he was, he was safe from them and though Truitt hoped fervently he would never lay eyes on him again, in his heart he wished him well.

He rubbed his cheek, still tender from Ellie's unrestrained blows. She had never hit him before. And he had never hit her, though honestly there were probably a few times over the years when he wanted to. It just was not done. Of course, there had been any number of times when Truitt had thought he and Mabeline would come to blows. More often than not their disagreements escalated into shouting matches but they had never gone beyond that. Again to be honest, Truitt had to acknowledge to himself that the thought of slugging it out toe to toe with Mabeline Williams was not a battle he was sure he could win.

The shame of hitting a woman notwithstanding, there was an element of fear involved as well. He could attest from recent experience that both Mabeline and Ellie packed quite a wallop. But in the space of two days, he had been assaulted by both women and, though he was definitely ashamed of it, he had struck his mother-in-law. Well, he had pushed her, anyway, and that was basically the same thing. It had to be the stress of the whole thing. The sweetest-tempered dog will bite when he's hurting and no could accuse Truitt of sweet temper lately. Not one solitary damn thing that was happening to him and his family made any sense.

The sunlight stole into the room with the dust swirling through the open portal where the door had been. Truitt watched motes of dust floating through the rays of light. Soon, it would be time to bring the others in and inform them of the conclusions he and Walter had reached the night before. They needed to have a voice, he guessed. Truitt picked up his pipe, poured a little more coffee into his cup and walked out onto the porch. He sat smoking and looking at the sky.

Walter was leaving, Truitt accepted that but, come hell or high water, he did not think he would ever be able to tear himself away from home. Everyone else would have to decide for themselves. One thing he knew for sure, Walter was right about holing up. They could not do that. There were other families in the valley and they had to know. The Tanners, the Larrimers, the Ways, the O'Daniels, the McWhorters; his brother-in-law, Freeman Williams. Every one of them was at risk. There was no way to justify not getting word out to them, no matter how dangerous that might be.

The clouds, coming together over the mountains, loomed like mountains themselves. Not wispy, like the day before, but dark, billowing on the horizon in large cumulus banks—threatening. Today, no later than tomorrow, thunder would echo through the highlands and torrential spring rains would be upon them. Truitt closed his eyes, turning his head as a gust of wind scooped dust from the road to scatter it across the yard. It stung the back of his neck, settled in his clothing, his coffee and the creases of his skin. He raised his hand, wiping it across the back of his neck before staring at the palm.

Truitt rolled the gritty dirt between his fingers. It was his soil, as much a part of him as anything could be. And he was part of it. He had spent his whole life with that soil. In dry weather, the dust covered him when he went to the fields, on his skin, filling his eyes, his ears, his mouth, blanketing him as if staking a claim. In wet weather, it clung to him like a jealous lover, pulling at his legs as he walked across it, trying to pull him down into it, groaning as it reluctantly gave way to his resistance.

"You could be more patient," he said to the grains

of dirt in his hand. "I'll be along by and by I reckon."

Grit in his coffee did not bother him as he drained the last of the brew, knocked the ashes from his pipe, rose and walked back inside. Walter sat at the kitchen table, eating one of yesterday's biscuits as he sipped his coffee. Truitt sat down across the table from him.

"Reckon we need to talk to the others, I suppose," he said.

Walter nodded while swallowing the mouthful of bread. He took another sip of coffee to wash it down before speaking.

"I reckon we do. You give any more thought to what you want to do, Papa?"

"It didn't take a lot of thought. I'm staying. We need to warn the others in the valley—I intend to do that sure enough, I can't hide in here no more—but I can't leave either. I've never been nowhere else. What would I do?"

"Well, you gotta think of Mama and the others."

"I am thinking of them. If they want to go, they're welcome. I'm just talking about me. I figure your mama can't get away from me fast enough anyway, after what happened yesterday."

"Well, you figure wrong then," Ellie said, from the foot of the stairs. She tied her apron around her waist as she ambled over to the stove. "I'm still not real happy about none of that, mind you, and I want a say in what happens from now on. But if I was to jump up and leave every time one of this bunch pulled some damn fool stunt, well, it ain't likely we'd ever need a front door on the place."

She refilled Walter's cup and Truitt's as well before setting the pot back on the stove. She patted Truitt's hand as she sat down next to him.

"Well," Walter said as he rose to his feet. "There's no sense wasting time. I'll get the others and we'll get this thing started."

117

Soon everyone sat at the table. Mabeline, like Truitt, wore a large bruise on the side of her face from her tumble over the porch rail and the slight swelling caused her appearance to be somewhat out of kilter. She looked old and tired. Truitt, besides feeling a healthy dose of guilt, felt once more his transient sense of pity for her. She fidgeted nervously with the hem of her apron as her eyes skipped from one face to another instead of focusing in the belligerent glare he was accustomed to seeing.

Mabeline's anxiety seemed infectious and Wilda and Margie had both caught a pretty serious dose of it as far as he could tell. The girls were always shy, staying in the background, keeping to themselves. Truitt sometimes wondered why everyone referred to them as "the girls" even though he did so himself. The Williams "girls" were thirty-five and thirty-three years old. Still when anyone mentioned "the girls" no one ever had to ask which ones.

Neither of them had ever married, nor had they ever entertained any serious suitors for that matter. It was not their appearance or their weight; size had never been an issue in these parts. Besides, they were not that large. If the truth be known, they were not much larger than Ellie and he still considered her one fine looking woman. Since the first time he had laid eyes on her sisters, however, they had constantly been together, constantly in their mother's shadow.

It occurred to Truitt he had never even seen them as people. If asked to describe either one, he was not sure he could do it. Each was about five-feet-five, each weighed around a hundred ninety or so pounds, each had mousy brown hair, brown eyes, a smattering of freckles sprinkling a chubby non-descript face. They wore their anonymity as comfortably as an old sweater.

Truitt's sense of sadness expanded to take in Wilda and Margie. When they died, if anyone ever spoke of them again, no one would be able to keep them straight. "It was Wilda who once . . . no, it was Margie . . . no it was Wilda who . . . well, it don't matter, it was one of the Williams' girls." They would be lucky if their names were spelled right on their tombstones.

He had known them for more than twenty-five years and they were little more than furniture. When they were gone it would be like an old chair removed from a room. For a while the empty space would be noted but, after a time, people would have trouble remembering the object which had occupied the space. Then, finally, no one would even notice the space any longer. Truitt found himself wondering why they had ever been born in the first place.

"Why are you looking at me like that?" Margie asked.

"Was I? Sorry. Just thinking, I guess."

He pulled his eyes away from her, feeling even sadder. Furniture could not feel anything but Margie's anxiety exuded from every pore. The poor thing. The poor, poor thing. Jesus.

"Listen, this is the way we got it figured," Walter said. "Me and Papa, we got to go from place to place, let folks know what's going on. We can't just let anybody go and blunder into these bastards. That just wouldn't be right. I think we ought to all get together someplace or other and maybe these monsters will think twice before they get to fooling around with a bunch of people."

"That's not all there is to it," Truitt said. "He thinks we ought to go on ahead and high-tail clean out."

"Yeah, that's right," Walter said, a bit defensively. "What's keeping us here? It's not like we got a pot to piss in is it? Rich folks like us got a lot to worry about leaving behind don't we?"

Truitt did not reply. He knew Walter had aimed the barb at him but he had said all he had to say about it

119

the night before. Ellie waited for Truitt to respond and, when he did not, she did.

"You know good and well we can't do that, Walter. There's been a McBride sitting here on this patch of land for over a hundred-fifty years. You just want to walk off and leave it now? We'll find some way of taking care of this without doing that."

"Mama, I been wanting to walk off and leave this place for years. I'm not interested in being no farmer and I never have been. God knows I tried but I just ain't got it in me. We all got to die sometime. I just don't want to die for something I don't even want."

"Now, if that ain't a fine way to talk," she admonished.

"It's the truth. Now's no time for lies. We can leave here, go somewhere else. You and Papa can take up farming again if you want to. And, as for a McBride sitting on this patch of land, I reckon we can leave it for Amos and his bunch."

Ellie caught her breath, face flushing with anger as she started up from her chair. Truitt took her arm, not sure what might happen next. Ellie sat back in her chair but her anger had not passed; she simply held her peace. Truitt broke the short, strained silence.

"When we get the word out, we'll have done what we need to do. After that, I reckon everybody's free to make up their own minds. Walter's a grown man and should have left a long time ago. It's a right thing, Ellie. Let it be."

Mabeline cleared her throat for attention, placing her hands on the table before speaking. They still shook slightly.

"Me and the girls will be coming with whichever one of you is going by Freeman's. Ellie was right last night, we ain't got no business here."

Ellie flushed. Truitt knew she felt guilty about the harsh words the night before. But he also knew, and so did Ellie, that once they were said they could never be taken back, not really.

"Mama," Ellie said. "Don't pay what I said last night no mind. I got scared and all about Amos. I felt like I'd just swallowed a mad dog and had to bite somebody. I didn't mean none of those things. You and the girls are welcome here and always have been. I was scared for Amos and took it out on you. I'm sorry."

"I hear you, but what you said was still the truth. I haven't done you no good here. None of us have. We've been all caught up in feeling sorry for ourselves since Freeman put us out and we ain't stopped for a minute to think of nobody else. Now, I worked like a damned mule to make something out of that place, it wasn't all Sean's doing. And I know good and well Freeman's old lady don't care for me. To be real honest, I wouldn't go out of my way to spit on her if she was on fire either. But I got a right to be there."

"What if he won't take you in?" Walter asked.

"Oh, he'll take me in all right," Mabeline said, the old familiar belligerency settling comfortably over her again. "Or I'll stomp a mud-hole in the middle of his ass and kick it dry."

CHAPTER TWELVE

It was not yet dawn. Tildy pulled the covers back, rose and slowly swung her legs over the side of the bed. She sat quietly, allowing the circulation to remove the numbness she sometimes felt in her lower limbs after a period of inactivity. After a moment she stood, walked into the kitchen and tossed a couple of pieces of wood into the black-iron stove. She pumped water into the pot, put it on to boil and went about the business of getting dressed. By the time she had finished so had the coffee. She filled the cup to the brim, spilling it over into the saucer.

Tildy abandoned the coffee long enough to start breakfast. Bacon sizzled on the stove and she was satisfied with biscuits left over from the day before. It was just too much trouble to make fresh ones. As soon as the bacon was done, Tildy scooped flour into the hot grease and in short order had a pan of gravy. She continued to think about her revelation the day before as she sat down to eat.

It surprised her, in a way, accepting the proposition of her own death, within the week, surely, so easily. Yet accept it she did. What else could she do? While she chewed her food, she thought of how any meal could now be her last. Somehow it made the act of eating seem quite important. She chewed slowly; concentrating on what she was doing; trying to be aware of the texture of the food as she ground it between her teeth, the crunch of the bacon, and the taste of the grease. It was as if she were trying to memorize the sensations of life, to carry them with her, if they could be carried.

As a girl she had been greatly concerned with death. Her father served as a deacon and Tildy spent a good deal of time with him, attending meetings, services, revivals, baptisms, where the backwoods preachers howled of fire and brimstone. At the age of fifteen; convinced, smelling the sulfurous smoke, hearing the wailing of the damned, she wound up in the hands of one of the revivalists who dipped her into the waters of Baptizing Creek. The water was cold, plastering her long dark hair to her back, sending gooseflesh crawling over her body. Water trickled down her face, dripping from her chin as she broke the surface, not just rising above the water, but above the earth, to salvation, to glory.

Her father shouted and clapped in the meadow, where the cross had yet to be erected. Tildy beamed at the congregation on the bank as she rose shivering from the water to scan the faces in the crowd. The faces were rapt, filled with the spirit, as was her own; until she turned to face the preacher. He still held her bare arm, the hand he had used to support her head during the baptism still rested on her shoulder but his eyes were riveted on her upper torso. Her bright smile faded.

The light, white cotton of her best dress clung to her body, transparent. Her breasts were outlined by the wet gauzy fabric stretching over them like a second skin. The nipples, hard and erect from the cold, pressed against the wet cloth in stark definition. The parson took his hand off her arm and, as if hypnotized, actually reached for them. She jerked back involuntarily, breaking the trance. With a shake of his head, the revivalist composed himself. He gave her what he surely assumed was a benign smile, but she had seen what she had seen and the minister's thoughts had been anything but holy. Suddenly, his left hand came up to the back of her neck as he clamped the right to her forehead.

"Hallelujah!" he shouted, bending her backwards to again plunge her beneath the surface.

She barely had time to catch a breath before the frigid liquid engulfed her. He pushed her much further down than he had the first time and she lost her footing. As her legs shot out from under her, she opened her mouth and the water flooded in. The preacher lost his grip, grappling for another handhold. Tildy coughed, sputtered, as he clutched her from behind to pull her up. His large, rough hands brushed her breasts and he pressed himself tightly against her from behind.

"Hallelujah!"

"Horny old bastard," she said to herself as she took a sip of her coffee. Her faith had been questionable almost before her hair was dry.

Over the years, she had spent a great deal of time examining her motivations for the baptism and had eventually come to the conclusion that it was nothing more than a reaction to her fear of death—more precisely, her fear of hell. It was apparent to her she could never be what her faith demanded. In fact, her own mother had told her so.

"You're an abomination—damned to hell-fire."

This had followed her mother's discovery of Tildy and her cousin, in a compromising situation, in the hay-loft. If one believed the stories of the adults, this was not an uncommon thing. After all, children have always been curious. But Tildy had been fourteen and Cousin Annie nine years older. If that alone was not enough to raise eyebrows, and it was, there was also the fact that Cousin Annie was a married woman and the mother of four children. Though Tildy's relationship with Annie had begun two years before, this was the first Ma Garrett had known of it. She had been less than pleased.

Tildy felt exposed, more exposed than ever in her life, even more so than when she stepped from the waters of Baptizing Creek with her white dress plastered to her. Still, years after the fact, the memory brought a rush of blood to her face.

"If it was up to me," her mother said, bringing her face close to the tear-stained and swollen face of Tildy, "I'd follow the Scripture and do what it says we should do with things like you. I ain't gonna do that because of your daddy. He dotes on you. God knows why, but he does. It would flat kill him to find this out. You pray, girl. You pray to God for mercy and listen to me. If I ever hear of you doing anything like this again, God might have mercy but I sure won't."

From that time to her father's death, six years later, she heeded her mother's warning. Pa wondered why she had so few suitors, good-looking woman that she was, and why she never married, but, as far as she knew, he never did ferret out the truth. Her mother also made it a point not to discover any further lapses on Tildy's part though they were there to discover had anyone held the interest.

Thinking back on it now, it may have been because her parents really did not want to know. If they did not see it, it was not there. Anyway, knowledge of Tildy's preference did not kill her father. Consumption did. She had been with him when the wet, tubercular coughs strangled the life from him. After that, she and her mother continued to share the same roof though their relationship had ended years before in the hay-loft. When her mother died, she and her brother, Delwin, who had also never married, lived together until he, too, eventually passed on leaving her alone.

Over the years, Tildy spent much of her time alone. There were lovers, of course , but that was tricky business while her parents had been alive. After their deaths, Tildy dropped all pretenses.

Delwin, surprisingly enough, was not affected at all.

"It ain't my life," he had told her. "And I'm not smart enough to know what's right and wrong for other people. I don't understand what you feel and I don't imagine it's all that important that I do. But I love you, Sis. Nothing you do is apt to change that."

She felt tightness in her throat when she thought of Delwin. Maybe she did not think of him often enough anymore. She had never been the recipient of such total acceptance at any other time in her life. She missed that. "Strange." Tildy Garrett was "strange." People did talk. She knew that, of course. And sometimes she was aware of folks—particularly the younger ones—looking at her like she was a two-headed snake or something. But that was life.

The choice had been hers. Not for her feelings for other women, she could not help that, but the choice to act on those feelings. To go ahead and be who she was. That was what people could not stand. There was a price to pay, of course. Her cousin, Annie—an on-again, off-again, lover for some thirty years—went through two husbands during their long-standing involvement. All the while Annie kept it secret, as well as she could anyway. And all the while Tildy knew, beyond the shadow of any doubt, that Annie condemned her as harshly as anyone else when her name came up in conversation.

Tildy stopped attending church services after her father's death. Her mother, likely figuring she was,

126

indeed, damned to hell anyway, never said a word about it. For a number of years, Tildy continued to read the Bible. She found her mother's quotation and it bothered her still when she thought of it.

"I am an abomination," she said aloud, as she had hundreds of times before.

No sooner were the words out, than Tildy felt the old feelings of rebelliousness and outrage rising up in her. She cleared the table, placing the dirty dishes in the sink basin. As she poured another cup of coffee, the anger still roiled within her.

"T' hell with it," she said. "What kind of damn-fool God would go around making up silly-ass rules like that and then go build a body so's they can't abide them?"

There was no answer. After all this time, how could she expect any? Tildy slammed the coffee pot down on the stove and threw her head back.

"Did you make me or not?" she yelled at the ceiling. "Well? Then how in the hell can you hold me accountable for something you done? If I go to hell, then I reckon I go to hell—but it won't be for lying."

Her voice sounded loud and a bit shrill to her own ears and Tildy was embarrassed by her outburst. He cheeks reddened as she peered across the room at the broken grandfather clock.

"I reckon my mind must be going."

She sat down at the table, watching the sunrise through the window. The sun climbed slowly in the sky, filling the small kitchen with light and barely noticeable warmth. Would she miss this if she died? Lordy, she was missing it now. She stared at the sun and felt a deep sense of regret at the possibility of giving it up. Even if there was no heaven, or hell for that matter, she would not mind dying if she did not have to give up the sun. It would not be so bad to lie in a grave somewhere where the soil was warmed by the sun, drenched by the sweet spring rain. Maybe,

127

after a time, becoming part of the soil, whipped up by the gusting wind from the mountains, carried into the air, blown over all creation. That would not be bad at all.

Tildy's third cup of coffee caused her bladder to remind her of its' presence. She got up slowly. It occurred to her that this was one element of humanity she would not miss at all, particularly in bad weather. Tildy opened the door to walk to the outhouse. The body of a man lay no more than fifty feet in front of her home. The sight startled her and she jumped backward, retreating back inside.

She squinted at the body from the safety of her doorway where the silver crucifix hung fastened to the door. The body lay still, motionless. Tildy could not be sure who it was. The man lay on his stomach, upper arms perpendicular to his trunk and bent so the forearms were on either side of his head.

Tildy turned inside and picked up the Navy Colt from the bureau next to the door. Keeping her eyes fixed on the prone form, she took halting steps across the porch, moving out of the shadows of the awning onto the sun-splashed stoop. Carefully, with tentative steps, she descended watching the man for any sign of movement.

He looked like Percy Way.

Tildy stood in the dust of the pathway which crossed the yard and ended at the stoop. Her body swayed back and forth as she fought indecision. It was Percy, all right. She had known him all his life and there was no mistaking him. A chill ran up her spine. Percy was dead—she had seen it in her dreams and she had never in her life been wrong.

Had he died here?

No. That was not possible either; she had seen the setting as clear as day. She knew how he died, where he died and what he had become. But, on the other hand,

128

here he was lying in the yard, in broad daylight, and that just was not possible. Tildy's mind swam with confusion.

She turned and climbed the steps to her front door. The clear vision of Percy's death grew in her mind as she pulled the crucifix from the door. The blood. The blood. She shook her head to clear it of the violent image. For the first time since childhood, Tildy ignored the vision. She did not downplay it or try to rationalize it, she had done that often enough in the past, but now she locked it away in some compartmentalized part of her mind from which it could not escape. Then, willfully, she started toward Percy.

With short steps, she crossed the yard, crucifix in one hand, pistol in the other. Both hands were held extended toward Percy. She stopped several feet away, craning her neck to look over the body. His eyes were closed. The left side of his face lay in the grass at the side of the path. Tildy watched the blades of grass in front of his nose and mouth but the brisk, spring breeze made it impossible to detect breath in the movement of the grass.

She took a step closer, reaching out her foot to give Percy a light kick in the ribs, then jumping back. No response. She took another step closer, pistol at ready, and repeated the procedure. Still nothing. She lowered the pistol and the cross. With a speed totally inconsistent with his size, Percy rolled over and sat upright.

"Mornin'," he sang out cheerfully.

Everything became clear to Tildy in an instant. The murderous teeth were punctuated by the hard, mad glint of his eyes. Pink skin shone on the left side of his face, as if a severe sunburn had recently peeled. He squinted against the glare of the sun and raised a hand to shield his eyes.

"Looks like it's gonna be a hot one, don't it?" he

said. "Awful early in the year for that, don't y'think?"

Percy had begun to rise when Tildy held the cross in front of her and advanced. His eyes grew wide at the sight of the crucifix and he fell back, scrambling backward across the ground, pushing himself along with his legs.

"Lordy, Tildy, please. Please get that thing away from me. No. Please. Don't bring it no closer."

"Get off my land," Tildy commanded, jabbing the cross in Percy's direction. "You clear out of here and I mean right now. If you don't, I swear to God, I'll ram this thing right down your throat. You hear me?"

"Yes ma'am. Yes ma'am, I do. Let me get up from here and you won't have no more trouble out of me."

Tildy stopped as Percy pushed himself still further away from her; away from her and the gleaming silver cross. He kept his face averted as he rose to his feet, arms crossed protectively in front of him.

"I'm gone, Miss Tildy. Just don't touch me with that damned thing."

"Then get," Tildy ordered, shoving the cross in his direction.

Percy moved with the serpentine speed of a diamondback. He seized Tildy's wrist and, with a twist of his own, broke the ancient, fragile bone. Tildy gasped in pain as the cross fell from her hand. Percy dropped her hand with a confidence born of strength. He knew she could not get away. If he allowed her half the distance to the house, he would still be able to catch up to her without breaking a sweat.

"Yep," he said, bending to pick up the cross. "What with all the damned sunshine and crosses and whatnot layin' around, it's awful tough for folks like me to make a livin'."

Percy laughed as he flung the cross away. He turned back to Tildy as she was bringing the Colt to bear on his mid-section.

"No!" he shouted, no trace of the actor left.

Tildy thumbed the hammer and fired. A thick, ropy gout of blood spurted from Percy's abdomen marking where the slug punched through. Tildy fired again as he fell forward and an identical jet of crimson burst from his side.

Her hand slipped as she attempted to cock the weapon again and she almost dropped it. Percy fell heavily at her feet as she struggled with the weapon. He swung his arm in a sweeping motion and cut her legs from under her. She landed on her back, feeling the explosion of pain as her hip broke.

"Now, you old bitch," Percy said, getting to his feet. "I'm going to teach you a thing or two about how to treat company."

Tildy struggle with the pistol, finally managing to cock it again as Percy reached her. She braced herself with her left elbow, the hand dangling limply from the broken wrist, and saw his eyes widen again as she raised the Colt. Not this time. No more mistakes. Tildy raised the gun to her head. Finally, she stood on the threshold and it was time to cross.

She pulled the trigger as Agnes fell on her from behind.

* * *

The men swung out in a semi-circle to close in around the small clump of short, bushy trees. Keeping pace with the thump of the drums, bare feet kicked up clouds of yellow dust where the thin top-soil met the dry stalks of the long grasses. Amos wore the skin of a lion, fashioned into a crude breech-cloth. Looking down at his legs and feet he noted, without surprise, the dark, ebony sheen of his skin. In his left hand he held a shield made of bull hides, stretched tightly over a wooden frame. In his right, he carried an assagai,

131

honed sharp as a razor, gleaming in the sun. He, too, advanced in a dancing march, feet rising and falling with the drumbeats. Each time his right foot came down, he swung his left arm backwards and jerked the right forward, jabbing with the assagai in a stabbing motion.

There was a low, coughing snarl in the small thicket, a cracking of branches as the beast rushed back and forth in the cage its sanctuary had become. The men swung around the thicket, closing the circle with every step. They sang in a language foreign to Amos but he understood the content, if not the words, of their song. He found the same words on his own lips, carried on his own breath, as the heat of the moment burned in his veins.

The brush exploded with sound as the animal rushed from cover, roaring in fury. Holding his shield in front of him, Amos raised the spear and ran forward. The long grass parted and he saw the tail, lifted high in the air, as the creature charged.

The circle closed around them and he braced himself to drive the weapon home as the animal quickly closed the distance. Powerful muscle rippled and bunched as the legs launched the beast through the space he had occupied a heartbeat before. He stepped aside at the last moment and thrust with the spear. He, too, missed the mark.

Amos spun to meet the next assault. The animal crouched several yards away and Amos' legs turned to water as he looked into its eyes.

The body was that of a lion, lean, muscular, dark mane framing the snarling face and gray eyes—the gray eyes of Tildy Garrett. He tried to scream but no sound came. His face contorted into a rictus of terror which was even more eloquent in its silence. Pulling his gaze away from those eyes, he backed away as his own eyes focused on the legs of the creature, trying to read the

132

tension that would announce a charge. A harsh laugh drew him back to the face.

Tildy smiled at him—or snarled; he wasn't sure. The mouthful of teeth sent shivers down his spine as he felt his bladder go. She laughed again as she saw the warm liquid running down his bare legs.

"Nasty feeling ain't it, boy? Yep, nasty feeling, fear. Kills you from the inside."

"Please—."

"Please what? Please don't hunt you? Well, why not? You're hunting me ain't you?"

She rose on her hind legs, dark tuft of the serpentine tail dragging in the dust. Taking slow steps forward, she flexed the fore-paws, armed with sharp claws. Her thin lips pulled back over gleaming teeth and Amos saw the hind legs tense for action. In a flash, he raised the assagai, hurling it forward with all his strength.

Tildy screamed as the sharp blade sliced into her body, punching through the mid-section with a violent, tearing sound. Amos raised his arms into the air and shouted. Brandishing his shield in victory, he leaped into the air as dark blood sprayed onto the dry earth.

Swaying from side to side, the monster refused to fall. It gripped the haft of the spear, paws now hand-like, and grunted as it withdrew the blade. Amos flinched as it made the same tearing sound with which it had entered. He looked on in amazement as the wound began to close.

"Hunter, my ass," she said with a sneer as she again advanced.

Amos turned to flee, shoulder muscles braced for the impact he knew would be coming. The circle closed around him as the song of the hunters became an incoherent howling. They pulled in closer still, bringing their feet down in perfect unison with the thump of the drums. Headdresses, imitating a lion's mane, were tied beneath their chins, swaying adornments that framed their faces—each face a duplicate of Tildy's. He fell screaming to the ground as they closed in on him and heard the high, shrill laughter of the old woman as it burst from dozens of throats.

* * *

Agnes Way was dead as she hit the ground.

She had hidden herself alongside the house to cut off Tildy's retreat in case the old lady had been successful in eluding Percy. Hurriedly crossing the yard, she came up behind Tildy as Percy knocked the woman to the ground. Agnes, at a dead run, flung herself in a headlong leap. She hit Tildy, pushing her head forward, just as the hammer fell on the old Colt revolver.

The muzzle flash scorched a smoking furrow through Tildy's gray hair, followed the contour of the old woman's skull and crashed into Agnes' face between her nose and upper lip. The slug exploded clear through, scattering the back of Agnes' head over the yard.

"Damn," Percy said, rising to his knees.

He still clutched his steadily leaking wounds as he disentangled himself from Tildy's legs. The pain had been intense but short-lived. By the time he struggled to his feet it had already subsided to a dull ache. The bleeding stopped soon afterward and Percy knew the gunshot wounds, like the burn on his face, would be completely healed in a short time. He steadied himself on his legs well enough to walk over to his dead wife.

"Damn," he said again, looking down at Agnes. "You always was impatient. Well, there's nothing I can do for you now, is there? Reckon I need to take care of matters at hand."

He knelt next to Tildy, cradling her head in his hands. He took a breath, exhaled and brought his mouth to her throat.

* * *

Amos sat up, his scream imprisoned by his clenched teeth. The ache in his jaw muscles told him that his teeth had been clenched for some time. He drew his knees up toward his chin and pushed himself up to his feet. Walking several yards away, he carefully kept his back to Chloe as he relieved his bladder.

The image of Tildy as the lion-beast stalked the edge of his consciousness, flinging itself occasionally against the barrier he was fortifying to keep it out. It was too unreal, too threatening to think about and it was only a dream. There was so much going on, so much no one could explain. Chloe had her dreams as well and none of them meant anything. It was just something the strain produced.

Amos buttoned his overalls before coming back to sit beside Chloe. The fire had burned down to nothing more than smoking ash beneath the sparse, blackened remains of the rabbit—now charred and un-definable as a lump of spent coal. He crossed his arms over his knees, resting his chin on them. Slowly opening and closing his mouth, he flexed the jaw muscles to work the stiffness out. The motion caused his head to fall and rise and he felt the nagging soreness of his gums. Amos massaged them with his tongue, pressing it against the sore gums and into the space where his tooth had been.

Who was he trying to fool? Tildy was dead—stone, cold, graveyard dead. He had known it from the moment he opened his eyes, even before. He had known it in the dream. Nerves had nothing to do with it. Tildy was dead. Why had Tildy appeared as a beast? Why had he been hunting her? But the wall of his consciousness held against the onslaught of truth. He

135

clung to the idea he would never see her again, conjured up the moment of that awareness, the premonition he had experienced looking at her standing on her porch. She was dead and that was the end of it.

He reached out his hand and shook Chloe awake. There was much to do today and the sooner they got started the better. Perhaps there was safety in numbers. In any case, he had a plan to get back in the good graces of his family—that is if they did not shoot him before he had the chance to demonstrate. He took the whiskey bottle from the hunting sack and uncorked it. He had perhaps a fourth of the contents left. Well, no need to waste good whiskey, he thought, raising the bottle to his lips.

CHAPTER THIRTEEN

Sara stepped off the road to conceal herself in the brush. Someone was coming down the road in her direction but they were still too far away for her to recognize them. It was the mule she recognized first, the big gray with white hair on its chin that gave it a goat-like appearance. Truitt and Ellie rode double on its back. The couple rode in silence, swaying from side to side with the mule's gait. Truitt held his shotgun balanced across his lap, his hat pulled low concealing his face. Ellie sat behind him, arms wrapped around his mid-section. They were directly in front of Sara before she made a decision. She stood and stepped out into the road, leveling the Colt at Ellie's back.

"Don't move," she commanded.

But Truitt moved, wheeling the mule so quickly that Ellie was unseated and tumbled to the ground. He was in the process of raising the shotgun as Sara thumbed the hammer of the Colt.

"It'll be the last move you make on God's earth, old man," she said, holding a bead on him.

He lowered the weapon and his eyes searched her face.

"Sara?"

"Are you all right?" Sara asked.

"Oh, I'm all right," Ellie answered as she gained her feet. She patted her backside. "The Good Lord knew they'd be days like this. He gave me plenty of padding." She brushed at her clothing while Sara stood holding the gun on Truitt. Ellie froze in surprise as she noted the expression on the girl's face.

"That's not what she's asking," Truitt said. "Is it, Sara? You want to know if we're the same people you're used to seeing."

"Are you all right?" Sara repeated, her lower lip trembling. The gun in her hand wavered as Truitt lowered the shotgun carefully to the ground, raised his hands to his face and, with his fingers, pushed his lips back from his teeth. He let his hands fall loosely to his sides. "We're all right."

* * *

Mabeline sat astride the little Jennie as Walter led it down the road toward Freeman Williams'. Wilda and Margie plodded along beside her. It was a long day. Freeman's farm lay eight miles east of the McBride's; Duncan Tanner's some three miles closer. The first farm they had come to, the Larrimer's, had been empty. Walter hoped the family had merely been out on a visit somewhere. He had gone inside, written them a note and tacked it to the front door.

He printed the note in block letters, the dark painful scrawl of a hand for whom the pen was a mysterious and complicated instrument:

MR LARRIMER
WE GOT TROUBLE. NO ONE WAS HOME TO WARN SO I LEFT THIS NOTE. DON'T STAY HERE. BRING YOUR FAMILY TO MCBRIDES BEFORE DARK. BRING YOUR

GUN. DON'T TRUST NOBODY. DON'T
TALK TO NOBODY. JUST HURRY UP AS
QUICK AS YOU CAN. IF YOU CAN'T MAKE
IT BEFORE DARK THEN STAY IN YOUR
HOUSE TILL MORNING. DON'T LET
NOBODY IN. NOBODY.

    W. McBride

They took turns riding and Wilda sat on the mule as Walter came from the house to take the reins. Next, the Tanners, then the Williams–where he would leave his companions–then a swing south to warn four other families and finally back home. By tomorrow morning, he would be on his way out of the valley for good.

He had been honest with his parents. He had tried, but he just was not a farmer. The soil never held the same meaning for him it did for his father. Truitt was married to the land while Walter viewed it in the same manner with which a poor yard dog might view the rope that anchored it to a tree. It was a shame it had taken something like this to force him into making that disclosure and his decision. But there it was. Now that it was out, he felt a sense of satisfaction, he felt relief, contentment.

Now he felt like a man.

Mabeline took her turn on the mule when they left the Tanners. Perhaps he should have expected old man Duncan Tanner's reaction to the news but he had not.

"You're crazy, boy," Tanner said. "I ain't never heard such foolishness in my life. Vampires my ass. What kind of goddamned corn you been into?"

Well, he had only committed himself to warning the others. It really was not in his power to cause them to believe him. He gave Tanner the warning and that was about all he could do. As he turned to leave, he spoke once more to Duncan.

"Look here, you don't have to believe a thing I say

139

about vampires and all. I got all I know from Tildy and she's wrong about a lot of things. But you'd better believe this. Something ain't right down here and there's some folks running the woods who'd just as soon kill you as look at you. Some of them might have even been your friends or family this time yesterday. Now, you keep that in mind. Then, if anything happens to your family, you'll know who to blame for it. Anyway, it won't cost you nothing but time to load up and come down to our place if you're a mind to. You go ahead and do whatever you want."

Walter thought about the warning he carried as he led the mule along the road. If the shoe was on the other foot, would he have believed Duncan? If the old man ran up to the door all lathered up about some sort of creature that was living and dead at the same time, drinking blood, hunting other humans for food and that any one of his neighbors might be one of these creatures, would he believe that? Not likely. In fact, he would probably think the same thing Duncan had; the messenger was crazy.

"Walter, I gotta stop," Wilda said.

Walter was startled. He gripped the shotgun at ready, quickly turning his head as he checked the countryside around them.

"What's wrong?" he asked.

"Nothing's wrong. I just gotta step out to the bushes for a minute."

"I reckon we could use a breather anyway," he said. He helped Mabeline down from the mule and sat down alongside the road to wait while Margie and Wilda disappeared into the undergrowth. Mabeline joined him. He sat silently, watching the little jenny crop grass. It was already past noon. By one-thirty, maybe two, they would be at Freeman's. Without the women, Walter would make much better time and would rejoin the family before dark. Whether or not the Tanners, or anyone else, would be there was anyone's guess. After a while, Mabeline intruded upon his introspective silence.

"What you're doing ain't right," she said, as a matter of fact.

"Huh?"

"You heard me. What you're doing ain't right."

"Look, Grandma, I don't want to get into that anymore. I talked it over with Papa, my mind's made up and I've said just about all I'm gonna say about it."

Mabeline took a container of snuff from her apron pocket, dipping a hefty load of the fine powder into her lower lip. A brown cloud puffed from her mouth as she spoke.

"I know all that but your Mama and Papa ain't looking at things too clear right now. You ain't either. You couldn't have picked a worse time to leave. If you packed up and gone last week, for instance, it would've bothered 'em–it would've bothered me, too, for that matter–but it would've been different. Then it would just have been leaving. Now, it's running out."

"Don't talk to me about running out," he shot back. "You're doing a pretty good job of it yourself."

"Naw, I ain't," she said calmly. "Soon as I claim what's mine, I intend to go back. I ain't about to leave nobody holding a bag. We're family, by God. I intend to live that way or die that way, whichever the Good Lord decides. When I decide to leave this valley–if I ever do–then I'll walk away. But I'll be damned if I'll run."

"Are you saying I'm a coward?"

"I don't reckon that's something you ought to be asking me."

Walter's face grew red, the anger inside him rising to conceal the shame.

"You got a nerve to talk to me like that after the way you've been acting lately. You're not about to be winning no medals for heroism either, by God."

"Never said I was, boy."

Walter heard the rustling of brush as the Williams girls returned, making their way back toward the road. He felt grateful because it marked an end to the uncomfortable conversation with his grandmother. The old woman just saw things too clearly sometimes; much more clearly than he wanted to see them. He looked at the gathering clouds above them. Before long, they would be soaked to the skin.

"Walter, I'm not trying to shame you. You're my grandson and I love you, whether you believe that or not. We got to stick together. That's all. After all, blood's thicker than water."

"Tastes a damned sight better, too," said a harsh voice behind them.

* * *

The body of the dead vampire, eighteen inches of stake protruding from its chest, lay where Walter and Ernie had dropped it two nights before. It was swollen, black with flies. Chloe looked at the body dispassionately as Amos led the way around it. Her lack of reaction was not lost on Amos. Just two days ago, such a sight would have sent her into hysterics. After today, Chloe was beyond that. Amos was grateful, on one hand, but he was not at all sure that in the long run Chloe's lack of emotional response would be the good news.

They had not made very good time, resting frequently during the long hike, as much from stress as any physical exhaustion. The only time, he felt, they had really kept anything like the pace he had hoped to maintain was when they crossed the meadow.

They carried crosses made from twigs picked up at their sanctuary and tied with bits of cloth. A dozen

142

extras were in Amos' hunting sack as well as the whiskey bottle and canteen which were both filled with water from Baptizing Creek. Chloe had her father's shotgun slung over her shoulders as she limped along behind Amos favoring the sore toe she had injured on rocks at the bottom of the stream. She was reluctant to approach the bodies lying in the field.

"I've never seen a body nowhere but at a funeral. I don't want to look," she said.

"I don't want to look either but I suppose we gotta."

"No. Let's go around. It won't make no never-mind."

"Chloe, you got to see this. It'll put your mind at ease."

"I doubt that. I doubt that my mind will ever be at ease again." The first body lay on its back, just as Amos had left it. Chloe looked at the dead, blue-hued face and her stomach lurched. She grew dizzy, swaying slightly. "My stomach either," she added.

"Watch this," Amos said, taking her hand and guiding her to one side. He kept her hand until she had steadied herself then he stepped forward and dropped a cross on the body. Jumping back quickly, he gripped her arm as the cross sizzled on the vampire's chest. Just like before, the creature literally fell apart, leaving nothing behind but ashes soon snatched away and scattered by the wind sweeping the meadow.

"Good Lord, what did you just do?" she asked.

"I don't know but it sure as hell works good don't it?"

They moved on to the next body.

"Oh, Amos, this one is just a baby."

The baby stared back at them, blood from the hole in its forehead caked on the dull, dead eyes.

"Let's see what this here water will do," Amos said, uncorking the canteen. He poured a stream over the thin chest and abdomen. The body seemed to swell as

143

the water hissed and steamed on the dead flesh. There was a ripping sound, like the sound of a sliced melon being pulled apart, and a rancid stench hit him full in the face. The boy's shirt swelled and crawled as if something alive were under it and the fabric ripped open, spilling intestines out onto the ground. The organs and flesh were again decaying before their eyes but this time the water seemed to be dissolving the body, melting it away.

"Oh, Jesus," Chloe said, falling to her knees and retching.

Amos covered his mouth and nose with his hand as he moved upwind. He felt a little embarrassed as he turned to Chloe. She emptied the contents of her stomach into the grass and wiped at her mouth with the back of her hand.

"I reckon the water works a bit different than the crosses do," he said.

"I reckon so."

Amos helped her to her feet then reached inside his sack for more of the crosses.

"What are you fixing to do?"

"I don't want to look at these things no more," he said. "I'm going to get rid of them."

They moved from body to body, dropping a cross on the chest of each in turn. In a few moments, no trace remained of any of the vampires slain in the gun-battle. The soldier was the last to go. Amos felt like he was doing the man a favor.

As they continued toward the McBride farm, Chloe made better time than before. Her eagerness to get as far away as possible from the scene was evident in the way she kept a hurried pace, rarely even taking time to favor her injured foot with a limp. Amos matched her stride for stride. The crosses had done the trick—the bodies were gone—but they would never be gone inside him. No matter how long he lived, or where he might be, no matter anything, he would always see the meadow in his mind and there would always be bodies lying in the grass. Amos had lost something, he knew that, but he did not know what it was nor how to describe it. The rolling hills and long grass rippling in the breeze would be ugly for a long, long time. Something was gone from Chloe as well.

"Are you gonna drop a cross on that one?" Chloe asked, as they swung around the body of the vampire lying near the farmhouse.

"Not yet. I need him to prove a point."

He stopped in the middle of the yard and called to the house.

"Papa! Papa, it's me, Amos. Don't shoot. Just come to the door and let me show you something."

His legs trembled as he waited for a reply, fully aware that any answer might come in a chest-load of double-aught buckshot. He breathed in short, shallow gasps.

"I don't think nobody's home," Chloe said.

"Hello! Papa! Anybody?"

He turned to look at Chloe, his expression a mixture of worry and relief.

"Well, let's go inside," he said as the rumble of thunder echoed across the valley. "It's about to pour down."

CHAPTER FOURTEEN

Thunder rolled across the valley and Burl Tanner looked up at the dark, gray thunder-heads. There had been no discussion among the group of where they were going, what they were doing, as they made their way down from Hog Heaven Hill. It was as if some silent command had passed from one to the other and been accepted by mutual consent.

No one had to tell Burl they were on the hunt.

For hours now he had maintained a loping run and was not even slightly winded. He had never felt so energetic in his life. The rippling of muscles, deep inhalations of air, were sensations which fueled him. The more he ran, the more he felt like running. Strange how a little dying could make a man feel so alive.

Rachael followed close behind him, along with Frank. Aaron and the others had split away on a hunt of their own. By early afternoon, Burl and his companions were several miles east of the mountains, near Duncan Tanner's farm. They passed cattle, which would have been easy pickings, and several deer—which they stood no chance of catching— but they were after other game. Frank was armed with a revolver and could have brought down any one of the animals with it if he so chose. But the understanding, once again unspoken, was clear. There would be no shots fired and when the time came to return to the mountains their numbers would be increased.

Frank quickened his pace, moving up beside Burl as they darted silently among the trees. A dirt road bisected the forest, cutting east and west through the center of it. Frank stopped and held up his hand. He inhaled deeply, testing the wind, then nodded in the direction of the road. There was indeed a smell, the smell of living beings and Burl had never experienced it in this way before. It shook him to his shoes. He quivered with excitement as he glanced at Rachael. She felt it, too. The three began to move once more, stealthily now, toward the road.

The muted voices of women, speaking softly together was much nearer. Burl concealed himself in the brush, alongside a tall oak, as the women approached. Frank and Rachael flanked him on either side. Margie Williams walked within ten feet of him, stopped, raised her skirt and squatted low to the ground. Wilda stood beside her. Burl exploded from his hiding place, throwing himself completely over Margie as he drove Wilda to the ground. He clamped his hand over her mouth. Margie drew a deep breath as she rose quickly to her feet but the scream was muffled by Frank's hand as he and Rachael fell on her from behind.

It was over in a matter of minutes. The kicking of their legs in the dry leaves began frantically enough but soon subsided away to nothing. Soft gasps and moans were carried away by the damp, chill wind running like a crier before the approaching storm. Iron fingers, clamped over the mouths of the women, relaxed as last breaths slipped unnoticed into the humid air.

These were not the only ones. Burl knew that as he stood looking at the bodies. He flared his nostrils into the wind. There were others. Frank and Rachael soon joined him, Frank again taking the lead as they moved away through the underbrush. In a moment of carelessness, brought on by his excitement, Burl brushed against a bush which became ensnared in his bibs. It rustled loudly as he pulled free. Walter, sitting alongside the road, glanced in his direction for a moment. Burl froze in his tracks. As Walter turned back to his conversation, Burl moved again. Frank was closer though. Burl heard his response to Mabeline's last remark. There was no further need for stealth. Burl followed the lead as Frank rushed forward with Rachael close behind.

He felt more powerful than he had ever felt before, charged with a sense of it, strong, heady, a power that only God must have known before, intoxicating. His lips pulled back over the descending fangs as excitement boiled over in him. The frightened look on the old woman's face increased the feeling. He snarled savagely as he followed Frank in for the kill. It seemed, however, that they underestimated the speed of Walter. The young man rose, spun and fired the shotgun in a blur of hiccup-quick motion. Fragments of Frank's head hit Burl full in the face a split second before Walter fired a second shot. The load of buckshot caught Burl in the abdomen, hurling him backward. His guts were on fire as he slammed roughly into the brush. Rachael froze, hands held claw like in front of her, face twisted in fury. She looked from Burl to Frank and back again before a heavy slug from Walter's revolver hit her in the shoulder and spun her around.

A spurt of blood marked the trail of the exiting lead, spraying outward, seeming to hang in the air. Rachael screamed, clutching the wound as Walter fired twice more. One shot caught her in the side, the other went wild as she fell.

Walter did not see her fall.

He turned toward Mabeline, who held frantically to the reins of the struggling mule. Walter scooped the shotgun from the ground, took two quick strides and leaped onto the animal's back. Mabeline swung up behind him, belatedly screaming encouragement for Wilda and Margie to run. Walter turned, firing three more shots before allowing the little jenny to have her head and run wildly down the road while Mabeline—shouting to her daughters—clung to him like a bad reputation.

"It ain't that easy, you son of a bitch," Burl yelled as he struggled painfully to his feet. He almost fell as he leaned over and tugged the revolver from Frank's belt then staggered out onto the dusty road. He spread his legs wide for balance as he sighted down the barrel of the gun and squeezed off four rounds.

One of the riders slumped, then tumbled to the ground as Burl blinked his eyes against the powder-smoke and dust. He thumbed the hammer and fired twice more but each time the hammer fell on an empty cylinder. Rachael joined him as he lowered the gun and let it drop into the dirt. The way she looked at him made him feel vaguely ashamed. She knelt and looked at his stomach wound.

"You're going to be all right here in a bit," she said, pressing her hand tightly over the hole in her own side.

"I know," he muttered as he reeled over to Frank's body.

Burl didn't bother to bend down. There was no need. A blind man could see Frank was dead. The whole top of his head was gone. There wasn't a bit of skull left that wouldn't have fit into a table spoon. Burl clutched the wound in his stomach as he waited for the pain to subside. It could be a sight worse. Rachael stepped closer, raising her long skirt to wipe at his face. Her efforts, though ineffective, were appreciated. Burl pulled away from her, walking back to the road.

"Whew," he said. "That sure packed a wallop."

Rachael followed him to the dark form lying in the dust forty yards away. The old woman lay on her back, her face bearing a look of surprise. No pain was evident but, even in death, there was enough of Mabeline's combative disdain to rob them of any sense of victory. The ground around her was stained with the blood still trickling from the destroyed body.

"This one's a waste," Rachael said. "There ain't no bringing her over now. You done put out the light and there ain't no way to get it back."

Burl said nothing.

"You see? This ain't right, Burl. Not for nobody."

"I know. But I just wanted to stop 'em. I didn't mean to kill the old gal."

* * *

The sounds of the slugs hurtling by were high-pitched whines. Walter held the reins in a death-grip, squeezing his legs tightly against the jenny's sides. Mabeline bounced roughly behind him, her arms wrapped around his waist. He heard a dull "thunk" like the sound of an axe biting into cord-wood. "Oh," was all Mabeline said as her grip on him tightened, then slackened and fell away. Another "thunk" as something warm and wet splashed onto his back. He felt his grandmother slide sideways to fall from their mount. He reined in the jenny, who fought the reins to a dancing stop several yards away.

Mabeline landed on her side and rolled slowly over on her back, eyes fixed skyward. Walter saw the exit wound in her forehead as she drew a last rattling breath before lying still. Just that quickly, Mabeline was consigned to memory. Well down the road, beyond the fallen woman stood Tanner, lowering the pistol. Walter dug his heels into the jenny. Mabeline was dead and,

150

for all practical purposes, so was everyone he had ever known. Burl and the rest of the vampires stood between him and home. They would stand there forever.

He gave the jenny free rein as the animal and Walter seemed to amplify one another's fears. Though the little mule ran with all her strength, Walter urged her harder as she strove even more mightily to put distance between themselves and the walking nightmares from the forest. Walter no longer had any intention of warning anyone of anything as he turned his mount southward. In fact, he was going to do his level best to avoid any contact— human or otherwise—until he got to a city. He would head southeast to the coast, then west. Mississippi, Louisiana, maybe Texas, anywhere but here.

The darkening sky grew heavy with moisture and the first large, heavy drops of rain began to pelt them. Walter wept openly, his tears increasing, falling with the blinding rain until both were coming in torrents. He pushed the jenny even harder as she slipped and splashed through the growing puddles.

* * *

The rain became a solid wall of water, like the falls of a river. Soon the dry earth was saturated by the inundation coming faster than the soil could absorb it. Even beneath the trees, puddles and rivulets formed. The storm built to a violent peak, abated and evened out to a heavy, steady drizzle.

Truitt led the way through the rain as Sara and Ellie followed astride the white-whiskered mule. He had done the job he had set out to do; everyone on his route had been warned and encouraged to meet at his place. What in the hell they would do from that point on he had no idea. Still, it sounded reasonable enough

151

that safety could be found in numbers. Jim O'Daniel had been taken aback by Truitt's story, so was Kyle Morgan and the others. But they had all agreed to come his place, and all had agreed to further spread the word.

The word was "madness."

Rain streamed from the brim of Truitt's hat and his clothes were soaked. Occasionally, he brought his hand up to wipe the water from his face. The rain made him extremely uncomfortable. It was not the wet clothes, or the chill, though both were unpleasant. He had been caught out in the rain before and, God willing, he would be caught out in it again. That could be taken care of as soon as he got home. Getting home, toweling off, dry clothes, a shot or two of good whiskey, a chair in front of the fire, all that would make his present physical discomfort more than worth it. It was the sound that worried him. More precisely, the lack of it.

Rumbling thunder, the crack of lightning striking something in the distance, wind driving the falling rain, all combined to make it difficult to hear anything else. The rain fell noisily among the trees, in the brush, pelting through the leaves with a rattling sound and shaking branches; noises that would mask any movement. A herd of bulls could dance jigs through the bushes and he wouldn't be able to tell a difference.

A couple of more miles—if they could only make a couple of more miles—and they would be home. He continuously swung his head from side to side peering, as well as he could, into the undergrowth lining both sides of the road. The gray, misty haze created by the storm limited his vision, added to his anxiety.

Sara and Ellie rode silently. Sara had been silent, for the most part, since joining them. She seemed incapable of discussing her recent experiences and answers to Truitt's questions, if they came, were simple

152

and direct. Truitt abandoned his interrogation, at Ellie's request, and, as he helped Sara up onto the mule, noted that she started at his touch.

Percy and Agnes were vampires. He had been able to get that much but further questioning simply brought on a new flow of tears. He let her be. If anyone could get more information from her, it would be Ellie. But now was not the time. Here was not the place. Besides, what else did he need to know? What more was there to know? Whatever else had occurred, it had rattled the girl to the point of distraction.

The deafening crack and boom of the storm pulled him back to matters at hand. First, get home, then whatever else had to be done could be considered. The rain became more intense, slapping heavily into them as the old mule lowered its head, ears flattened against the wind. Following the mule's lead, Truitt pulled his hat brim down further over his eyes and leaned into the storm.

CHAPTER FIFTEEN

First there came the sound, a rhythmic creaking which she could not identify initially, then the sensation of the rough, pine planks beneath her. Tildy's cheek pressed into the wood and she could feel the grainy texture of it, smell the dusty odor. The creaking was her rocker. She could feel that, too, vibrating through the floor of the porch, passing from one plank to another, spreading like ripples on the surface of a pond. Tildy rolled over, took a deep breath and opened her eyes.

The sound of the rocker ceased as she sat upright. There was no pain in her hip, though she knew she had broken it just a short time ago. She brought her left hand in front of her face. Not only was the wrist healed—the hand and forearm worked in perfect order—but the wrinkles had vanished, the liver spots disappeared. The hand was hypnotic. She could hardly pull her eyes away. It was beautiful, a hand worthy of any lady, a young woman's hand.

"Hidey," Percy Way said, cordially.

Tildy turned to look at him.

"You ain't none the worse for wear," he said. "In fact, you don't even look half your age, if that."

There was a change in his appearance, too. When she had seen him earlier, she had been too frightened to concentrate on much of anything about him, other than his teeth, though she noticed the pink, burn-like wound on his face. Now, she could see something else. Percy had become younger somehow. His hair, much thicker, was also darker, totally devoid of gray. And, of course, she could still fill a lard bucket with the renderings of his backside alone but he did not look a day over thirty. Tildy knew damned well he was at least twenty-five years older than he appeared.

With the tips of her fingers, she traced her own face. It was smooth, astonishingly smooth, young girl smooth, the deep crevices of wrinkles ironed out into a warm silken sheet stretched tightly over the bones. Feeling her way down to her mouth, she ran her finger over her teeth and gasped.

"Not bad, huh?" Percy said.

Reaching for the column post, Tildy pulled herself to her feet. She discovered she had no problem rising; the joints in her knees did not even pop. For years now, she had experienced aches and pains with almost any movement and now there were none. She took several steps then retraced them to be sure.

"Everything seems to be working fine don't it?" Percy said, as he returned to rocking.

"What did you do to me?" Tildy asked. Even her voice sounded stronger.

Percy laughed.

"Why, I gave you a present, Tildy. You had one foot in the grave and the other on a slick spot. I got you out."

Thunder rumbled down the mountain like a protracted groan from the bruised skies.

"I killed myself," she whispered. She spun around, striding over to the rocker and bending down until she was nose to nose with the startled Percy. "I killed

155

myself, goddamn it. Shot myself in the head. How can any of this be happening?"

Percy rocked back and dug in his heels stopping himself from rocking forward again. He grinned at Tildy.

"You missed. Missed your head anyways. But you didn't miss Agnes. No, ma'am, you didn't miss her at all."

He pointed toward his dead wife's body.

"I'm a vampire?"

"That you are, Tildy. That you are. I keep telling folks it ain't all that bad but you folks can be so damned unreasonable that it's like talking to a stump."

Tildy leaned against the porch rail and looked up at the sky. She laughed, a high musical sound she hadn't heard in over half a century.

"Done it to me again haven't you," she shouted eyes still skyward. "Yep, you've sure enough done it to me again."

"What?" Percy asked, puzzled by her behavior.

"Nothing. You might as well come on inside before it starts raining again. Don't reckon I've got anything to lose by inviting you in at this point do I?"

"I wouldn't be too sure," he said, following her through the door.

* * *

Two-by-six planks hung over side of the doorway creating a lip. Amos nailed the planks inside the opening to decrease the width so the smaller door from Mabeline's bedroom would fit more snugly. Amos centered it as best he could, however, there remained a small open space around three edges. The catch was different and would not work so again he had to improvise. He hinged the door to swing outward and, with material taken from the barn, constructed a huge

156

slide-bolt mechanism which spanned the entire width of the mother-of-invention doorway.

"There. That ought to keep out a grizzly bear," Amos said, stepping back to admire his work.

"Yep, if a grizzly bear didn't have sense enough to know about windows."

"Either way," Amos said, grinning at Chloe. "He'd still have to make a little noise to let us know he was coming wouldn't he?"

"I reckon he would."

Chloe moved about the house, lighting every lamp and candle she could find against the darkness of the storm. That done, she started a blaze in both the fireplace and black-iron stove. The wet, heavy air pressing down outside seemed to flatten the smoke from the chimney and it backed into the building.

"We need more cross-draft," Amos said, rubbing his stinging eyes. He went from window to window on the lower floor, raising the windows a crack and driving a nail in the frame on each side to prevent them from being raised any further. He repeated the procedure upstairs before returning to the kitchen. The strategy worked just fine.

Chloe had every available pot filled with water and heating on the stove as she busily filled the porcelain bathtub she had dragged in from the porch. Amos watched as she poured the water in the tub, steam swirling around her, filling the air. A bath was something they both could use. He sat down at the table, studying himself in the hand mirror he had taken from his grandmother's room.

"Dang," he said, moving his lips around with his fingers. This was his first opportunity to really examine himself and he truly was a mess. The black eyes were tinged with green and purple like the storm clouds outside, one so bloodshot that it looked like a red bead from Wilda's favorite necklace. His entire head was

157

swollen. The loss of the teeth caused him the most pain. He had really been proud of his smile and the missing tooth, along with the jagged remains of another, were just icing on the cake of his overall ghastly appearance. It was depressing. He looked like something the cat had dragged in and then been too uppity to eat. Amos almost tossed the mirror aside in disgust but caught himself before he let it go. Things were bad enough already. The last thing he needed was seven more years of bad luck. He carefully laid the mirror on the table.

Chloe had her back to him as she bent over the tub to test the water. Her form, outlined by the lamplight through the fabric of her dress, mesmerized him. The dress clung to her buttocks, riding up slightly as she bent over, exposing her legs. Amos' gaze followed them down to her ankles. Just looking at her made him want to envelope her, pull her inside, make her part of himself. It was odd, this "love" business.

Chloe turned and looked at him.

"Will you stay with me while I bathe?"

"Huh?"

Chloe was already wriggling out of her dress. "I'm not too pleased with the notion of being in here by myself while I'm in the tub," she said, pulling the dress over her head and letting it fall to the floor. "And it's not like I have any secrets left with you as far as that goes is there?"

"No, I reckon not."

"Besides, I feel safe with you. Not as afraid."

This pleased Amos and frightened him at the same time. He cleared his throat awkwardly and tried not to blush.

"Well, all right, then," he said.

Well, all right, then? God, what kind of thing was that to say? Some champion he was.

Chloe gasped as she lowered herself into the water.

Then she sighed in appreciation. She scrubbed herself with the harsh lye soap Ellie made, smeared liberally on wash cloths made from discarded clothing. Amos attended her while she bathed, pouring fresh water into the tub to keep it warm, scrubbing her back and helping her out when she finished. Amos sat down at the table, watching as she stood nude on the kitchen floor and tossed her head forward, vigorously toweling the long auburn hair. The motions of her arms caused her breasts to grow taut, quivering. Her whole body seemed to vibrate. Amos felt himself grow taut as well.

Chloe put on one of Ellie's dresses, which was too large for her and hung everywhere. She sat down at the table and nodded to Amos.

"Your turn," she said, pulling Wilda's hair brush through her hair.

"Reckon I'll shave first."

"You've never needed a shave a day in your life. I don't imagine you suddenly need one now. Go on and get a bath while you still got hot water. You don't have any secrets left from me either."

"Naw," Amos said, blushing again. "I don't reckon I do."

But, even as he lied, he pulled his chair closer to the table trying shove his legs and his troublesome erection underneath, away from Chloe's view.

Chloe knew and Amos knew she knew, but both feigned ignorance. She smiled, small, tight, controlled but definitely amused as she stood up.

"You get on into the tub and I'll fetch some more soap."

Amos undressed hurriedly and climbed into the tub before Chloe returned with another lump of the harsh soap. He was well concealed by the water. They both had been filthy and the water was covered by a gray scum that was the color of mud by the time he finished bathing. The lye soap removed all the accumulated dirt and a layer or two of skin as well. Chloe took more hot water from the stove, carefully checking the temperature, then knelt alongside the tub and poured the water over Amos. With a clean rag, she scrubbed his chest in circular motions. The heat of the water and Chloe's soft touch was soothing as she gently moved around to his injured ribs, tenderly cleaning the bruised flesh. For the first time in days, he felt himself relaxing. Fatigue settled over him, tension abating in strained, knotted muscles. He allowed himself to be carried away by the sensations, leaning his head back against the cool porcelain as Chloe continued to bathe him.

It began to rain again. The storm settled over the valley, wind and thunder creeping inside as a muffled roar. Rain slammed onto the roof, against the windows, and, in a short while, tentacles of water reached into the house from underneath the shabbily repaired doorway. Feeling their way across the floor, they left muddy trails in the dust on the old pine planks. The rain had a hypnotic quality. Amos floated away. Not asleep, not awake, but somewhere in between.

* * *

The bleating goat struggled, spraying rainwater from its sodden coat all over the room as Percy dragged it through the doorway. Percy, too, was drenched with rain, grit, and bits of debris clinging to his naked body. He gripped the horns of the thrashing animal, jerking it into the air as he gave its head a savage twist. The goat's body swung out at a sharp right angle to its stationary head, the neck giving way with an audible crack. It flopped back limply, dangling in Percy's hands, legs twitching slightly as if the muscles were reacting to some dim memory of life. Percy extended his arms, holding the goat out in front of him.

"Well?" he said.

160

Tildy moved forward, pulling her lips back over her teeth. It came as no surprise. It did not seem at all out of the ordinary now. A simple need, as powerful and demanding as the simple need to breathe, drove her forward. She did not stop to think about how natural it felt for her as she bit into the soft flesh of the throat for the first taste, her second baptism, a new life.

* * *

Amid the familiar surroundings of home, Amos felt secure, in control. The hot bath and dry clothes helped immensely. He and Chloe fried some bacon and made coffee. A half-dozen of Ellie's big, cat-head biscuits were left in a pan on the stove. They tore the biscuits in half, soaked them with bacon grease and placed hot slabs of bacon between the biscuits. They ate in silence.

Afterwards, sitting together in front of the fireplace, they listened to the storm as it waxed and waned. Amos wondered where the family had gone but he did not discuss it with Chloe. Anyone could show up anytime and in any condition. The Long Tom shotgun had been within his reach almost every minute since their arrival. His hunting sack, holding the containers of water from Baptizing Creek and the pine twig and rag crosses, hung from the peg next to the doorway. He found himself almost wishing he and Chloe would be left alone. It would be nice if the whole world would go away and leave nothing but him, her and the safety of the house–if there actually was any safety to the house. Everything was so unpredictable he could not really assume they were any safer here than they had been on the way.

Chloe's head fell against his shoulder and he looked down at her face. Her eyes were closed. Soon she began to snore softly. Amos laid her gently onto a

161

blanket on the   floor and covered her with another. He picked up both shotguns, placed one on the table and, turning a chair to face the doorway, sat down and laid the other across his lap. He was taking no chances.

CHAPTER SIXTEEN

Walking was difficult. The mud sucked and pulled at Truitt's feet as he led the mule towards home, slipping and sliding with every step. Ellie walked beside him, with equal difficulty, while Sara rode silently on the mule, wet hair plastered to her face. She still had her father's Colt stuck in her belt but, unlike Truitt, she was not constantly searching the roadside for someone, or something, to use it on. Her eyes focused directly in front of her, she had looked neither left nor right throughout the trip. Ellie fell in alongside the gray mule, gripping the animal's neck as she looked at Sara with concern.

"Are you all right, honey?"

Sara nodded without meeting Ellie's eyes.

She really did not want to talk about it. Nothing would ever be all right again. For that matter, as far as Sara was concerned, nothing had ever been all right in the first place. What do people want to know when they ask that question? She wondered. Did they have some idea of what *all right* might be? She didn't. Whatever they were talking about was foreign to her. She had not a clue. Was it *all right* to afraid of your father; to lie awake nights wondering if he would be coming to you–for you? To be raped by him while the body of your mother lies downstairs? Was it *all right* to hate him; to want him dead? Was it *all right* to spend the night on a roof while whatever monstrosities your parents had become rutted alongside the carcass of a dead mule like a couple of animals? Was it *all right* to feel the way she felt about other women? All right or not, that was the way it was. Would Ellie think her *all right* if she were to tell her all that? Was it *all right* just going about the business of being human, living and dying the way you were supposed to, not becoming anything you were not meant to be–was that *all right?*

Maybe *all right* is simply handling whatever happens for no other reason than because it just happens and there's nothing at all anyone can do to change it. In that case, Sara was all right. She was the most all right person she had ever heard of and it did not feel at all like she would have imagined.

"Yeah, I'm all right," she said.

They crested the last hill, overlooking the McBride farm, and Truitt came to a stop. The old mule halted just as suddenly, rocking Sara forward as he planted his front hooves in the mud. A trail of smoke rose from the chimney of the farmhouse, as well as the stove-pipe, disappearing into the gray vastness of clouds hanging over the valley. Lamplight shone in every window.

"I don't suppose you left the stove and lamps burning did you?" he asked Ellie.

"Why, no. No, I don't think I did."

"Looks like we've got company then," he said, eyes searching the grounds around the buildings.

"I wouldn't be surprised," Ellie said. "Ain't that the point of what we're doing out in this weather? Trying to get folks to come on out here?"

"Yep. But who'd be able to get here quicker than us? Nobody passed us on the road."

Ellie searched his face. She did not like the conclusion Truitt seemed to be reaching.

"Looky here, Truitt. Walter's been out among folks, too. Maybe this here's somebody he got to come out and they're in there drying off."

"Yep. And maybe it's somebody else we never invited," Truitt said, loosening the guns in his belt.

"God, I hope it's Daddy," Sara said.

Both Ellie and Truitt stared in surprise. The heavy Colt was in Sara's hand and her eyes burned with a rage that was frightening in its intensity.

"Now both of you listen to me," Ellie said sternly. "There ain't going to be no more of this 'shoot-first' idiocy going on today. You hear me? So don't either one of you get to feeling trigger-happy. We're going on down yonder, holler at the house and listen to whoever's inside it. You two understand what I'm saying?"

"We hear you," Truitt said, answering for them both.

Sara still held the Colt as they started downhill.

* * *

Howling like a live thing, the wind whipped and whistled around Tildy's cabin, rattling rain on the roof and against the windows. The carcass of the goat lay just beyond the front stoop, rainwater puddling around it. Trace blood floated in rusty streaks on the surface as the driving rain splashed beads of gritty water into the dead, cat-like eyes.

Inside, Tildy lay back beneath the covers watching Percy as he crossed the room to climb into bed with her. It was a funny thing. She had never before felt anything like desire for a man. Now, she found herself bedding possibly the least likely candidate imaginable. It was not even desire for a man—or a woman either for

165

that matter—but an unfocused drive burning inside her.

"In all my life, I've never been to bed with a man," she confessed. "Damned near a whole century in fact. Now here I am. Hardly been dead a whole day yet and screwing you."

"That sure is something, ain't it," Percy agreed, wasting no time as he rolled over on top of her.

It was something. It was something she did not understand; something which had been growing inside her since she had swallowed the first rich, hot mouthful of blood. It was as if she had been carrying a seed inside her all along, waiting for this evening, this transformation, this thirst, to germinate. And the blood awakened it like spring rains on a crop. No, more like an ember in a neglected hearth, unnoticed, invisible until coal-oil is splashed into the ashes. Then the sudden blaze. Then this new kind of burning. Anyone would do, anything. Percy entered her and she knew more than ever things had changed. Preferences had nothing to do with it. The blood lit the fire in her, a fire she had not felt in many, many years. She would put it out with whatever was available.

* * *

The whiskey in the coffee greatly increased the feeling of warmth Amos experienced. Following the bath, the meal and Chloe's affections, he had shed most of his fatigue as well as his aches and pains. He took another sip of liquor-laced coffee, leaned back in his chair and placed his feet on the table. His mother would have given him fits for that if she had been around to see it. He smiled to himself at the small triumph. What she did not know would not hurt him.

His smile faded as the fleeting thought of his mother brought him around again to the question of where she was. Nothing was missing from the house but the guns and mules. If the family had fled, they had done so in a hurry, taking a little of nothing with them. It seemed unlikely they would have run away like that. If they had not, however, then what had become of them?

A movement from Chloe caught his eye. She rolled over on her back, lying in front of the fire with the blanket kicked half off. Her right arm was drawn up beside her head, fingertips resting lightly against her cheek. Muttering something unintelligible, she gave a slight kick of her leg before settling back into quiet sleep.

Amos looked around the room. Faded stains splotched the floor, though it seemed someone had attempted to clean them up. They were still visible. He knew they were blood stains. The question was: whose blood? Whose blood and how did it get there? Whoever had been doing the bleeding apparently had bled a great deal—too much from all indications. And now everyone was gone. God, if something had happened to someone, he prayed it was not his parents.

Amos' face grew hot as if someone in the room could read his thoughts. It was wrong to wish evil on someone else. No. Nothing like that had happened. They had simply left, that was all. There was nothing here at this old place worth dying for and they had just walked out the door. Away. It was for the best and no one would blame them for it. Of course, they had left him, too, but that was understandable. After all, they thought him a vampire and, if the shoe were on the other foot, he probably would have thought the same. He would probably have reacted the same way as his father, as Walter.

The hell I would have, he thought. *If the shoe was on the other foot, I'd have waited. I'd have listened. I'd have been careful as hell. Maybe I would have made them give me some proof, but, by God, I would have at least listened.*

He rose from his chair to refill the coffee cup, took

167

a couple of sips and laced the remainder with whiskey. He knew he would have to be careful with the liquor– all he needed right now was to end up drunk. Amos capped the bottle and set it on the table as he sat back down.

He would not have left without them. Come hell or high water, he would not have left. Both he and Chloe had been safe at Baptizing Creek and could have stayed there. They could have but they did not. It would have been simple enough to keep them fed without risking too much in the way of exposure to the vampires. But he had come home–brought her with him. Now, they were in a situation they could not predict, possibly in much greater danger then they had been in at the creek. They risked everything to come home and home was deserted.

As the intensity of the storm increased, the small tendrils of water creeping under the doorway spread halfway across the floor into the kitchen, growing larger as they continued their relentless invasion of the farmhouse. Amos noted the progression of one as it crept toward the sleeping Chloe. If the rain did not let up soon, the rivulet would reach her, pull her from sleep with its icy touch. The small streams of rainwater looked like the rivers he had seen on maps in his old geography book. Snaking this way, that way, but always following the easiest path to the ocean, branching out vein-like over the land, breaking from one flow to join another, they spread like cracks in a window pane, forming a spider's web pattern on the floor before coming together, all at once, to form a puddle. Amos sat, lost in the movement of the water, until a shout startled him out of his chair.

With a shotgun in each hand, he faced the door.

"Hello in there!"

Amos moved to the window and carefully pushed aside the dripping curtains with the barrel of a shotgun.

Rain, driven by the forceful wind, blew through the ventilation space. Outside stood the sodden Truitt McBride his shotgun held at ready. The old mule stood at the side of the smokehouse, someone on its back. Amos' mother stood beside it. So, they had not left after all. Amos wanted to throw the door open and rush out to greet them but caution held him back. Earlier Truitt had mistakenly believed that Amos was a vampire. It would not be wise for Amos to mistakenly believe that Truitt–and the rest of the family, for that matter–were not. Besides, given his father's previous behavior, there was no way of knowing what Truitt would do if Amos suddenly appeared in the doorway. Amos's hands tightened on the shotguns. If push came to shove, he might have to defend himself.

Kneeling, Amos shouted back.

"Yeah, I hear you!"

"Amos? That you, boy?"

"Yeah, it's me."

Truitt glanced over his shoulder, assuring himself of a clear path of retreat as he backed toward the smokehouse. The strategy was not lost on Amos. Amos also saw his mother peering around the corner of the structure, her face just below the pale scar in the wood where Walter's shotgun had torn part of it away the day before. Truitt faced the house as he continued to back cautiously toward Ellie.

"You get the hell out of there, you hear me. Nobody's invited you in. I told you yesterday, you don't have a place with us. So, go on and get out. Get your ass out of there and I'll let you go on with your business."

"You will?" Amos said, sarcastically. "Well now, that's mighty white of you and sure enough the Christian thing to do. But I think you're going to have to listen to me today."

"I don't have to do a goddamned thing, boy. Now

you get out of there before I come in and get you."

Although Truitt's talk was full of bravado, he was still in slow retreat. Chloe joined Amos at the window.

"Mr. McBride. This is Chloe Way. We're all right, Mr. McBride. You don't have to be scared of us. We won't bother you."

"You're bothering the hell out of me right now," Truitt shouted back. "Now get the hell out of my house."

Truitt thought he might just be able to extract himself from the vulnerable position he had placed himself in if he could just get another twenty feet of edge. Just a few more steps and he could break for the smokehouse with a good likelihood of success. Amos saw that, too. Truitt was not listening to anything he or Chloe had to say. He was simply stalling for time. Amos pushed the barrel of the shotgun through the narrow aperture, letting it rest upon the sill. He cradled the butt to his shoulder, thumbing back a hammer.

"God All Mighty, Amos. What are you doing?" Chloe said, surprised and frightened.

She scrambled forward to stop him but his finger was already squeezing the trigger. The explosion of sound crashed through the room, loud, throbbing, pulsing through the air and into both their skulls. A thick drift of powder smoke moved across Chloe as she stood in silent incredulity, her ears ringing.

Truitt froze in his tracks as buckshot tore into the earth two feet away from him, cutting off his retreat toward the safety of the smokehouse. A geyser of mud and water sprayed eight feet into the air and showered down on him.

"Now, you stop right there and listen to me, damn you," Amos shouted angrily. "I can blow you out of your boots anytime I'm of a mind to do it and you know that's a fact. There's no way you're coming in here or going anywhere else unless it's by my leave.

170

You got that?"

Truitt swallowed hard, muddy streams of water rolling down his face. It was no idle boast on Amos's part. Of all the members of his family, Amos was the best marksman, no argument, no contest. At this range, he could deliver on his threat with his eyes closed. That knowledge paralyzed Truitt.

"I'm not moving, son."

Amos left the shotgun lying on the window sill where his father could see it and with the other held at ready, he walked to the door.

"Open it," he said to Chloe.

"What?"

"Open the goddamned door," he said testily.

Chloe drew back the hastily rigged dead-bolt as Amos moved up behind her. She pushed the door open and the gusting wind caught it, tearing it from her grip and almost pulling her outside in the process. The door slammed into the side of the house with a force that seemed to shake the entire structure. Amos appeared in the doorway with the shotgun leveled at his father's chest.

"Son is it now? You turn me away from here like a dog, threaten me, try to kill me and I don't know what all. Now, I've got the upper hand and it's 'son' again all of a sudden."

There was no mistaking the anger in Amos's voice and Truitt was completely aware of his vulnerability. But he was puzzled as well. Surely these things did not have a sense of family? At least it could not be proved by Bill and Percy Way. Searching his mind for something to say, he was as surprised as Amos when Ellie rushed from the safety of the smokehouse to get between them.

She slipped and splashed through the mud and water, arms flailing wildly to keep her balance. Her legs flew out from under her as she ran and she belly-flopped into the mire, sliding over it like the last skip of a stone hurled across the surface of a pond. She skidded to a stop, bounced up and, with her muddy face set in determination, positioned herself between her son and her husband.

"Well? What are you two gunslingers waiting for? Don't mind me standing here. I don't have a say in what goes on anyway."

Amos and Truitt both shouted a warning for her to move but her only response was a contemptuous glare that would have done her mother proud.

"Kiss my muddy backside, the both of you."

Amos, bewildered by this turn of events, stood on the front porch with the wind driven rain stinging his face. He did not know what his next move should be. Truitt was in the same boat. It seemed they had reached a stand-off and neither of them was able to take the initiative.

"Dang," Truitt said, making the first move. He threw the shotgun down in the mud and reached for his revolver when Amos hurried to the edge of the porch.

"Jesus Christ, Daddy, get that gun out of the mud before the shells are ruined. We're going to need every round we have come sundown."

A wave of relief left Truitt so weak that he slumped down in the mud as he retrieved the shotgun. For the first time since the night he had lost Amos in the meadow, he allowed himself to feel hope. His son did not act or sound like any vampire—at least not like any he had imagined which was really the most questionable of leaps of logic. But it was his hope and now the rain felt clean, fresh, washing away pain, washing away fear. Maybe it would wash away the guilt as well. God knew, a good cleaning was in order.

"Stay where you are," Amos said. "I'm going to show you something."

Sara stepped haltingly out of the shadows to join

172

them as Amos disappeared into the house. Chloe did a double-take at the sight of her sister.

"Sara," she whispered. "Sweet Jesus, it's Sara."

With a squeal of joy, she started out the door but Amos stopped her.

"In due time, Chloe," he said, stepping between her and the door.

"What are you up to now?" she asked suspiciously as Amos rummaged in his hunting sack.

He removed a cross with a flourish and brandished it in the air. Giving her a broad grin, he tossed it up and caught it on the way down.

"I'm about to prove that point I told you about, sweetie."

CHAPTER SEVENTEEN

The rain stopped by early evening. A heavy cloud cover still rolled slowly across the sky and periodic claps of thunder sounded in the distance but, for now, it seemed, the storm had played itself out. Tildy sat at the table with her hand mirror, examining herself by the light of the coal-oil lamp. She dragged a brush through the thick hair, deep, dark brown, almost black, without a touch of gray. She looked the same as she had seventy years ago. There was something to be said for this life after all.

Still nude, she rose from her seat to examine her body. Her skin had become tighter, as if it had somehow shrunk. Her sagging breasts no longer sagged, no, far from it, nor did her buttocks. The varicose veins, wrinkles, liver spots, gray hair, all were gone; all the marks of age time had etched upon her. God knows how, but three-quarters of a century had fallen away in the space of hours. Tildy turned her head, craning her neck back over shoulder to look at her behind.

"It's a nice one, all right," Percy said, from the doorway.

Tildy glanced over at him. He, too, was still nude,

leaning casually against the doorjamb between the bedroom and the kitchen. It had to be a dream. Delwin would be back any day now from the war with Mexico. Or were the troops out facing the Yankees? When did anyone come home? 1865? Was Percy Way even born then? If he had been, he still would have been just a baby. Tildy gazed intently into the mirror, pulling her lips back over her gums. The "fangs," if that's what they were, descended at her will, keen and sparkling in the yellow light, giving her gray eyes a hardness unknown to the Tildy of 1865. It was no dream.

"What in the hell is happening to me?" she asked, placing the mirror on the faded oil-cloth of the table.

"I'm damned if I rightly know," Percy said, scratching at the inside of his thigh. His ample stomach quivered, shaking with his movement. He was as pale as the belly of a mud-cat, white flesh covered with wiry coils of dark hair. "First, you feel younger. Then I reckon you start to look younger, too. It sure surprised the hell out of me when I looked in the mirror."

"When does it stop?"

"Huh?"

"I said, when does it stop? Are we just going to go on getting younger till we're nothing more than a couple of little old snot-nosed kids sucking on a sugar-tit?"

"Y'know, I ain't never give it much thought."

"That's one thing that didn't change much, anyway. You've never give much of anything much thought."

"Oh, I don't know, Tildy. Here you got all this savvy and all but it don't seem to have done you much good, has it? Old, ignorant Percy still managed to nail your ass, didn't he?"

With a laugh, Percy crossed the kitchen to the door leading outside. He left the door open as he walked onto the porch and relieved himself over the railing.

Maybe he's right, she thought. Here I am talking like I know what I'm talking about when I know I know nothing. God, I've been so wrong about so many things. And look where it's gotten me. Not that it was important now. The legends she had heard from her grandfather were more fantasy than fact. She knew that now, in a way she could not define. And, even if she could define the knowing, it felt every bit as tangible and reliable as the visions.

Tildy understood the revelation of her own death now as well. It was not death, not really, but something else. Her heart had stopped, surely, her breathing, too, and her blood had flown from her veins to nourish Percy, yet it was never really death. That was why the image had been so hard to fathom.

Like getting old was hard to fathom.

She had known old people all her life but had never understood the process of becoming one. Even when she grew old herself, it baffled her. One day the aches, the pains, the forgetfulness, all just flooded in and she was old. Until that time, there had been no basis for understanding. The same principle applied to becoming . . . what? A vampire? Is that what I am? She had viewed them as evil, wicked things; objects of fear to be avoided, stamped out. Now, it was different. She did not feel either evil or wicked though she knew, to those who still lived the other life, she would appear to be both. It was a bona fide cinch she would be frightening to them. But how could she be held accountable for that? After all, it was not her doing. In fact, she had done everything in her power to avoid the change, the contagion, whatever the hell it was. Still, they would judge her.

Tildy Garrett, the old queer woman, was now Tildy Garrett the old—or maybe not so old—bloodsucker. Wouldn't people have a field day with that? It did not look like she would ever be just plain old Tildy Garrett. But then, whoever is just plain old anything? She felt Percy's gaze upon her as she crossed the floor to her bedroom. It had been a long time since anyone, man, woman or otherwise had looked at her like that.

Percy was a predator. She had known many predators in her time; the preacher who baptized her was one; Burl Tanner another. The woods were full of them and there was no mistaking those for whom the hunt was everything. If Percy had become evil in his new life, then the journey had been a short one. Tildy had never failed to notice the way he looked at his daughters. And, perhaps because of her own experiences, she read that look as accurately as a book. In this regard, the transformation made no difference.

There was a difference in her, however. She immediately recognized the importance of the visions. It was not just about feeding–at least not altogether— the smell of the blood, the taste, was exciting and there was no denying that, but there was more. After all, the satisfaction of feeding could be met by the flesh and blood of animals, just as in the old life. The idea that human blood was the only food for vampires was just a legend. She and Percy had both eaten from her larder and the act was as pleasing and satisfying as at any other time in her life.

But the blood was a tonic and resurrection the thing. The purpose of the vampires in the valley was one of territory and domination; the goal not just to feed but to breed. Maybe the evil, if it was evil, lay in the manner they went about it. No one asked for volunteers–they more or less took whomever they wished regardless of what anyone thought about it. If a crime, it was more rape than murder. The Lord knows that rape is nothing new. Not here. Not anywhere. Murder either, for that matter.

Earlier, while in bed with Percy, a vision of the

177

long-dead Annie came to her, rising in her memory to
stand like a tombstone, marking the end of the old life.
There would be other women, other men, too. It really
did not matter anymore. What would the people who
had known her before have to say about that? Old
Queer Tildy, ass tilted heavenward as she rolled atop
the feather mattress with a . . . what? A man? Was
Percy even a man anymore? What would people say
about that? What would they think? Was she even a
person anymore? As Percy himself said, "It sure was
something."

Percy entered her from behind, driving her forward,
pressing the side of her face into the quilt. She lay
awhile after he finished, tracing the pattern–if it could
be called a pattern–with her finger. Flower prints,
plaids, solid colors, all faded from hundreds of
washings and almost as many mendings over eighty-
plus years, with the same random impulsiveness with
which the quilt had been created in the first place,
belied the idea of pattern. The very randomness of
material and placement was the quilt's only pattern.
She had sewn the pieces of fabric together haphazardly,
using whichever piece she laid her hands on first as she
drew them blindly from her basket. The quilt was
perhaps the most totally spontaneous thing she had
ever done and, like life itself, made no sense at all.
Perhaps that was why she was so fond of it, why even
the memory of the creation was such an intense
pleasure.

Tildy lay across the bed feeling more human than
she had in years. It would be a real shame if she were
no longer human.

* * *

"It looks like Tildy was right about religious
things," Amos said, as he walked through the door.

His boots were soaked through and made squishing noises as he walked. Truitt followed, dripping water in a trail from the door to the fireplace. Chloe and Sara still clung together, weeping in turn while Ellie stuck close, attending them with the single-minded attentiveness that gave mother-hens their reputations.

"I guess she was at that," Truitt said, removing his hat. He shook the water off, spraying droplets across the room. Ellie, automatically, thought to reprimand him, then, just as quickly let it go. With all the dust, smoke, blood and water in the room already, shaking off a little rain would not hurt anything at this point. But Truitt caught himself.

"Sorry, Ellie," he said, dripping into a small puddle gathering around his feet. "I wasn't thinking, I guess."

Amos payed no attention to either of his parents and when he spoke, it was as if he were simply thinking aloud.

"But it still makes no sense to me. No sense at all. A body shoots some of these things and they die for good and all, shoot some others and they jump up and run off. Sunlight don't bother them a bit but drop a little old raggedy cross on them and they fall all to pieces. I just don't get it."

"I don't get it either but I'm right proud it works," Truitt said.

The creaking of the hand pump drew his attention to the kitchen where Ellie strenuously pumped away. A rusty-red trickle of water spurted from the pump, growing clearer and steadier as it became a stream under her efforts. Chloe and Sara took pots of water and set them on the stove.

"You two drag that tub outside and dump it," Ellie ordered, indicating Truitt and Amos with a small inclination of her head. She was once again in charge of her own domain and expected no discussion. "We'll get the bath water ready and I'll fix a bite to eat once

179

we've cleaned up a mite."

They were careful to avoid spilling the dirty water as they dragged the tub across the floor. Not careful enough, however. Splotches of water marked their trail as it sloshed over the side of the tub, puddled on the floor. Amos and Truitt finally managed to get the tub to the edge of the porch and tilt the contents over, a frothy tide drifting over the sodden surface of the yard. They dragged the tub back inside. No one would bathe on the porch tonight.

"It'll be a few minutes," Ellie said, pouring the first of the pots of hot water into the vessel. "You all need to get some dry clothes on now. We all do. We're going to have to take turns and there's no sense being wet and miserable while we're waiting."

Amos, dragging his hands across the familiar unpainted walls of the farmhouse, followed the slightly stooped figure of his father to the second floor. A strained silence lay between them. It was not as if they were not speaking, they were, but both avoided speaking of certain things—such as the events that occurred between them just a short time ago. And this silence lay over them like the storm hanging over the valley. They had stood, armed and ready, each prepared to take the other's life if necessary and, of course, if they could. Truitt would not meet Amos's eyes and Amos knew his father was ashamed. Amos, too, was ashamed. It was as if some secret part of them had been exposed to the world; their fear and confusion put on display for all to see. Amos felt like a window peeper because he recognized those emotions in his father.

He felt a real need to acknowledge the emotions of his father and to speak of his own feelings but he did not know how. And the desire was even more acute because the words were not there. If he were to speak, to try to convey understanding, identification, absolution—and to seek it for himself—he would leave them standing naked before one another with no defenses left to protect their manhood. Why was it so difficult? Women could cry, carry on with one another and no one cared. But this was different. He had shared more of himself with Chloe in two days than he had in a lifetime with this man he loved so desperately. Why couldn't he and Truitt cling to one another, weep with one another, speak with one another. It was a shame. He wanted that contact with Truitt but it was just not done. No, sir, it's just not done. A man is a secret that everybody knows but nobody talks about.

"I'm glad you're home," Truitt said, stopping outside his bedroom door.

"Glad to be home."

Truitt patted Amos on the back before entering his room. Amos went to his own room and peeled the sodden clothing from his body. He dried himself with a dirty shirt he picked up off the floor and dried his hair with the same shirt while laying out fresh clothes. Amos had lived in this room all his life. If he were suddenly stricken blind, he would still be able to locate every article in the room, every stick of furniture, every picture on the wall, everything. In the room, he felt secure, safe and closer to sane than he had felt since this whole thing started.

His feet hurt as he sat on the edge of the bed to put on fresh socks. The flesh was wrinkled, prune-like and tender from many hours in his wet boots and the sketchiest of attempts at hygiene. The odor, too, was unpleasant. He lay back on the bed, flexing his toes and gazing at the ceiling. Of course, he could tell Truitt it had only been a bluff; that there was no way he would harm him, but he was not sure if that was the truth. He would like for it to be. He would like to believe that there was no way he would harm his father but, if not for his mother coming between them, Amos was not sure what might have happened. A rap at the door interrupted his thoughts.

"You done in there, yet?"

"Not just yet, Daddy. I'll be down in a minute."

"Everything's all right?"

Yeah, fine. Fine. Perfect. Not a thing wrong. Hunky-dory. How could his father–anyone of them for that matter–ever even bring themselves to ask such a question? The whole world and everything in it had gone to hell. What could possibly be wrong, Papa? But he could not say that either.

"Yeah, fine. Everything's just fine."

He listened to the receding footfalls as his father left to join the women. After a moment, Amos rose and picked up his boots. With a sigh, he went downstairs.

His mother and Chloe were stringing a quilt across a line they had stretched through the kitchen. Ellie looked up at him as he descended the stairs and smiled. He could see her genuine relief, her contentment with having him home. Poor Mama. You don't understand. You just don't know what's coming.

"Privacy's sake, you know" she explained, totally unnecessarily. "Just because everything's turned upside down around here, that don't mean that me and these girls are going to act like hootchie-kootchie dancers in some Atlanta carnival show."

"More's the pity," Truitt said, draping his sodden clothing over the back of a chair near the fire. "That would sure be some show."

Amos sat his wet boots in front of the fire next to Truitt's. Steam was already rising in odiferous tendrils from the dark, wrinkled leather.

"I wonder about old Tildy," Truitt said to Amos. He packed tobacco into his pipe and lit it with an ember from the fireplace while he let Amos think about his observation. He paused, puffing while the tobacco caught and fragrant smoke swirled about his face. "I hope she's doing all right and all. You reckon we need to go see about her? When the others get here, I mean?"

"No, Papa. No use bothering about Tildy."

Amos spoke softly, with a quiet conviction. Truitt questioned him no further. The rain came again, pounding relentlessly on the roof, filling the room with a rhythmic, liquid roar.

CHAPTER EIGHTEEN

Sam Larrimer clucked to the mules, giving them a light slap with the reins as he pulled the wagon into the yard. He was not sure what was afoot. Seth's note had lacked detail. But there was enough information to make him uneasy as he became one of the first to arrive at the McBride farm–particularly considering his cargo. He looked over his shoulder at the kids sitting in back of the wagon, drenched, outside the tarp that would help keep them dry. Two bulges in the tarp told of the bodies underneath. Mabeline Williams and a stranger whom he did not know. Or, at least, he didn't think he knew him. The man's own mother wouldn't recognize him now. Both were shot to death. The children shivered inside their wet clothing but it would take much more than a cold rain to force them under cover with the dead. They rode silently, rain streaming down their faces.

The wagon splashed into a rut outside the house, giving everyone a good jostling. Sam looked at the face of his youngest son, Roy. Roy bounced with the motion of the wagon yet kept his eyes fixed on the contours of the bodies beneath the duck cloth. He stared as though he expected them to rise–feared that they would. Or perhaps he was seeing them as they were when the Larrimers had found them. It was likely that he would be seeing them for a long time to come. Though only six, Roy had become a lot older today. They all had.

Sam stopped the wagon in front of the stoop, setting the brake before climbing down to greet Truitt, who had come out of the house to meet them. The intermittent rain abated as the two stood speaking softly on the porch. A moment later, Truitt stood before Ellie with his hat in his hands. Clearly uncomfortable, he looked as if he would rather be just about anywhere in preference to where he was.

"Your mama's dead," he said, simply.

* * *

It was almost time to leave. Tildy lay in the darkness of her bedroom listening to Percy move about in the kitchen. Whatever else had happened to the man, however he had been changed, there was certainly nothing wrong with his appetite. In fact, Tildy thought, if a body were to take away all of Percy that wasn't appetite, he'd fit right handily into a thimble.

She'd had another dream.

It did not seem to matter, human or not, if such distinctions could be made anymore, she still had the dreams. Percy was a dead man. She would not tell him, of course. It would make no difference, even if she was inclined to warn him, which she was not. When the time came to choose, he would choose, and being who he was, he could only choose certain things and that alone sealed his fate. She would also see Amos again, soon, and not under the best of circumstances for a reunion. The trouble she had foreseen coming in the other life was rapidly developing. She had been foolish to think she would

185

have no role in it, foolish to think it could be avoided. She sat on the edge of the bed with echoes of tribal drums from a land far away throbbing faintly in her mind. The hunt was on. No one knew the hunters from the hunted.

* * *

Slow rain fell on his face as Burl lay back in the blanket of dead leaves. His shirt was open and Margie sat beside him, tracing the ragged red tear of the wound in his abdomen. It had stopped bleeding some time ago, closing tight with bright new skin forming over it. A little while longer and no trace at all of the wound would remain. Wilda sat across from them, naked, her breasts jiggling as she brushed damp leaves from her hair. She noticed Burl watching and smiled at him.

He had known Wilda all his life, just as he had known everyone in the valley all his life. But he had never seen her smile like that before. Of course, he had never seen her naked before either. He had never seen her give herself to another woman as she had with Rachel. It seemed that this was a week for firsts. It occurred to him that Wilda, and Margie, too, had spent their entire lives dead.

They heard the wagon creaking down the road and watched from concealment as Sam, Kyle, and Win Larrimore loaded first Mabeline and then Frank into the back of the wagon. Margie and Wilda started in anticipation but Burl held them back simply by raising his hand. They had nothing if not time. It was certain someone else would eventually come by. The wagon disappeared down the road and Burl had fallen backwards into the leaves, the newly-alive Margie bucking energetically atop him while Rachel and Wilda looked on.

186

The continuous sobbing was interrupted only long enough for Ellie to engage in vicious self-recrimination.

"I . . . I talked to her . . . like some kind of dog."

"It's all right, sugar," Truitt crooned, as if talking to a baby. "Your Mama knew you loved her. She knew you didn't mean none of those things you said."

Ellie shook her head.

"How? How could she know? I didn't tell her. I never got a chance to tell her much of nothing. I sure didn't show her. Now, every time I think of her, I'll see her sitting there with her head down and me lighting into her like all of this was her fault or something. Now, she's dead."

Sara sat alone, watching. She had to bite back the words on the tip of her tongue. Good, she thought. Good for her. Anybody who dies comes out of this lucky. It's those of us who don't die who are going to be in the deep shit.

The clouds rolled overhead, hanging between the earth and stars. As the darkness of the storm gave way to the darkness of night, Percy and Tildy left the house. Tildy was surprised by the acuity of her vision in the little light left available to her. She had always had good vision but this was something else entirely. They approached the body of Agnes Way lying crumpled near the muddy path. Percy stepped over her without a second look and Tildy noted the way the blind eyes of the woman, fixed in her shattered face, seemed to stare at him in recrimination. She is dead, Tildy thought, but if she could be pissed she would. Wouldn't anyone?

Percy stopped to wait for Tildy who stood quietly by the body.

187

"Poor old Agnes," he said. "She didn't even know what hit her. You blew the old girl out like a candle, by God."

"And don't that bother you at all? After all, she was your wife. You two have been together damned near thirty years or so. Seems like you'd be a mite upset with her passing."

Percy stopped for a moment, seriously considering Tildy's question.

"You'd think so wouldn't you," he said. "But it don't. It don't bother me at all. Should it?"

Tildy shook her head and stepped over the prone form.

"I don't know. It bothers the hell out of me though."

"I never figured you to be so soft, Tildy. Well, don't fret none, you'll get used to it."

"Lord, I hope not."

They walked down the slope, into the trees, leaving the body of Agnes Way where it lay.

* * *

Usually, even at a funeral, the children were exuberant. But Roy Larrimer was very subdued. Sara watched him. He sat still, staring blankly at the wall across from him, oblivious to those around him. There were only rare opportunities throughout the year for all the youngsters in the valley to get together. Even if the gathering was centered around a calamity or tragic event, the children tended to make the most of it. Not now, though. The other youngsters, even those who had not seen the bodies, were just as still. It was as if they had been infected by the anxiety of the adults. Sara thought it sad to see those young faces so quiet, so somber.

As usual, just like any other get together, people

188

divided into groups along age and gender lines. The children sat together while the women whispered among themselves as they busied themselves with the endless tasks of women that would outlive mankind itself. And the men stood off by themselves to discuss the situation and to question Amos and Chloe. There was certainly plenty to discuss and more than a few questions. As Sara watched and listened and waited her turn as a witness, Duncan Tanner was just putting the finishing touches on his tirade of how everyone must have gone crazy at the same time.

"Goddamn, boys, this is 1905. You people talk like a bunch of superstitious injuns or something. Now, I'll allow that something ain't right, but this 'vampire' shit has got to stop. People don't just get up and walk around once they're dead unless their name is Lazarus."

"Oh, yes, they do," Chloe said emphatically. "It sounds crazy enough, I guess, but it happens anyway. I seen it. Amos seen it. Mr. and Mrs. McBride, Sara, we all seen it. I don't like to think about it. God knows I sure wish it wasn't so but I'm not about to let on that I'm crazy or let you convince me that I'm seeing things just so you can feel better. I've got no intention of pretending that what's happened never happened. Because it did. And it's still happening. Like it or not, that's the way it is."

"Then I reckon I'll believe it when I see it," Tanner replied, stubbornly.

"I'm thinking you'll sure enough have that opportunity, Mr. Tanner," Amos said. "I guess we all will. Those things are going to show. You can bank on it."

"And Burl's with them," Chloe said. "I saw him die, Mr. Tanner. I know what happened after that. When you see your son again, he ain't going to be your son anymore."

"Little girl, if you seen him die, then I ain't going to

see him again. This is foolishness, Chloe. I know you don't mean to tell no stories and that you've been scared half out of your skin but I've already buried a child–so has Truitt–and there's nothing harder. But it is final. I've never seen her again. Never. And never will. Dead is dead and that's that."

Chloe rolled her eyes heavenward, throwing her hands up in exasperation.

"I reckon you've got to believe what you've got to believe."

"I reckon I do."

"And I reckon we've got work to do," Truitt said, tiring of the debate. "You all can conjecture on the mysteries of life and death after we bury our dead. It's time to get them underground. You all do agree we have dead?"

Duncan nodded and rose to join the burial detail; if his beliefs had been challenged by Chloe, then the events at the funeral party totally obliterated them. The dead were lain out on tarps, which Truitt was prepared to cut into sections for shrouds. The stranger, Bill Way, Ernie Weems and Mabeline Williams lay on the dirty fabric shoulder to shoulder as Truitt knelt with his knife in his hand.

"Just a minute, Papa," Amos said, joining the men with his hunting sack hung over his shoulder. He reached into it and took out a cross from Baptizing Creek as he knelt beside his father.

"Here, now, what's this," Duncan Tanner protested. "Does the boy think he's a priest now, too?"

Amos did not answer he simply dropped a cross on the chest of the stranger. Duncan Tanner had absolutely no explanation at all for what followed. A cross on the body of Bill Way confirmed the unbelievable. Ernie and Mabeline were laid to rest a hundred yards west of the barn. The wet soil caved into the graves, settling and forming basins rather than mounds. The graves were puddles before the stern-faced men made it back to the house.

Sara watched from the window. Her feelings were so jumbled they were difficult to identify at any particular time. Her reaction to Ellie's grief was a generalized sense of anger. At least Ellie knew what became of her mother—body and soul. At least she knew. But what of Agnes Way? Chloe had Amos. Who did Sara have? Sara had nothing but her rage. She nursed it, fed it like a fire in a winter hearth, growing it progressively hotter. Tomorrow, perhaps the next day, she would have the blood to drown it.

* * *

Wind rattled through the rain-heavy leaves, swaying branches and sending cold droplets pattering down beneath the trees. Burl sat up and looked at Rachel, sitting silently in the darkness gazing westward. Without a word, he stood and pulled on his overalls. Clouds scudded over the dark sky and the stars shone through the random breaks in the cover. He helped Margie to her feet.

"What?" she asked, bending to pick up her shift. She pulled it over her head, wriggling and squirming as she pulled it over her hips and straightened it.

"Hold still a minute and feel it," he said.

"Feel what?"

"Just keep still."

Margie stood still, her head tilted back slightly, arms dangling at her sides. After a moment, she turned to face the west as well. The very air was charged with meaning. Unheard, unseen, but felt, clearly and deeply as life itself. It told of movement, power, joining. It called her. It called them all.

"Yeah," she said. "Yeah, I see what you mean."

They wound their way quietly through the trees,

back toward the highlands.

* * *

The fire in the hearth popped, crackled and sent a
bright cloud of darting embers swirling up the flue.
Sara pulled her blanket tighter around her as she stared
into the flames. Sleep was out of the question as she
thought about the morning.

The men had already decided that they would ride
out at first light. Why wait for the strangers to bring it
to them? After all, Duncan, Amos, Truitt, everyone
knew the lay of the land. They had all been born here,
hunted here, farmed here and generations had lived and
died here. The strangers, the "vampires," could not
avoid them, evade them, hide from them. All the men
knew every inch of the woods, the mountains, the
ridges, the creeks, and would cover every inch until the
invaders were either driven out or destroyed.

Sara, of course, had not been invited to ride along
but it did not matter. Her mind was made up and there
was no changing it. If she was not allowed to ride
along, then she would follow. If she were not allowed
to ride at all, then she would walk. Come hell or high
water, she intended to have some part in it. She already
had a part in it.

It was not something she had asked for or sought
out. Sara would have been perfectly happy if Duncan
Tanner was right about them all being crazy. But they
were not. She would have been perfectly happy if her
father had simply disappeared and had never returned
to bother her and Agnes—even if that meant Chloe
disappearing as well. But it had not happened that way
either. Percy had done things to her and there would
be no forgiving or forgetting. He had done things to
her mother. Sara had been dragged in through no fault
of her own and she was damned if she would let

192

anything go.

Sara sat upright on her pallet. Several other women and many of the children lay around her. People had been arriving all evening as word got around. Freeman Williams and his family had come with Win Larrimer. Freeman had arrived too late for his mother's burial but had spent a good deal of time at the sodden grave-site. So long, in fact, Truitt became concerned and fetched him back. Red-eyed and silent, Freeman had gone directly upstairs. Like many of the others, his face bore evidence of his terrible resolve. Tomorrow's sun would set on a bloody, bloody day.

But morning was many hours away. Sara rose and stuck the .45 in her belt. The gun had never been more than an arm's reach from her since she had dug it from her father's bureau. She stretched her hands toward the fire to warm them for a moment, then walked outside.

* * *

At the foot of Hog Heaven Hill, dark figures slipped from the shadows of the trees. Little more than shadows themselves, they drifted across the wet grass like wraiths. Tildy was among them, pulled eastward toward a joining by the same unseen force that drew the other band westward. The would meet in the valley, near the McBride farm. Something was afoot and excitement grew in her with each step she took. It was like a new-found instinct. She looked at the others and knew they felt it, too. Everyone came together like geese preparing to fly south. None of them fought against the urge, none resisted, none questioned. Tildy found the feeling stronger than anything she had ever before experienced.

Odd, but awfully natural.

193

CHAPTER NINETEEN

Crickets and frogs created a cacophony of sound following the rain. Truitt sat tilted back in a kitchen chair, legs crossed and propped atop the porch rail. His shotgun rested across his lap and he seemed relaxed, though nothing could be further from the truth. Lanterns hanging on the porch columns bathed the yard in an ocean of yellow light. Truitt, pipe clenched between his teeth, was shrouded in a cloud of tobacco smoke, as his eyes flitted nervously over the perimeter of light. He had been constantly jumping at shadows since night had fallen.

He sat just outside the door while Duncan Tanner and Sam Larrimer sat posted at each corner of the building. There had been little conversation between the men as they peered into the darkness beyond the circle of light, eyes straining for the slightest movement, ears attuned to the faintest of sounds. The creak of the plank floor beneath Sara's weight almost tumbled Truitt backwards from his chair.

"Damn it, girl. Don't do that. You scared the living hell out of me."

"Sorry," she said, managing a grin. "I didn't mean to give you a fright. I just have to go to the outhouse."

Truitt shook his head. He took his pipe from his mouth, exhaling a lung-full of smoke. "I don't reckon that's such a good idea. Too risky. You go on back in the house. I imagine Ellie's got a few slop-jars started by now."

"Nah, I've never been so delicate I couldn't go outside. Besides, I got this gun here and you can see the outhouse right from where you're sitting."

"That's true enough, I guess but it's still too risky. There ain't no use taking any foolish chances when --."

Sara ignored him and walked out into the yard.

"I don't want you to think that I'm asking permission, Mr. McBride. But if it makes you feel any better, I'll take this with me."

Sara leaned forward and pulled a cross from the ground. It came free with a loud sucking sound that sent gooseflesh crawling across Truitt's skin. Sam and Duncan came over to flank him as Sara crossed the yard.

"Now, what's that one up to?" Duncan asked.

"Going to the outhouse," Truitt said. "Don't want to dirty the house up none, I guess."

They watched her shadowy form as she reached the building and disappeared inside.

"If that don't beat all," Sam said.

"You ain't never lied," Truitt said. "I'm damned if I ever want to go the outhouse at night again."

Sam nodded. "You and me both."

"Let's go on back where we're supposed to be, Sam," Duncan said, resting his shotgun over his shoulder. "We don't want nobody slipping up on us while we're chewing the fat about that hard little girl's outhouse business."

Truitt continued to stare at the silhouette of the outhouse as Duncan and Sam returned to their positions. Sara was going to be all right. He had been worried about her for a while and he tried to leave her

195

alone, let her pull herself together. But Duncan was right about one thing—Sara was one hard, young woman.

Maybe Ellie and Chloe could talk to her tomorrow. She might be more talkative if no men were around. There was no doubt that Sara had little use for men and even less trust in them. Still, even a hard case like Sara had to talk to someone. Whatever she had been through had taken its toll and would eat her alive if she tried to handle it alone.

Sara had always been quiet, self-contained, private. But there was an undeniable strength about her as well. Of all the Way girls, Sara was the one most likely to stand up for herself, and her sisters. The most likely to draw a line on the ground and dare you to step over it. There had been some kind of conflict between her and Percy for years and, though Truitt did not know exactly what it was, it seemed pretty clear that somehow or another Sara had managed to come out on top. It was evident to anyone paying attention that when she and Percy were together, they circled one another like a pair of game-cocks.

Truitt had watched Sara grow up. Something had happened. She did not begin her life hard and mistrustful. Sara had been no different than any other little girl he had ever known. No, she had not been born tough, suspicious, guarded, withdrawn, hard. Something had caused her to become that way.

Something like Percy Way.

There was another Percy people did not know. Truitt did not really know that side of him either but he knew of it. He had seen it from time to time. That, in itself, was no surprise. There is always part of a person that even the people closest to him are not aware of or, if they are aware, they have no way of knowing, of understanding. It was like that with Percy. Percy had a way of looking at his girls. It was not decent. No, it was not decent for a man to look at his children like that. There were other things, too. Hugging them the way he did, sitting them in his lap in ways that weren't proper. Things Truitt had gone out of his way not to notice.

But he had noticed.

Even when the girls were nearly grown, Percy insisted on putting them to bed, wrapping the covers around them, kissing them on the lips. Once, Truitt had been sitting at the Way's table, drinking whiskey, when Percy returned from his fatherly duties, his face flushed with more than whiskey. Truitt was surprised, horrified, as Percy pulled at the crotch of his overalls before sitting down. He had an erection and he saw clearly enough that Truitt saw clearly enough. He grinned.

"Can't help it," Percy explained, his tongue loosened by the alcohol. "You got boys so you wouldn't know. It ain't easy raising the finest clutch of gals these parts have ever seen. Any one of them would flat tear a young man a new ass."

No wonder Sara did not trust men.

Truitt leaned forward and tapped his pipe against his boot heel. He was embarrassed by these thoughts. He told himself he did not know anything for sure. But the lie did not set easy with him.

* * *

The thumping of the drums grew louder, tangibly filling the air. Amos felt the sound-charged waves pulse against his skin as the high grass of the veldt rippled around him. The shaft of the assagai was slick, slippery with sweat and the muscles of his forearm cramped with the effort of a tight grip. His eyes narrowed against the yellow dust as he scanned the grasslands. This time, he knew the prey. Sing-song

197

chants accompanied the skin drums, mingling with the bass coughing sound of the hunted. The roar began like distant thunder but became harsher, louder, with each step he took. The grass parted and Tildy rose before him.

She no longer had the lion body nor the face of an old woman. Her bare shoulders were pale, smooth in the blistering sun and were in sharp contrast to the dark cascade of hair flowing down her back. He stopped, staring, as she walked toward him. She was naked, her young body firm as she stepped into the clearing where he stood.

Amos could not take his eyes off her. She stopped several feet away, smiling, stunning him with her beauty. He was swept by the same powerful feelings he had experienced with Chloe at Baptizing Creek. Tildy drew her hands languorously over soft curves, raised her arms, beckoned him. Amos moved toward her as if in a trance. An aura of warmth surrounded her and he wanted to step into that aura, pull it tightly around him, sink into it, smother himself with it. Tildy's smile widened, as did her arms and she extended him the invitation. She made a sound like a soft purr as he moved into her. She tightened her embrace and the lazy half-closed lids of her eyes flew wide open as she gasped and shoved Amos away from her.

He could not believe it himself.

He had brought the wicked blade of the assagai up between them and shoved it into her. Amos stabbed just below the rib cage, thrust upward toward the sternum and deep, through the cavity of the chest and out her back. Six inches of the long blade protruded between her shoulder blades. The mirror surface of gleaming steel flashed brilliantly in the midday sun. Amos was entranced by the light dancing off the metal as Tildy bent forward at the waist, turning in a slow, descending circle. Amos stepped back, waiting for her to fall.

She did not.

Tildy completed the slow circle, facing him again, standing upright as she pulled the spear from her body in one easy motion. There was no blood. From start to finish not one drop of blood spilled from her. The blade of the weapon still gleamed as if it had just been forged. Amos stared at her chest. A four-inch gash gaped just below her breasts. The sound of her heart echoed like a shout from a mountain cavern, growing fainter and fading away as the wound closed before his astonished eyes. Tildy let the assagai fall at her feet.

Her calm expression told him nothing but as Amos looked into her gray eyes he thought he saw both sadness and pity.

"You don't understand," she whispered.

"I don't understand."

* * *

Truitt fumbled with his tobacco pouch as he refilled the bowl of his pipe, tamping the tobacco nervously as he stared at the dark silhouette of the outhouse. He struck a match and held it to the pipe, sucking noisily as the tobacco caught. He spit several times to clear his lips of loose grains that had found their way to the mouthpiece. It was sure taking Sara a long time.

Movement caught his eye and he looked back as the door of the privy swung open. He could not see anyone, they would be invisible in the shadows, of course, but the corner of the door, framed in a patch of sky against the tree-lined horizon, signaled Sara's return. Good, he thought. It's about time.

* * *

Amos backed away as Tildy advanced on him.

199

"No need to fear me, boy," she said. "I've never meant you no harm."

Amos shook his head violently and clutched the wooden cross hanging on his neck. He wore it like a fetish and it felt warm to his touch. Amos yanked the talisman free, snapping the thin leather thong around his neck. With the cross held at arm's length in front of him, Amos backed slowly away. Tildy reached forward, curling her long, thin fingers around the failed protection of the rag and twig icon from Baptizing Creek. She pulled it gently from his hand. Nothing happened. Nothing at all. The ground disappeared beneath him and Amos tumbled backwards into space.

He did not have time to scream as he splashed into a body of frigid water. The icy liquid rushed over him as he fought his way back to the surface. Sputtering, he rose in the waist-deep flow and looked around him. The oak cross loomed in the meadow. He was standing in Baptizing Creek. Tildy stopped at the edge of the stream. She let the cross fall from her hand. Amos watched speechlessly as it twisted in the current, floating past him.

"You don't understand," she said.

Her pale skin glowed in the sunlight, framed against the verdant trees crawling up the mountain. Again, she held her hand out to him. Amos waded slowly toward her. He was not surprised to find that he, too, was naked. She took his hand, helping him up the bank into the soft, lush grass. Tildy took him in her arms, caressing him as she slowly knelt before him. Her lips and tongue traced a tingling trail from his chest to his stomach. His legs trembled.

"No!" he shouted, grabbing her head in both hands and holding her tightly against his stomach. He coiled his legs beneath him and drove her upward and back, tilting them both over the edge of the bank. Together, they tumbled into the creek.

200

* * *

Truitt leaned forward, pipe-stem clutched between his teeth. Something was wrong. The outhouse door had swung outward and still stood ajar but there was no sign of Sara. Where was she?

"Sam," Truitt called softly in a stage whisper.

"Yeah?"

"You see Sara out there anywhere?"

"Nah, I can't see much of nothing."

"Me either," Duncan Tanner said.

"Sure is taking that gal a while, though. She coulda done had a baby by now," Sam said.

"Sara! Youuuuuuu, Sara!" Truitt called loudly. There was no response as both Sam and Duncan joined him by the steps. The three of them shouted but there was still no response. Truitt did not like the look of things.

"Grab us one of them lanterns, Sam. Duncan, you stay here and wait on us."

Duncan stood on the porch as instructed, nervously licking his lips and shifting his weight from one foot to the other as Sam and Truitt crossed the yard to the outhouse.

The building was illuminated by the approaching lantern and the men could see through the open door that it was empty. There was no sign of Sara.

* * *

Gulping a mouthful of air, Amos held Tildy in a death-grip as they fell through the air. A geyser of water marked their point of impact as the force of their fall carried them to the bottom. With his eyes tightly closed, Amos released Tildy and kicked against her, propelling himself away. He rose as quickly as he could and, with a shake of his head, flung the wet hair out of his eyes. Air bubbles rose to the surface several feet away. So ended Tildy. Amos leaned forward, peering into the water.

Tildy floated below, her hair billowing about her head like tentacles as she rose to the surface. She broke the plane of water with hardly a ripple and continued to rise into the air. A light, white cotton shift was plastered to her body, concealing nothing, fitting tightly as a fine silk glove. She arched her back, spreading her arms wide as she rose to the heavens.

"You don't understand."

The water swirled, rippling violently as if caught by an earthquake. Tildy rocketed skyward, the water from Baptizing Creek following her like the tail of a comet to gather into heavy clouds that blotted the sun from the sky. Amos stood on the dry, pebbly bottom of the creek bed, shivering in the sudden darkness as the wind rose, sobbing across the meadow in whistling gusts. The sky grew darker yet, stitched by fiery threads of lightning. Thunder boomed, rumbling like cannon fire. Amos fell to his knees, covering his head with his hands.

"Hallelujah!" Tildy shouted.

* * *

The wooden cross lay in the mud next to the outhouse. Truitt held the lantern low to the ground as he examined the two sets of boot-prints in the mire. One set was definitely made by a man–large, heavy, deeply imprinted into the ground. There was a smaller set as well, no doubt Sara's. Only the large prints led away from the building. Truitt picked up the cross and raised the lantern as he followed the trail. It led toward the trees. He and Sam followed the tracks for several yards before losing their nerves. Sam stopped and

202

cleared his throat.

"I don't reckon it's none too smart for me and you to go following this fellow all alone tonight, do you?"

Sam was right, of course. Truitt knew that. The one set of prints leading away told him all he needed to know. Sara was not walking. He saw the few red drops staining a rust streak on the black ground around the door and knew that Sara had made a terrible mistake; that he had made a terrible mistake. He should never have let her go out alone. His frustration, close to the surface at best, now got the better of him.

"Hell no, it ain't. But what's good sense got to do with anything here lately? I let her come out here by herself and now I got to find her and that's all there is to it. Goddamn it all, anyway. Goddamn it all to hell."

"Hold on now. Ain't none of this your fault. Sara's grown and she's hard-headed to boot. She can't put none of this off on you and nobody else will either. Anyway, it'll be light before too long. We'll find her then or know the reason why."

Truitt kept his eyes on the dark trees. Sam wasn't much at argument but then Truitt was not in need of much convincing.

"I reckon so," Truitt agreed, after a moment for decorum. "I got me a feeling that it's too late, anyway. We'd better get on back to the house. I'm getting right good at breaking bad news to folks lately. Must be because I'm getting so much practice."

They plodded heavily through the thick mud, Truitt walking with his head down, concentrating on his feet.

"Hold it! Hold it! Hold it, Duncan! It's us Goddamn it!"

Sam was already diving for the mud when Truitt looked up into the muzzle flash of Duncan Tanner's shotgun. It blinded him as he was swept by the hot, violent wind of the concussion. He threw both shotgun and lantern into the air as he tumbled backwards into the mud.

"I got the son of a bitch!" Duncan shouted exuberantly from the porch. "By God, I got the son of a bitch!"

* * *

Gunfire.

Amos opened his eyes and sat upright. It was not thunder; it was gunfire. Scrambling to his feet, he grabbed his shotgun. He did not stop for his boots as he hurried out the door.

CHAPTER TWENTY

Tildy, lying in the meadow, felt herself lifted and carried into the sky. The wind whipped against her as she rose, popping the fabric of the cotton shift, streaming her long hair out behind her. Trees, mountains, streams, all fell away beneath her as she rose higher and higher.

"You don't understand," she muttered.

"What?" Percy asked. He knelt several feet away beside a smoldering pile of twigs and branches. Tildy opened her eyes and regarded him sleepily.

"Huh?"

"What did you say?" Percy asked.

"Oh, nothing. Reckon I was just talking in my sleep a mite. What are you doing?"

"Trying to get a fire started."

Tildy shook her head as Percy dropped to all fours to blow energetically on the weakly glowing embers. They glowed a bit stronger under his efforts but faded again the minute he stopped for another breath. His only reward was a larger plume of greasy smoke.

"Damn," he said.

Aaron and the others sat just beyond Percy, watching him wordlessly. The wood was sodden.

Tildy was amazed that Percy displayed such a remarkable lack of common sense.

"Percy, what in the hell do you need a fire for anyway?"

He stopped, looked at her with a vacuous expression and shrugged.

"I don't know. Just thought it'd be nice to have one."

As he turned back to his task, Tildy watched the plume of smoke rising from the McBride farmhouse. If Percy succeeded in building a fire, which was unlikely, then it would be like sending a message to the people down there. That did not matter really. Everyone knew where everyone else stood. Everyone knew, at least in a general sense, where everyone else was located. It did not make any difference who knew what.

She got up and walked away from the group, up the slight incline of the hill. She was sharing dreams with Amos, she knew that. And, like Amos, she was not sure of the meaning. Since joining Aaron's group, she had been experiencing a growing sense of awareness, of revelation perhaps, that she had been trying to piece together.

It was as if she shared a common consciousness with the others that Percy, for whatever reason, was unable to tap into. Or maybe the man simply had his own agenda. She knew, that for all the information her grandfather had provided, he had left out a great deal. For instance, the creatures were not invaders from some foreign place. The hills, valleys and high mountains were their homes as well.

Aaron walked up behind her. He stood silently watching her for a moment before he spoke.

"Ye'd be beginnin' t'understand ere ye not?"

Tildy turned to face him.

"Yeah. Yeah, I reckon I am."

206

"There's folks like us all over the world, I'd reckon. The first of our line come from a place called Africa a long time back. She come as a slave I've been told, sometime in the 1600's. It didn't take her long t'change that though. She held land in Virginia a bit o'time before the law was changed t'where black folks couldn't hold no slaves or indentured servants– especially white ones. She got drove off from there. Of course she brought some others with her when she came here. She was in these hills long before yer granddad or mine ever arrived."

Tildy sat down and motioned Aaron to a place beside her. It was time she found out a little about who, or what, she'd become.

"The Indians were here."

"Aye, they were. A few got brought over, the rest lit out. Guess there ain't nobody's land that wasn't somebody else's before."

"Guess not," Tildy said, pulling a long blade of grass and placing it between her teeth. She chewed at it thoughtfully a moment. "You're not from here," she stated simply.

"No No, I'm not. I farmed over Chickamauga way till I ran into a couple of our companions in the woods one day. That was a while back, bout 1709 if I recollect correct. Time don't mean a whole hell of a lot anymore but that's the year that somehow sticks in m'mind. I come back here with them. There was three, maybe four-dozen or so of us living around here at that time. You people drove us out."

"I was born here," Tildy corrected.

Aaron smiled at her.

"Aye, I reckon ye was. The ones that come before ye, the settlers, they drove us out. That weren't right. We didn't look them up."

"Well, like you said, whose land ain't been somebody else's at one time or another? Anyway, I know that was a bad time. My granddaddy told me of it."

"Ye don't know nothin'," Aaron said, his face hard. "There was killing like ye'd not believe."

"On both sides I'd imagine."

"Aye. We did our share all right. Some of them we brought over, some we just killed outright. Yer people got plumb crazy. A bunch got together a dozen miles beyond Baptizing Creek and marched their way to Hog Heaven Hill killing all that was big enough to die."

"They killed a lot of their own folks," Tildy said. "Granddaddy told me about that, too."

"Aye, they did. They had some foolish notion that the only way we could die was to have a stake drove through our hearts. I'm here to tell ye the killin' weren't pretty."

"Killing never is."

Aaron smiled.

"Well, ye'd be right about that but let's just say this was uglier than most. Anyways, we lit out. It weren't worth it back then while there was a lot of country left."

"And now there ain't."

"And now there ain't. It's gettin' smaller all the time. Oh, there's some places out there yet, I'll not be denyin' that. There's been some of us gone to cities and whatnot. But in a city, ye got to live alone, stick to yerself, not get close to nobody. A lot of us don't cotton to that."

Tildy gazed into Aaron's eyes. They were soft, gentle, not at all threatening. Perhaps they would have been in the other life . . . no, not unless she'd known of his status—then she would have seen him as threatening. If she had met him under any other circumstance, she would have had no qualms at all. His fangs were retracted and his long brown hair moved gently in the slight breeze. Aaron had gone somewhere else, she did not know where. But suddenly he was distant. Perhaps lost in a history that would always be second-hand to her.

"Who are you Aaron? Who am I? What are we?"

Aaron came back, at least partially. The distant look remained even as he answered.

"I'm Aaron Taggert, born to Brian and Margaret Taggert once of Shropshire, who come to the Carolinas indentured. And a loyal subject of the British Crown, at least I was when I was born, when this country was legally England.

"Ye know that changed with the revolution. I was as much rebel as anyone else and fought the Redcoats as hard as any man. Aye, but I was a hard Colonial to keep down with such a small ball of lead.

"Ye blessed me a vampire but that means not a thing t'me. I'm a human born. I don't know if that name still holds for me. I reckon, if you get right down to it, I'm just Aaron Taggert, trying to play out the hand that's dealt me. As for ye? Girl, I'd be sparse the first idea."

Tildy grinned. "I don't either but I'm around a hundred years old. I'm hardly a girl."

This time Aaron laughed.

"Not t' insult Sis Tildy, but ye'd do t' keep it all in perspective. I got great-grandchildren running around in the world out there old as ye."

Aaron stood and dusted at the back of his pants. He trailed his hand through Tildy's hair as he turned to go.

"Try not to let it weigh on ye. Ye'd be havin' eternity t'figger it out. I'd vow it takes ye every bloody second."

He moved easily away toward the rest of the group. Tildy rose to her feet and called to him.

"Aaron, what happened to the woman?"

"Which woman might that be?"

"The black woman you were telling me about."

Aaron grinned.

"Sadie Meachum. That'd be her colonial name, her American name. Her own name? She called herself "the lioness" in her old language, the one she talked back in Africa. She used to say we was all lions, so I hear, since, in a way, she was our mother. I ain't never seen her myself, but I like to think she's out there somewhere."

Tildy could hear the thump of the drums, see the swaying yellow grass of the veldt as she turned her head from the mountains to look into the valley and back again.

"We can go out there somewhere, too, Aaron."

He faced Tildy as he shook his head.

"Them like us, Tildy, we've never been out of the shadows of these mountains and don't want to be. This here is our home."

Tildy turned away from him, looking down at the farmland as Aaron walked away. She stood for a long time.

"This is home," she echoed softly.

* * *

Amos hurried through the door just as Duncan descended the steps. The smell of gunpowder still hung in the air. Truitt lay sprawled in the mud fifty feet away, just inside the circle of light covering the yard from the lantern Duncan carried. Sam was rising to his hands and knees several yards away from Truitt—his extinguished lantern still clutched in his hand. Amos vaulted from the porch to run slipping and sliding through the mud to where his father lay. Both Sam and Truitt were covered with mud and water.

"Oh, Lord," Amos said, kneeling by Truitt.

Truitt moaned, as Amos raised him to a sitting position.

Amos ran his hand through his father's hair, brushing it back to search for a wound. There was none. No blood anywhere. It seemed Truitt had simply gotten the wind knocked from him.

"Dang," Truitt said.

"What happened, Papa?"

Truitt shook his head to clear it. A wave of anger washed over him as he got his wits about him.

"Where's that goddamned idiot at?" he demanded.

"Who?"

"Duncan Tanner, that's who. The fool almost blew my head off."

Sam had regained his composure, to some extent, and helped Amos get Truitt to his feet.

"He wasn't shooting at us," Sam said. "Look yonder."

Sam pointed to a body lying fifteen feet away. It was the body of a woman. Amos started to go examine her but Duncan stopped him.

"Watch your step now, lad. I think I got him all right, but he might just be playing possum."

"It ain't a him, Mr. Tanner. It's a her."

Amos led the way to stand over the fallen woman, her dark blood flowing and forming a puddle at his feet. He looked up at Duncan, who had stopped in his tracks, head jerking as if he had just been slapped. Even in the darkness, Amos could see the blood draining from his face which grew eerily pale in the yellow light.

"Oh, sweet Jesus, I done shot Sara."

"No, sir," Amos said. "It ain't Sara. It's Wilda. And I reckon she needed killing now."

Truitt retrieved his shotgun and stood with Duncan and Sam. Each of them seemed rooted in the earth.

"Now ain't that a hell of way to talk," Duncan said, indignantly. "That's your mama's sister you're talking about; your own flesh and blood. Here she come running out of the woods to join up with us and I cut her down like some kind of mad dog."

Duncan, seized by a paroxysm of guilt, spoke with a trembling voice. Amos felt no sympathy. Instead, he found himself angry, filled with rage toward the man.

"I'm damned if you got the sense to pour piss out of a boot when you're wearing it. Don't you get it yet? This here thing wasn't about to join up with nobody. She was going to kill them. Now, has somebody got to pound you between the eyes to get your attention?"

"I'll tell you what, you little peckerwood. If anybody's going to be doing any pounding here it'll be me."

Duncan took a threatening step toward Amos but Sam restrained him. Duncan allowed himself to be ruled. A shout from the porch drew their attention. The shots had awakened everyone and several armed men stood on the porch undecided about their next move. Inside, the remaining men, women and children crowded one another for available space at the windows. It had been Freeman who shouted. He repeated his question.

"What in the hell's going on out there?"

"Duncan's done nailed one of them critters," Sam called back.

Like the others, Amos was watching the porch. He had his back to Wilda as she pulled her legs up beneath her and rose silently from the ground.

* * *

Tildy rubbed the nail of her forefinger back and forth across her upper lip as she sat alone on the hilltop. Things were coming to a head. That was a lead-pipe cinch. But what of the dreams; what was she to make of them? She needed time to think things out and something inside her told that kind of leisure was

212

soon going to be a hard commodity to come by. Tildy had figured out the significance of the crosses and Baptizing Creek but she had not shared that with anyone. The others likely knew already.

Miles beneath the ground, somewhere in the highlands at the source of the stream, the flow of water became infused with an element that was poison to them. She did not know what it was and it did not much matter but her dreams told her it was there. Sort of like her well at home which had such a high iron content. It had nothing to do with faith, damnation, curses or retribution. At best, it was an allergic reaction–though quite a dramatic one. How it tied in with ideas of Holy Water and the mystic protection of crucifixes was relatively easy to figure out. Even with that knowledge it continued to puzzle her.

She was most puzzled, however, by her connection with Amos. They were blood relations, of course, through her mother's sister, but they were connected on another level as well. When she put her mind to it now, she could see things through his eyes. She wondered if he could do the same with her.

Tildy smiled. It occurred to her that all her relations, any connection she had with anyone now was a blood relation; Truitt, Amos, Percy, Aaron, anyone, everyone. But still, she was different; a part of them and apart from them at the same time. She could feel it in the same way she had always felt it in the other life. The knowing set her apart. The knowing, both then and now, would always make her different.

She lay back in the grass to look up at the clearing sky. The rain, done for now, would come again tomorrow, maybe tomorrow night, the next day at the latest. Just like every spring. For that matter, it would rain almost daily for the next few weeks. Always has. Always will. The remnants of the clouds drifted past the pale yellow crescent of the moon. Every night the crescent moon would grow larger, become more luminous, until it was full and filling the meadow with a ghostly light. She tilted her head back even further, again experiencing a feeling of rising above the earth. The high, clear, night sky seemed to swallow her up as the stars spread above her. She felt as if she might spiral away with them, into infinity.

What if I just say to hell with it? she wondered. Just say to hell with it, turn around and climb back up that mountain to my place? Just let the whole damned thing lay? Why not?

She raised herself to her elbows and looked down at the farm house. Too bad. Too bad old Annie was dead all these long years. Tildy considered how she could have brought Annie with her. Just the two of them, sitting up on that mountain till times weren't long. Neither would ever have to get old, ever have to die, ever give up the sun, the stars, nothing. But Annie's dead; turned to dust years and years ago. Besides, she was hardly good enough company to consider for an eternity. Sara? Now there was a thought.

"Dang," she said, softly. "Don't look like I've changed all that dadburn much either."

Amos dreamt. She could feel the dream stealing over her like morning fog. She could see it and see through it at the same time. Poor Amos. He was even more puzzled by all this than she was and the Good Lord knew he was a lot more frightened. She eased herself back down and allowed herself to slip away-- Africa, Baptizing Creek, Heaven.

The sharp boom of the shotgun, muted with distance, rumbled up from the farm house to the top of the hill. Tildy leapt up in time to see winks of flame from the porch and yard seconds before the sounds once again came echoing up to her. Soon, she could see figures scrambling about in the yard, crossing it,

214

stepping into shadows beyond the light.

Now what? There would be no going back to the cabin just yet. Whatever was taking place below tied directly into her. That much was certain. She could not run from it. Maybe she did not even want to. She felt the excitement boil up inside her again. Whoever she was, she was not the same Tildy she had been this time last night. Staring intently down from her vantage point, she watched silently for several minutes. It was killing business below. Soon the darkness lit up again with short, violent winks of flame from muzzle flashes as shadows danced in the orange light. The reports of the guns mingled together, rolling across the valley in one long sound.

Movement caught her eye. Along the tree line to her left several figures headed quickly up the slope in her direction. Instinctively she curled her lips back, as the muscles in the upper jaw pressed downward, forcing the killing teeth to descend into place. Her body tensed. She relaxed a bit as she recognized Burl Tanner. He carried someone thrown over his shoulder like a sack of grain. Two women followed, Margie Williams and someone else she did not recognize.

"Look what I found," Burl said, dumping the still form of Sara Way onto the grass.

CHAPTER TWENTY-ONE

Sara stepped from the outhouse head on into Burl
Tanner. Clapping his hand over her mouth, he dragged
her back into the shadow of the building. Sara
struggled to break free as he held her tightly around the
waist with one hand and prevented her from crying out
with the other. She still carried the wooden cross she
had pulled from the yard. She swung it over her head,
feeling it make solid contact with Burl. He released her
waist, caught the cross in mid-swing and tore it from
her grasp. It was not possible. She had seen what
crosses did to vampires but Burl held it as easily in his
hand as she had. He tossed the cross down into the
muck and stripped the revolver from her belt.

Sara knew she was dead but she resolved to go
down fighting. Twisting her head from side to side, she
worked her mouth open and bit down with all she had
into the flesh of Burl's hand.

He grunted and Sara felt his body stiffen with pain
but he did not cry out. Instead, he spun her around to
face him, tore his hand from her mouth and swung.
Sara drew a breath, preparing to scream, but she never
got the chance. In the darkness, Sara never saw the
punch coming. His fist whistled through the air

connecting solidly between her eyes, an explosion of light and pain, followed by a dark nothingness.

He snarled as he stood over her, glancing toward the house. McBride still sat in his chair undisturbed by anything. If Truitt's vision were half as good as Burl's, he would be blazing away. If Truitt's hearing had half the acuity of Burl's he would be pumping his legs toward the outhouse at the first catch of Sara's surprised breath. As it were, Truitt sat smoking quietly while Burl knelt beside Sara and lifted her onto his shoulder. There was no need for any real effort at stealth. Even with the added weight of the young woman, Burl rose easily, moving quietly and quickly toward the trees. The women were waiting as he entered the shelter of the branches. They crowded around as he laid Sara on the ground. It did not take long at all.

They were still kneeling alongside Sara when Truitt and Sam came from the house to look for her. Wilda tensed when the men began to follow Burl's tracks. She trembled with excitement. A burning inside her was not entirely related to the hunt. She had wanted Truitt for years; since he had first come to call on Ellie. No one knew—she had gone to great lengths to keep it secret—no one, not even Margie, who knew her better than anyone alive. Now, it no longer mattered. Now, Truitt drew near and she would take him.

The two men stopped some fifty yards away and spoke quietly together. Wilda almost snarled in frustration when they turned back to the house. Rachael put a restraining hand on Wilda's arm, realizing her intent, but Wilda shrugged it off. She rose to her feet, slipping silently into the open and quickly closing the distance between herself and the target of her blind intentions. Had she started just a few seconds sooner, Duncan would not have had the light to spot her until it was too late. Just a few seconds sooner and he would not have been able to fire into the ensuing melee without fear of hitting either Sam or Truitt. As it was, it was still close.

The first load of shot ripped into her upper left shoulder, spinning her around as the surprised Sam dived into the mud. The shot passed so close to Truitt that it ripped his hat from his head in passing. Another round came a heartbeat later, catching her in the small of the back, lifting her from her feet and hurling her through the air. Wilda landed face down in the mud and her body was on fire with pain as she rolled over onto her back, kicked for a moment, then lay still. Something insider her told her the wounds were not much.

Just lay still. Just give it a minute.

She lay motionless as Amos attended Truitt. After a moment, the boy came to stand over her. She did not twitch, blink, or even breathe. Someone shouted from the porch and Amos turned away from her. That was a mistake. The pain dissipated as she gathered her strength, drew her lips back and rose to her feet.

* * *

Chloe elbowed her way in, pressing her face so close to the glass pane her breath fogged it. She wiped the glass with her hand, holding her ground as others pushed and shoved for position. Duncan, Sam and Truitt stood facing the house. Amos stood behind them, several yards away. Sam appeared to be arguing with someone on the porch. Chloe's heart felt as if it stopped when she saw the dark shadow detach itself from the earth to rise behind Amos.

"Look out," she screamed, bolting away toward the door. She shoved her way through curious neighbors but heard Amos cry out before she reached the porch. Confused and startled shouts from the men greeted her

218

as she ran outside.

* * *

Amos, looking toward the house, had neither heard nor sensed Wilda behind him. He stood with his arms at his side and Wilda wrapped her arms around him with an iron grip, pinning him helplessly. He began to leap about frantically, bending his body forward for all he was worth in an attempt to avoid her teeth. Wilda danced the leaping Amos around in a circle as he struggled with all his might.

"Ain't this fun?" she said, giggling.

"Let him go, damn you," Truitt roared, bringing his shotgun to his shoulder. "I mean it. I'll blow your fat ass clean into the next county."

"Fire away, hardcase," she challenged. "You can blow me anywhere you want to long as you know this little peckerwood's coming with me."

She tightened her grip on Amos and his breath left him in a whoosh. He felt like he was caught in a vise as she squeezed him even harder. He was certain his injured ribs would give way.

"Oh . . . God . . . you're . . . killing . . . me."

"That's about the size of it, little man. Course, maybe you need killing now," she said, flinging his own words back at him.

"Stop it, Wilda. Stop it," Truitt said, lowering his shotgun. "Don't hurt him."

Wilda relaxed her grip slightly, allowing Amos a little breathing room. She smiled at Truitt. "That's better. A lady always appreciates a sweeter attitude from the men-folks."

Amos sagged in her arms, eyes rolling as his breath came in harsh, rasping gasps.

Truitt took a more diplomatic tack. Holding the barrel, he let the stock of the shotgun rest on the muddy ground as he spoke with his sister-in-law in a contrite tone of voice.

"I didn't mean nothing by it, Wilda. You just scared me. That's all. Don't none of us want no trouble. I'm damned proud to see you've not been hurt none. I've always thought a lot of you. Now, you just let my boy go and you can go on about your business. Ain't nobody here going to mess with you."

She laughed, hugging Amos close to her body almost affectionately.

"Well, that's right Christian of you, Truitt. All I got to do is turn this little horse's ass loose and you'll just mosey on back to the house, right?"

"That's about the size of it."

Wilda tossed her hair back and laughed again.

"I can't check right now, my hands are full, but did someone write 'stupid' on my forehead? Who do you think you're talking to?"

"I mean it. Let my boy go. I'll do whatever you want me to."

"Suppose I want you to come with me?"

Truitt didn't hesitate.

"I'll do that, too."

Freeman, Kyle and Win came down from the porch, fanning out alongside Sam, Duncan and Truitt. Others followed their lead. Wilda fixed her brother with a murderous glare.

"Well, look here," she said. "If it ain't the country squire himself. Don't get no ideas about being a hero, Freeman. Don't none of you get no ideas like that. I'll break this little bastard's spine before you can spit."

Freeman's eyes could not have been wider as he stared, speechless, at the strange beast in the familiar disguise of his sister's body. Duncan, on the other hand, was not so awestruck. He broke the twelve-gauge down and ejected the empty shells, calmly sliding two fresh loads into the chambers and snapping the weapon closed while the obviously enraged Wilda looked on. He spat a stream of tobacco juice off-handedly, almost casually, in her direction, his every movement studiously taunting.

"Won't do you no good, bitch," he said, in a cordial tone of voice. "I'm going to kill you anyway."

Duncan drew the hammers of the shotgun. With a roar of rage, Wilda tightened her grip on Amos. His scream of pain cut off, his face became a rictus of silent agony.

"Have it your way," Wilda said, lifting her nephew into the air.

A new level of pain coursed through Amos as he drew his knees up toward his chest, struggling for breath. Truitt reacted with lightning speed, flipping his shotgun up and gripping it with both hands. The struggling Amos, drawing his legs up, exposed the lower limbs of Wilda. Truitt shot from the hip, squeezing off a round and the kneecap of Wilda's left leg exploded, the leg nearly severed by the close-range blast.

The woman howled in pain as the leg collapsed beneath her. She momentarily loosened her grip on Amos as she fell to the ground. A moment was all he needed. He flung his body sideways as they hit the ground and felt Wilda's strong arms slide away from him. He rolled fifteen feet away as all hell broke loose around him.

Nearly a dozen men rushed forward to surround Wilda, firing at point blank range. Round after round tore into her, sending geysers of mud, blood, flesh and cloth flying through the air. She died almost instantaneously, but the men fired into her body until nothing was left but an unrecognizable lump. Armageddon could not have been more sudden, more violent. Armageddon could not have been louder. As the last report rolled away to echo through the hills,

Duncan stepped forward to look down at what was left of Wilda, chewing his tobacco nervously, energetically.

"There," he said, spitting on the body, "let's see you get up now, goddamn you."

Amos cradled his ribs as he struggled to a sitting position. He was covered with mud and blood–some of which was his own–in his hair, his nose, his mouth. He spat out clods of bloody earth, trembling with fear, thinking there might be bits of lung there as well.

"Good Lord," he said, rocking himself back and forth. "She killed me. Good Lord, I think she killed me."

Chloe rushed across the yard as Truitt and Duncan helped Amos to his feet.

"You're all right, boy," Truitt said, soothingly. "Ain't no real damage been done."

As Chloe embraced him, Amos winced, stiffening in pain and catching his breath with a sharp hiss. She realized what she was doing and stepped back, a look of concern on her face. Amos brought his hands to his chest as he coughed weakly.

"Dang," he said.

* * *

Sara opened her eyes to the star-peppered sky, lying motionless with the wind tugging gently at her hair, blades of grass tickling her cheek. She was afraid to move, remembering only the frightening figure of Burl Tanner appearing out of the darkness. It took her a moment to work up the courage even to breathe. She sensed the others around her, sensed that the worst had happened.

"You can go ahead and get up now, if you're of a mind to. Like it or not, you're among the only friends you're likely to have from here on out."

Sara turned her head toward the voice and found

222

herself staring at a stranger; a dark-haired young woman with striking gray eyes.

"What . . . what happened?"

"Huuummmph. You were there, girl. You know what happened."

The plaid shirt was still stained and tacky with blood as Sara brought her hand to her throat. She felt her way across her face, saving the mouth for last, knowing what she would find there.

"Good Lord."

"It is a bit of a shock, I reckon. But give it some time, Sara."

"Who are you? How do you know me?"

The woman threw her head back and laughed, dark hair streaming behind her.

"Why, I've known you all your life. And you know me, too. Just give it some time."

Sara leaned forward, eyes wide in surprise.

"Tildy?"

"None other. Welcome home."

"Welcome home?"

"Yep, welcome home," said a male voice behind her.

Sara spun around to find Percy kneeling several feet away.

"Hidey, baby girl," he said with a grin. "Miss me?"

CHAPTER TWENTY-TWO

"You done what?" Ellie shouted, placing her hands on her hips. She leaned into Truitt, her face a scant two inches from his own. "Now the Good Lord knows you've pulled some bone-headed stunts in your time but this just about beats all I've ever seen. You let that girl go out there all by herself? Knowing what we're up against? Have you taken leave of your senses? Lord, Lord. Sometimes you're just not worth killing."

Truitt said nothing. He watched Chloe make a fuss over Amos, who lay on a pallet in front of the fire with his head in her lap. She held a cup of whiskey-laden coffee that Amos sipped occasionally while she brushed his hair and crooned encouragement to him. It was clear that she felt something for Amos and that her ministrations were not entirely of the motherly variety.

Her care was genuine but Truitt also thought she did it as much to take her mind off things as for any other reason. While it was true that Amos had been bruised, battered, soaked to the skin and scared half to death, there was no real physical damage worth noting, nothing that wouldn't be a memory by this time next week. So, Chloe sat comforting Amos in order to comfort herself.

And while Truitt considered the situation with Amos and Chloe he was unable to escape the fact that Ellie expressed no such kind feelings for him. He could not blame her. Her mother was dead. Wilda was, thankfully, dead. Margie and Walter were missing. The strain had to go somewhere. Besides, maybe he did deserve it. He should have stopped Sara. And he had put Amos in the gravest of danger for at least the third or fourth time over the last few days. It seemed like he mishandled everything he tried to do.

Sam and Duncan watched as well. They watched him and he could feel their eyes. They, at least, had compassion for him but it was of the "better you than me" variety. He had shed his wet clothes and sat wrapped in a dry blanket. He pulled the blanket tighter around him, wishing he could hide in it, avoid all the eyes—the compassionate and the not-so-compassionate. Shivering, he took a sip of the laced coffee, feeling it burn its way into his system, creating a warm glow.

"Damn it, Truitt, I'm talking to you," Ellie said.

"That you are," he admitted. "You're sure enough doing that all right. Talking and talking and talking to me. You've been talking to me since I first walked in the door and you haven't stopped yet. You've been talking to me so much that it's a wonder my ears haven't fallen off."

"Well, somebody needs to talk to you. What in the world were you thinking? Letting Sara go off like that? Don't you know anything?"

Truitt slammed the cup down on the table. The liquid hung in the air the briefest part of a second before following the descent of the cup, splashing over it and onto the table.

"I know a few things, by God. I know enough to farm this place, keep you all fed and clothes on your back. I know that none of you have ever gone hungry on my account. I know enough to understand that

225

everything I've touched here lately has turned to shit. And I don't need you to remind me of that."

He stood suddenly, walking across the room to the stairway. He climbed three steps then turned back to Ellie with another thought.

"I'm a farmer, Ellie. That's all. And that ain't much. What am I supposed to know? I know plowing. I know crops. I know mules. None of that does me much good now. What I don't know is who died and left me general of this damned army."

Ellie said nothing as Truitt climbed the stairs and disappeared down the hallway. "Don't you think you were a mite hard on him?" Duncan Tanner asked, sitting down at the table across from her.

"Of course I was. I always am. I hate it but, God help me, I just can't seem to stop myself."

"I reckon it's hard on everybody. After what I've seen tonight, I ain't got much choice but to believe what Chloe and you all been saying. You know, if I believe that, then I got to believe that my own boy is worse than dead."

Ellie did know. She patted Duncan's hand as she got up.

"And I reckon I'd better go make it up to him," she said.

She climbed the stairs slowly. Truitt, too, was in a great deal of pain. She knew that. He had lost the same people she had and couldn't expect him not to feel that. But Truitt had also killed people–the young boy, Bill, her sister. The business with Amos and now Sara, Walter and Margie disappearing, it was all too much for either one of them. If they were going to make it, they would have to rely on one another. They were going to need one another's strength and support. Without that, the grief would be too much. Without that there would be nothing.

At the top of the stairs, she paused. She could hear

him in the bedroom. Ellie had been expressing all her pain in the guise of anger but the unfamiliar sound of Truitt's weeping planted a seed of pity that sprang forth for Truitt initially but suddenly blossomed for her as well. Her eyes stung with tears and she knelt in the hallway. Ellie crouched on the floor, lowered herself into a prone position and buried her face in her hands. It would be a little while yet before she could go through the door.

Chloe heard Ellie's sobs and toyed with the idea of going to her for a moment. She decided to leave the woman alone. After Sara's disappearance–she could not think of it as death, though she knew in her heart that it was–her own emotions were too close to the surface to predictably contain. She, too, blamed Truitt. She held her tongue but secretly enjoined a tongue-lashing by proxy at the table. Of course, she knew that Truitt was no more worthy of blame than Sara herself, or any of the others really, but someone had to take the heat. It might as well be Truitt, since he accepted the responsibility so readily.

Amos moaned, turning his head in her lap. Chloe placed her hand on his brow, stroking him gently. She wondered if Amos was always a troubled sleeper or if this was something brought on by current circumstances. She made a mental note to question Ellie about it, discretely of course, as soon as the opportunity presented itself.

He had bad dreams. She had watched him since the first night in the meadow and every time he slept, night or day, for any length of time, he would toss, turn and mumble in the grips of whatever fantastic terror he might be experiencing. Now it was happening again. Chloe hoped it was a passing thing.

Catching a movement from the corner of her eye, Chloe turned her attention to the top of the stairway. Ellie pulled herself to her feet, tugging down the hem of the dress which had ridden high up on her hips. The shadow on the wall was a mime, mimicking Ellie's every move, reflecting the quick, flitting motion of her hands as she smoothed the dress, pulled back and fluffed her hair and finally wiped her eyes. A prickle of gooseflesh crept across the back of Chloe's neck as Ellie leaned forward slightly, turned and once again brought her hands to her hair. The shadow looked exactly like the form Chloe had seen rising behind Amos a short time before and a jolt of fear shot through her. The fear passed and the shadow disappeared as Ellie entered the bedroom.

* * *

Sara looked at Percy without speaking.

"Well?" he said. "Didn't I tell you? I told you it would be different and, by God, it is ain't it?"

Keeping her silence, she turned away from him. The smile faded from her father's face.

"Look at me when I'm talking to you," he demanded, grabbing her roughly by the shoulder and turning her back to face him. "You and me been together for while, baby girl. And we're going to be together a damned sight longer, too. So, you might just as well get used to it and drop that uppity attitude of yours right now. I done told you, you're mine."

He moved toward her unexpectedly, pressing her backward into the grass. She was surprised by the ease with which she broke his grasp, pushed his hands away. His face darkened, twisted into the cruel and frightening visage she had seen in her room, as his lips drew back to reveal the twin daggers of canines that lengthened before her eyes. Sara felt her own descend as a red rage flooded through her. But a shadow fell over them and Burl Tanner was suddenly there. He stepped between them, facing Percy.

228

"Yours? Seems to me that I'm the one who brought her over," Burl said, not at all fazed by Percy's most intimidating stare. "I reckon she's just like the rest of us and that means she ain't nobody's. Nobody's and everybody's at the same time and only when she wants to be. That's the way it is, Percy. You might consider getting used to it if you intend to stay."

"She's mine," Percy argued. "I'm her daddy and can't none of you deny that. That gives me some rights, by God. Now, you can say anything you want but family is family and that's a fact. I raised her and I say she's mine."

"You're the only one who does then," Tildy said, siding with Burl. Aaron followed her lead, standing beside them. It took only a glance to tell Percy all he needed to know about how the power was divided.

"Well, old hoss," Aaron said, cordially. "Looks like ye'd be havin' a decision t'make. How's it t'be?"

Percy glanced from face to face, trying to control his anger and succeeding only slightly. After a moment, he was calm enough to let the fangs retract. He smiled, falsely contrite.

"Hell, I didn't mean nothing by it. It's just . . . well, I've always been a family man and she is my daughter and all. She just hurt my feelings, I guess. I don't know why she acts like this."

Aaron nodded, looking away as he spoke. "Just so we understand each other," he said, sitting back down on the damp ground.

"C'mon," Tildy said, taking Sara by the hand. "Take a walk with me."

* * *

After all the years together, it seemed they could communicate without saying a word. Truitt and Ellie held one another without speaking, lying still in the quiet darkness. He understood she needed him and hoped she understood he needed her. They might not make through this night, much less another one. What if she did not understand? She had certainly been rattled by her mother's death but then who wouldn't have been? No, it was not that. Ellie was upset, of course, more because her mother had died and Ellie had not had the opportunity to say to her the things she needed to say; things that would remain locked inside her because the opportunity had passed. And how common was that? Truitt did not want to find out. He did not want that to happen with him and Ellie because there was too much he needed her to know. He just did not know how to say it.

"I love you," he finally whispered.

She held him tighter, nuzzling her face into his shoulder. "That's no secret. I love you, too."

"I know I don't act right sometimes and maybe I ain't as good a man as I ought to be, but the Lord knows—."

"Hush now. I understand all that and I ain't complaining. I knew when I married you I wasn't getting no Solomon but I wasn't looking for one, either. Besides, you didn't get no Queen of Sheba."

Truitt chuckled and gave her a squeeze. "No, I guess not. But I wasn't far off." He settled back and closed his eyes.

* * *

The fog was thick. Amos heard voices all around him but he did not see anyone. He waved his arms in frustration, trying to clear the mist. Selecting a specific voice, he walked toward it, taking tiny steps for fear of falling. It seemed he was moving in the right direction, the voice straight ahead, but he drew no nearer to it nor did he ever seem further away.

230

"Who are you?" he called. "Where are you?"

The mist parted, creating a pathway that stopped at his feet. At the other end, a shadowy form appeared and walked toward him. Amos tried to back away but the fog closed in around him, solidifying, trapping him like the cricket he had once found frozen in a patch of ice; the creature's useless legs free only to wriggle–if it had been alive to wriggle them. He recognized the heavy gait and plodding side to side carriage of his grandmother.

"Well," she said, stopping in front of him and spitting a stream of snuff over her shoulder. She looked him up and down, obviously appraising him, then grinned. Her teeth were stained with tobacco and bloodstains were splattered over her clothing. The head wound distorted her, pulling her features out of shape. Discolored, swollen flesh punctuated the exit hole in her forehead.

"Well," she said again. "It looks like you sure enough caught your pecker in the wringer this time."

Amos opened his mouth to speak but could not find his voice.

"Walter turned out to be the only one of us with any sense at all," she continued. "He lit out, Amos. He sure enough lit out. And don't you go blaming him none for that."

"I'm dreaming," Amos finally choked out.

"Sure you are but what's that got to do with anything? Your dreams been telling you what to do all along but you been screwing it up. Walter was right, I'm here to say. There ain't no other choices, boy. Them that don't light out right now ain't never going to leave and that's the Lord's own truth."

"But I'm dreaming."

"That don't make no nevermind. That don't change a thing."

She turned, walking back down the eerie passageway

through the mist.

"Wait," he called out. "Wait a minute, Grandma. Where are we, anyway? Where are you going?"

"Don't rightly know, myself," she answered, disappearing into a thick swirl of smokey gray fog. The fog disappeared just as suddenly and Amos was free.

* * *

Rage burned hotly inside him as he followed the two women. He had been denied and there was never a time when such denial did not fill Percy Way with rage. He snarled deep in his throat as the muscles in his upper jaw tightened and the killing teeth snapped down into place. He could not follow his desires now either. It would not be safe. But a time would come, he told himself. A time would come. Tildy looked in his direction. He could feel her eyes on him, knew she was aware of his presence. Percy bit down in frustration, driving the teeth into his own lower lip, relishing the taste of his own blood. A time would come for reckoning.

Tildy pulled her shift over her head, letting it fall to the ground as she continued to look at Percy. She could see him well enough in the starlight, just as he could see her. She kissed the back of Sara's neck and Sara responded, tilting her head, catching a quick breath, and grinding backwards into Tildy. Soon, Sara was naked, too.

Percy breathed heavily through his mouth as he watched, blood trickling slowly from the punctured lip where the tissue was regenerating so fast that he could feel the wound closing. He brought his hand down and rubbed his open palm over the tight bulge in the crotch of his overalls.

"Forever's a Godawful long time, baby girl," he said in a harsh whisper.

CHAPTER TWENTY-THREE

Bacon fat spat and sizzled in the black iron pan. Smoke from cooking meat rose, mingled with numerous other odors in the house, and swirled and congealed into an overpowering atmosphere that assailed Amos's nostrils in a way that was less than pleasant. It was too close in here; much too close. Unwashed bodies, tobacco smoke, liquor, coffee, blood, fear, all jumbled together, heavy, pungent; Amos walked onto the porch to escape. He found Win and Kyle Larrimer standing guard. He nodded to them, noting the somber expressions of the youngsters as they nodded back.

Kyle was fourteen and Win sixteen but Amos thought of them now as youngsters. That was what the past few days had done to him. He was ages older than his peers. Events had created a distance between Amos and any vestiges of youth he could recognize. He felt old, older than he could ever have imagined, older than he ever wanted to be.

He had been awake a while, hours before the rest of the household had begun to stir. The encounter with Wilda had left him little room for sleeping. But that was good. It had given him time alone to think. There was certainly a great deal to think about. Not just events, though events alone were enough to boggle his mind, but about the visions as well.

It had taken an eternity, or so it seemed, to find his way back to his body after the fog released him. The voices continued to whisper to him and, as he moved slowly through the mist, hands feeling in front of him like a blind man, shadowy figures rose before him then disappeared again. Amos, listening closely to the voices, began to recognize them after he had heard them a few times and some were voices he knew from the before life, the life where the sun rose and set and the seasons passed and the people one knew remained the people one knew. Yes, that was before; the before life; the past life; the life that was no more.

Occasionally, a face appeared, looming, floating, disembodied, startling, only to vanish as quickly as it had appeared. The ghost of the young boy his father had killed hovered about, features ruined by the rude restructuring the heavy lead projectile visited upon his face. The soldier was there. Bill Way, Tildy, all swam around him like bluegills at the creek swarming a kicking grasshopper, darting in one at a time to strike at it. He found his way back, to his body, his pallet by the fire, to Chloe but the voice of Mabeline echoed in his mind throughout the morning. Now he sat on the porch trying to make sense of it all.

"Your dreams been telling you what to do all along, but you've been screwing it up."

As he processed the images, attempted to fathom the meanings, Amos allowed himself to consider everything, every possibility and he discounted nothing, disputed nothing. He took things as they were, piecing images, taken at face value, carefully together. The final result of his evaluation was hardly encouraging and left him with a sinking feeling of despair. The people of the valley were lost. For them, there was no victory.

The door creaked open behind him and his father joined him on the porch.

"Getting nigh onto time we get started," Truitt said, peering at the sky. "I got me a feeling that this is going to be one long day."

"I got to talk to you," Amos said. "Can we walk off a piece so we can be alone?"

Truitt nodded and walked toward the barn, Amos pacing him. After fifty yards, and well away from anyone, he stopped.

"So? What's this all about?"

"You're going to think I'm crazy," Amos said.

"Won't be the first time."

"Yeah, but what I've got to say don't make a lot of sense."

Truitt chuckled softly but there was no humor in the sound. "Hell, what does? Everything's crazy, boy. Everybody. Not a blessed thing makes sense to me anymore." He took out his pipe and tobacco, prepared a smoke and waited for Amos.

Amos was not sure where to begin. He should have done this before daylight. This was a discussion suited for midnight, when moonlight and shadows painted the most fantastic of tales with the hue of truth or, at least, the possibility of truth. In the sunlight, Amos felt foolish, embarrassed. In the tricky reality of daylight where the most profound of unpleasant truths were seen through the lenses of wishful fantasy, Amos had clear vision. He could no longer see things that way. Goddamn it all to hell, he thought. He just could not see things that way. He did not doubt himself any longer. He could not pretend that there was hope any longer. The only hope that he could find was the most unreasonable hope that he was wrong.

And he was not.

"Walter was right," he said. "I know it as sure as I know my own name. If we go up against these, these

235

monsters, these vampires, whatever they are, we're going to lose. And there's no sense making out like there's any other possibility. The only chance we have of getting out of here with our souls is to pack up and leave, right now, this minute. We should have left last night. Sundown will be too late."

Truitt looked at his feet, rubbing at the stubble on his chin thoughtfully. He did not seem surprised. For Amos, it only confirmed what he had been feeling for some time. Still, he did not like to hear it said aloud.

"Yeah, I know," Truitt said. "I knew before we ever got back to the house that first night. I knew like you know, I guess, like Tildy. But I can't see it as clear. If they really want us, there's nothing we can do is there?"

"No, sir, not a thing. We can fight but it won't change much."

Truitt nodded.

"Walter knew it, too, didn't he?"

"Yes, sir, he did."

"And he ain't dead is he, Amos?"

"No, sir, he ain't dead," Amos wanted to comfort his father but he did not know how. "He ain't one of them either," he added. "He just left. That's all."

Truitt squatted on his heels and pulled a blade of grass. He inserted the long stem into his mouth and squinted up at Amos, who stood with the sun at his back.

"I thank God," he said. "I thank God for that. How is it we know things? You, me, Tildy? How is it you know all this?"

"God's own mystery, I reckon. Just do. It ain't nothing I asked for, believe me. I see things with Tildy's eyes sometimes. And I saw Grandma last night. In my dreams. She told me some things."

"You see things clear all right. With me it's all muddled. Maybe I'm just not smart enough to figure it out. I don't know. But I think I'm blessed for that. I don't envy you, son, but I believe you. I just don't think anyone else will."

"I don't think I should be too concerned about that, really. That's what worries me. I think that before this day's over, there won't be a soul left unconvinced."

Truitt stood up, spitting the grass stem from his mouth.

"By then, it will be too late won't it?"

"Yes, sir," Amos answered, looking towards the mountains. "For a lot of us. For a lot of us, it's too late, now."

* * *

The sun climbed higher over the eastern mountains spilling an ocean of light down the dark slopes like a flow of golden liquid. Droplets of water clinging to the trees and foliage glistened brightly in the sunlight, going out in a blaze of glory as the sun burned them away. Tildy lay atop a gentle slope in the meadow and watched sunlight spread over the valley, flowing toward her and Sara.

Sara's head rested on Tildy's thigh and Tildy absent-mindedly ran her hand through the girl's hair as she watched the new day, wondering what that day might bring. She and Amos would meet again today and there would be blood.

Lord, there would be blood.

* * *

They certainly did not look like fighting men.

No, they looked exactly like what they were– farmers. Truitt sat astride the fidgeting gray-whiskered mule, holding a repeating rifle and looking every bit the reluctant general. His shotgun hung over his back, strung from a cord, and a pair of revolvers was stuck in

237

his belt. Nearly everyone among them rode mules and mules broken to the harness at that. These mules were resentful every time they had to carry someone on their backs and the hustle, and the excitement, and the confusion and the fear was doing nothing to improve their attitudes. Not one of them, mule or rider, was having his best day.

Sam, Freeman and two other riders were the only ones with horses. Sam had even affected a soldier's look—or, at least, had attempted to. His late father's Confederate cavalryman's belt was strapped around his waist and held a .36 caliber Navy Colt and a heavy saber. A gray infantryman's cap, pushed back on his head, seemed totally out of place; particularly since it was complemented by a badly faded red-checked flannel shirt that had seen entirely too many winters and equally faded overalls.

At another time, on some other morning when the sun was up and the world was as clean as the spring rain could make it and her happiness with Amos was not tinged with grief and death and loss and terror; in some other valley where human beings did not murder and drink the blood of other human beings; in that place, in that time, Chloe would have found them comical. Not today. Not here. And if she had been moved to amusement, their set faces, and horrified eyes would certainly have stifled it. These men, and some were barely that, were going out to perform a frightful task. Chloe could tell them what they might encounter but that would do no good. It had done no good the night before. And Amos rode with them.

He, of all people, knew what they were up against. He knew their cause was lost and still he rode with them. Amos had spoken his mind but, as Truitt had predicted, there were not many prepared to listen.

Amos had walked her to the smoke-house that morning to collect a slab of bacon. They had made

238

love in the cool darkness, the rough planks pressed into her back and buttocks, her skirt bunched up around her waist. She clutched him tightly and the force of their effort rattled the walls, causing the meat hanging from the rafters to bounce and sway as if an earthquake were rumbling through. Neither of them gave any thought to the tenderness of Amos's ribs as they clung together. They gave no thought to the fact that the smokehouse had served as both a larder and funeral parlor over the past few days. The act of life drove all thoughts of the dead away from them. Chloe was amazed to find herself crying as she reached her climax and pushed through to the other side. If it had not been for the wall, she felt both of them would have collapsed together.

Amos's breathing became even as he nuzzled his face into her neck. Eventually, he raised his head and she felt her muscles tighten to hold him inside her, gripping him, reluctant to let him slip away from her. He blushed as he arranged his clothing, even turning away from her to tuck his shirt-tail in. She loved him as much for his sporadic modesty as she did anything else. She loved him? Well, how about that, she thought. She loved him.

"I, uh, I ain't much good with words," he said. "But, you know, well, you know how I feel about you. I mean, I, uh, think a lot about you and, well, you mean a lot to me."

"I know what you mean, Amos," she said, partly for his sake and because it was true. He was, indeed, having a difficult time expressing himself. "You might just say, 'I love you, Chloe'."

"I love you, Chloe," he said in such a rush that it almost sounded like one word. He spit it out like a willful kid with a mouthful of castor oil but Chloe embraced the words anyway. It would take some time, some practice, but she would give him every opportunity to work on it–if they had the time.

Amos sighed in relief and picked up his rifle and the side of bacon. "I reckon we'd better be getting on back to the house before somebody comes looking for us," he said.

"I guess so," she said, following him. She could not help but smile. She hoped he did not have to do anything else as hard as saying "I love you," today.

Now she watched him ride away.

The warm feeling she had held with the memory of the morning settled in her stomach. It settled there and trembled.

* * *

They crossed the meadow toward the tree line where the forest began at the foot of Hog Heaven Hill. Tildy stopped and looked behind them. The high grass swayed in the wind and crows circled aimlessly over the meadow. The others stopped as well. Aaron stood beside her.

"You feel it?" she asked.

"Aye, I feel it."

There was nothing in the meadow, nothing on the horizon. But there was certainly something on the wind, blowing inside her, through her.

"Aye," Aaron said again. "Aye, I feel it, too. We'll grow no older waitin'.

CHAPTER TWENTY-FOUR

The motion of the mule rocked Amos from side to side as the animal plodded through the grass at a leisurely pace. The sun was at his back as he rode toward the mountain. It was going to be a beautiful day. Already the temperature was climbing and the wind sweeping gently down the slope was soft, wet, fragrant and alive. The morning mist burned away early but the ground was still damp from the thunderstorms the day before. The hooves of the sure-footed mule made sucking noises pulling from the soggy earth only to sink into it again with the next step. Amos rode easily, appreciating the warmth of the sun. It might be the only pleasure he experienced today–the only pleasure other than Chloe.

Amos had to ride with the men. He did not know why exactly but he had to. Perhaps it was loyalty, perhaps curiosity, he was not sure. Perhaps it was because he was merely a fool, choosing to die with friends and family rather than to live on his own. It made no sense, to him or Truitt. Both of them knew, beyond the shadow of a doubt, that they were riding into defeat, death, and God knew what else.

He had not been surprised when his attempts at

explaining his visions were met with skepticism. He had expected that, after all and it was understandable. Why would Duncan Tanner, Sam Larrimer, his uncle Freeman, any of them, simply walk away, leaving everything they knew, everything they loved, everything they'd worked for? Why would they abandon everything on the strength of his dreams? Still, some of them entertained the idea. Others, like Sam Larrimer, became angry.

"I can't give you proof," Amos stated flatly. "All I can say is what I've said and there you have it. There's not a soul in this room would be happier than me if I was wrong. But I'm not, whether you believe me or not, it's the truth. If we don't get out of here today, we're not going to."

Some of the children began to cry and pulled closer to their mothers. Sam looked at the crying kids, a flush of color sweeping up his neck and across his face. His big, bulbous nose seemed to absolutely shine.

"Now look what you've gone and done," he said. "You didn't have no call to go scaring women and kids like that. What's the matter with you, boy?"

The question was not rhetorical. It was clear that Larrimer expected an answer and equally clear he did not expect an acceptable one. Amos stepped away from the fireplace and closer to Sam.

"It's not meanness, Mr. Larrimer," he said, raising his hand and pointing eastward. "It's the truth. Over yonder's the coast." Amos pointed in various directions, stabbing his finger in the air as he made his point. "Yonder's the mountains. Yonder's Alabama. Yonder's Kentucky, the Carolina's. There's lots of country out there yet."

"Well I reckon you're up on your geography," Sam interrupted belligerently. "But over yonder ain't our land. This here is. You telling us that we should just shuck it all, without even putting up a fight?"

Amos dropped his arms, sighing in resignation. He glanced from face to face and shook his head as he spoke again.

"Without a fight? Hell, man, I've been fighting for all I'm worth for the better part of a week. I've been fighting monsters—we're not up against people; I've been fighting myself, my own weakness, my child's mind, telling me that all I have to do is close my eyes and everything will go away; and I've been fighting you, too, all of you who tell me that I'm crazy and refuse to believe your own eyes. Maybe you're the crazy one, Mr. Larrimer. If we were up against people, I'd be for standing our ground, too. But if them things out there are anything like human beings—."

Amos stopped for a moment and collected himself. Larrimer waited for him to finish.

"Well," Amos went on, calmly, evenly. "If them things are human beings. Well, I'll smile and kiss a pig if they are. You seen Wilda." Amos stepped close to Sam, in intimate, earnest proximity. "Good Lord, Sam, you seen Wilda. She took two loads of buckshot, jumped up and damned near broke me into pieces."

"Yeah. Yeah, I saw that all right. But, by God, she's still laying out there ain't she? Them things are powerful strong and they take a lot of killing. I'll give you that. But they do die."

Amos shook his head and walked over the window, looking outside as he spoke.

"There's nothing more I can say. I don't know what else I can tell you. But you saw Wilda. She was my aunt; she helped raise me, loved me, and I loved her. And you saw what she was like. Margie's out there, too. Margie and Sara and Burl and Tildy and Mr. Way and the Lord knows how many others. I'm not talking about killing strangers, Mr. Larrimer. I'm talking about killing our friends and relations. Is it worth it? Is anything we got worth that? You willing

243

to do that to Kyle? Win? Maybe even little Roy?"

The question took Sam aback. He glanced quickly at his children. Roy stood silently, meeting his father's eyes, waiting for an answer.

"That ain't the way it is," Sam said, side-stepping the issue. "They ain't out there, they're here. They're all right and they'll stay all right if we do what we're supposed to do. And we're supposed to protect our own, provide for them, not drop everything and run, dragging them off to God knows where every time trouble comes our way. My kids are fine and they're going to stay fine because I aim to put an end to this shit right now. Today."

A murmur of approval swept through the assembly and Amos noted the general nodding of heads as most of the men agreed with Sam. He had known before he ever started that he would not change much but still he had a sinking feeling, the feeling of defeat.

"I ain't no coward, Mr. Larrimer. I'm scared, sure enough, but I won't run from a fight. If you all go, then I'm going, too. But listen to me. Even if we do come out on top—and we won't—things will never be the same around here again. If we kill every one of them, we won't feel safe around here ever again. This place is ruined, for good and all. You think me, you, or any of these good people here are going to shut their eyes here ever again? Sleep through the night again? As long as we stay, they stay with us, even if it's only in our memories. Now, if we're going to fight, we'd best be on our way."

Fifteen minutes later, they were.

* * *

"There's over thirty of us here," Sam said, reigning his horse up beside Amos. Sam's face was partly shadowed by the bill of the cap he wore but Amos didn't need to see his face to detect the attempt at bravado.

"I know that. But you still don't understand what we're up against."

"Well, they're powerful strong, I seen that much last night, but they ain't stronger than a Long Tom. We're going to be all right, Amos. Let your mind rest easy."

"Mr. Larrimer," Amos said, careful to keep his voice even and matter of fact. "My mind's at ease. But my mind's at ease because I've made my peace with what we're doing, not because I'm whistling my way through a graveyard. I'm not real sure about the particulars but I am sure about the outcome. We are not going to be all right. Not by a long shot."

"Suit yourself," Sam said.

"Looky yonder," Win sang out, standing in the stirrups and pointing. Amos looked in the direction indicated. A head protruded above the grass. A man leapt from hiding and fled across the meadow toward the forest. Three others rose like apparitions to follow him. Sam drew his saber, waving it above his head as he spurred his horse to a gallop. He brought the saber down in front of him, pointing at the four running men as he raced after them.

"Let's get them, boys! Charge!"

"Jesus Christ," Truitt swore, riding up alongside Amos. "Charge? Charge? Who the hell does Sam think he is? Stonewall Jackson?"

If Sam imagined himself a soldier, he was wrong. He was even more in error if he thought his companions were. There was no order, no discipline, no chain of command. Sam covered fifty yards or more before anyone in his group made the first move to follow him. Kyle was the first, then Win, then most of the group decided to go.

The running figures were well out of shotgun range when the mounted men opened fire. Once again, the meadow was filled with the roar of gunfire and billows of powder smoke rolled thickly over the grass. The reluctant mules balked, spun and bucked, unseating fully a third of the riders before turning and bolting for home. Several of those who managed to stay in the saddle found themselves involved in a retreat they had little to say about.

The animals that remained continued to spin, milling, bumping into each other and screaming frantically as their riders kept firing weapons. Two men were shot down by their own comrades as their mounts carried them into the line of random fire. One of them was Freeman. Duncan Tanner rode recklessly along the dangerous line, shouting, waving his hat.

"Stop shooting! Stop shooting, Goddamn it! You're shooting your own fool selves!"

The gunfire subsided as Amos made his way through the confusion. Dead and wounded men were on the ground and not one was a vampire. What an army. Casualties without an enemy shot being fired. Sam and a handful of others disappeared into the forest. Blood pulsed in Amos's ears like a drumbeat and the gooseflesh crawled across his neck at the realization of what was happening.

"No! Not into the woods!" Amos shouted. "Don't follow them into the woods!"

Spurring the mule into pursuit, Amos rode as hard as he could. He continued to shout but his exhortations fell upon deaf ears. Caught up in the excitement of the chase, the men did not hesitate but entered the woods at a gallop, darting around and between trees. The single-minded chase strung them in a ragged line covering fifty yards or so, leaving each man to his own resources.

The vampires fell on them from the shadows, pulling the men from their mounts. Burl Tanner rose in front of Sam's horse. The old gelding planted its feet

246

in the dirt to avoid trampling a human being and Sam pitched violently forward in the saddle, his hat tumbling from his head. He regained his balance, if not his dignity, and stood in the stirrups as the horse tried to back away from Burl. Sam swung the saber with all his might, guiding the heavy blade toward Burl's head.

Burl made no attempt to move as Sam's down stroke stopped abruptly, the saber and Sam hopelessly caught in a tangle of wild grape vines dangling like a canopy from the pines. The gelding continued to wheel and Sam was pulled from the saddle, still trying to extricate himself from the vines. He heard the horse bolting back toward the meadow as he fought to free himself, toes barely touching the ground. He could not reach the pistol in his belt. He would die without firing a round.

Laughing aloud, Burl came for him.

"Hidey, general," Burl said.

He seized Sam's arms and tore him effortlessly from the grip of the vines. Sam's eyes widened as Burl pulled him close, biting into his throat. Eyes bulging now, tongue lolling from his mouth, Sam fought for air. The sky, broken by the limbs of trees, danced in his vision, spinning, swirling and sinking into a quiet darkness. There were screams all around him but Sam heard none of them.

He never even heard his own.

* * *

Truitt dismounted and knelt beside Freeman, who groaned as Truitt rolled him over. The shot had entered his back, pellets careening, ripping him to pieces inside as they tore through vital organs. Truitt took one look and knew Freeman would not survive. Blood poured from the ragged tear and, as Freeman coughed, a stream of dark, oxygenated blood gushed

247

over the front of his shirt. His frightened eyes found Truitt, and Truitt did not have the poker face to make things easy on him.

"Dang," Truitt said, cradling Freeman's head.

Freeman tried to speak but his body died around the words, sealing them inside forever. His head lolled, eyes rolling back as Truitt let the body slump limply back to the ground. Men picked themselves up and tried to catch their bolting mounts. Truitt had seen Amos enter the trees and his heart had sunk. Death lay beneath the trees.

"Lord, get us out of this one," he heard Duncan Tanner say. "Get us out of this one and I'm gone."

* * *

Nine men rode into the forest. None rode out. The terrain was relatively easy for a man on foot but it was another matter for mounted men. Amos heard their startled screams as he pulled back on the reins, halting the mule well clear of the dark edge of the forest. It was not just a loss of nine men for their side, he knew, but an equal gain in force for the other. Three more, dead in the meadow, would do more to convince the others to leave than any amount of talk on Amos's part.

He clucked to the mule, digging his heels into the animal's flanks as he urged it toward the group of men in the clearing. Amos saw the vampires rise from concealment in the grass, rushing the men.

There were two groups of vampires. Amos was caught between them.

* * *

Sam had not been a soldier, nor had Truitt, but Aaron had. He had fought the French, the British twice and the Indians more times than he could count. In fact, Aaron was an old hand at combat and he was quite good at it. He watched from the high ground as his guerilla troops waded through the confused men of the valley, easily outmaneuvering the ragged army of farmers. It would not be long now.

* * *

Several of the men froze, staring as the creatures descended upon them in an unexpected onslaught. Truitt, too, stood immobile, too shocked to react. Duncan Tanner, wisely leaping from the back of his mule, fired his shotgun no more than ten feet away. The jarring report brought Truitt to his senses as a charging vampire did a complete back flip, landing heavily on the ground as a misty spray of blood hung in the air. Duncan dropped the shotgun and pulled his revolvers from his belt. He took careful aim and fired, dropping another vampire.

People scurried in every direction, making it hard to tell friend from foe. Some of the panicked men ran toward the trees, others dropped their weapons and ran for home, two stood helplessly unable to defend themselves as the vampires pulled them down. A dark-skinned woman crossed in front of Truitt, pursuing a fleeing man. Truitt shot her in the back of the head.

"Stay together! Stay together!" Duncan shouted, moving into position beside Truitt. Pull on in slow. Take aim, damn it, take aim!"

Truitt followed his lead, grabbing young Pat Coughlin, Duncan's nephew and pulling them into line with them.

"Don't just stand there, man. Use that gun," Truitt said.

Pat fired. Another vampire went down, only to leap to his feet again. Both Truitt and Duncan swung their weapons to bear on their wounded enemy. This time, he stayed down. The stragglers caught on and the men closed ranks, sporadic fire becoming a withering barrage. The vampires fell back.

"Pull on back out of here slow," Duncan ordered. "Keep 'em at a distance. Pick your shots and make them count."

The vampires held at bay now that the farmers made a more orderly retreat. When it was apparent that they were not being pursued, Duncan called a short halt to take account of their losses before continuing to the McBride farm on foot. The losses were horrendous, nineteen men, almost two-thirds of their original force. Duncan looked at Truitt, utter hopelessness etched into his face.

"We should have listened to Amos," he said. "There ain't nothing in the world worth this. Nothing in the world. When we get home, I'm quits. The sun won't set on me in these parts."

"I reckon you'll have plenty of company," Truitt replied.

CHAPTER TWENTY-FIVE

Amos wheeled the mule to the right and urged the animal into a gallop, riding parallel to the trees and well into the meadow. The vampires were fast but they weren't four-legged fast. None of them could keep up with the mule, not as long as they remained in the trees anyway.

His hat fell off his head as the rough-gaited beast bounced him in the saddle. Amos gripped the pommel, allowing the animal to have its head as he squeezed tightly with his thighs. The next thing he knew, he was airborne. The terrified mule, running in a dead panic, bore down on a fallen log in the high grass. It veered away at the last moment and lost its footing in the wet soil.

Amos was thrown from its back as the mule tumbled head over heels, regained its footing and continued on its way without a backwards glance. Amos, too, was on his feet in an instance, running into the underbrush with the same fear-driven intensity.

He wasted no time as he tore through the brush. He knew exactly where he was going. And, though he had no idea where any of the vampires might be, Baptizing Creek lay only a few hundred feet away. If he

251

could make it to the creek, he could stop to consider his next move. If not, well, there would be no next move to consider.

As he ran, he pressed his hand against his hunting sack, holding it tightly to his side so that it would not tangle in the brush. He clutched the Long Tom in his left hand, using it to ward off twigs and branches in an unsuccessful attempt to protect his face from their lashes.

The wet fabric of the sack, as well as the broken glass rattling inside it, told him that his shotgun was now his only weapon. Even if he made it to the creek, he had no other container for the water. There was no sign of the creatures as he exited the trees, increasing his speed as he headed with single-minded determination for the creek.

* * *

Chloe sat on the porch with Ellie, watching some of the younger children playing in the yard. The muffled explosions of the guns stopped the youngsters in mid-step. There was not one word of argument as Mrs. Tanner ushered them into the house. Chloe stared over the rolling terrain of the fields. Even at this distance, smoke seemed to be visible but maybe it was a trick of the eyes. She scanned the horizon but could see nothing beyond the crest of the first hill. Several moments later, another volley of shots rang out followed immediately by yet another. Even to her untrained ear, the roar of organized volleys sounded measured, purposeful, effective. The men were giving them a fight.

"Lordy," Ellie said, nervously, flitting with the collar of her dress.

The children who had thundered up the steps only moments before, came to the windows, pressing their noses against the panes, trying to see what Chloe imagined, a rag-tag army cutting down the foe. But Ellie flinched with each new echoing wave pealing across the valley. Chloe wrapped her arms around Ellie's shoulders and led her inside.

"Rest easy, Mrs. McBride. Rest easy. The men are giving them what for now."

Ellie did not respond. She stared toward the meadow as if she could cover the distance by force of will. The gunfire abated and silence reclaimed the countryside. Inside the farmhouse, silence only intensified the anxiety. Soon, the women and some of the more adventurous children, ventured back onto the porch in a flood of chattering conjecture. But all they had were questions and answers would take time. They all were willing, even eager, to embrace the most positive possibilities, to assume an attitude of bravado, of hope. They reassured one another that the venture had undoubtedly been a success. Caught up in this, they did not notice when the first riderless mule crested the hill.

"Here comes somebody now," Roy Larrimer said, pointing at the animal.

Chloe moved over to the porch railing. The mule was joined by two others, veering eastward, away from the farmhouse. A sinking feeling swept over her. She leaned against a column post. It was not long until she saw the figure of a man, running, staggering and stumbling toward the house.

"Oh, Lordy," she whispered.

* * *

Amos gasped for breath as he ran, ribs and lungs on fire. Once again, he was convinced that Wilda had broken something inside him. The sharp pain coursed through his chest, stabbing him with each inhalation.

He breathed through his mouth, fighting back an almost overpowering urge to just give up, sit down, catch his breath and allow whatever was going to happen to happen. He coughed and a warm liquid jetted into his mouth. Amos recognized the taste. He spat a clot, watching it arch outward to splat onto the grass. Dark blood. Lung blood.

"I knew it," he grunted aloud, legs pumping furiously. "I knew it. The fool done killed me."

He felt, rather than saw, the group of vampires running swiftly along the creek to intercept him. A glance to his right confirmed what he already knew. Burl Tanner led a group of five trying to position themselves between him and the safety of the creek. He veered left, running even faster, pushing himself to his limit as the distance closed between them. He hardly felt his feet touch the ground.

But Burl moved faster. Every time Amos glanced his way, Burl was gaining on him. Amos took one last look ahead and then back to Burl. Suddenly he knew. They would not catch him. They could not catch him. He had done it. The distance they had to cover was too great.

It would not even be that close.

In a matter of seconds, he would be on the other side, catching his breath, while the empty-handed monstrosities snarled and gnashed their teeth in frustration. Already Burl's companions had slowed to a walk, giving up the chase. Burl, too, accurately gauging his chances for success, also gave up pursuit. Amos laughed aloud, turning back to concentrate on the ground before him.

He barely had time to note the figure appearing from nowhere before a jarring blow sent him reeling backwards and the world was swallowed in a sea of darkness.

* * *

The mood of those waiting at the farmhouse plummeted to a depth beyond despair as the sorry group of survivors straggled back in. Mrs. Larrimer, suddenly widowed and almost childless, was beyond consolation and had mercifully collapsed. When finally brought around, it was as if a part of her had checked out on its own. She was unaware of and far removed from those who grieved around her.

Duncan Tanner wasted no time. He hardly paused long enough to put his two cents into the explanations which were demanded by frantic women who had contributed family members to the carnage of the lost cause. The men, particularly Truitt, were assailed from all sides. Truitt did his best to explain but was obviously overwhelmed. Duncan came to his rescue, terse and to the point as ever.

"Listen to me, all of you. If your men ain't back by now, they ain't coming back. Get your things together. There ain't no time for mourning and there ain't no time to waste."

Duncan Tanner was a down to earth man, thoughtful, practical, and not at all given to snap decisions. No one could ever accuse him of being skittish or hysterical. Those who knew this—recognizing the unfamiliar note of hysteria in his tone—swallowed their questions, immediately preparing for flight.

* * *

Thick, gray, almost solid, the fog parted again, creating a path for the dark figure lumbering through it. The fog banked to both sides and Mabeline seemed to be strolling through ash-hued snowdrifts. Amos watched her approach. This time the fog did not hold him immobile. The familiar rolling gait was as

255

unhurried as always, yet determined Mabeline was no different in death than she had been in life. Amos stood silently, waiting for her.

"Well," she said, stopping an arm's length away. "It don't look like you paid too much mind to what we talked about last time, Amos."

Amos said nothing. Having his nose rubbed in it in his first few seconds of the afterlife was not a good indication.

Mabeline picked distractedly at the hole in her forehead. "I can't say I'm particularly surprised by that, I reckon. Talking to you has always been a bit like talking to a stump."

"Am I . . . am I dead?"

Mabeline grinned widely.

"Dead? Naw, you ain't dead. Not yet anyway. But don't let that worry you none. It ain't all that bad. Being dead, I mean. In fact, I kind of like it."

"Where am I?"

"Why, you're here."

"Well, I don't know where 'here' is and if I'm not dead then why the hell am I wherever it is I'm at?"

Mabeline considered this for a moment.

"I don't rightly know."

"You don't rightly know what?"

"Either one, I reckon." She paused to spit a stream of snuff and glanced around her as if his question had caused her to pay attention to her surroundings for the first time.

"This here sure don't seem like anything I ever believed hell would be like. And, I reckon, given the circumstances of my life and death, that's where I could expect to find myself. I ain't seen no booger-man, no lake of fire, nothing like I ever thought torment would be. Then, on the other hand, it's a damned sight away from what I thought heaven would be like, too. But, like I said, it ain't all that bad. As for why you're here,

256

you must be looking me up. Far as I know, I ain't been haunting you."

"Hidey Amos. Hidey Ma."

Amos and Mabeline both turned as Freeman came out of the fog.

"Uncle Freeman? What in the hell happened to you?"

"Damned fool got himself killed trying to be a hero," Mabeline said, with a laugh. "One of them idiots you were with shot his ass."

"Yep," Freeman agreed. "I reckon I'll sit the rest of this dance out."

Amos looked his uncle over. He did not appear any different from when they left the farm that morning. There were no wounds, no blood, nothing.

"Then why . . .." Amos began.

"Because you didn't see him dead," Mabeline interrupted. "And, by the way, if you were to start thinking about me like I was before I got shot, then I wouldn't look such a sight myself."

Amos glanced from one to the other. Freeman stood with a grin on his face, watching his mother as she continued to finger her wound. Amos closed his eyes, willing the time away. He rolled the time back to the morning Truitt had prepared for spring plowing. It seemed like ages ago. He pictured Mabeline standing on the porch, watching his shouting father running toward her. When he opened his eyes again, she stood before him unmarred.

"Well," she said. "That's a damned sight better."

"How did you . . .?"

"Beats me. Just works that way."

Figures drifted in the mist around him. All of them speaking in hushed tones. All of them speaking at once. He felt his legs grow weak, wobbly. He had a sense of drifting, hanging in the air.

"Looks like you ain't going to be here long, boy."

257

Mabeline said.

Amos could not breathe. He was choking.

"What's going to happen?" he gasped harshly.

"I don't know, Amos. I just don't know. You didn't leave like I told you to. You had to go on with Freeman and that pack of fools that killed him. Now, you've really got yourself in a tight."

"I have to know," Amos pleaded, barely getting the words out as his throat was constricted.

"No, you don't," Mabeline said angrily. "You ain't got to know nothing. Maybe that's been the trouble all along, thinking we got to know something when we ain't got the foggiest notion of what we're dealing with or where we stand. Maybe some things just ain't for us to know. Now, you get on back out there. The next time we see each other, I suspect you'll know about all you're going to know."

Freeman raised his arm in a casual salute as Amos streaked away through the fog with the wind whistling in his ears. The figures of his grandmother and uncle dwindled to nothing in the space of a second as he hurtled away.

He stopped with a violent jolt.

* * *

In a few hours, shadows creeping down the mountains would drive away the coward sun, sending it slinking into hiding behind the peaks, pulling the last tentacles of reddened light along with it. Chloe watched from the porch still, dreading the creeping shadows, the chill of evening. There had been a time—ages ago it seemed now—when darkness had been pleasant, welcome, romantic. That time was gone and she would never get it back. She gathered Ellie's shawl about her shoulders, peering at the horizon for any hint of movement. Her hopes faded much faster than the slow demise of sunlight.

She was weary—tired of stoicism, tired of dealing with it all, tired of pain. Duncan barked orders like a master sergeant as the people prepared to leave. Chloe left the porch and climbed the stairs to Amos's room where she sat on the edge of the bed, staring vacantly out the window.

"Chloe?" Ellie said, entering the room. She took her time as she sat down beside the girl and waited patiently for her to answer. Chloe seemed to be considering what to say next and Ellie expected a drawn-out explanation. She did not get one.

"I'm not going," Chloe said simply.

Ellie put her arm around the girl and sighed.

"I didn't figure you were. I'm not going either."

CHAPTER TWENTY-SIX

The rumble of gunfire filled the air, mixed with the stench of gunpowder, the screams of the injured and dying and the rich, overriding smell of blood. Tildy had certainly been on the mark when she foresaw the blood. She looked up at Aaron, standing on a small rise like a general overseeing his troops. Tildy would not take part. The struggle was all but finished anyway. By nightfall, the survivors would be heading out of the valley.

There would be no reinforcements. Each and every fleeing soul would keep this jealously locked away, a secret not treasured but feared. If they ever mentioned it again it would only be among themselves, whispered from one to the other in still silences of late nights as they reassured themselves of their sanity. Never would any one of them ever try to convince an outsider such things had actually occurred. Aaron came over to join her and she looked up, startled. She had not noticed him leaving his position on the rise.

"That'd be that, I reckon," he said, sitting down beside her. "Them that's left broke and run."

* * *

A blue-bottle fly buzzed ceaselessly in unconcerned arrogance. Spiraling quickly skyward when confronted by a waving hand, it stopped its flight, dropped suddenly then picked up its wing-beat to again circle Percy's head. He shifted his weight from one leg to another as he crouched low in the undergrowth just inside the tree-line where the meadow ended.

Seen from atop Hog Heaven Hill, the meadow stretched below like a body of water. From up there Percy had seen how the margins dipped deeply into the trees in some places, like bays on an inland sea. He had positioned himself in the deepest part of one of the bays. Not just any bay, but the one nearest the flow of Baptizing Creek. The stream flowed along behind him beyond a small breadth of trees and another meadow bisected by the water. Sara was less than a hundred yards away. If anyone attempted to skirt the meadow, they were ready. And anyone who wanted to stay out of the trees until the very last moment would have to run across the top of Percy Way.

Percy knew Burl and the others would be heading in his direction. Aaron had arranged that, positioning his forces where, when the second wave engaged the farmer/soldiers, any stragglers would be cut off and forced this way. Burl's group would move toward him, driving the enemy, as they finished their work in the trees.

Percy smiled to himself as he squatted on his haunches. He held a three-foot length of pine limb, about two inches in diameter, and had been patiently whittling a point on it with his pocket-knife. He hoped Aaron or Burl, or that bitch, Tildy—he did not care which—would venture this way alone. If not, then there would be another time. The blue-bottle fly made another pass at his face and he swatted it away testily.

Percy did not care how they ran their business but

he had no plans whatsoever to relinquish his claim on Sara, Chloe either for that matter. In his estimation, they were his and always had been.

The rage rose up inside him again as he thought of Sara, still rejecting him time after time, and the manner in which the others supported her. It would not be long before all of that changed. As for Chloe, he would bring her over himself. Nothing, or no one, would be able to prevent that. Percy slashed savagely with the knife, the wood peeling away in long, pale curls fragrant with the turpentine smell of wet pine sap.

A crashing in the brush froze Percy, his eyes fixed in the direction of the noise. Amos McBride appeared through an opening in the trees, angling away from Burl Tanner and toward the creek. Percy, up and running in a heartbeat, plotted his course to intercept Amos. He was already in the clearing before Amos cleared the trees. Amos would take the shortest path to safety. Percy knew that as he dropped flat in the tall grass, carefully raising his head to watch as Amos headed directly for him. Burl and the others were giving him a race, running like deer as they closed on him. But Amos was no slouch himself. It appeared, left unimpeded; the boy would succeed in eluding them.

Percy was determined to impede.

As he sped toward safe haven, Amos looked over his shoulder. He was within spitting distance when Percy suddenly rose from his hiding place. Amos was no more than two steps away when he turned again and saw Percy. Percy laughed out loud at the astonished expression. He swung his fist in a wide back-hand that landed alongside Amos' head, sending him into a senseless cartwheel to earth. The boy landed hard, lying motionless as Percy strode over to stand over him.

"Not you, boy," Percy said, as his fangs descended.

"You ain't coming over. I'm sending you somewhere else and I'll be sending that queer aunt of yours and her friends along behind you soon enough."

Percy glared at Burl and company, who had slowed to a walk and were watching him as they approached.

"Fuck them," he muttered, leaning down to seize Amos by the throat. He straightened; both hands wrapped around Amos's neck, and lifted the boy high in the air. Amos moved weakly, his unconscious body struggling vainly to protect itself, eyelids fluttering open then closed in rapid succession, the whites showing as the eyes rolled back in his head. Percy shook him back and forth with a jealous, hatred-driven ferocity.

"Hey! Hey, Goddamn it," Burl shouted, hurrying forward, now aware of Percy's intent. "Goddamn it, Percy, put him down. You're going to kill him."

"It won't no accident, that's for sure," Percy shouted back with a laugh.

Rachael ran over, trying to force him to release Amos. She succeeded only in angering him. Percy gripped Amos with one hand, freeing the other to strike savagely at Rachael, knocking her to the ground. His clenched fist smashed her lips back against her teeth, sending a rivulet of blood down her face.

Rachael bounced back like a rubber ball. Leaping to her feet, she shook her head, growling from deep in her throat.

"I'm going to rip you apart like the pig you are, you son-of-a-bitch."

"Rip me?" Percy said, giving Amos another shake. "Anytime you feel like a frog, why, you just go right ahead and jump, little sis."

"You're the one who'd better be thinking of jumping," Tildy said, stepping out of the forest.

Percy, turning his head toward her, noted she was flanked by Aaron. He stood indecisively, the limp Amos hanging from his hands. The boy's face was purple with engorged blood, his head lolling to one side.

"I'd be puttin' the boy down, Percy," Aaron said evenly. "There'll not be another chance fer ye. If ye don't turn him loose right now, killing that boy is going to be the last move ye'll ever make."

With a howl of rage, Percy pulled Amos close then heaved him through the air. Amos hit the ground, breath whooshing from his body. He lay still for a moment, then inhaled with a long, tremulous gasp. Percy kicked at the ground, tearing divots free and sending them flying through the air as he strode in an angry circle. His voice rose until it was a bellow.

"Just who in the hell are you, huh? Who in the hell are you to keep telling me what to do? I caught that boy myself, didn't I? I reckon, by God, I can do as I please with him."

Tildy felt her own anger boiling inside. She stepped in front of Percy, stopping him in his tracks, bringing her face up nose to nose with him.

"You hush. You hear me?"

His eyes widened in surprise. Without being conscious of her actions, she had seized him by his shirt front, pulling him even closer. He looked over her shoulder and met the hard eyes of Rachael, the equally hard eyes of Aaron and Burl. It dawned on him he was very close to being a dead man, and this time there would be no getting up and walking away from it. Percy withered.

"Now, I'm telling you there ain't no sense in this," Tildy said. "We done what we set out to do. It's over, you hear? There ain't no need to kill nobody."

"Damn it, that ain't the point," Percy said, defending himself. "I caught this boy. He's mine to do whatever I please with. Now, if you all want me to let him go, well then, I reckon I can do that. But I don't cotton to the way you all try to give me orders. I'm a

264

man and a man just can't take——."

"Are you a man?" Burl said, stepping forward. His voice was even but cold as a winter night. "I'm damned if I've seen sign of it. I've been looking for a man all day long and ain't found one yet. Maybe I just ain't turned over the right rock."

Tildy shoved Percy away from her, standing between him and Burl. Maybe it would be best to just allow Burl to do what he clearly intended to do and save them all a lot of trouble. There was no chance Percy would ever change. He would always be a problem, a liability. She knew that, but now was not the time. It was not the time. It was not the place. And Burl was not the one for the job. She held her arm out to Burl, gesturing him back. He complied reluctantly as she turned her attention back to Percy.

"Don't fool yourself, Percy Way," Tildy said. "You ain't never been a man a day in your life and you ain't likely to be one any time soon."

Percy fought hard with his anger. He was on very shaky ground and knew it.

"I ain't done nothing to you," he said. "Why are you all treating me like you do?"

"You weren't trying to bring Amos over," Burl said. "You were just going to kill him, for no reason, and that just ain't right."

"Well——."

"Ain't no 'well' to it," Tildy said. "You ain't getting another shot at this, Percy. If you don't decide to straighten up, then you can't stay."

"You might be right about that, Tildy. The last part, anyway. Why should I stay? You ain't done nothing but treat me like a dog ever since I brought you over. You was a wrinkled old bag without the good sense to die and I gave you life again. Now look how you're acting."

"Don't let on like you ever thought of me," Tildy

265

shot back. "You never waste a minute thinking about nobody but yourself. I don't owe you one damned thing."

"And, by God, I don't owe none of you nothing either. I'm gone. I don't need you."

"Handle it as ye like, old hoss," Aaron interjected. "But don't cause us no more trouble. I'm here to tell ye, if ye do, ye won't be a livin' t'regret it."

Percy spun angrily on his heel, striding away from the group. He stooped, picking up the pine branch. Turning to face them once again, he pointed the sharpened end of the stake at Tildy.

"Just so there ain't no misunderstanding. If you want to fuck with me, come on. But I ain't going to be the only one to die."

* * *

Lights shone through the fog. Orange, dancing unearthly light flickered, undulated, leaped from ground to sky and back again. Shadows moved in the light. Lions strolled to and fro, yellow eyes gleaming as they stepped from the darkness. An incessant drone of voices hummed in the gray and moving mist, drums and animal sounds underpinning the cacophony.

Amos's head swam as he opened his eyes. The damp earth was chill, numbing against his back. He tried to swallow and the pain in his throat caused him to gasp as he raised himself up on an elbow to focus his rebellious eyes on an unbelievable scene.

A campfire burned brightly, sending plumes of smoke and crimson sparks high into the chilly spring sky. Lying in the circle of firelight were several couples, rutting as obliviously to one another–and to him–as if they shared the same intimate privacy he had shared with Chloe just that morning.

"Oh, God," he whispered, bringing his hand up to

his throat. "Oh, God, I didn't make it."

* * *

Truitt stood on the porch, watching the last of the refugees disappearing over a rise in the road. Preparations had been hasty, goodbyes even hastier. He had not been surprised by Ellie and Chloe's unwillingness to flee. In fact, he would have been much more surprised if they had embraced the idea. He was even more surprised, considering his experiences earlier in the day, by his own desire to stay.

"You can't do no good here," Duncan argued. "They're all dead—or worse. You can't not know that. What good will it do to stay here and get yourself killed?"

"No good at all, Duncan. But I can't get Ellie and Chloe to go. And, if they're not going, then I'm not going either. That's all there is to it."

"Looky here," Duncan said, whispering conspiratorially. "I'll help you. We'll hog-tie them, fling them into the back of the wagon here. It ain't got to be this way."

Truitt shook his head. For the first time ever, Duncan Tanner seemed an old man. The flesh sagged along his jawbone, shaded by the brim of his hat. His eyes were feverish as they glinted from beneath the shadow of the hat. Truitt wondered if his own face bore the marks the last few hours had etched in Duncan's.

"Yes it does. It has to be just this way. We can't keep them hog-tied forever and if I know Ellie, and I reckon I do, she'd be headed back this way before we could spit. It'd be easier to bail the creek with a thimble than to move her off this place."

"But—."

"Ain't no 'buts', Duncan. Now you go on and get

267

your family out of here. You need to put some miles behind you before you lose what light's left. If Amos makes it back anytime soon we'll catch up with you."

Duncan shook his head in sad resignation as he turned to go. His shoulders slumped forward slightly as if under some heavy weight, a weight he had not borne the day before. Truitt's heart went out to him, it went out to them all. Duncan stopped alongside his wagon and turned to face Truitt.

"Amos will be back," he said. "You know that. Sooner or later. I don't reckon it matters much either way. But you ain't going to be catching up with nobody, Truitt. Don't you understand? When Amos makes it back–and he will–you and yours' will stay here forever. Forever, man."

Duncan coughed and spat on the ground. Placing one foot on the wheel hub, he swung himself up into the wagon bed. A few blankets, pots and food, along with extra ammunition split from the stores of the lost neighbors, were all he carried. That and what was left of his family. Everyone was in the same boat. There would be no stopping, no side-trips to various farms to collect goods, furnishing, memories. And perhaps it was for the best. No other memories were strong enough to override the most recent ones and the recent ones would never be left behind. With each passing mile, with each turn of the wagon wheel, everything Duncan Tanner had ever been would fall away until, no matter where he stopped, he would be a stranger to himself.

Stepping over the wagon seat, he picked up the reins and settled himself down. He released the brake, pulled his hat brim down lower over his eyes. Duncan slapped the reins against the rumps of the mules, clucking to the animals as he led the ragged caravan away from the valley. He nodded silently to Truitt as he passed.

Truitt felt an unexpected tightness in his chest. Duncan, Sam, even Mabeline, were as much a part of him as anything else could be. This was more than a parting. It was an amputation. There was no anesthetic, nothing to kill the pain, and the missing part would leave a raw, painful wound, throbbing relentlessly until his last breath. No power on heaven or earth could ever make things right again. Amos was right. If God himself took a deep breath and blew the vampires from the face of the earth, nothing would ever be the same. The valley, the people, everything had been changed—eternally, irrevocably changed. Tears welled in his eyes. He fought them back as he hurried his stride to pace alongside Duncan's wagon.

"Duncan," he said. "You've been a good friend to me and mine. You need to know that. I hope to God to see you all again, but you need to know you've been a good friend. I think a hell of a lot of you."

Duncan leaned down, his face hidden in the shadow of his hat. Truitt did not need to see his face. Duncan's voice told him all he needed to know.

"We ain't going to see each other again, old hoss. At least, not in this here life. God bless you, Truitt."

Nothing else was said. Truitt stood in the yard as the wagons creaked by, their wheels churning the still wet soil into mud. When the last one passed, he stepped up on the porch to watch them until they were out of sight, to watch a lifetime of connection, of friendship, trail over the horizon.

"God bless you, too," he said. "And God forgive me."

CHAPTER TWENTY-SEVEN

The air was heavier. High in the night sky, dense clouds moved across the stars, erasing them like chalk from a blackboard. Night sounds filled the air, crickets, peeper frogs, cicadas and the occasional deep bass of bullfrogs on the creek. It would rain again before morning. The fire still burned brightly. Embers popped and crackled as the wood shifted, collapsing into the flames. Amos sat with his legs drawn up, staring at the others around the fire.

It was a scene from hell. He awakened to sights and sounds of random copulation, made eerie in the firelight. The pain in his throat caused him to immediately jump to the conclusion he had been transformed. He fell back, closing his eyes, opening them again at the sound of Sara's voice.

"Don't look like he's dead after all."

Her face, initially hidden in shadows, glowed as she leaned forward. She turned back to those around the fire. Amos saw her clearly when she turned—naked, breasts high, firm, the almost invisible down of hair covering them, catching the light, shining weakly around distended nipples. Sara noted his gaze.

"Ain't you the fickle one?" she whispered teasingly.

"He ain't dead by a long shot, Tildy."

A jolt of fear rocked him at the mention of Tildy. He struggled awkwardly to his feet, backing away from Sara.

"Leave me alone. I've never done nothing to you. You just keep away from me."

"Settle down, son," Tildy said, as she joined the puzzled Sara. "If I wanted you dead, you'd be dead by now."

Amos was having none of it. The images from his dreams flooded his consciousness as if a psychic dam had given way. He felt as if he would drown in those images as he backed away slowly, all the while keeping his eyes on Tildy. Like Sara, Tildy, too, was nude. This only heightened his fear. Panic took control and he ran blindly toward the cover of darkness. Burl Tanner came from nowhere to cut Amos's legs from under him in a diving tackle. Amos grunted as he hit the ground. Struggle was useless. Wilda had taught him that. The world spun dizzily as he tried to focus on the hazy figures swimming in the night sky.

"You want to stop acting the fool and listen?" Tildy asked.

Amos was angry now. Burl had released him, rising to stand over Amos. Tildy and Sara also leaned over him, filling his clearing vision.

"If you haven't killed me, then whatever you got for me has got to be worse."

"You're talking foolish, boy," Tildy said, squatting on her heels beside him. "Why, just a few days ago you were up at my place and all you had was questions. You must've wised up a considerable bit since then if you got all the answers now."

"You're evil! You're . . . you're a . . . a . . . "

"Abomination?" Tildy asked, chuckling.

"Damn right," Amos shot back.

"Now what would you know about that?"

Burl and Sara stood to one side. They exchanged smiles and the interaction was not lost on Amos. He grew angrier still.

"What in the hell are you two doing?" he said, standing and squaring around to Burl. "Go ahead and grin. Your time's coming. When it gets here you're both going to be in hell popping like a couple of chestnut logs."

The killing teeth were down in an instant. Burl drew his lips back over them and they glistened wetly in the light, sending shivers down Amos' spine, as Burl's eyes narrowed in a threatening glare.

"Might as well go to hell, Amos. If I go to heaven, I reckon I'll have to make all new friends."

Tildy interceded before things escalated too far.

"Now hush up, Burl. There ain't no use being testy. The boy's got a right to be scared. All of us were."

She never rose. Still squatting on her haunches, she plucked a long blade of grass, sticking it in her mouth and chewing thoughtfully. Finally, she looked up at Amos.

"I been thinking about this for a while, Amos. Talking to you, I mean. Now I got the chance, I don't rightly know where to start."

Amos stared at her silently. Tildy smiled, rising to her feet and stretching her hand out to rest it on her great-nephew's shoulder. He shrugged out from under her hand as if it were ablaze. Tildy's smile never faded.

"I always thought a lot of you, you know. And I've always been honest with you. The last time I talked to you, I told you the truth as well as I knew it. If I was wrong about some things, well, I wasn't lying because I believed them to be true. You say I'm evil–and a couple of days ago I'd have agreed with you. Now, I ain't so sure."

"I am," Amos said, without hesitation. "I've never been more sure of anything." He pointed his finger

272

accusingly at Tildy before sweeping it over the rest. "All of you are. I'm not about to pretend that I've ever been real religious but I seen what crosses do to you. What water from the creek yonder does to you. You can say what you want, but if God hasn't got a hard-on for you, then I ain't standing here."

Burl laughed. He bent down and picked his overalls off the ground. Fishing around in the pockets, he came out with a silver object. He held it out to Amos. Amos' eyes grew wide. Burl held the silver crucifix Tildy had hung on her door. It was not possible.

"Don't look so surprised, Amos," Tildy said. "Hell, I been in your dreams. If you'd paid them any mind, you'd have known that little old trinket was worthless."

"But I saw them work," Amos stammered.

"Naw, you didn't. You saw some wood and some water do some things. I can't rightly explain it all myself. Maybe it's got something to do with God after all." She turned, walking slowly back toward the fire. Amos followed automatically, flanked by Burl and Sara. Tildy did not even seem to be talking to him anymore. It was as if she were speaking to herself, or perhaps something–or someone–beyond.

"I do know there's places like the meadow–places we can't go–the ground itself is poison. There's something in that meadow. Way deep. And whatever it is, it's in the water, too. We never could go there, no more than you could walk through fire. No more than a fish could come out of the creek and have a seat here. Nope, it don't have the first thing to do with curses or preachers, or the revivals, it's just something in the ground, in the water, in the trees. Hell, a stick from that meadow was all you needed. It didn't have to be a cross. I reckon people have known about places like this for years. Taken comfort in them long before the first Holiness preacher ever scared the shit out of his flock in the meadow yonder."

"Then . . . but . . . "

"I don't know, Amos. We always thought we knew some things didn't we? If God's there—if he made us, I mean—then how come I'm evil? Sara? Burl? All the rest of us? We didn't ask for this. None of us ever went out of our way to do nothing wrong. Don't you think you think it's a pretty chicken-shit little old God that'll punish folks for something they can't help and ain't got no say so about?"

Amos didn't know what to think. Tildy made it all sound so reasonable. Certainly Bill Way, Burl, Sara, none of them had sought out the fate that had befallen them. But, on the other hand, no sooner had they been changed than they had attempted to bring violence and death on other innocents. The alternative life could not be as guiltless as she would have him believe. And a mad dog was a mad dog regardless of the sweetness of his prior nature.

"Well, you poor victims of circumstances managed to slaughter about half the valley inside of a week. You're going to have to pardon me if I don't feel too awful damned sorry for you."

"And just what in the hell were you doing out there today? Shooting quail?"

"I was protecting myself, damn it."

"So were we. We just did a better job of it. This here valley's ours now, Amos. You know that. You've known it for a while. I'm giving you an opportunity. None of us had a choice, but I'm offering you one. You can stay or you can go. If you go, and run into Percy out there, it's going to be your ass. He means to kill you—and would have killed you if it hadn't been for Burl and Rachael. You can go on and wade the creek yonder, live like some kind of hermit or something. Or you can come over with us. It ain't all that bad, son. It really ain't all that bad."

What of Chloe? Was she waiting for him at the

274

house? Would Truitt and Ellie wait? Percy would, he was sure of that. He looked toward the creek, where he and Chloe had spent the terrifying nights. Somewhere, deep inside him, he knew he wouldn't leave. But he couldn't force that awareness into his consciousness. Somewhere, deep inside him, he knew Tildy knew as well.

"Well?"

"I . . . I don't know, Tildy."

Tildy gazed steadily at him for a moment. She removed the blade of grass she had been chewing and let it fall to the ground. She rolled her eyes and sighed.

"Ain't never been a McBride in the history of the world was ever worth a damn at making up his mind."

She drew close to Sara and whispered. "Take him," she said.

"No," Sara said, shaking her head. "It ain't my place to do that. It just ain't my place."

Tildy stood silently a moment.

"No, I reckon it ain't," she said, turning back to Amos.

* * *

The smoke from Truitt's pipe was pulled slowly along toward the fireplace. Caught in the updraft, it spiraled up the flue, mixing with wood smoke, carrying embers in its wake.

"You done?" Ellie asked.

"Hmmmnnn?"

"I asked if you was done."

"Yeah. Yeah, I reckon I am."

Ellie took his plate. Chloe was already busy clearing away the table. The meal had been opulent. Enough food had been left at the farm to feed many more than the three people remaining. They could have lived for weeks on leftovers alone. Truitt watched the women complete their tasks. How could anything, under the circumstances seem so normal? They worked silently, mechanically going through the motions while their minds were elsewhere—the same place his kept going, out into the darkness with Amos. There was nothing left for them to say to one another. The hopeful lies were useless now. And not one of them wanted to speak openly of the fear they all shared.

* * *

Percy sat with his back against the wall of the smokehouse. He spun the sharpened pine limb between his hands as if attempting to make a friction fire. Occasionally glancing toward the house, he could see the women moving about, crossing back and forth in front of the window. He wondered what they'd do if he simply walked in—unannounced, uninvited. Percy pulled his legs up toward his body, preparing to stand. No. No, he wouldn't do that. No need to borrow trouble. He settled back against the wall, taking out his knife to idly whittle the point of the stake.

The wind had picked up again. From across the mountains came the distant rumbling of another storm as it sailed down toward the valley. Bright embers danced like fireflies leaping sporadically from the chimney. Percy stopped whittling, watching the sparks rising high into the night sky, fading away as they died.

He smiled.

* * *

Amos gasped, panting in Tildy's embrace. He knew the others were watching. He knew he was the focus of their undivided attention. He knew this was madness. But, for now, he was drowning in her body and felt no need to rise for air. In a very far corner of

276

his mind, an image of Chloe stood obliquely like a half-developed photograph, quickly fading. Thoughts were gone. Fear was gone. Pain was gone.

"Now," he said, throwing his head back, breathing faster.

Tildy gripped him tighter, locking her legs around his back, thrusting to meet him. Her dark hair framed her face, her gray eyes catching the firelight, blazing in the darkness. The descending fangs glistened as she parted her lips, bringing them close to his throat.

"Now," she whispered.

CHAPTER TWENTY-EIGHT

The window panes rattled loudly in the gusting wind, announcing the approaching storm. Chloe found herself jumping at the noise each time it occurred. She could not sleep. She had tried. It would have been nice to escape consciousness but sleep just would not come to her. Ellie, on the other hand, exhausted, snored softly on a pallet by the fire and Truitt, nursing his pipe, sat beside her.

"Looky here," Chloe said, softly, to avoid disturbing Ellie. "You go on and get some rest. I'm not sleepy so I'll keep watch for a while."

"I can't sleep either, girl. Looks like we'll both stand watch."

She reached for the coffee pot, sitting among the coals at the edge of the fire, and re-filled both of their cups. The metal cup soon absorbed the heat of the steaming liquid and she had to set it aside.

"Mr. McBride?"

"Hmmm?"

"We've killed ourselves haven't we?"

Truitt looked over at her. Was she asking for honesty or reassurance? Perhaps both? An honest answer was frightening and God knew she was

278

frightened enough. He stared away into the flames.
The truth would have to do. Besides, what could he
say that would frighten her more?

"God knows, Chloe. God knows. Try not to think
about it."

"But I do think about it."

"I do, too."

His face changed in the wavering light of the hearth.
It was Amos's face, or Amos's face as it would be given
twenty-five years or so. The dark black hair was a
sharp contrast with the carrot-top red of Amos but the
features of the face were the same—lean, sharp, almost
angular, with a slightly oversized nose. She would
never get the chance to watch the years chisel Amos the
way they had his father. Amos would never have the
deeply-lined, weather-beaten look of Truitt. Amos was
dead. Her heart sank at the thought but she could not
drive it away. Amos was dead and the rest of them
would join him in a very short time. An extremely
weary part of her sighed in relief and resignation.

* * *

He emptied the contents of a five-gallon can of coal-
oil into a washtub. A number of heavy limbs, placed
on one end inside the tub, lined the rim like a picket
fence. Percy left the limbs soaking and returned to the
barn. He had three lamps and another container of oil
when he returned. Leaving the lamps beside the tub,
he quickly moved across the yard to splash the
remaining coal-oil against the walls of the farmhouse.
He doused the structure on the chimney side, along the
back and, finally, the opposite end of the building,
leaving the front untouched. Percy set the empty can
on the ground and returned for the lamps.

One by one, he lit the lamps, covering them with
cloth as he carried them to the windowless, blind side

279

of the building where the chimney rose into the air. He collected the fuel-soaked torches, piling them next to the lamps and splashing the oil remaining in the tub as high as he could on the walls.

"Now, by God, let's see what you think of this shit."

He shoved a torch into the ground, lighting it from the lamp. Turning, he heaved the lamp high into the air, watching as it arched downward onto the roof. The glass exploded on impact and the lamp rolled clattering down the slope of the roof, leaving a fiery trail of burning oil behind it.

* * *

The thump on the roof startled Chloe. She squealed involuntarily as the loud clatter of the rolling lamp pulled her eyes to the ceiling. Truitt, on his feet in an instant, clutched the shotgun tightly in his hands.

"What is it? What is it?" Chloe demanded.

"Hell if I know," Truitt said, peering intently at the white pine rafters as if he could see through them.

The unexpected sound was repeated, then repeated again. Ellie sat upright on the pallet, awake and alert.

"What's . . . "

"Hush," Truitt said. "There's somebody on the roof."

His heart pounded as he moved across the floor, feeling and hearing the blood pulsing in his ears. He made his way to the front of the house to look out a window. Even before he got to the window, he knew what was happening. The popping, crackling sound—faint at first, but becoming louder—was something he was not likely to misidentify. The orange glow of the burning roof, reflecting down on the dirt of the yard, only served to bear further evidence of their predicament. He was back across the room in a split second, grabbing his revolvers from the table and sticking them in his belt.

"The sons-of-bitches are burning us out. Well, by God, it's about time we got on with it."

Ellie clutched her husband's arm as he turned toward the door. She leaned away with all her weight, spinning him around to face her.

"Don't be a fool, Truitt. Whoever's out there wants us to run out. That's what all this is about."

Truitt angrily snatched his arm away from her.

"For once in your life, try giving me some credit. Don't you think I know that? But we ain't got no Goddamned choice. We either get the hell out or roast like spitted pigs."

Everything was frozen for Chloe. Time, everything. Truitt and Ellie stood looking at one another for an eternity. The hungry crackling grew more demanding as the house burned. Whoever was out there not only wanted them out but knew exactly in which direction he wanted them to come. The shattering of glass jolted her back from her paralyzed state as a flaming torch crashed through the window, setting the old, yellowed curtains ablaze. She and Truitt spun at the same time and she was almost deafened by the report of his shotgun as the shot ripped away the lower portion of the window-sill and the remaining shards of glass. One by one, the windows shattered as torches were hurled inside. Truitt stalked through the thickening smoke, reloading the shotgun and firing again without ever seeing a target.

Outside, Percy was unfazed by the random shooting as he methodically went about his task of lighting torches and throwing them inside. He made his way along the walls to the front, stepping up on the front porch after tossing the last branch.

The smoke stung Chloe's eyes as she took a long, wide-blade carving knife down from a peg just inside the door of the larder. She fell in behind Truitt and Ellie, already making their way to the front door. Ellie stopped Truitt again as he drew the bolt on the crudely crafted door.

"Give me one of them guns," she said.

Without a word, Truitt pulled a revolver from his belt and handed it to her. Ellie pulled back the hammer.

"You can't let me and Chloe end up like that," she said. "You know that don't you?"

"Yeah, I know," he replied, his voice choked with both smoke and emotion. "If the time comes, I'll do what I got to do. I always do what I got to do."

"I know you do, Hon."

He turned again and kicked the door open. Holding his shotgun at ready, he strode through the open doorway in a cloud of smoke pulled out by the draft.

* * *

Calmly retracing his earlier frantic steps, Amos walked silently along with his new companions as they headed for his home. All his aches and pains were gone.

He couldn't help but think that it was an odd sort of evening. As he reached his climax, Tildy had leaned forward, kissing his shoulders and neck, running her tongue across his throat. His eyes had bulged in surprised terror as she suddenly sank her fangs into him, locking her jaws in bulldog tenacity.

Of course, he had fought her. Of course he had. Even if he had given in somewhat willingly, he still had no choice but to fight at the end. He guessed that was just nature. His breath cut off, no way to cry out, the struggle had been brief and silent. She pinned him to the ground, drained the life from him. His vision dimmed and life, as he had always known it, slipped away from him.

He was vaguely aware of the others watching impassively as he grew weaker and his resistance trailed away. The horrible sucking noise rose to a crescendo, filling the universe as he surrendered to it. Somehow he still managed to note his orgasm. He died inside her. A blackness descended, soon giving way to the swirling, foggy world he visited in dreams. Voices again and Mabeline stood before him.

"Reckon you know all you need to know now, boy? Done let your little head lead your big head right into some pretty deep shit ain't you?"

"It had to be this way," he said.

Mabeline shook her head, disappearing into the fog. Her voice drifted back to him.

"Don't reckon it matters none. Since that's the way it is."

Amos had no idea how long he stayed away. But, when he returned, he knew he was forever altered. Lying naked where Tildy had left him, he raised himself on his elbows to look down at himself. For the first time in days, he was able to breathe deeply without experiencing pain. The large, splotchy bruises he had acquired from his fall were gone. Amos drew his legs up, rising to a sitting position as he brought his hands to his face. His missing teeth were back and then some.

"Dang," he whispered in amazement.

Now, marching along with those he had recently sought to destroy, he felt as comfortable as if going to a church social. Life—any life—continued to be strange. The intermittently gusting wind blew into his face. He pulled up short, startled from his introspection. The pungent odor of burning wood filled his nostrils just seconds before he heard the first report of gunfire. Both came from the direction of home.

CHAPTER TWENTY-NINE

The flames leaped high into the night sky, filling the air with plumes of fragrant smoke. Percy pressed himself against the wall, waiting. He had positioned himself so that the door would swing away from him. He would have unimpeded access to whoever came first through the portal. Thunder rumbled in the distance as the storm made its way over the peaks. Percy glanced at the flashes of lightning flickering above the trees along the dark ridge on the horizon.

"Hold off," he whispered. "Hold off just a few more minutes. Then, even if the bottom falls out, it will be too late."

Percy's heartbeat quickened. He felt the killing teeth descend into place as he heard the sound of the bolt being drawn. The door slammed open and the oily barrel of the shotgun, gleaming in the twisting light, emerged inch by inch from the doorway. Percy's muscles tensed. He waited until he saw Truitt's work boot swing across the threshold, then he sprang into action.

With a snarl, Percy seized the gun in both hands, shoving it upwards. He felt the hot rush of shot as it burst from the barrels, faster than thought. Splinters of wood and bits of smoldering shingles flew through the air, raining down on them as the lead pellets tore through the fire-weakened roof of the porch. Percy laughed as he brought the weapon back down, swinging it outwards in a wide arc.

Truitt, taken by surprise, instinctively clutched the Long Tom as Percy used it as a lever to swing him away from the door, into the porch railing. The timber gave way with a loud crack, spilling Truitt into the yard. A sharp, blinding pain in his left side caused him to gasp as he hit the ground. He knew, without any doubt, some ribs had broken. He struggled to rise, fumbling for his revolver as he struggled to his feet. He flinched at the harsh sound of the discharging pistol Ellie held. She screamed from the porch.

"You son of a bitch!"

Percy held her by the wrists and pulled her toward him, shaking the pistol from her grasp in the process. A dark stain spread across the front of Percy's shirt where Ellie had gotten her licks in. Truitt raised his own weapon, struggling to train it upon Percy. Even the slightest movement sent a fresh wave of pain coursing through him and he reeled on his feet as he tried to focus his pain-dimmed eyes.

"Reckon I could have this dance, Mrs. McBride?" Percy said, grinning as he held the struggling woman tight against his chest. He lifted her off her feet. She kicked and wriggled, feet six inches above the plank floor. Percy spun in a circle like a swain at a waltz. Ellie spat into the grinning face. Percy only laughed.

"Ow," he said, "that made a lot of difference."

Ellie could feel the hot, sticky blood against her skin. He had taken the heavy lead in the mid-section and had hardly flinched. He wiped his face on her shoulder and noticed Truitt in the yard.

"It's a done deal, Truitt," he said. "You might as well get used to it."

The large-bore barrel of the Colt wavered and trembled as Truitt gripped it with both hands, trying to keep it trained. He drew back the hammer. Percy again seemed amused.

"Now, don't be like that," he said. "If you fuck with me, I'll just have to squeeze this old whore until her guts pop out."

He raised her slightly, jerking his arms inward. Ellie screamed.

"This has got to stop," Truitt said.

"Drop that gun and it will."

Truitt saw Chloe slide through the doorway behind Percy. He quickly pulled his eyes away from her, away from the bright glint of the carving knife. He was not quick enough.

"Don't you try anything foolish, girl," Percy said, without so much as a glance behind him. "I know you're there. Damned if I'm shy about killing any one of you."

"Do what you got to do," Ellie gasped, writhing in Percy's arms. "Good Lord, man, do what you promised."

The roar of the heavy pistol pealed through the air. Percy lost his grin and his mouth fell open in surprise as the long tongue of flame leaped toward him and the weapon bucked in Truitt's hands. Percy was aware of everything at once. The sight and sound of the shot, the wince of pain on Truitt's face—both at the pain of the recoil shock and the knowledge of what he was doing. Percy even heard the high-pitched whine of the whistling slug as it covered the short distance in the smallest fraction of a second to slam into the woman's body. He felt her stiffen as the slug punched through her and into him. It penetrated only slightly, velocity spent passing through Ellie. The slug had broken her spine. For him, it was little more than an annoyance.

For her, it was much, much more.

Percy staggered backward a step, holding the limp, dying body of Ellie in his arms like a rag doll. It took a few seconds for the knowledge of what had happened to sink in.

"You crazy bastard," he said incredulously. He was genuinely amazed. "What in the hell did you do that for? There was no call for you to do something like that."

Truitt said nothing. He merely took aim again with his pistol.

Percy charged across the porch with a roar. Truitt squeezed the trigger and another slug slapped into Ellie's body. He was thumbing the hammer for another shot when Percy hurled Ellie toward him. Truitt saw Chloe plunge the knife into her father's throat just as the body of his wife hit him chest high.

* * *

Truitt had no idea how long he had been unconscious. Cold, heavy rain-drops pelted down on his face and a heavy weight pressed on his chest. Truitt opened his eyes. The rain came down harder, spitting and hissing into the still burning ruin of his home. Ellie lay across him. He gathered his strength, pushing against her to free himself. She moaned. Covered in his wife's blood, he fell backward into the rapidly puddling rain, vaguely aware of the dim figures coming out of the shadows and moving into the flickering light. A deafening clap of thunder heralded a new wave of darkness sweeping over him, pulling him down into its depths.

* * *

Hot blood sprayed everywhere as Chloe drove the knife home. It was as if a dam had burst, a crimson flood spraying into the air, raining down on the porch, raining down on Chloe. Percy wheeled to face her, bringing his hand up to grip the haft of the knife. He pulled it from his flesh, staring at the blade unconcerned as the blood continued to jet from the wound.

"I wouldn't have thought you had it in you," he said to Chloe, strangling a bit and making a gargling sound as the blood rose in his throat. He held up one finger to indicate she should wait a moment and completed a very theatrical swallow. "Ah, that's better." He pressed his hand to the wound to staunch the flow of blood. "As I was saying, I wouldn't have thought you had it in you, stabbing your own daddy like that I mean. But I guess you've got the gumption after all."

He took his hand away from the wound and the flow of blood had lessened by more than half in the few seconds it took his new biological function to seal off the damaged veins and capillaries. Chloe leaned against the hot, smoking wall of the house, oblivious to the temperature. She could not believe what she was seeing. The blood slowed from spurting to a heavy flow to a trickle to nothing and the wound closed before her eyes as she stood speechless.

"Hell," Percy said. "I've had worse than that on my pecker."

Chloe tried to rush past him but he caught her arm. She screamed and struggled to no avail as he held her firmly.

"I told you I'd be waiting, didn't I? Didn't Daddy tell you he'd be waiting?" He brought his hand up between her legs, rubbing and grinning lecherously. "It's about time you and me took care of some unfinished business don't you think?"

Chloe screamed as he clutched the front of the cotton shift and pulled it apart, ripped the front of the garment away from her body in one effortless motion.

All the while, his iron grip on her neck held her immobile. He completed the task of disrobing her, shoved her roughly against the wall and held her there while he unfastened the bib of his overalls.

"This here's just something you're going to have to get used to, sugar."

She braced her hands against the wall, shoving backwards with all her strength. But all her strength was not nearly enough. It was far from enough. All of her struggles were useless. She felt the hardness of his erection as he easily spread her legs with his and moved himself into position. She screamed as he entered her, slamming her against the wall with each thrust. Rough splinters dug into her cheek as he pressed her head against the wall.

Oblivious to the smoke and flames, Percy actually lifted her from the floor as he climaxed, hammering away at her with the abandon of a wild animal. Burning wood and embers showered down around them as the roof collapsed into what had been the living area of what, such a short time ago, had seemed a sanctuary. Percy shoved her away from him and she hurtled over the steps and landed roughly in the yard. Chloe skidded to a stop, pulling herself up on hands and knees as she spun to face him, smarting from her numerous scrapes, scratches and bruises. She made no attempt to get to her feet as she stared at him. What good would it do? Her auburn hair framed her face; shone in the firelight as if it, too, were burning. Percy descended the steps and she had never seen anything more frightening; like he was walking out of hell.

Percy moved slowly, unhurriedly, as if he had all the time in the world. He worked his jaws open and closed, cruel fangs exposed. The burning building shifted again as the timbers gave way, fiery sparks swirling crazily through the air. His thick body glistened from the heat and from his recent exertions.

A sheen of sweat shimmered on his pale skin. Naked, except for his boots, he carried his overalls in his hand as he left the burning porch. Still semi-turgid, his penis swung obscenely with his movements as he approached. Hot anger swept across her and she rose, threw herself at him and clawed at his eyes. He had no difficulty evading her attack as he brushed her aside.

"I'm going to kill you," she raged. "Do you hear me you son of a bitch? I'm going to kill you!"

Percy laughed, catching her arms as she renewed her assault.

"Looky here, Honey. I done told you that I'm already dead. At least in the way you understand it. Come on, let me show you what it's like."

He pulled her close, his head darting down at her like a rattler. She felt the sharp pain as the canines punched through her flesh, opened her vein. In a very short time, it was over.

* * *

Truitt was drowning. He gagged as he tried to breathe, coughing painfully. The sound of rushing water filled his ears. He could feel its cold touch as it lapped against him. His eyes popped open and he raised his head, spitting a mouthful of cold rain. It came down like a solid wall. The smell of burning wood lingered in aromatic traces all around the clearing where the wreckage of his home smoldered and smoke still rose from the ruins. His eyes adjusted to the darkness and he tried to focus on cause of the grunting and panting several yards away. Two people struggled in the rain, rolling and kicking through the puddles, sending mud and water splashing in every direction.

It was Percy and Chloe.

CHAPTER THIRTY

Amos saw the bright glow of the burning house while still some distance away. Tildy saw it, too, and quickened her pace. Lightning flashed as the storm crossed the valley, cold, pelting rain coming down like a fury. The flickering orange light began to fade in the downpour as they made their way toward it. The gunfire had ceased.

* * *

Chloe opened her eyes and, through the driving rain, could see Percy sitting several yards away. Both of them were naked and Chloe felt the gritty, wet soil of the yard clinging to her skin.

"Hidey," Percy said. "You weren't gone long at all, sugar."

Chloe stood, shaking back her hair, sending sprays of droplets flying. She knew well enough what had happened but somehow it did not much bother her. What bothered her was Percy, still sitting back and grinning at her like some kind of idiot. Chloe ran her tongue over her lips, starting with surprise as she felt the teeth. She almost smiled. It should not have been surprising at all. Nothing should be surprising anymore. She rubbed her body, flinging off the mud and grit. Percy rose and took a step toward her. She took a step back. Her action was not lost on him.

"Well, you goddamned uppity whore, you," he said, his face flushing with anger. "Don't you back off from me. I'm still your old man and we're going to be together a long, long time. You might just as well start towing the line right now."

"No. Our time together stops right now."

Percy shook his head.

"What is it with you? What is it with everybody? This life is different. Better. It ain't the same as it was. I done a good thing for you."

He continued to advance as he spoke. Chloe stepped forward, shoving him violently in the chest and driving him backwards.

"A good thing? A good thing? Rape? Murder? Whatever the hell it was. All you've ever done your whole miserable life is take. Well, old man, you got all you're ever going to get from me."

Lowering his head like a bull, Percy rushed her. She tried to side-step but the muddy ground cost her a second. He drove his full weight into her mid-section and they tumbled into the yard, splashing mud high into the air. They grappled, rolling through the mire, silent but for grunts, heavy breathing. Her strength amazed her as she held her ground against the heavier Percy. It was a short-lived confidence, however. His superior size began to tell as the advantage swung his way. Finally pinning her to the ground, he knelt upon her arms, holding her virtually immobile.

"Well," he said, grinning down at her. "You might just be a little off if you think I done got all I'm going to get from you. You damned sure ain't got all you're going to get from me."

Chloe's head shot forward, killing teeth snapping

292

empty air as he pulled away. She gasped as he spread her legs again.

"No, goddamn you, no!"

* * *

"Ellie?"

There was no response, other than a weak, wet cough. Truitt rolled over and cradled her head, lifting it so she could breathe. His own breath was a dagger, piercing him with each inhalation. She opened her eyes. Truitt brushed her hair back as she struggled to speak.

"Get . . . get your gun . . . "

"Hush, now, hush. We're going to be all right."

"No," she said, coughing again. "No. We ain't going to be all right. I can't move. Can't feel my legs. You got to finish what you started."

Chloe's scream pulled his eyes away. He saw the violence taking place not twenty feet away. Chloe lay on her back, struggling futilely, while Percy methodically raped her. Truitt lowered Ellie's head to the ground and felt around in the mud for his revolver. If it could be ended, it should be. Survival was no longer his concern. A madness had settled over the valley—meaningless, random, violent. It had to stop.

His searching hands finally found the familiar grip of the pistol. Truitt clutched it firmly as he got to his feet. Neither of the combatants noted his presence, so intent were they with one another. He took small, tentative steps toward them, pausing to steady himself after every step. Even then, he came perilously close to falling several times. If he went down, he might never get up again.

Percy panted and gasped with his efforts as Truitt approached. Truitt could see Chloe's face, lips pulled back over threatening teeth, and heard the long, continuous snarl emanating from her throat, broken only by the rough thrusts of her father. A deep sense of pity took him off guard. Chloe had to die, too.

Sheets of wind-driven rain pummeled him as the storm reached an apex. Peal after peal of thunder crashed through the night air accompanying the jagged trails of lightning. Truitt raised the Colt and took aim—barrel eighteen inches away from Percy's head, trained just behind his right ear—his finger tightened on the trigger.

Then Truitt was airborne.

He did not know what hit him as he spun crazily away, the Colt flung from his hand. He landed on his back, a shock of pain running from head to toe and back again. Just before he lost consciousness, a bright flash illuminated the night and a strange, jolting crash of thunder rang in his ears.

* * *

They moved into the muddy perimeter to stare at the sight in the yard. Anger rumbled through Amos as a snarl from deep inside his chest.

"Goddamn," Tildy, standing next to him, said in disgust.

Amos started forward but Tildy, in gentle restraint, placed her hand on his chest.

"Looky here," Burl whispered, nodding in the direction of Truitt.

They watched as Truitt rose from the ground, pistol clutched tightly in his fist. No one made a move to stop him as he staggered toward Percy and Chloe. It was only when he raised the gun that Sara was goaded into action. She crossed the yard in quick strides and snatched something from the ground. Catching Truitt's wrist, she hurled him away from her with no more effort than if he had been a dish-rag. The Colt spun out of his hand, flying thirty feet through the air before hitting the ground.

The gun went off on contact. Truitt had inadvertently packed the barrel with mud when he fell beneath Ellie. The barrel split backward like the skin of a half-peeled banana, sending slivers of hot steel flying. Sara had, unwittingly enough, likely saved Truitt's life.

Percy's head jerked up at the sound of the explosion. Sara stepped in front of him to connect with a wicked backhand. Chloe scrabbled away through the mud as Percy got to his feet. Sara seized a handful of Percy's hair, before he had time to recover, and snatched his head back. He was raising his arms to break her grip when she lunged forward. Her right arm swung into his middle and Amos stepped back in surprise as he saw Percy's broad back suddenly bulge, then tear, as the sharpened point of the pine limb punched through the skin to protrude six inches from his flesh. He screamed–a long ululating wail–as he attempted to pull the stake from his body. Bright red blood sprayed onto the ground as he staggered in a wide circle.

Percy, fell to his knees and clutched the end of the stake protruding from his chest with both hands. He grimaced in pain as he withdrew it from his body. The limb pulled free with a wet, tearing sound, blood gushing from the massive hole. He dropped the stake, bringing his hands to his chest in an attempt to staunch the flow. Sara laughed as she strode over to him. Everyone came forward, standing in a circle around the two. Chloe joined them, taking a place beside Amos. Percy remained on his knees, looking up at them. He coughed clots of blood, watching in shocked surprise as they splatted onto the ground in front of him.

"Oh," he said, simply. "Oh."

Sara squatted beside him, picking up the bloody piece of wood. "I should have done this years ago," she said, cupping his chin in her hand, tilting his face up to hers.

"Why?" Percy asked, bloody froth dribbling from his lips into her hand.

"Why?" she repeated, incredulously.

"Why?" he asked, as if he honestly didn't know.

Sara brought her hand away from his chin, letting her fingers trail caressingly across his cheek.

"Because, Daddy, some things just don't ever change."

Percy grunted as Sara drove the stake into him again. His mind refused to accept the reality of his shattered heart. A large, bloody bubble formed on his lips as his last breath left him. The bubble popped as he fell forward, spraying Sara with bloody spittle. Her fangs retracted as she looked at Tildy. She smiled, brightly, flecks of her father's blood spattered across her face like freckles.

"Dang," Amos whispered.

* * *

Truitt was aware of being moved. He felt himself lifted, repositioned and settled back in a yielding but firm warmth. Soft hands brushed the wet, matted strands of hair from his face. He turned his head to meet Chloe's eyes. He had nothing to fear. He was broken up inside.

He was dying.

Chloe looked no different than she had before the fire, except for the fact she was sopping wet and entirely naked. Her wet hair was plastered to her head, rain trickling from it to trail down her face, dripping from her nose and chin. She held him gently, kneeling behind him, leaning forward over him to keep the rain out of his face. Someone else called his name softly.

"Truitt? Truitt, can you hear me?"

"Tildy?" he said, turning to find her.

"Yep," she said, coming out of the darkness to squat on her heels beside him.

"What . . . what . . . "

"Hush, now. You ain't in no shape to be carrying on a conversation. You ain't in no shape to be doing anything except what you're doing."

"What I'm doing," he repeated faintly.

"You're dying, Truitt. So's Ellie. Neither one of you got much time left."

"Ellie?"

He looked around him as well as he could. There were people milling all around. Some he knew, some he did not. Sam Larrimer, Burl, Win, Kyle, Margie, strangers, and, finally, Amos, down on his knees alongside Ellie's broken and bloody form. Nothing frightened him any longer. Well, so this is dying. Not so bad. His head swam as the darkness loomed over him like a storm from the mountains. As it came down and surrounded him, he met Amos eyes.

"Nobody else dies tonight," Amos said.

Truitt looked up past Chloe to the dark heavens and beyond. A flash of lightning exploded silver light over the wet yard and sheets of rain blew over them, crawling slowly across the valley as if clearing the way for the dawn.

EPILOGUE

The old man sat behind the wheel of the fifty-six Chevy, waiting for the attendant to make change. News on the radio crackled intermittently with disruptive static. He was too far between stations to get a steady signal. The gas jockey found him leaning over, fiddling with the dial when he returned.

"Here you are, old buddy. Fourteen bucks and change."

The old man smiled as he took the money.

"Most days, we can't get anything on the radio out here," the attendant chatted on, not paying attention at all to the old man's interest or lack of it. He wiped his hands with a shop rag and squinted at the sky as if it had something to do with what he was saying.

"Besides, there ain't nothing on there worth hearing anyways. Nothing in the world anymore but war and protest and 'yah-yah' music and women with their titties flopping. Maybe if Nixon gets elected he'll straighten things out. I don't know what to think anymore. Seems like the whole damned world's gone crazy."

"Sure enough seems that way," the old man said. "Well, you take care now."

He pulled the gear shift into drive, moved slowly

away from the pump and steered stiffly across the gravel to the blacktop road. He stopped, looked carefully in each direction several times and pulled cautiously out onto the road.

The attendant noticed the Texas plates and shook his head. If the guy had driven all the way from Texas, it must have taken him a month driving like that. The old boy was ancient, older than dirt. Eighty-five maybe but at least eighty. Eighty if he was a day. Must be terrible to be old and alone like that. He watched the car until it disappeared around the bend. Yep, it must be terrible. It must be.

The old man could not have any family; none that cared for him, anyway. Otherwise he would never have been allowed to make a trip like that all by himself. The gas jockey reached into an icebox sitting just outside the doorway and fished out an RC before walking back inside the station. Maybe the old boy did have people. Maybe he had come up here with them and was just out for a drive by himself. Or maybe there was family here he had come to see. Sure. Of course. Somehow, it made the gas jockey feel better to think so.

It was still early in the day. The sky was overcast and scattered showers had drifted by throughout the morning and early afternoon. As the sun peeped through the clouds, the wet stretch of road glistened like a satin ribbon. A faded red and white billboard sign announced; "Welcome to Lion Country." Beneath the greeting was a picture of a male lion in full stride and beneath the picture, "Lion Oil Company." Spread across the horizon, the looming forested mountains huddled together like blind giants unable to feel their way past their own massive bodies.

The old man drove slowly, with the bat-wing cracked, breathing the wet air. The radio signal faded altogether and he leaned forward to turn the switch off. There was no need for news, no need for music. He pressed down on the accelerator, increasing his speed. His destination was not far and he was anxious to be there.

An old gravel road branched west off the blacktop toward the mountain the locals called "Hog Heaven Hill." He slowed, steering the Chevy onto the gravel, disappearing into the pine shadows. A few small farms, open fields, then woods, open fields again, the countryside swept by until he was almost at the base of the mountain. Fourteen miles from his turn-off, the road dead-ended at the edge of a forest. He pulled the car to the side of the road and switched off the ignition. An open pack of Camels lay on the dash. He shook one out and lit it as he thought about the man at the gas station. Yes, indeed, he could have told the guy some things about craziness, about a world gone mad.

He could have told him about France, where men ran at one another and slaughtered and slaughtered until there were none left to pour over the walls of the trenches. He could have told of gas attacks. He could have told him of cancer. He could have told him of terror—a terror so great it would make a man run away from everything he had ever known. Terror that could make a man leave everything—everyone—who had ever meant anything to him and simply run away. But there was no need to tell the man anything. Live long enough and a body's sure to find out for himself, if not sooner, then later. Maybe it is best if people live as long as they can without finding out just how crazy the world is.

In his case, it just happened to be sooner.

The old man smiled, grinding the cigarette out in the ashtray. He took a .32 caliber pistol from the glove box and stepped out into the damp grass, slipping the pack of smokes into one pants pocket, the small automatic into the other. He leaned back inside for his sweater. This time of year, the temperature dropped rapidly after sundown and he expected it would take him that long to reach the summit. He draped the sweater over his shoulder and began the climb. It was a long one, over treacherous footing. He had to stop frequently to catch his breath. So many years on the Gulf Coast had conditioned him to thick, heavy air and he found himself gasping for breath with every step.

He lost his footing several times, falling to his hands and knees. Though he moved slowly, carefully, by the time he reached the top of the mountain, most of the day had gone behind him and his pants were torn and muddy from the falls. The muscles in his legs quivered and shook from his exertion—his knees, as well as the palms of his hands, scratched and bloody—as he moved into the clearing atop the mountain. At least he would not have to retrace his steps back down this time.

He sat heavily on the damp soil to catch his breath. It was not as easy as it once had been. Age made it difficult, malignancy made it damned near impossible. He coughed and felt the death in his chest, wiped his fingers across his lips and saw the blood. It took several minutes before he was able to rise.

With the slow, halting steps of the aged, he made his way to the ridge overlooking the valley. The fields and farms stood as they had so many years ago. No modern roads and few power lines marred the countryside. Ghosts were in the valley, their faces drifting up from the fields. Faces that had been reduced to dim images over the years were suddenly remembered in sharp focus—Williams, Ways, Larrimers, Tanners, McBrides. He could almost see Truitt harnessing the mules; Amos, walking up from the creek with a string of catfish; Tildy, sitting in her rocker with a chaw of sweet-twist in her mouth. He could see himself, astride the gray jenny, riding away.

He found himself suddenly emotional, more emotional than he'd been in years. Walter cried, tears

301

rolling down his face, following the channels of deep creases cut into his skin, etched and craggy as the mountain itself. He wept softly, quietly, without disturbing the deep silence of the high, still world around him.

There was no sound. The traffic noises, the squawking sea-birds, the rhythmic surf which had filled his ears and mind for so many years, were absent. He had forgotten how silent the mountains could be. He was unaware of the shadow as it fell over him. The hand on his shoulder gave him a start and he almost cried out as he turned to stare at the figure framed in the red light of the setting sun. He raised his hand to shield his eyes, squinting.

"Papa?" he whispered, as the man knelt beside him. He seemed much younger than Walter remembered him. "Papa?"

"Shhhhh, hush now, you're home."

ABOUT THE AUTHOR

Howard Bushart lives and writes in Seabrook, Texas. He is chairman of the Allied Health Division at Lee College in Baytown, Texas where he teaches in the Mental Health Services Program. Bushart is the principal author of the non-fiction work *Soldiers of God; White Supremacists and Their Holy War for America* Kensington, 1998. His writing interests also include short fiction, poetry and screen plays.

Visit Howard L. Bushart on FaceBook
howardlbushart@yahoo.com